In 2011, Toby Soames dies from a freak accident on Hampstead Heath; Charlie Falk simply disappears. Two years later, Australian Adele Soames returns to London to be nearer her son and the places he loved. She is joined in her pilgrimages to the heath by Charlie. Charlie tells her things; unnerving things about his last day alive.

Enter DS Xandra Bentley, a member of Adele's grief support group at St Bart's. Xandra has worked on a number of cold cases of missing boys in the area and Adele's information reignites her interest. As new evidence comes to light, Adele has the creeping dread that she is bringing danger closer to home.

EX

ALICIA THOMPSON

A NineStar Press Publication
www.ninestarpress.com

Ex

© 2024 Alicia Thompson

Cover Art © 2024 Jaycee DeLorenzo

First Edition, September 2024

ISBN: 978-1-64890-801-9

Also available in eBook, ISBN: 978-1-64890-800-2

CONTENT WARNING:

This book contains sexually explicit content, which may only be suitable for mature readers. Depictions of death of a child, references to child abuse, and homophobic slurs.

Notes on the text: The majority of the chapter title definitions and spellings have been sourced from the *Collins English Dictionary*, 1980

To Vivien
(You know what you did)

What memory owes to love;
what love owes to memory.

Prologue

Exigent

Def. Pressing, demanding.

November 2011

ONE MINUTE TOBY is downing a glass of milk at the island bar while she prepares dinner, the next he is flat on the floor. Adele turns just in time to see her son's eyes roll back in his head, after he jumped off his stool to demonstrate something from his game.

Her spoon clatters on the floor tiles as she runs to her son. She crashes to his side, her fingers at his neck, her ear to his mouth. Nothing. Her brain goes cold and blank as she swiftly arranges his body and commences CPR, her hands pumping in time to her mind chanting *No!...no!...no!*

As she goes through the frantic process of trying to revive her son, her glances pinball from one surface to another around the room. Where the hell is her phone? Leaving her son to hunt for it is unthinkable.

Tears of despair run down her cheeks as her efforts produce no response. After what seems like hours, her phone rings. It's a few feet away just above her head on the buffet table. Clutching at it, she puts it on speaker and slams it on the floor so her hands can fly back to her son.

"—Adele? Are you—"

"Roof! *Help me!* Call an ambulance. To the house. It's Toby!"

Chapter One

X Marks the Spot

Def. Ground zero

January 2014

SHE DIDN'T WANT to go, but she went anyway. It was like falling into a rhythm. She locked the door behind her and walked to the end of the street. Brushing past wet rose bushes in a neighbour's garden on the corner, she walked downhill to South End Green where the shops started, putting one foot in front of the other on the greasy, rained-on pavement.

She averted her eyes from the mothers hurrying along with uniformed children taking them to appointments or for shopping;

she plunged her hands deeper into the pockets of her trench coat, focusing on where she walked and the whooshing of passing cars. A melee of food smells assailed her as she ran the gauntlet of the restaurants and takeaway shops. The trip back from the park had always been fraught, with her hungry son wanting her to give in to grease for dinner, not to mention his favourite red velvet cheesecake at Dominique's. Fish and vinegar smells blended into hot fugs of curry, then segued back into raw fish and seaweed to fried fumy noodles. Already there were mothers at counters with children in tow. But not her. Not today. Not any more.

At the train station, she crossed the road. The street turned uphill, and progress was slow. She had let herself go these last few years living in Australia, even without the excuses of less daylight hours and the higher cost of healthy food.

After passing the car park, she turned up an unmarked entry point into the heath. She paused and took a deep breath of trees and wet grass, partly to cleanse herself of the polluting streets, but also as if she was entering Narnia and all would be the same as she had left it. The pebbles on the path crunched underfoot and the odd drop of water leaked from the networks of naked branches to hit her glasses or run down the back of her neck.

As she left the path and staggered up a grassy bank, the view opened up and she was there. From her vantage point, she gazed down over an expanse of playing fields backed by thick woods. And there, as she had expected, was an after-school soccer game in progress, small figures running back and forth in bright colours, a few parents on the sidelines.

She had always preferred to watch from the raised bank. Having a redheaded son meant she could easily follow his game, and there was a bench. Her bench.

She walked over to the bin nearby and extracted a discarded newspaper. She crumpled a few sheets and wiped the remaining rainwater off the slats of the bench. She settled down, tucked loose strands of hair back behind her ears, and burrowed her cold hands into her pockets. She could pretend for a little while, at least.

There were no redheaded children in this game—although she looked, of course she looked—which was probably just as well, and time passed as she watched, but didn't see, the small figures running back and forth, yells and whistles drifting up, providing a disembodied soundtrack to her thoughts.

Some time must have passed when she felt the bench give and vibrate, signalling that she had company. She glanced sideways, not without annoyance, to see a young boy grinning at her as he rustled a paper bag on his lap. Freckles littered his nose and cheeks, and his thin hair fell in shoelace strands over his forehead. He produced a speckled banana from his bag and proceeded to peel it.

"Are you here to watch the game?"

Momentarily distracted by his bony knees and thin bare legs, one wrinkled grey sock around his ankle, the other halfway up his calf, as he banged his school shoes against the bar underneath the bench, she wondered if he was cold. She looked back at his face, watching him stuff banana into his mouth.

"Yes. Yes, I thought I would. Just for a bit."

He nodded. He had the unpleasant habit of talking with his mouth full, and through the banana and the gap in his front teeth, she saw as well as heard him say, "I'm Charlie Falk."

His forwardness made her smile. "Well, I'm Mrs Soames."

Charlie clucked his tongue and grinned. "Yes, I know. You're Toby's mum."

Her heart lurched and suddenly, he seemed different to her: not a cheeky half-urchin invading her peace, but a window onto something...something...

He was still banging his feet in a rhythm on the bench rung, a thrumming beat and vibration that now seemed to portend that *something*. She swallowed, trying to release the sudden tightness in her throat.

"You—you knew Toby?"

He nodded vigorously, chewing his last gob of mushy fruit as he put the skin in the bag and screwed it up into a ball. "We played football together."

"Oh...I see." It was hard to believe this scrawny child was the same age Toby would have been now. Her son had been big for his age, true, but more than two years on, he would have been almost twelve now. She gazed out over the playing field, vaguely aware of little moving figures, seeing only her redheaded son dashing around, kicking the ball. He had loved soccer—football, she mentally corrected herself. He was always scolding her for that.

"Mrs Soames?"

She jerked her head back in Charlie's direction.

"Are you all right?"

"Yes, yes, I'm fine." She fossicked in her coat for a tissue. She removed her glasses and dabbed at her cheeks. "It just makes me sad coming here. Happy and sad at the same time, if that makes sense. It makes me remember things." She stood up, feeling the cold and the hardness of the bench, wanting to be home in the warm.

Charlie got up as well, walked over to the bin, and lobbed in his scrunched-up ball. He turned to look back at her, his face suddenly serious and wise. "It's good to remember things." He zipped up his jacket. "Goodbye, Mrs Soames. Maybe see you again."

She half lifted her hand as he turned and walked off down the slope, round a clump of bushes, and out of sight. Walking back down the slope to the dirt path, she marvelled at all the loose threads that had pulled her back to this knotty place. Penelope must start over and weave up the unravelled mess. Again.

Chapter Two

Exile

Def. A period of forced or voluntary absence from one's country

IT WAS A relief to be home and make herself a hot cup of tea. She had walked home in the creeping gloom, sadly aware that it was only four o'clock. Bad enough this cold and miserable weather, but only three days ago, she had been enduring a heatwave in Sydney's inner west. She took a first blissful sip of tea and stared out of her kitchen window. There would be crocuses soon, two long beds of them in the gap between the boundary hedge and the path that went down the side of the house. The parks would be glorious.

She wandered out to the living room and cleared a spot on

the sofa to sit amongst the chaos of boxes and wrapping materials. It would be strange living here on her own. No Toby, no Rufus. Just her, bouncing around all these rooms, with only her own things and herself to answer to. This house only knew her as a married mum, but now it would have to get used to her as a newly divorced childless woman.

Her family and friends had all tried to talk her out of coming back to London to live, to this house of all places, but she had her reasons. Of course, there was no shortage of people to point out the irony of the English husband staying in Australia and the Australian wife returning to London, but here was where she felt closest to Toby, and all the memories associated with him; and truth be told, the happier memories of her time with Roof, before he became distant and sour. That person she had left behind. The kinder one, the man she had fallen in love with, was still discernible in this house they had shared for eight years.

Burrowing her stockinged feet under some folded clothes, she pressed her hot mug into her sternum and allowed her eyes to close, silently blessing the gods of central heating. She also had reason to bless the more English system of renting places furnished. With the tenants gone, all she'd had to do on arrival was make her bed and fall into it. A phone call had brought about the arrival of her tea chests, and after turning some of the boxes inside out looking for crucial items, she had left the scattered mess to be dealt with when the jet lag had worn off. That had been her rationalisation, anyway.

Her eyes flew open. Somewhere, her phone was ringing and she knew who it would be. She dodged around boxes to get to her coat hanging near the door and rummaged in the pocket. She flipped the cover open. Yes, it was Franny.

"Hey there. Just off my night shift, so thought I'd give you a call for the drive home. How was your flight? Settling in okay?"

They talked for a while about the usual ups and downs associated with international travel. Adele asked for, and received, updates on their parents and her niece and nephew.

"I still can't believe Roof let you have the house. You don't just give away something that's been in your family that long overnight?"

But he had. Roof had changed a lot since they'd lost Toby. He'd been adamant about moving to Australia and starting fresh, declaring he never wanted to live in this house, or even London, ever again.

"Well, it was his decision to make. Being an only child, he wasn't putting anyone's nose out of joint, except for some cousins in Suffolk, and I'm not sure they even cared that much."

"Do you think he knew you'd go back? Do you think that's partly why he did it?"

Adele laughed. "Seems an extreme way of getting rid of an ex."

There was the sound of a car horn and Franny swearing.

"I wish people would learn how to use freaking roundabouts. Sorry. I keep thinking there has to be someone else, but he just seems too mopey for anyone to consider him a romantic option these days." She paused. "But you never know."

No, you never knew. And her focus had been elsewhere at that time, on returning home to Sydney and trying to fit back in and trying to revive her career in a country where she no longer had professional connections. It had been easier for Roof. He had left Magnus Design to freelance, but he still did the odd job for his old firm and maintained his professional connections online. As to there being someone else, she found herself not minding if there was or not. It was a sad thing to feel so dully neutral, but there it was.

"Anyway, I just thought I'd check on you, luvvie. I worry about you and I'm sad you're back on the other side of the world, just when I was getting used to having you around again."

"I'll miss you all, too. But there'll be free accommodation when you come to visit...I'm still working on Rosie to come over for a gap year."

"Oh, don't you get me started on that girl's plans, or non-plans. She's driving me mental."

"Well, that's why a gap year away from her mother might be the best thing for her. *And* you."

Franny gave her a noncommittal *hmph* followed by the announcement that she had arrived home and would call again soon.

Adele smiled and tossed her phone onto the clothes piled near her feet. Her sister had worked hard to build a solid family unit, and Adele felt bad that she had been benefiting from that investment while her own family unit had disintegrated. The Sanders had been her bedrock and sanity these last two years: more evenings had been spent round there than with her husband, and for all Franny's complaints about the kids, they had treated their aunt more like a confidante than a nuisance. She had already exchanged several messages with Harry about his latest school project online and liked a few of Rosie's pictures with her boyfriend.

She folded her arms and stared into space. But now it was just her. She had missed London. Pined for it, even. It felt right being back. Sydney had seemed so small by comparison, although the weather and lifestyle had been energising. For her, if not for her marriage.

She surveyed the carnage of bubble wrap and newspaper, the unrelated oddments here and there. Tomorrow she would get her big girl pants on and clean and put everything away where it belonged. Clear the decks for Day One of her New Life, whatever that was going to be. Emptiness sprawled out in front of her, but it was up to her to fill it; she just didn't know what with yet.

Reluctantly, she hoisted herself out of the sofa's embrace and made her way to the kitchen. She did have some plans, actually, she consoled herself, and they currently amounted to eat, read, bath, and bed, in that order. It was enough for now.

Chapter Three

Ex Voto

Def. Offering in fulfilment of a vow

SHE WAS MOVING under water. Not just the slow heaviness, but with the distortion of sound and the disconnection with those above the surface. At some point, she hoped her ears would pop to release a gush of warm water, restoring clarity and briskness.

It had taken a week, but everything from the boxes had found a home, and a list had been made of new items to shop for. Shopping and sleeping were now her two favourite activities, and the shopping was combined with some sightseeing to remind herself why she loved London, although in reality, a lot of it was spent nibbling snacks on park benches or on the Embankment staring into space.

It was a matter of enjoying it while she could, as soon enough she would have to get back to work. The contract editing work she used to do for a small publishing outfit was still on offer, and the emails told her a large manuscript would soon be on its way.

Today she was in her office, getting herself set up for the work's arrival, and being distracted with social media and messaging friends. When she realised she was watching the same cat video a second time, she took a deep breath and closed it all down. She hated being sucked in by the continual stream of vapidity, but it happened frequently and all too easily.

She rubbed her eyes and looked around the room as if expecting judgement from somewhere in the corner. The office, bedroom four, had been her workspace, and Roof had used the third bedroom next door. The second bedroom had of course been her son's, and she started walking to it now.

Adele stood in the doorway looking at the single bed and the chest of drawers. His toy trunk and a few other personal items had been moved to the attic. Apart from photo albums, this was where her son now resided, and she would no doubt give in to mooching around here, too, before long.

She sat on the edge of the bed. The déjà vu of sitting in the same spot where she'd read so many bedtime stories to her son evoked a kind of muscle memory, until a tsunami of sadness engulfed her, and she was weeping and gasping for breath. His cheeky face and that wild red hair against the pillow, his wriggling when she tried to kiss him. All abruptly stolen from her—and for what reason?

She stood up and wiped her palms over her wet cheeks. Took a deep breath. Pinched the snot from her nose. The view from Toby's window showed their back garden, Roof's pride and joy, in all its landscaped glory: paved, trimmed, and hedged, with a few nicely shaped trees; trees that had been growing even before her parents were born. Over their sky-reaching fingers and the intervening houses, she could see the roof of the park and was comforted to think of what it sheltered. Toby had loved his view of tree tops: a forest that contained Robin Hood, Knights of the Round Table, and The Magic Faraway Tree. He also liked to imagine he could see the distant spire of St Michael's, high up on the ridgeline at Highgate, which doubled as the royal palace or the tower holding the princess.

She took another full breath and exhaled hard as if it would help throw off the heaviness she laboured under. When she left the room, she pulled the door firmly shut behind her.

*

AFTER A CUP of tea and an apple, she wrapped her scarf around her neck and pulled on her trench coat. The image of St Michael's had jarred her into action.

Half an hour's walk saw her taking the steps leading down to the canal path at Gloucester Avenue. It had been a grim day, and threads of mist still hung around the rushes and shrubs on the opposite bank. The air was solidly cold. She pulled her scarf up over her mouth, which at least stopped her blowing white smoke.

After the anonymity of the public roads, Adele now felt more closely observed by passers-by. She kept her head down, gloved hands wedged in her pockets, putting one foot in front of the other, not making eye contact with anyone. When she reached the bridge, she climbed the steps and turned into a quiet street lined with holly hedges. A stone church was partly shielded by a large yew tree near the corner. She crossed the road and walked up the few steps to the front door, which was open.

The building seemed small and compact from the outside, but on the inside, it was airy and capacious, and, of course, cold. She sidled into a pew near the back and sat down. She brought her gloved hands out of her pockets and clasped them in her lap. Closing her eyes, she breathed in the familiar odours of cold stone, polished wood, and musty carpets, and with them, a sense of calm.

Adele had never been much of a churchgoer. Special occasions sometimes, or with friends and their families, but not as a regular member of a congregation. She was not confirmed and preferred to observe the ceremonies from afar.

It was after Toby had died, when she had asked for stronger sleeping tablets, her doctor suggested she join a grief support group at St Bartholomew's. She hadn't lasted long in the group, but in the short time she had had left before their departure, she had kept coming to the church itself, simply to sit and think and imbibe the atmosphere. Sometimes she was lucky, and there might be choir practice, other times it was the local ladies fussing over the week's flower arrangements or polishing the brass. Mostly she tuned it all out, and just breathed in the space, letting it do its settling, soothing work on her.

This was her third visit since she had returned to England, and she was relearning when the quiet times were. Today, she was vaguely aware of someone moving around up near the altar, organising things maybe, checking the wine and wafer supply, perhaps. She raised her chin toward the light coming from those tall windows, mottled with their patchworks of deep reds, purples, greens, and blues for saints' robes, then the golds for halos and bars of holy light.

Adele shifted her weight on the pew and heard it creak; the echo seemed to reverberate up to the roof. It was followed by the sound of footsteps coming toward her down the aisle. She opened her eyes when they paused at the end of her pew.

"Hello, I hope I'm not disturbing you. You seem to be more than just a passing tourist, so I thought I'd introduce myself. I'm Joanne Dysart, the parish rector."

The woman in front of her had an air of comfortableness—a plain comfortable face, a comfortable ample figure, and comfortable clothes: a simple pairing of slacks and jumper.

"I—hello. I just come here to sit… It…it does me good."

"I'm very glad to hear it." The rector smiled benignly but made no move to leave.

Adele looked into her lap and consulted her gloved hands.

"Are you all right? I sense you're struggling with something. I'm here to help, even if it's only to listen."

The kindness and warmth in her voice was turning an unwanted key, and Adele had to press her lips together for a moment. Eventually, she took an unsteady breath. "Thank you, I'm okay. I just need...time."

The rector nodded and dipped her head slightly to get a better look at Adele's face. "Am I right in thinking we've met before? You look familiar."

Feeling ashamed at being somehow caught out, Adele stood up, ready to leave, except she had to walk closer to this woman to do so.

The rector raised her hands in protest, and there was that honeyed voice again. "Please. You don't have to leave. I can—oh dear."

She moved forward to where Adele stood leaning heavily on the prayer rail, almost choking with the effort not to cry. "Why don't you come out the back, where it's more private, and I can make you a cup of tea?"

Adele nodded and sniffed, allowing herself to be led up the aisle and out a side alcove to a small office. The rector hastily removed a pile of papers from a chair and urged her to take a seat. Adele watched as an electric jug on top of a bar fridge was flicked on and two cups were pulled down from a shelf.

"Do you take milk? Sugar?"

"Just milk, thanks."

As the rector bustled around clearing space and making the tea, Adele took off her gloves and looked around the cramped but cosy space. Two rows of bookshelves above the desk were crammed with religious texts, counselling materials, and self-help books, most bristling with tabs. Some larger hardcover books at the end were about church architecture and art and the local area. The desk, like the chair, was covered in papers and scribbled notes. Loose cords extending like tendrils from under the papers indicated the presence of a closed laptop.

"I'm sorry. I'm keeping you from your work."

"Nonsense. Don't mistake all this for work—it's my way of looking important and busy. Very handy when I'm trying to get out of something or delegate a job."

She gave Adele a cheeky grin as she put a mug of tea on the corner of the desk for her. Taking her own tea, she made herself comfortable in her chair and spun around so she could face her guest.

"So, I think I've figured out where I know you from. You came to our grief support group a year or two ago. Am I right?"

Adele rubbed her lips together and stared into her mug, her voice not much over a mumble. "Yes. You must have a good memory. I didn't stay long and it's a few years ago now."

The rector beamed, pleased with herself. "I'm good with faces. Don't ask me to remember your name, though."

Adele looked up quickly, her eyes wide. "Oh, I'm so sorry, I'm

Adele. Adele Soames."

Her hostess shook her head. "No, no bells rung, but I do remember you. You lost your son, I think?"

Adele swallowed. "Yes. It's been over two years. I shouldn't still be like this, I—"

The rector leaned forward. "It takes as long as it takes." She patted Adele on the hand. "But sometimes we need help in adjusting to things and getting unstuck from endless unproductive circles of pain. Those aren't good for you, or your remaining loved ones."

"There's only me now. My husband has his own circles of pain, and we've decided to deal with them separately." Adele glanced up at the rector's face, but she was simply sipping her tea and listening. "We left England for Australia to start over, to escape the memories, but it didn't work; in fact, for me, I think it made things worse." Her eyes shifted unseeingly to the upper window above the rector's head. "It seems I need to stay close to the memories."

Adele let her gaze return to the rector's face which still wore a kind but impassive expression. "So, I've come back here to...deal with things. To deal with myself, if that makes sense."

The rector nodded slowly. "Yes, it does make sense. But don't feel it's all on you. Ask for help where you need it. Don't suffer unnecessarily, Adele."

"Does anyone ever get over the loss of their child? Ever?"

"I don't think so. But maybe being with other parents who

have their own losses might make you feel less alone. Less guilty."

Adele looked away and angrily flicked tears off her cheeks.

"Guilty? Oh yes. My son died right in front of me, Reverend."

"Tell me what happened, if it helps," she said softly, passing her the box of tissues from the desk. "And please do call me Joanne."

Adele held her mug tightly in both hands and finished off her tea. She continued to clutch the empty mug in her lap. "My son played soccer—football, sorry—after school. He was football mad. Collected all the cards, loved watching the games. He was a devoted Hammers fan. Much to his father's consternation. *His* whole family support Arsenal." Adele laughed. "Not that it all meant much to me, of course.

"I wasn't watching on the day that it happened. Rufus was away for work, and I had something on. It was easy for Toby to just walk down the hill himself, and he often did.

"He came home and was behaving normally, giving me his usual rundown of his game, until he stood up to show me something. The last thing he said was, 'Mum?' Then he collapsed."

Adele was breathing faster, unconsciously shredding the tissue in her hands. She raced over what happened next, trying not to let the images take hold.

"I don't know how much longer it was before they came and took over, but it was no good. He was gone. A severe brain haemorrhage."

While Adele had been talking, Joanne had got up and filled

a glass with water. She placed it in front of her. "Was there any sort of family history...?"

Adele looked up at her grimly. "No. I wasn't informed till later: there had been an incident during Toby's game that afternoon. A kick had misfired, and the ball had smacked into the side of his head. He went down like a sack of bricks. They all crowded round him, but he was just a bit dazed. He said he was okay to keep playing."

"Oh, goodness. Did the teacher or coach not inform you?"

"I don't think anyone present thought it was anything to worry about. The fact that he just got up and kept playing..."

Joanne shook her head. "So abrupt. So sudden. I see why you've had trouble adjusting." She gazed up at the ceiling for a moment, as if gathering her thoughts. "How did your husband take it?"

"He was in Manchester and couldn't get back till late that night. He met me at the hospital where we spent hours filling in forms and trying to get answers. It was the longest night of our lives...and all of it for what? It couldn't bring him back. It was just empty and pointless, but we gnaw at the bones left as if it matters."

"But it does matter. It matters to you and how you live with it afterwards. There has to be a way for you to reconcile what happened and find peace."

Adele shook her head and brought the glass of water to her lips.

"Rufus was in a state of disbelief, as was I. When we finally went to bed, there was this unspoken thing between us that we'd wake in the morning and it would all have gone away. It was just too unreal to accept. But in answer to your question, Roof did what men often do. He buried himself in work and basically shut down. Although his pain did burst out in angry flashes when he'd been drinking, which ratcheted up further after Toby's death. I looked for comfort with my girlfriends and family over the phone, but I quickly realised I was wearing them out with the same old, same old, and I had to get myself together or lose my friends. That's when I started the counselling here."

"But you didn't stay."

"No." Adele took another sip of water. "Apart from the fact that we would soon be leaving anyway, I couldn't handle hearing about all the lost children. It felt like a mass haunting when I was with the group. All those lost souls and us sad sack parents left moaning about it. I decided it was better to dig my own way out of my hole."

Joanne gave her a direct look. "So, how's that going for you?"

"Not so good. It's why I've come back."

Joanne stood up and rubbed her hands together. She leaned down around the corner of the filing cabinet and flicked a switch and an electric heater whirred into action.

"Sorry, I should have put that on earlier."

They sat for a while, and Adele was surprised that she felt comfortable enough not to break the silence, that there was no un-spoken expectation or demand being placed on her. She placed her glass on the desk and looked at her watch. It was getting late. Joanne reacted to her expression of surprise and stood up.

"Yes, it *is* that time, isn't it." She clasped her hands in front of her. "So, I'll summarise my thoughts, which you can take or leave. I'm a practical woman first and foremost and I don't believe in pushing people when they're not ready, but I do believe in encouraging them in the right direction to make their own decisions." She gave Adele another one of those warm smiles. "It's clear that you benefit from being here, and I welcome that as a positive start. You can come and see me any time you like, come to services or not, make an appointment to see me at other times. Just to chat, whatever you wish. But eventually I'd like to see you come back to our weekly group. There are some people here who it might be good for you to meet, and vice versa. Will you give it your consideration as a vaguely staged plan?"

Joanne held out her hand, and Adele took it. Joanne gently placed her other hand over Adele's and pressed them together, and rather than it feeling awkward, she felt comforted. Like she'd been blessed.

"Please don't feel you have to do this on your own. There's always help if you are willing to ask for it."

Adele took a longer route home via the lamp-lit streets. It gave her time to think before she faced the challenge of filling her evening. Her feet were like ice blocks, so she walked briskly in the hope of getting some circulation happening. By the time she was putting her key in the door, she was aware that her mood had lifted. There was still a remnant of sadness, but the heaviness had abated, and she was left with a warmth and steadiness hovering around her that she hadn't felt in a long while. She had Reverend Joanne to thank, that much was obvious; but how she'd done it was more of a mystery.

Chapter Four

Exoneration

Def. Officially absolving someone from blame

THE MANUSCRIPT FOR editing had arrived. It was currently in excess of one hundred and fifty thousand words, and while it was from one of their better selling authors, she had instructions to cull wherever possible. Or at least to negotiate with the author and see what could be done.

She spent the afternoon on the sofa doing a first read on her tablet with her notebook at her side. The work was dense and lacking the momentum of his other novels, and as a result, she was finding it hard to get into it. In her younger days, she would have taken that as a direct challenge to rejuvenate the text and trim it to a leaner, more angular framework, but right now, on her third cup of tea, she was feeling bogged down and uninspired. She was also out of practice. It would take a few days, but she would soon be back into a routine and have her swing back.

She looked up from her screen and out of the front window. It was the end of the school day, and some old internal clock still told her that her son would be home soon...or be at soccer practice on the heath. She swung her legs off the sofa and went in search of her sneakers. Some exercise would do her good. Then she would be fresh for another session after dinner.

Striding up the hill, she was pleased to notice she was less puffed and that her legs felt stronger. There hadn't been any rain these last few days, so the path was dry and abrasive underfoot and the odours exuded by exposed earth and foliage were thinner and more subtle than when recently doused in water.

It made her smile to realise that the expansive feeling in her chest and mind was similar to when she sat in St Bart's. Even though the church was enclosed, it was something to do with the soaring roof and the empty storeys of space above her head, as if her aura had room to expand as much as it needed. No limits. Nothing pressing down on her head, pushing her into a small airless space.

But the rich green colours, even those on offer in late winter, were another level again. Coming from Australia, the greens outside of the winter months still seemed unreal to her. Straight from a child's paint box. Impossible. Even the greenest of greens in Australia, usually non-native and brought about by careful and expensive irrigation, were somehow different to the verdancy you found in London parks and beyond. The effect of harsh versus soft light. No wonder it took early painters in Australia time to get the hang of their new colour palette. The gardens were full of snowdrops and crocus shoots, and some premature warmth had triggered the unfurling of nascent leaves. Adele's eyes drank it all in and she never tired of it; in fact, it was an unfailing antidote to feeling weary and stale.

At the top of the bank now, she headed over to her bench, only to find she already had company.

"Hello, Mrs Soames!"

"Hello, Charlie. How come you're here and not playing in a game?"

"I'm getting some special coaching."

She supposed that explained why he was again wearing shorts, although he still wore his school shoes with those untidy socks. Even worse, he was stuffing his face with another brown banana. Could his mother not give him fresh fruit?

They sat in silence while she settled in to watch the boys below running backwards and forwards to the scream of whistles and parents on the sidelines shouting encouragement. Still. After all this time. It was unbelievable after what had happened. A collective act of callousness.

Her gaze slid to the boy fidgeting beside her, and for a

moment she was captivated by his bony knees expanding and contracting as he swung his feet, the crusty scab on his left knee developing a life of its own. Charlie's shoes banging on the bench rung brought her thoughts back to the present, and she turned to face him.

"Charlie? The other day when we were talking, you said you played football with my son."

"Mm-hmm."

Adele fiddled with a ring on her right hand through the wool of her gloves. "Did you know him well?"

"Not really. He was in 5B and I was in 5C. Different buildings."

"But you played in the same team after school."

"No, we played on *opposite* teams."

"Oh, I see." She looked at him and smiled. There was that gappy grin of his again. "Who won the most games? Your team or his?"

"We were ahead, until...until..."

Adele looked at him keenly now. His expression showed uncertainty, and his eyes were those of a child who thought he might be in trouble. "Until the accident, you mean?"

Charlie swallowed and nodded.

Adele felt a quiver in her stomach, anticipating what she was going to ask, but she went ahead anyway, speaking softly. "Tell me, Charlie. Were you there that day? When Toby was hit with the ball?"

Charlie looked frightened, and his hands crushed the paper bag in his hands into a tight ball in his lap. "Mrs Soames..."

"It's okay, Charlie. You can tell me."

"Mrs Soames." He was almost weeping now. "It was *me*. It was me who kicked the ball."

Adele gasped, winded. "Oh, Charlie..." Her voice was barely above a whisper.

"I'm sorry, Mrs Soames! I didn't mean to! It was an accident. I kicked it and he was there—"

Her hand was over her mouth, trying to hold back her crying, if only for the sake of the child next to her, and all she could do was close her eyes and nod vigorously.

When she was able to breathe without gasping, she wiped her face and pulled out a tissue to blow her nose, all the while aware of Charlie's anxious, horrified face.

She took her glasses off and cleaned them on a corner of her trench coat. "I'm sorry for crying like that, Charlie. Losing my son still upsets me, I can't help it. But you—" She almost choked on her words and had to clear her throat. "Charlie, it was an accident. Nobody would have said it was your fault. Surely?"

"Some of the kids did. They said I killed him."

"That's a dreadful thing to say to someone. What did your teacher say?"

"He said we weren't to talk about it. It would upset Toby's parents."

Ah, yes. A memory was coming back to her. Roof had asked

at the school, wanting to know exactly what had happened, as if it somehow made a difference to the end result. He just wanted to *know*, he said. It must have felt too close to home for him. Roof had often taken Toby for games, and he'd even helped out with the weekend matches and away games when he could. He had arranged to speak with the coach and Toby's teacher. Would there be a report, he wanted to know.

He had come home angry and frustrated. The school had closed ranks. They didn't want any specific child being blamed for the event. It was scarring enough for all those who had been there after they found out what had happened. The boy in question would be getting some counselling, as would the other boys who were present.

"It's not like I can't find out myself. Their not telling me is the worst form of bureaucracy. It's unnecessary cruelty."

She had watched as he downed a glass of whiskey while telling her this. "What difference would it make, knowing it was boy A rather than boy B?"

Her husband had glared at her. "I just want to *know*. I have a right to know how my son died and by whose hand, even if it was an accident."

Adele had silently agreed at the time, but now she felt that Charlie also had the right to some privacy and protection for his involvement in an event he could neither help nor fully comprehend.

In control of herself now, she turned to see he was still

watching her anxiously. The wind blew his fringe up and she longed to reach out and smooth it down, to bless him. Instead, she held out her hand palm upwards and smiled. "Give me your hand, Charlie."

He reached out and hesitantly put his hand in hers. Even through her woollen gloves it felt like ice. "Oh dear. Give me your other hand, too." With both of his hands now in hers, she gave them a vigorous rub. She began to laugh as it reminded her of a silly game she used to play with Toby. Charlie also laughed, but he was still eyeing her warily.

Adele stopped rubbing, but she maintained her hold on his freezing hands, giving them a good squeeze. She dropped her chin and looked directly into his face. Speaking slowly and deliberately, she said, "It was not. Your. Fault. Do you hear me?"

He just looked up into her face, almost in confusion.

"Charlie, it was not your fault. If there's anything to forgive, I'm forgiving you, okay? I'm sorry if anyone tried to make you feel bad for something that was a complete accident. It could have happened to anyone."

Charlie nodded wordlessly, a tear slipping down his cheek.

"Oh, please don't you cry, too. You'll start me again." She laughed and patted his shoulder with one hand while the other hunted for another tissue in her pocket.

They sat a little while longer on the bench, not speaking. Just staring out at the game, still going on, as the light became a little dimmer.

"What time is your session, Charlie? Is it after the game down there?"

"Yes." He got up, walked to the bin, and lobbed his rubbish in. He lifted his hand. "Goodbye, Mrs Soames."

"Goodbye, Charlie. See you again."

Charlie turned to go, then stopped and turned back to her. "Mrs Soames? Do you think Toby forgives me too?"

The expression on his face made her heart twinge painfully. "Oh, sweetheart…" Adele squeezed her face into a smile. "He wouldn't dwell on it. He'll be too busy kicking goals with the angels."

Chapter Five

Xbox

Def. A home video game

INSTEAD OF HEADING home, she decided on a whim to walk down the slope to where the game was taking place. The boys were the same age group as Toby had been back then, so three school years on she didn't expect to recognise any of the parents. She approached the sideline and tried to imagine Toby was out there, all elbows and knees, with his fiery mane blustering in all directions. One of the fathers had once asked where he got his hair colour from. Her standard joke was the milkman, because in fact, they didn't know. The real joke was that Roof's nickname among his uni mates was "Red".

The ball was kicked her way, and she could feel the vibration of their stampeding feet, the referee trying to keep pace. She winced and grimaced at some of the more violent jostling, and once, when the ball received a sweeping kick and immediately smacked into the legs of a defender, she had let out a gasp. The game moved on at top speed, but that resounding whack reverberated in her head.

On the opposite side of the field in her line of sight were some older boys and a few adults, one of which was a man who walked up and down, gesturing and yelling. On her side of the field, a solid-looking man, presumably another parent, also stood watching the game, a sports bag at his feet. He wore tracksuit pants and a jumper with the hood over his head. Something about his shape and the way he held himself looked familiar. Adele took up a position a little behind him out of view. Her focus kept switching from the game back to the man, her brain trying to nut out the problem. When he turned his head toward her to follow the action, it clicked: Stephen Lane. Of course. He had been Toby's team coach. So, he was still here, still going. Well, good for him. The continuity pleased her.

Toby had liked Mr Lane. She had known him, and his wife (what *was* her name again?) on an exchanging-pleasantries basis from the soccer games and also from the occasional "play date" Toby had had with Stephen's son when he'd been younger. But after the accident, they had spoken more often. Stephen had paid them a visit at the house to express his deep sorrow: losing one of "his kids" had impacted deeply on him and the team. He personally delivered one of the arrangements of flowers they had received on behalf of the school, and at the funeral itself, Toby's team had sung the school's sporting anthem in farewell.

So, when the final whistle blew and the kids all ran to their bags, Adele loitered, waiting to see if she could say hello. Stephen didn't make a move to join the milling parents. After a while, he raised his hand and gestured impatiently. An older boy, whom she had noticed on the side lines earlier, broke away from the others and trotted across the field carrying some shin pads and a dirty shirt. Stephen took the gear off the boy and stuffed it into the bag at his feet. He was hoisting it up onto his shoulder when he noticed her. His face was uncomprehending at first, then his eyes brightened in recognition. He let the bag drop back down to the ground.

"Adele! What are you doing here? I thought you'd gone back to Australia."

"I did, but here I am again, turning up like a bad penny."

He walked up to her, smiling, his eyes flitting all over her face. She'd forgotten how good-looking he was. Or perhaps she simply hadn't noticed before.

"It's so good to see you're still doing the soccer games."

"Ohh..." Stephen's smile vanished, and his expression darkened. He lowered his voice. "Actually, I'm not."

When Adele opened her mouth to respond, he shook his head. "Long story." He turned round and gestured to the boy to come over. He put his arm around his thin shoulders. "You probably won't recognise him now, but this is Freddy. Freddy, you remember Toby's mum?" The boy was tall and gangly with a shy grin and a mouth full of metal, but it was his large brown eyes under thick angular brows that defined his whole face. He was going to be a lady-killer.

"Hello, Mrs Soames." He held out his hand.

Adele's heart melted as she took it for a light shake. "Oh, Freddy," she said quietly. "It's just Adele, now."

The boy's eye sought confirmation from his dad, who smiled and nodded that it was okay.

She explained as quickly as possible why she was back, not wanting to dwell on it or receive his sympathy. Just a practical explanation, no more.

He nodded, concern in his eyes. "I'm really sorry to hear that, Adele. It's sadly common for marriages to hit rough patches after the loss of a child."

"Yes, well." She forced a cheerful smile. "Maybe it just exposed something that might have happened anyway. Either way, I felt I had to be back here, near Toby."

"It's a long way from your family."

"Oh, my brother's still up north, and I speak regularly with my parents and sister and her kids by phone and Skype. Sometimes you speak more when you're distant."

Stephen laughed. "I suppose that's true. Time goes by so quickly. I haven't been round to my sister's in over a month. Which way are you heading? Can I give you a lift anywhere?"

"Oh, I can walk home, don't let me trouble you."

Stephen looked up the slope and at the bag of gear at his feet. "Come on, walk us to our car and I'll drive you home. We can make room, can't we?" He looked to his son who nodded. "It will be dark in half an hour."

His smile told her to say yes. On the way, he updated her on some of the teacher news and some happenings at the school. "Oh, and I suppose I should mention my own news."

Adele looked away from Freddy, who was running up ahead to the car, to catch the facial expression that went with Stephen's curious tone of voice.

"My marriage didn't survive these two years, either."

"Oh, Stephen. I'm so sorry. Nothing to do with...?"

"No, no. Of course not. Just the usual boring rubbish complaints women come out with. Tania had played away on me before, but this time the grass was green enough to jump the fence. My son now lives with a stepdad rather than his real one. I get to have him every second weekend, although I've swung it so I pick him up from his after-school games now, as well. It's pretty shit, not to put too fine a point on it. I miss him far more than I miss Tania, to be honest."

"I don't know what to say, Stephen. I really feel for you."

There was a pause, and Stephen let out a terrible laugh. "I've just won the tact award, haven't I? Complaining to *you* that I don't get enough time with my son. I'm so sorry."

She reached out and squeezed his arm. "It's fine. I didn't take it that way. How *is* Freddy anyway? Toby used to love going round to yours to play Xbox."

"Yeah, they did that a lot early on, didn't they? You've got a good memory. He's fairly robust, I think. His mum and I are still on civil terms, which helps." He shook his head. "Xbox, eh. That all feels like ancient history now…BF as it were." He looked at her and laughed. "Before Football."

"You're not wrong there. Roof was trying to get him off electronic games so he wouldn't be one of these nerdy computer-obsessed kids who did nothing else." Adele laughed wryly at the memory and how it had backfired on her husband so badly. "And so instead he became a nerdy obsessed football fan who lived and breathed West Ham United."

Stephen grinned. "Boys, eh. It's one obsession after another. Then it becomes beer and girls."

"Or cars and their mates."

Stephen gave her a humorously resigned look and shook his head. He'd stopped in front of a white station wagon—estate, she corrected herself—and let his bag swing to the ground.

"Here we are. Now I was thinking—and I'm sorry I can't offer tonight as I have to get his nibs home—and you're allowed to say no, naturally, but our local pub does a great steak special on a Wednesday night…if you'd like to join me? I'm sure you've got lots on now you're back—oh, thanks mate." Freddy had already crawled onto the back seat to push gear out of the way, clearly intending for Adele to sit in the front.

Adele was surprised at the sudden surge of happiness she felt at this humbly-bumbly invitation. "Gosh, well, I did have plans to work and eat cheese on toast all on my own, so I don't know…"

Stephen was loading gear in the back of the car and so didn't catch her tone or see her face. "Oh, look that's totally fine, I understand. Just being spon—"

"Stephen? I was joking! I'd love the company and pub grub beats cheese on toast hands down. A pint of something wouldn't be too bad, either."

"Oh!" He laughed and stood back as he closed the hatch, a relieved look on his face. "Sorry. I've kind of lost the knack of asking an attractive woman out." He bowed and waved his arm towards the front seat. "Madam, your chariot awaits."

She made herself comfortable and clipped the seatbelt on, feeling a small internal glow at being classed as an "attractive woman". It had been a long time since she'd felt that she was anything other than a grieving parent, or a sad and ignored wife.

*

STEPHEN DROPPED HER off, but not before making a plan to come and get her the following evening. She walked inside and hung her outside clothes up, glad to be back in the warmth. She prepared herself a light meal and settled down to do more work on the manuscript. She surprised herself by keeping at it till almost 9.00 p.m., her energy levels weirdly high after her earlier work and traipsing around in the cold. She closed her laptop and smiled. A date.

Her heart was light and fluttery at the mere thought of a little flirting and fun, things that were almost alien to her now. And if she was honest, the potential for something more in the physical line was creating a pleasant fizz. Technically, she had been single only a short time, and some would think this too soon to be even considering someone new, but the reality was quite different.

She had hoped so hard that the move to Australia would revive her stymied relations with her husband; dissolve the impersonal chill that had emanated from him ever since they'd lost Toby. She hadn't wanted to admit that the only thing holding them together had been their son. But what had begun in London grew steadily worse in Sydney to the point where it was akin to living with an antagonistic stranger holed up in the study and the spare bedroom. In the marriage counselling sessions she had attended alone, her counsellor had constantly reminded her that she was worthy and deserving of love, but this was the first time in over two years that the possibility of testing this idea out had presented itself. Maybe leaving Roof in a different country had burnt a mental bridge.

"Give yourself time to heal," Franny had said. A grim smile slid over Adele's lips as her older sister's lecturing about frying pans and fires echoed in her ears. Easy for her when she hadn't been starved of warmth and affection, not to mention respect, for over three years.

She got up and took her plate and cup to the sink, admonishing herself. Stephen was just being friendly, pleased to revisit an old connection. It was sad to hear about his marriage breaking up, but she couldn't deny that it was setting off little thought explosions, loosening up thinking that had been petrified for a long time now. Fantastic ones, but couldn't she have some fun imagining?

It had never occurred to her to see Stephen in any other way than as a sexless teacher or the father of Toby's friend. It was just easier, and she'd had too much else to worry about, namely, how to keep her miserable husband engaged and happy, or latterly, how to just keep out of his way and not provoke an argument.

Heading up the stairs, she switched off the downstairs lights as she went. It was still early enough, and she felt like indulging herself. Making herself feel smooth and clean. And maybe even more than that.

She turned on the bath taps and poured in some of the expensive bath crème her brother's kids had given her for Christmas. She lit candles and turned off the overhead light. For a moment, she just stood in the dim flickering chiaroscuro and breathed in the sweet hot vapour rising from the tub. It wasn't often she made time to treat herself like this; working mothers rarely got the chance, so she couldn't help a feeling of naughty indulgence as she watched the pile of bubbles inflate under the gushing tap.

She peeled off her socks and pants and all the layers on her top half, freeing her skin to the air, releasing it from tight elastic and other constrictions. She lifted her curls off the back of her neck, twisting and securing them with a clip. The water level was steadily rising, and she reached in to test the temperature. It was only then she realised she was missing something. She skipped, naked, into the office, ducking low in case anyone could see from the street, and turned on her small CD player. She already had the perfect music ready to go. Adele ran lightly back to the steamy bathroom and turned off the taps so that Sade could make her sultry presence felt.

As she eased herself into the milky water, her mind stalled. Ahh. *Heat*. So delicious. So...encompassing. She lay prone, just gently moving her hands back and forth, circulating the water, enjoying the throbbing pulse of the music. How perfect it would be to have a lover scrub her back right now, or be in the tub with her and exchange some foot massages. It was a lifetime ago when Roof had last done anything like that for her...antediluvian for anyone before that.

Now, she was free to imagine anyone. A complete fantasy figure if she liked. But that wasn't necessary. She was already visualising Stephen's strong and capable hands massaging some scrub into his palms, prior to sliding them down the length of her back right down to the crack of her bottom as she leaned forward. *Mmm*. And he would be naked, of course, ready to get in the bath with her. Solid broad shoulders and, she was sure, a manly amount of hair on his chest. She wasn't into this modern kick of completely hairless men. Yet she had ended up with a weedy cerebral kind of guy.

She smiled serenely. Sex was all between the ears, ultimately. Her ending up with Roof proved that. But for the moment she just wanted to delight in the concept of a large dominant body with gentle, capable hands and a warm, inviting smile in the eyes. That was it in a nutshell, actually: *warmth*. Kindness, even. It had been too long.

Her hand drifted down between her legs to accompany her mental choreographing of what might happen if Stephen "came in for a drink" after their night out. Her eyes flashed open. Did she have any condoms? She had better pop to the shops tomorrow. How awful to get him all the way here to fall at the last, looking like an inexperienced teenager. Although surely he would bring some. But maybe he wasn't ready for that. Maybe he really was just being friendly... No. Surely not. But what if he didn't find her attractive? It had been a while, and...*shit*. Maybe visualising a perfect fantasy man was a better idea after all.

Determined to block out the sabotaging thoughts, she settled back to give herself an efficient and intense orgasm so she could get on with the job of shaving her legs and scrubbing her arms and shoulders till they were soft and pink.

As the drain hacked the water down, she wrapped herself in a fluffy bath sheet and rubbed cream into her newly smoothed arms and legs. She took a little more cream and rubbed it over her chest and down to her stomach. Having a child had left her muscles a little wobbly in that area, but on the whole, she had been lucky. Her hand paused in its thoughtful back and forth movement. She was only thirty-eight. Maybe another child could still be possible, given the right father. Again, Stephen's warm smile appeared in front of her, and she heard the love in his voice when he had spoken to his son.

She went into her room and allowed the towel to drop to the floor. The light from the hall was enough to see by, and she caught a side glimpse of her silhouette in the mirrored doors of the wardrobe. She stood up straight and viewed herself more critically, hands on hips, wondering what Stephen might see. She sniffed. Supermodel she was not, but hell. Not everyone wanted to go to bed with a broomstick.

She pulled on her kitten-covered flannelette pyjamas, noting with pleasure the looseness of the waist elastic. All the walking she had been doing of late was helping a lot: even Franny had commented that she was looking trimmer when she'd stood up during a Skype call this last week. She turned back to face her reflection and put on an exaggerated sultry pose, her hands pushing up her hair. She let it drop, laughing at herself. How could he resist?

Chapter Six

Ex Parte

Def. In the interests of one side only

THE MIDWEEK CROWD was fairly modest, and they found a table in a quiet corner of the Lord Nelson's front room to set their beers on. Stephen placed the buzzer for their meals between them. He watched as she peeled her coat off and draped it over the back of her chair. He had a frown on his face.

"So, you're going to have to explain something weird about Toby that never made sense to me."

She paused in bringing her drink to her lips. "Oh? What's that?"

"Why the Hammers?"

She laughed and extended her glass toward his. "Cheers, by the way. Oh yes. The bane of Roof's life." She rolled her eyes in an exaggerated fashion. "Serve him right, I say."

"I suppose it could have been worse. He might have gone for Tottenham."

"No, my son was a weird one. What can I say. He didn't think he should follow a team 'just because Dad does', so he did some 'research'. I don't really know what that entailed, but I know he was impressed by the fact that the three key players who ensured England's only World Cup win were all West Ham players."

"But that was over fifty years ago for god's sake, and they've been rubbish ever since. What a relief he never invested on the stock market."

Adele sighed into her glass. "I know. But whatever the logic was, it made him happy, so who was I to say anything. And it did amuse me to see the two of them on match days when their teams played each other. He used to give his father as good as he got."

"Yes, he used to cop it from his classmates as well."

By the time their buzzer started flashing and farting, Adele was surprised at all the conversational ground they had covered and how easy it was to talk to this man she hardly knew. His face was open and interested, with a touch of vulnerability that seemed to invite confidences. They were in need of more beers, so she hopped up to get the next round while he collected their meals.

Focusing on applying cracked pepper to her veal limone, she

said, "I'm sorry to hear you're not coaching any more. You were so good with the boys."

She glanced up and passed him the pepper. He took it from her but made no effort to use it.

"I had no choice, Adele. That bitch Susan Loftus made sure of it."

"What? The principal? What happened?"

"Some parents got in her ear saying it was unacceptable for me to continue as a teacher, let alone a coach. It didn't help that my own colleagues were gossiping behind my back, talking to the media. That fucking Anna Thomsett—"

"Oh my god, you nearly lost your job?"

"Oh, yeah!" Stephen nodded his head vigorously. "It really was touch and go for a while there. To lose one boy was bad enough, but to lose two in close succession...especially when I was in the firing line—"

"*Two* boys? Stephen, what are you talking about?" Adele had planted her knife and fork on either side of her plate, her hands tight fists around her cutlery.

Stephen stared at her for a moment with his lips parted to speak. Finally, he said, "Did you not know? It was just after..." He frowned and rubbed his chin, expelling a ragged sigh. His shoulders slumped, his momentum lost. His eyes focused somewhere in the middle distance over her shoulder. "I'm just trying to think if you were still here or whether you'd already left. No, you must have still been here..."

He was speaking more to himself than her, so she dipped her head impatiently to get him to look at her.

"Stephen? Please. What's all this about?"

"It was some weeks, maybe a month, after we lost Toby. The parents of another boy in the team reported their son missing. The last place their son had been seen was at the after-school game with me."

It was Adele's turn to frown, trying to dredge up her memories of that time. She waited for him to continue.

"I had nothing to report that was of any use. Sam Norton, the only parent there that day, was also grilled, and the boys were all questioned, but no one had seen or heard anything that seemed to have any bearing on the situation."

"That must have been just as we were preparing to leave. Life was a blur then. I was putting in long days of packing and calling freight companies and teeing up arrangements in Sydney... Someone mentioned it to me in passing, I think I do remember now, but I was too frantic and distracted to give it more than half a thought." Adele looked down at her plate. "That's terrible, isn't it. I'd just lost my son but had no time to consider someone else who had lost theirs." She raised her eyes back to Stephen's. "They didn't find him?"

"No. There was extensive searching with sniffer dogs all over the heath. Posters put up in the local area. Any time a child goes missing, the issue gets raised again, but no one has ever come forward with anything new or helpful."

Adele reached over and placed her hand over Stephen's. "Now I'm impressed that you even kept going with the teaching."

Stephen half laughed, half grimaced as he pulled his hand away and took up his cutlery. "It was a close thing. I was a key suspect for a while, and in the absence of new information, in some people's minds, perhaps I still am. There was talk of linking it to other known cases in the area, but nothing stuck. It scared people and made them more cautious. A few boys left the team around that time, although no parent said that was why."

"It sounds like you've been going through your own private hell these last few years. I had no idea. I'm so sorry."

"Yes, well, it didn't help when Tania left, firing up the gossip mill again."

There was a pause in the conversation while they addressed themselves to their meals, although Adele's veal felt like rubber in her mouth as she absorbed these not-so-new facts. Strange that Roof hadn't mentioned it, either, when he had had the closer connection with the team, helping out from time to time as he had, but of course, like her, his thoughts would have been elsewhere in those last panicky days of trying to cut ties and leave. Or maybe he *had* known and deliberately kept it from her, worrying that it would paralyse her all over again. It weighed heavy in her chest, knowing Roof had been carrying this additional burden on top of everything else. Not only that, but with his wife a mess and no other close confidants, he had no choice but to bury his pain. No wonder he had sunk inside himself.

What had started out as a gently flirtatious and fun evening now felt heavy and depressing. They both tried talking about other things, but the missing boy seemed to hover between them for the duration of their meal.

As she stood up from her chair, Stephen came round to help her on with her jacket. "We'll have to try this again when we're both in a better headspace. I'm sorry. I haven't spoken with any-one about Charlie for a long time now and it just brought it all back to me... I wish they'd find out what happened so we—"

Adele had turned sharply, and the look on her face stopped him.

"The boy's name was Charlie?"

"Yes. Charlie Falk. The family left—"

"But that's not possible."

Stephen just stared at her.

"I mean, it couldn't. I've just...but maybe there's..."

Stephen had taken her by the arm, and they were heading for the door. Out in the cold air, her head cleared of its fuzziness. "Is Charlie Falk a common name, do you think?"

Stephen gave her a sideways look as he opened his car door for her.

"I wouldn't have thought so." His voice sounded cautious. "Why?"

She waited for him to circle the car and get in. There had to be a logical explanation. By the time Stephen was eyeing her war-ily as he buckled his belt, Adele was determined to make light of it. "My memory's not the best these days. I was talking to a young kid in the park the other day. He was telling me about some special coaching he gets. He's a Charlie, too, and now I'm remembering his last name as Falk, but I'm probably just jumbling everything up."

Stephen's face relaxed. "There's probably a few around. There's a Charlie Weatherhead in one of my classes...but I don't do any 'special coaching' these days, for obvious reason."

Adele nodded. No point in arguing. This boy was Toby's age, but his name couldn't be Falk, and that was that.

*

IN THE SHORT time it took for Stephen to negotiate the way back round the park to her street, she was regretting the loss of lightness and fun that she had so been hoping for. Stephen slowed down the car and leaned forward to look up at the upper windows of her neighbours' homes.

"I'd forgotten what a posh street you live in. A lot of detached houses."

"Yes. Roof's family had money, and there were no siblings to share it with." Adele fiddled with her fingers in her lap. "He didn't like talking about his childhood much, but from what I could gather, Roof's family life was seriously...lacking. I think he'd long ago come to the conclusion that money alone doesn't bring happiness."

"So, he gave it to you without a fight?"

"He *offered* it. Like he was keen to cut ties with his past. Our past, too, which made it a little harder for me. But here I am. There's nothing to say I won't also cut ties and sell it, but for now, it's a familiar bolthole while I figure things out."

Stephen whistled. "It's a luxurious position to be in." He'd turned the engine off and was resting both his hands on the top of the steering wheel, apparently lost in his own thoughts.

Adele squeezed her fingers a bit tighter in her lap. "Listen…"

Stephen turned his head with a look of enquiry on his face half visible in the shadows.

"I feel bad the conversation got stuck on such sad topics tonight; I suppose I should have expected it, but it's early yet. Would you like to come in for a drink? Just chill out with some music and chat for a while, even if it is just therapy talk? I went out and got this bottle of spiced rum that I'm keen to try—you could have a taster in some coffee if you didn't want to go overboard."

There was a bitter edge to Stephen's laugh as he turned back to face the front. "'Therapy talk'." He reached over to pat her knee. "Sure. Let's give it a try. Sorry I've been a bit of a sad sack tonight. I don't want to hardwire you in my mind with the past, but I guess we've got to chew it over to get beyond it, haven't we?"

He followed her up the front path, and she was keenly aware of his presence close behind her as she opened the door. She had left a lamp on beside the corner sofa, which now emitted a cosy glow to accentuate the central heating.

"Oh, very nice."

"Take a seat, and I'll put the kettle on." She glanced over towards her stereo system. "Why don't you pick something out and put it on?"

She was just pouring hot water into their mugs when she felt, rather than heard, the soft accents of Dido smoothing over the holes of quiet.

When she placed their mugs on the coffee table, Stephen had already made himself comfortable and was flicking through the novel she'd left there.

"Any good?"

"Yes, I'm enjoying it. Australian author." The leather sofa cushions let out a hiss as she lowered herself into their comfort. She leaned over to tap the book's cover, a black-and-white photo of a woman farewelling her soldier sweetheart leaning out of his train window. "The author found that photo while doing library research and was inspired to write a whole book around how they got to that point and what followed."

She brought her mug to her lips for a thoughtful sip. "The best part, though, is how each chapter is a different character's perspective on what happened. It's like piecing a jigsaw together. Everyone is looking into a different window of the house, and you have to figure out how the rooms fit together."

"Is it crime? Unreliable witnesses and so forth?"

"No. Just good old human drama. He said, she said."

"Ahh. The old he said, she said." He rolled his eyes and took up his mug. "A toast to the lady of the house. May she find happiness."

Adele curled her stockinged feet under her and snuggled into the opposite corner of the sofa where she could easily observe her guest. He did seem tired around the eyes and his hair curled a little on his collar like he was overdue a cut. It made her want to reach out and smooth it with her fingers. Perhaps he could do with a little feminine care in his life. She smiled at him over the rim of her mug.

Stephen stretched his arms, settled back in the sofa, and looked around. "I can see you downsizing to something more cosy and manageable before too long. This is a big place to knock around in all on your own."

"I know. I still expect to hear Toby racing down the stairs or Roof calling me from the study. How about you? Still in the same place or did you have to move?"

"No, Tania was surprisingly good about the house. She moved in with the new man, so she didn't need it; it's mortgaged to the hilt anyway. I had to make up for it in the support payments, though, don't you worry."

"Less disruptive for Freddy."

"Yes."

"He'll be eighteen before you know it. Do you think you'd ever go there again? Have more children?"

"Haven't thought about it. Probably not. I'll be too old for that caper soon. The thought of going back to sleepless nights and nappies...would have to be a special woman."

"I've been thinking about it. Whether it would help fill an

ache in my heart—not that Toby is replaceable—but a focus for my care and love. It's part of why I feel so...directionless."

"But do you think that would have been the same if you and your husband had closed ranks? It might have made you a stronger unit, together."

"Maybe. And decided to have another child together...or not."

"So, there wasn't anyone else? He just drifted away from you? Is his mental health okay?"

"If there's anyone else, he's completely covered his tracks. I wanted him to get help. It feels like he's been spiralling down for a long time, further and further from my reach, till in the end it was like living with a stranger. I woke up one day and questioned my whole life and where it was all going."

"It's hard when you think you could fix things by just trying a bit harder. I went through that until I realised there was a reason why Tania wasn't responding to my efforts. She was already getting serviced elsewhere."

"I—I see." Adele frowned. "But...but this was while you were dealing with traumatic things at work."

"Yes." He reached up and ruffled his hair as if to loosen his thoughts. "I guess I took my eye off the ball, but I gather it had been tentatively going on for some time beforehand. The tension and stress at home was just an excuse for her to up the ante."

"But...you're cleared now? You said the boy was never found, so how...?"

"I don't know if I'll ever be 'cleared'. It's hard to have a rock-solid alibi when no one knows for certain what the relevant timeframe was. After the game, I went home and had a shower. Tania came home shortly after. So, there is a gap of time when I could have got up to no good, assuming that is the time something happened, but it might have been later."

Adele nodded slowly. "Did he live close enough to walk home alone?"

"No, I think he caught a bus. He was last seen walking up the hill from the playing field."

She pursed her lips. So many times, Toby had walked home that way on his own. He had got to an age where she and Roof had felt increasingly comfortable trusting their son. It was horrendous to think it might have been her own child encountering a stranger in the bushes before making it out onto the road. It made her worry for her park bench boy, still out and about, with dusk closing in.

Stephen moved towards her. "Hey," he said gently. "Such a big frown on such a pretty face." He reached over and trailed the backs of his fingers down her cheek.

The tenderness in his voice would have been enough, but the touch of his hand drew an immediate response from her affection-starved heart. She leaned in and was soon kissing him with a hungry enthusiasm. After some jostling for position on the squishy sofa cushions, Stephen pulled back to take a breath.

"Wow. I can't remember the last time I had such an exciting

response to an advance."

She laughed nervously. "Too much?"

"No! I'm flattered. I've always thought you were a hot sort."

He was now lying full length and had manoeuvred her to be alongside him. She hooked her leg to pull herself on top of him, and like two schoolkids with their parents out, they took full ownership of the sofa. It had been so long since Adele had enjoyed simply kissing and cuddling and feeling bare skin under clothes that she lost track of time. Eventually, the empty silence left by the CD ending brought her back to a fuller awareness. She sat up and pushed a dangling curl behind her ear.

"What's the matter?"

"Nothing at all. I'm having a lovely time." She settled her hips more firmly over his, delighting in his responsiveness. She reached down and slipped her hand under his shirt that had inched its way up to his lower ribs. She allowed her head to fall to one side as she regarded him. "Would you like to go upstairs? Making out on the sofa is very nice, but we're all adults here and allowed to do things with a little more style if we so choose."

"Oh my." He grinned up at her. "Didn't we just have Christmas?"

She slithered off his body to a standing position without losing too much of her dignity. She ducked over to the stereo to give Dido a slightly louder reprise, then turned to lead the way upstairs.

The balls of her feet thudding up the stairs jarred all the way up to her palpitating heart. She should have skipped the rum shot in the coffee and just slugged some neat. Too late now. She was on her own. Then a smug smile spread over her lips. *Well, actually, no. I'm not...*

Once in the bedroom, it turned into a frenetic race to tear their own or each other's clothes off, and they were soon rolling around on top of the covers, a tangle of arms and legs.

"You saucy thing," he groaned into her stomach.

Desire had wiped away the last vestige of Stephen's mild manner, and his gentleness had been replaced by an urgency tinged with desperation. His cock jabbing at the inside of her thigh produced a moment of sanity. "Just—just a moment—I have some...things..." She extricated her arm and reached towards her bedside drawer.

Stephen breathed hotly into her neck. "Ohh. Okay." His nibbling teeth were sending electric currents down to her toes. "Been a long time since I've had to worry about *that*."

There was a hiatus of held breath while they both manoeuvred everything into position, but almost before that had happened, Stephen had crushed his weight onto her, expelling all the air in her lungs. With no further preliminaries, he jammed against her as if he had to fight his way in, thrusting hard and fast as if he had lost all awareness of her.

She was no longer in the moment, but outside it. He was hurting her, but she didn't dare say anything to ruin the mood. After a decent interval, she breathed in his ear, "Could we...uh, change?"

She heard a sudden intake of breath, then he drew up on his knees. Before she could suggest anything, he'd flipped her over and it was the same thing, only more furious and from a different angle. It wasn't helping that the condom now felt like sandpaper. She reached underneath herself, hoping she might be able to accelerate her own progress, or at least distract herself from feeling like a mere vessel, but it was all she could manage just to stay steady and avoid head-butting the bedhead.

A moan of discomfort escaped from her, and she heard Stephen say, "You're just loving this, aren't you?"

She bit her lip. "Mmm."

She felt him straighten up and grab her bottom more firmly, spreading the cheeks apart. "You have such a fantastic arse, Adele, I've just got to—"

"No!"

She scrambled away from him, cupping her bottom with her hand, but not before he'd made a clumsy, painful stab at her anus.

They lay collapsed, side by side, panting, Adele's mind zinging with confusion and disappointment. Her chest was tight with misery, all the worst fumblings of her sexual youth coming back to her, waves of shame and frustration crashing on her in equal measure. She heard Stephen groan and expel a deep breath. Finally, he spoke.

"Are you okay?"

"I—I think so. I'm sorry, I wasn't, I didn't expect—I've never..."

"Never? Really?" The incredulous wonder in his voice was doing nothing to reassure her. "Not even with your husband…?"

She steeled herself. "Actually, I'm not into it." She took another breath. "I don't…I don't have a G-spot up my bum like you do." She had felt the need to take the higher ground, but her voice just sounded prissy and peevish.

In the interval of quiet, her eyes searched for his face in the dark to see if she could gauge his thoughts. She heard him chuckle softly.

"All the women I've ever been with loved it."

She opened her mouth to speak, but snapped it shut, her naivety and inexperience apparently indefensible. The constriction in her chest had intensified, making it harder to draw breath. She was grateful when he rolled off the bed to head into the en suite. She lay in the dark, staring upward at nothing, her breath coming in short staccato pulses, wondering how she was going to get rid of him.

The toilet flushed, and his shadowy form blocked the dull light coming from the bathroom window. The light increased as he bent over looking for his clothes. She allowed herself to relax a little. She slid her legs off the bed and plucked her dressing gown from its hook behind the door. Stephen was now sitting on the end of the bed pulling his shirt on.

As they wordlessly made their way down the stairs, Dido was still at it, sliding through "See You When You're 40" for the second time that evening. When they got to the door, she crossed her arms in front of her, pulling her dressing gown tight. She felt small and pathetic with him looming above her in the dark as he turned towards her.

He reached out to ruffle his hand in her hair. "Well, I'm sorry that didn't go exactly to plan."

"No. A pity."

There was a pause as if he expected her to say more.

"It would be nice to try again...maybe when you're feeling more...ready?"

Her mouth opened, but the only sound she emitted was inarticulate. He seemed to take it for agreement as he nodded and leaned down to kiss her cheek.

"I'll give you a call."

With the click of the door, her insides collapsed and tears of self-disgust pricked under her lids. She turned to face the empty room, challenging each piece of furniture as if it was mocking her.

She padded over to the stereo and summarily ejected Dido mid song. She snapped the CD back into its case and jammed it back on the shelf, somewhere out of order, which was fine. She didn't expect to be playing Dido again for quite some time.

Chapter Seven

Excursion

Def. 1. A short journey 2. A deviation from a regular activity or course

IT WAS GOOD to dump her suitcase in the luggage area and collapse into her seat. The train trip up to her brother's was just long enough to enjoy for its own sake, but not so long that she became bored and restless. Out of habit, she had booked a window seat with a table, as she and Toby would sit opposite and play cards to pass the time. Now she was regretting it, as she would most likely end up surrounded by a family for the whole trip.

As the train pulled out, she stood up far enough to inspect

the electronic readouts above her neighbouring seats. She groaned inwardly. All three said reserved from Milton Keynes, which didn't give her much time. She swayed and jolted two carriage lengths to get to the snack bar, collected a watery coffee and a toasted sandwich, and swayed back again. There would be just enough time to enjoy her food in peace and have a loo visit before erecting her fortress wall of a laptop screen.

Apart from the extortionate cost, something identified all rail food as the same. Some hot steamy fume or rubberiness. Yet it hit the spot. She screwed up the greasy paper and popped it into her empty coffee cup. The action reminded her of Charlie.

She stared out of the window. Part of her was sure he'd introduced himself as Charlie Falk. She had been amused at his chutzpah, but the German sound of his name had also struck her as unusual at the time.

But clearly there must be more than one in the area or she had simply got it wrong. She sighed and got up to go to the loo.

Edging back into her seat with clean hands and an empty bladder, she noticed that the grey buildings and back gardens of London's northern suburbs had thinned out to broader and flatter buildings with some expanses of greenery visible.

She opened her laptop, but something about the speed of the scenery zipping by mesmerised her and her fingers rested inactive on the keyboard while her thoughts returned yet again to her evening with Stephen. She had found it hard to knuckle down to work since then, feelings of inadequacy and the virulent need to mount defensive arguments in her head constantly interrupting her normal flow of thinking. She'd also worked through three packets of biscuits in two days, feeling worse for each one.

Getting horizontal and naked with someone was surely a test of who a person really was, but she was still adjusting to the shock, and if she was honest, disappointment, of finding that Stephen's courtesy and kindness had seemingly fallen to the floor with his clothes. Was she too demanding? Or was she just—shudder—daggy and old-fashioned? Or had years of being married to one man turned her into a judgmental prude? She couldn't help but feel that the fault must lie with her...and yet...

She sighed and activated her fingers on the keyboard, bringing her screen to life. By the time the train pulled into Milton Keynes, she was well into her second read-through of *Far From the Tree* and was converting some of her scribbled notes into electronic comments for the author.

Her companions turned out not to be a family, but three lads who looked to be in their late teens. From snatches of conversation that filtered through, it seemed they were planning to hit the Manchester clubs over the weekend. Instead of black words on a white screen, a vision of Toby as a young man was before her, his hair perhaps long and tied back like that of the boy diagonally opposite her, telling her how he was going up to stay with his Uncle Peter for the weekend with a mate and her worrying about what his real plans were. She blinked hard to remove the sudden sting in her eye. Of course, Peter's son Jeremy would have been with him, and *he* had always been a good kid. Her favourite of Peter's children, if it came to that. The girls tended to the precious and whingy side, and she always found herself on the trip home counting her blessings that she'd had a son.

The next hour and a half passed quickly enough, and she was soon murmuring to the boy next to her that Stockport was her stop. Rain had been spattering the window for some time, and it was all but dark, even at half four.

On the platform, ejected from the cocooned warmth of the train, a sharp slice of wind cut up her leg, lifting her coat. Flecks of icy water hit her cheeks and glasses as she looked up and down the platform and another cold gust pushed at her from a train speeding back to London.

It was funny to think it had all started like this. Her scratching her pennies together for an overseas trip, starting with a stay with her older brother in not-London. A stay that had been extended when she found some work at a local pub and extended beyond that when a smart young man on a business trip from London had popped in for lunch and a quick pint. Eons ago, and surely different people from her and Roof.

Adele walked to the taxi rank and wondered whether she should call. Simone could be a bit scatty sometimes, and it was possible she had forgotten about picking her up. She squinted out into the gathering rain to see if she could recognise their green Peugeot. She pulled her trench coat tighter around her to fend off the probing fingers of icy wind, instead trying to focus on Peter's warm and cosy living room and a hot drink. Watching other travellers being met and embraced and loading themselves into comfortable, warm cars, she was just beginning to feel sorry for herself when a voice startled her from behind.

"Aunty Del?"

She spun around to see a thin blonde girl with a large full-lipped smile. She hesitated for a moment before saying, "Connie? Is that you?"

The girl laughed and dived in to give her a hug. She picked up Adele's bag and indicated which way they needed to go. "Mum has a committee meeting tonight that she completely forgot about—" Connie rolled her eyes at Adele in a humorous "surprise-surprise" fashion—"so she sent me to fetch you. I've had my licence six months now, so you needn't be too nervous." She turned back and flashed Adele a mischievous grin.

Adele was just grateful to be inside an enclosed space away from the nasty weather. She marvelled that such a small improvement could result in such relative pleasure. It would make being inside the house even more delicious.

Connie kept up a lively conversation for the fifteen-minute drive to Heaton Chapel. By the time they pulled into the driveway in Holly Grove, she knew what subjects her nieces had passed and failed in their degrees so far and what the current boyfriends' names were (David in Connie's case, Iain in Clarissa's) and how Jeremy was struggling with his A-levels. "But I'll let Dad tell you all about that," she said mysteriously.

Peter was on the phone when they walked in. He beamed an elated smile at her and came over to give her a quick kiss on the cheek, then gestured to the study, where he disappeared and closed the door.

"Mum's got you set up in the downstairs guest room. I'll just pop your bag in there and you can freshen up while I put the kettle on. I'm guessing you'd like a hot coopa tea?"

Adele reached over and squeezed Connie's arm. "You're an angel." She headed to the downstairs bathroom, feeling guilty for labelling her nieces unfairly in her memories. Connie, at least, had apparently grown into a caring and friendly young woman.

Divested of her coat and having run a brush through her windblown hair, Adele was feeling a little more relaxed and looking forward to clasping her hands around that "hot coopa tea".

She came out to the living room and settled herself among the cushions of one of the sumptuous leather sofas. She loved this room. The dark-red walls were something you'd rarely see in Australia, either because it suggested heat or shrank a room, but here, it spoke of a rich cosiness. The shining wood of the skirting boards and built-in bookcases enhanced the look even further. To complete the picture, a scented candle stood in the middle of the coffee table, sparkling in a red glass receptacle. She was just bringing it to her face to inhale the hot sweet vapour when she heard a door click, then Peter was collapsing into the sofa opposite with a put-upon sigh.

"Hopefully that's it for the week." He glanced towards the

kitchen. "You right in there, luv? Need a hand with anything?"

Adele smiled fondly at her brother. He still retained his Australian accent after all this time, but rather than sounding comfortably familiar to her, it made him seem the odd one out in his family of Mancunians where all their Us rhymed with push rather than shove. She had long gotten used to hearing Simone referred to as "Moomeh", or now the kids were older, "Moom". And she in turn called Peter "Loove", as often as not, which sounded generous and encompassing to Adele's ears.

"So, have you settled in okay? Seem like you were never gone?"

"Yes, it's all the same. Except it's not."

"Ah, well." Peter's mouth set into a grimmer line. "I did suggest coming up here to be near us. You could still do that. Rent the damned thing out and stay away from the memories."

"Yes, I know. But I'd rather be in London. It's too cold up here." She grinned at Connie as she set down a tray of tea ware and a plate of biscuits.

"*That's* what central heating's for, my girl! Besides, it's not like London calls for the tropical shirt any more than it does here. Or you could head over to the south of France for a while. Give yourself a real break."

"Oh, you know, but there's all those French people over there." She looked at Connie, and they both laughed, recalling a family joke.

Peter smiled ruefully. "Just seems silly you living all alone in such a large house. It will be expensive to keep it up. A smart flat would be more convenient. Easy to clean, more secure? You could probably buy two, or even three, for what you'd get for that house, and have an income stream to boot."

Adele sighed. Always the practical one. "Yes, eventually, I will probably have to. Roof gave me the house, but no money to go with it. I've got my job back, so that's a start."

"You could always take in a lodger...or two," said Connie brightly.

"Oh yes, and who exactly did you have in mind?" Her father reached over to poke her in the ribs.

"Guys, guys, I've only just got back. All I know is it feels like the right thing for now. I've got so many changes to adjust to, staying in the same home with the same shops and transport options where I know my way around just eases the stress for me a bit."

"Okay, but don't let the place beggar you."

Adele reached over the table and patted her brother's hand. Turning her attention to the tray's contents, she said, "Ah. What McVitie's specials do we have here? Ooh, Jaffa Cakes."

Peter had worked as an engineer at the nearby biscuit factory since he first came to England. He'd met a local girl, had three children, and lived a solid, relatively uneventful life. It wasn't just the living room that felt warm and cosy to Adele; her big brother represented safety and security to her, if not a little bit of dullness, but that was eminently forgivable in someone who was loving and kind. She hadn't dismissed his suggestion to come and live near them out of hand, but her better judgement told her she had to learn to be strong on her own, or risk becoming needy and dependent.

"We haven't planned anything specific for the weekend. I thought we'd see how you felt when you got here. Sim suggested taking you out for a drive to Lyme Park tomorrow and having a big family dinner with everyone here Sunday night." Peter looked at Connie. "That's right, isn't it?"

"No need to go to any trouble. It's only me. I just wanted to see you all. We don't have to do anything. I'm happy to sloth around on the sofa."

"Plenty of time to do that on your own at home." Peter gave her an arch look. "Although I hope you're not spending all your time mooching around. That's not good for anyone."

Adele gave Connie a look of mock despair.

"You can't half tell you're the *older* brother, Dad."

"Not so much emphasis on the word old, thank you very much."

"So where are Clarrie and Jem?"

Caught with a Jaffa Cake, Connie covered her mouth as she spoke. "Clarr's out with Iain doing some shopping—she'll be in later, though, and Jem's upstairs."

"Upstairs? Oh. Busy studying, I guess?"

Her brother frowned and took a biscuit. "Unlikely."

Adele looked at her niece for further information, but Connie just shrugged.

"He'll come down when there's food on. And speaking of, are you hungry? We'd better get that casserole humming. And I'm well overdue for my end-of-week glass of red. You'll have one with me, Addie?"

"Got anything Australian?"

Peter grinned. "I just might…"

They spent the next while in the kitchen bustling around together, getting the table set, pouring wine, putting some music on, and getting the food heated. Adele accepted a glass of Hunter shiraz from her brother and clinked his before taking a sip. This was so what she needed to soften some of the raw edges of her heart.

While Peter went to the bottom of the stairs to call his son to dinner, Adele said, "So who's this singing?"

"Lisa Stansfield. I thought you'd recognise one of Dad's oldies."

"Oldies! Lisa Stansfield is still alive and singing, I'll have you know. I loved her stuff when I lived here. I just didn't recognise this one. Glad she's gone more cruisy. Suits her sexy voice."

Connie gave her a playful poke in the arm. "I didn't say she was *dead*. Calm down."

Adele was grinning as she turned to the sound of footsteps down the stairs, but it was all she could do to keep it high on her face when she saw her nephew. The boy walking up to her had changed beyond recognition: a foot taller with stooped shoulders, his black hair now extending well down his back, and a silver ring hanging off his bottom lip. Now he was closer, she even detected black eyeliner.

Hearing her own laugh sound nervous, she tried to cover with humour. "Lordy, Jem. You kids are really trying to prove how long I've been away. I hardly recognised Connie at the train station, and now you! Can someone show me a photo of Clarissa before I get a third shock? I'm getting old, Connie tells me, so it might just do me in."

Jem smiled shyly at her and walked into her open arms, or to be more accurate, he folded himself around her smaller frame.

She couldn't stop looking at him. His cute-young-boy-ness had morphed into an almost feminine beauty. The usual first question of "How's school going?" bubbled to her lips, but she sensed it would be tactless, and nothing else could get past that standard opener, so she just smiled awkwardly, feeling like a dill.

"Come on, son. Put this on the table and we're ready to serve." Peter handed him a trivet and armed himself with some oven mitts.

Adele couldn't keep the smile off her face. It was so lovely sitting down to a meal with her family. Her eyes kept returning to Jeremy throughout the meal and she had to bite her lip several times, as she was dying to ask him about his hair and makeup and what was behind it all, but she had no wish to provoke her brother.

They were just finishing up their meal when they heard Clarissa breeze in. Adele looked at Connie. "Are you ready in case I have a stroke?"

Even before Adele could turn in her seat, Clarissa had bounded up to where she sat and breathlessly thrown her cold arms around her aunt's neck.

"Aunty Del, Aunty Del! So sorry I wasn't here when you arrived. How are you?"

Apart from a little extra roundness, which actually suited her, Clarrie was the same girl she remembered, just more cheerful. Maybe these boyfriends were doing the girls good.

"I'll just dump this stuff upstairs and fix myself up. Be back in a tick. It's pretty wild out there!" She grabbed her hair on either side and pulled it out horizontally from her head.

Peter smiled and stood up to clear plates. "Always has marvellous timing, that one. Right on dessert."

"Yeah," muttered her nephew next to her, just loud enough for her to hear. "And she has the figure to show for it."

Adele raised her eyebrows but said nothing.

Dessert was an apple pie, and the smells were already wafting from the open oven door as Connie brought it out to cool. "So, we have custard, cream, or ice cream. Self-serve and take your pick."

Jem pushed his chair out. "I might give it a miss, thanks. Pretty full from dinner."

Adele couldn't help her face falling. "Running away already? Are you coming with us tomorrow?"

Her nephew gave her an ironic smile and shake of the head. "Not my thing, sorry."

"How about Sunday?" She was aware of sounding a bit desperate. "Brunch? Just you and me?"

Jeremy snuck a look at his father's back as if expecting him to comment. "Sure...if you like."

"It will be more like 'linner' by the time Sleeping Beauty gets out of bed."

Jeremy pulled a face at his sister.

"So, lunch then. I don't mind. There's no fixed schedule... although we'll need to save room for dinner, don't forget."

Adele watched the retreating back of her rake-thin nephew and wondered if he was deliberately not eating enough or whether it was just accelerated growth. She took a bowl from the kitchen bench and queued for some pie. She was just picking up her spoon as Clarrie blasted back into the room with all the energy of a puppy.

"Oh, pie! Have you heated the custard? Oh no! You've *got* to have hot custard!"

"So, heat some then. No one's stopping you."

"Hot coosted's nice, but cold cream is even better." Adele winked at Connie. Some of the old dynamic between the two sisters were still there, it seemed. Maybe that's why she remembered them as whingy: it was the impact they had on each other. But now they were growing up, perhaps their grating against each other was lessening. It wasn't like she didn't understand what was going on. She and Franny still had their moments when they'd been together too long.

Connie came up behind her and gave her a playful jab. "I bet you'll want to pla-ay a ga-ame of Scrabble later on, ehh?"

Adele grinned and poked her back. *Touche.*

Clarrie landed in the seat next to her. "So, Aunty Del, what do you think of our Jemima, then?"

"Clarissa."

"Oh, come on, Dad. You don't make it easier by being all stuffy about it."

"I just think giving the thing oxygen is asking for trouble. We need to make sure he gets the right kind of help." Peter had already ploughed through his pie and was picking up his empty plate. He came around behind Adele, leaned over, and kissed her on the top of the head. "Sorry, kiddo. Been up since five, so I'm pretty beat. I'm going to turn in early so I'm bright-eyed and bushy tailed for our day out tomorrow. A nine o'clock start okay with you?"

She nodded and watched him head up the stairs. Turning back to her nieces, she said, "Right, now *spill*, you two. What's going on?"

Connie shrugged. "Jem's gay, and Dad can't handle it."

Adele's mouth fell open, and she turned to Clarrie for confirmation.

"Yep. And he's been skiving off with our dresses for a long while now."

"More mine than yours, these days."

"Oh, *meoooow*! Can I get you a saucer of milk to go with that pie?"

"Stop it, you two. Just give me the facts."

"Those *are* the facts, Aunty Del. Dad came home one day and caught Jem in full dress-up mode. Make-up, Mum's heels, the lot. He thought—" Connie covered her mouth and started laughing.

Clarrie continued, "Dad thought it was some friend of ours all dollied up. I reckon Jem could've almost carried it off if Dad hadn't recognised the new handbag he'd given Mum for her birthday."

"Oh gawd," Adele groaned. "What happened?"

"Went off his nut, of course," said Connie cheerfully.

Adele wiped her hand over her mouth. "Girls, this isn't funny. At least not for Jem it isn't."

Connie stopped laughing and made an attempt at being serious. "No, you're right, Aunty Del, but humour is the only thing that's going to get us through this when Dad can't accept what's going on. Sending him off to see a counsellor isn't going to change him, I don't think."

"Cross-dressing doesn't have to mean you're gay. You don't think it's just a passing thing? Exploring boundaries, trying things out?"

"Hmm. I don't think so," said Clarrie. "The signs have been there for a long time if you knew what to look for. It actually explains a lot of things in retrospect."

Connie nodded in agreement.

"But...but there's nothing else going on is there? He's not um..." Adele lowered her voice, "anorexic or anything?"

"I reckon he is. I've heard him throwing up in the toilet," said Clarrie.

"That would be more bulimia, Clarr, but I don't think so. He was probably out drinking too much with his girlie mates."

It was a lot to take in at short notice, and Adele's head was awhirl with questions. "You've been talking a lot about your father's attitude, but what about your mum's?"

Connie shot a look at her sister. "Oh, she's okay with it up to a point. She's a bit stuck between Dad and Jem and trying not to take sides. She's always one to avoid rocking the boat."

"So, after what point is she not okay, then?"

"He doesn't bring male friends home any more, put it that way." Clarrie got up and helped herself to another wedge of pie. Connie watched her and shook her head at Adele.

"So, theory's okay, but actual practice will take a while."

"Yep." Connie nodded. "A long while."

Adele sighed and slumped in her chair. "Oh dear."

Clarrie leaned towards her and threw an arm over her shoulder, pulling her in for an apple pie-scented kiss on the cheek. "But apart from that, it's all happy families, Aunty Del, and we're very glad you're here."

Chapter Eight

Exploration

Def. 1. The act of exploring an unfamiliar area 2. Thorough examination of a subject

YESTERDAY HAD BEEN a long but joyous day. Luckily, the wild weather had cleared to leave fresh and brittle colours behind, with wet roads and pavements covered in sodden leaves the only remaining evidence of the stormy night before.

After a full English breakfast at a pub on the way, Peter and Simone had taken her to explore Lyme Park, which consumed the greater part of the day. They'd viewed the rooms, paused for cream teas in the café, and walked around the grounds where Peter had taken their pictures with their arms "around" the Darcy statue in the lake.

Then, after they'd got home and surrendered themselves to the sofas and tea and biscuits, Adele had been rigged into what became a marathon series of Scrabble games with Connie and David. Glasses of red had progressed to sips of scotch by 11.00 p.m., and the arguments over valid words were getting sillier and sillier. David had then proposed a game of dirty word Scrabble, and after seeing dubious words on her rack all night, Adele found to her embarrassment that she couldn't come up with a decent one to save herself. So much for being the "with it" aunt.

She now lay in bed with a smile on her face, aware that it was after 8.30 a.m., but with no reason to get up other than to make tea and return to her cosy nest and read for a while. If Jem was up late, she could put in a few hours on the manuscript, but there was no rush. She was doing okay for time, having put in some late nights the week just gone so she could enjoy her break guilt-free.

She tiptoed out to the kitchen and made herself a tea. She could hear murmurings upstairs and the flush of a toilet, but no one was venturing down yet. Lovely. She took her tea back to bed and settled in to read some of her new novel. Except she couldn't seem to get past the first paragraph of the next chapter. Her mind kept picking up little snippets of conversation and recalling things people had said and what they meant or didn't mean. And how her lunch would go with Jem and what they would talk about. And could she be of help in any way?

She had not brought up the subject in front of Peter, but at one point there'd been a moment with Simone in the ladies' toilet. Looking in the mirror as they washed their hands, Adele had said, "Simone, tell me. Is everything okay with Jem? The girls told me what's been going on."

Simone had looked a bit startled but laughed it off. "Oh yes, we'll get past this."

Adele frowned. "You say that as if it's a temporary thing?"

"If it's temporary, we'll get past it, and if it's not, *Peter* will just have to get past it. He's already adjusted a little bit here and there, not that anyone but me would have noticed, but he has. We'll get there in the end, Adele, don't worry. He loves his son."

Adele had nodded and followed Simone out of the toilet. She wasn't so sure it was something you "got past", but it was a more positive and accepting attitude than she'd been led to expect by the girls. Perhaps Simone was just playing the longer game and waiting to see how the cards fell. Maybe that's why she was still happily married and Adele wasn't.

Roof had enjoyed coming up here and had often done so on his own. The design work he'd been doing with McVitie's when she first met him had continued, making the occasional trip necessary, except then he stayed with the Walmsleys, not in a hotel.

For them, the break had been sudden. When Toby had died, the whole family had come down—or up, as they say, which seemed illogical to her—for the funeral, but within two further weeks, Adele and Rufus had packed up and left the country, with only Adele making a last visit for goodbyes. This was then followed by two years' worth of superficial conversations that had communicated little. Even Franny hadn't understood the full extent of where things had got to, until in her kitchen one morning, Adele had turned up in tears with a large suitcase saying, "I'm done."

Adele had grown sick of making excuses for her husband's distant and loveless behaviour. Since Toby had started school, it had been about how hard he had to work, trips away exhausting him, and recovering from drinking with clients. Then when Toby had died, he'd gone into a spiral of despair and blackness where she couldn't reach him, and didn't have the energy to anyway, having her own mental anguish to cope with.

She had hoped the new environment and change of lifestyle in Australia would refresh both their hearts and their marriage, but it hadn't. Roof spent ever longer hours on his computer holed up in his study and the spare room, claimed as his bedroom from the very start, with him not even bothering to put his clothes in the wardrobe in the main bedroom when he unpacked. The line had always been, so he "didn't wake her coming to bed late", but when she'd queried his unpacking in the spare room, he'd said, "I think it just works better this way for both of us."

The last time they had sex was the night following Toby's death: a distraught, mutual, mindless comfort, which neither had had the heart to revisit. Then one day she had just woken up, literally and figuratively, and realised her marriage was a farce and it wasn't ever going to get better if only one of them was trying. Even before they left the UK, she'd broached the possibility of them seeing counsellors, either together or separately, but his reaction had been so angrily dismissive that she hadn't raised it again. That was around the time she'd given up on the support group at St Bart's.

Adele's book was still open on her lap and her tea mug empty when she heard the coffee grinder whirr into action, and the heavenly smell of freshly ground coffee wafted into her room. She wandered out in her T-shirt and pyjama bottoms and found David bent with his head to one side, tinkering with the expensive coffee machine Peter had bought in the early years of their marriage "to ensure we stay together".

"Do you have a licence to run that thing?"

David stood up straight and laughed. He was dressed similarly to her, but she couldn't help but notice that he filled out his T-shirt with a lot more tautness than she did hers. "Oh, sure. It's a bit temperamental, but it still does the job."

Adele eyed the two mugs lined up on the bench. "I don't suppose I could get you to add one for me?"

"Of course. Not too worse for wear after last night, are we? Do you realise we went through more than half of Pete's Glenfiddich? I'll have to get him a replacement."

Adele smiled. It was strange but nice at the same time that David seemed on such comfortable terms with her brother. He'd been with Connie for a less than a year, but they seemed fairly settled together, despite their young ages. David was in his first year of working as a junior engineer, so that probably qualified him as a decent son-in-law as far as Peter was concerned. Adele accepted the cup of creamy caffeinated goodness he handed her and nodded as he excused himself to go back upstairs.

The coffee was pure excellence and she wandered over to the front bay window to stare out as she took blissful sips. Maybe there would be a wedding to plan for soon, she mused. Then Franny might come over, and—

Something hit the kitchen bench and she spun around to see Jeremy putting the kettle on. "Oh, you scared me!"

He gave her a smile. "I like to creep around."

"You're up earlier than I expected. You still up for brunch?"

"Sure."

"Where would you like to go?"

"Nothing much round here. How about we catch the train into Manchester? Plenty of cool places there you might like."

"Done. It's nearly ten now. I'll race in and have a quick shower. Is a ten-thirty leave time doable for you?"

"Wow. Okay, I'll have to skip the full make-up routine, then."

She laughed and headed for the bathroom, not quite sure whether he was joking or not.

*

THEY CAUGHT THE train into town and emerged from Manchester Piccadilly into a rush of people where they just blended in. Adele had eyed Jem's outfit, noting the bagginess of his shorts and the loose round-necked top under his flared coat. It kind of worked, but it was definitely a feminine look: how feminine only became clear to her when they sat down on the train and she realised the baggy shorts were actually a skirt.

"Lucky you've got such great legs," she commented as she plucked at the material of his skirt, pretending to inspect the quality.

He led her out of the station along some streets with heavy traffic until they came to Sackville Gardens. Adele paused to read the plaque for a bronze statue of a man seated on a bench, who turned out to be Alan Turing. When they came to a canal, Jem waved his hand in a flourish.

"You are now in the Gay Village."

That explained the rainbow banners and colourful balloon displays. Adele looked with closer attention at the shop fronts facing onto the water.

Jem led her to a side alley that took them to a brick archway with "The Flag Pole" curving over their heads in red letters. It took about three seconds for Adele to realise she was by far the oldest person there, and one of the few females, if you excluded the staff. They took the last vacant table in a corner at the back. A waitress placed a couple of menus in front of them. "The water's self-serve." She gestured vaguely behind her.

Adele knew what she wanted, so while Jem frowned over the choices she gazed around the room. The walls were raw brick and covered in poster art and screen prints. Roy Lichtenstein and

Andy Warhol provided the primary colour power to the décor, and the furniture was all chrome and varnished wood set on a polished concrete floor. The latter meant the acoustics were set to loud, but it all added up to a high-energy vibe.

"I'll get us some water." She passed tables of smart-looking young men with chiselled facial hair all engaged in focused or laughing conversation, some absorbed by their devices or laptops while they worked and sipped coffees.

She returned to her seat and placed a glass of water in front of Jem. "So, is this where you meet with your friends?"

"Sometimes. I'm on a waiting list to work here, actually, but it's a long list."

"I can't see any male waiters. Do you think you have a chance?"

Jem grinned and leaned across the table so she could hear his lowered voice. "Aunty Del, none of the wait staff are girls."

Adele leaned slowly back in her chair. "Ohhh. I seeee." She laughed and took a second, more educated look. Now she saw strong jawlines, heavy make-up, and some hairstyles that must be wigs or hairpieces.

Jem was watching her look, with either a pleased or superior smile on his face. She wasn't sure which. "So, what do you think?"

"I tell you what I think. I want to hear about *you*, nephy. Tell me the whole story. What's going on for you these days? It seems I've completely lost the plot as your devoted aunt."

Adele had to wait for Jem's answer as the waitperson—"Fay",

according to her nametag—took their order. She watched as he/she flirted outrageously with Jem and studiously ignored his frumpy companion. Jem was in his element.

Jem smiled fondly after Fay as she sashayed back to the bar. He turned back to Adele with a more serious expression and clasped his hands on the table in front of him. "Okay. What do you want to know?"

"How long have I been asleep for? When did you realise?"

Jem frowned and pressed his thumbs together. "I've always joost been me. The realisation was more that what 'me' was, didn't accord with what other people thought 'me' ought to be. I think I was about five, and new at school. There was some playground game where you had to catch someone and kiss them. Well, no one told me it had to be someone of the opposite sex..." Jem's shoulders shook as he laughed.

"Oh dear. At least they were only five-year-olds."

"Yeah, I learned quickly. I also have a memory of watching this old film with the family on some wet afternoon, chariot races and stooff—"

"*Ben-Hur*, maybe?"

"Yeah, that sounds right. Naked chests, sweat, and deep booming voices...that guy stretched out on the table after being trampled by the horses...anyway. It featured in my dreams for a long while afterwards...maybe still does!"

"Ha. Have you heard of Gore Vidal? Famous homosexual writer. He worked on that screenplay and deliberately put suggestive stuff in there and instructed that actor who was 'stretched out on the table' to work it, so it wasn't just your imagination."

Plates descended on their table and there was silence as they gathered up their cutlery and arranged serviettes.

"So, what made you come out, then? That must have taken some courage."

"My friends, mainly. I have some who were out already, and while it was hard for them, at least they got to be themselves. I've got some really nice girlfriends too...which is just as well, as bringing a male friend home now would create parental panic."

"Your mum seems to think your dad will come round eventually."

Jem's expression flickered. "'Eventually' is a long piece of string."

"It's better than a door slammed in your face. I'll bet some of your friends have had that."

"True." Jem sighed and concentrated on sawing at a strip of bacon.

The food was good, although their coffees had been slow to arrive. Adele held her cup up with both hands for a sip.

"So, is there...anyone special?"

Jem's cheeks glowed a delicate shade of pink. "No...not really." His eyes shifted sideways to the bar area.

Adele laid her cup down and likewise looked sideways. Two waitresses stood talking waiting for coffee orders.

"Fay?"

"No, the other one. Alice. Alfie, when not working. He left school last year, so I only see him here now."

Adele took in the blonde curls and the square jaw. "I see." She looked back at her nephew. "So, have you got a working name?"

"Yes. When I'm togged up, I'm Crystal."

"Must be an expensive business, all that gear and make-up. Are you thinking of trying to be a professional drag queen, or just keep it as a fun thing?"

He settled his chin on his hand, still glancing over to the bar intermittently. "Don't know."

Adele reached over for his other hand and gave it a squeeze. "I'm sure it will all be fine in the long run. I'm happy for you and worried at the same time, if that makes sense."

He nodded.

"Hey. I tell you what. Why don't you come up and spend a weekend at mine soon? It would be nice to have the company."

Jem's face brightened. "I have some friends in Islington. I could catch up with them at the same time."

"Well, yes...you could. But I have to be the responsible aunty, don't forget, or your parents will never trust me again. Let's see. How about we throw a formal dinner party where they all come in their poshest frocks?"

Jem's eyes widened. "That would be *awe*some," he whispered.

"Then we have a plan."

Chapter Nine

Extempore

Def. Done without preparation

ADELE'S NURTURING TIME with loved ones was capped by a family dinner and promises to do it all again soon. It all seemed ancient history by Tuesday lunchtime, however, when she was knee-deep in pear-shapedness. She had risen early, intending to put in a solid day of work, only to stand naked and freezing in her shower stall, listening to grinding noises in the pipes and no hot water. Just when she had given up and leaned in to turn the taps off, an explosion of cold water had doused her and left her groaning and her teeth chattering uncontrollably.

With her dressing gown wrapped tightly around her and a towel turbaned around her head, she had called the emergency "superhero" plumber number on her fridge. It was lucky her house wasn't flooding, as the superhero response rate approached geriatric. After a few hours of banging and clanging that took till 2.00 p.m., she was told the whole tank needed replacement and they'd be back the next day with a new one to install for her, and "here's what you'll be up for, luv." Adele had felt the colour drain from her face as she signed the docket, trying to block her brother's warning about "expensive houses" from echoing in her ears.

Her work day utterly destroyed and her nerves frayed and irritated, she wanted out. A long walk. A comforting chat. She wondered if Joanne might be around. Even if she wasn't, a calming sit in her pew would help. She went to grab her trench coat and scarf.

A light wind gusted leaves and bits of rubbish around in willy-willies, so it was pleasant to finally arrive at the church and have its large empty space occlude all exterior noise and thought. The space appeared to be empty, so she decided to take a pew closer to the altar today, to sit more in the light where she could make out more detail in the stained-glass windows and the inscriptions carved in the wooden lecterns and choir stalls.

To sit more in the light... She smiled, her hands clasped in her lap. Her weekend with family had been like an injection of happy juice, and she was still full and high from it, even given the events of that morning. She was delighted her nieces had nice boy-friends, that her brother's marriage seemed healthy and mutually respectful, and that her nephew was on his way to finding himself. All she had to do was hold her own end up and create her own happy.

She inhaled, expanding her chest and lifting her shoulders, then exhaled gently. She had a lot to be grateful for: a roof over her head; enough resources to cover her bills, even this big emergency one; a job that she enjoyed and could control the pace of, that paid reasonable money; a wonderful supportive family, and her health and wellbeing. She opened her eyes and lifted her face up to the glowing colours emanating from the three tall windows over the altar. They were so—

A pew far behind her creaked. Her flowing sense of calm was replaced by jagged bouncing thoughts. She wasn't good with people sitting behind her, watching her. It was why she normally sat near the back. She moved to the side, as if she was looking into a bag next to her, and used the opportunity to quickly glance behind her. But it stretched to a longer look, as her eyes were still full of light and she was looking back into the gloom. At first, she thought it must have just been one of those adjusting creaks that happen all the time with temperature changes, but she finally discerned a shadowy figure near the back and, throwing caution to the wind, kept staring until she could see who or what it was.

It was a little boy, his head barely visible over the prayer rail. She turned back around, confusion muddling her thoughts. It was

Charlie. It must be. But here? Why?

By the time she'd cycled through these thoughts a few times to no purpose and concluded that she should walk back and speak with him, she stood up only to find he'd gone. She hurried out to the front entrance. From the top step she had a good view down the street in each direction, and she thought she saw a small figure in grey turning near the end at the corner. She ran down the steps to see if she could catch up with him.

She realised, as she started puffing hard, that she had managed to put thoughts of this little boy and her conversation with Stephen out of her head the whole weekend, but they had been bubbling away on a subterranean level, just waiting to burst back into her front-of-consciousness. There were shops up ahead, and he was ducking around the people walking towards her, causing her to lose sight of him. She hurried on, though, not even sure why it seemed so important. After a few more turns, she'd even lost track of what street they were in, but thankfully, at the end of this one, she saw him turn in at the front gate of a house. Now he'd arrived somewhere, she slowed down and caught her breath. She removed her scarf and stuffed it in her pocket, letting the cool air freshen her damp neck.

The gate he had opened had been grey and near what she could now see was a rose bush of some description. She pulled up in front of the gate and placed her hand on it. She frowned and looked around. There was a "To Let" sign in the garden. She stood back and checked the gates on either side. No, neither of them were grey. It had to be this one. Maybe he'd slipped down the side of the house to take a short cut.

She lifted the latch, which was surprisingly stiff, and entered the front garden. She looked down the sides of the house. One was blocked up with unpruned hedges, the other she could walk down. The path opened out into a small back yard with a high fence enclosing all three sides. No back gate or gap for escaping, no outbuildings or trees to hide a small boy. She looked to the back of the house. A plain patio with no furniture. Windows that looked very locked up.

Adele let out a frustrated huff and returned the way she had come. She stood for a moment out on the street and removed her glasses, giving them a good polish on the corner of her trench coat. *Blind, batty, or both?* That was the question.

She walked to the corner and noted that she was in Putney Street. The house was number 37. She at least knew where she was, roughly. At the T-intersection was a small grocer's shop facing down Putney Street. She crossed the road, realising she was short of milk and bread. A chocolate bar might also be necessary.

She gathered up what she needed and went to the counter where an elderly man stood browsing a newspaper. He looked up over his glasses as she approached. As he processed her items and put them in a bag, she decided she had nothing to lose by asking.

"I'm sorry. Do you know anything about the house across the road that's to let?"

He leaned forward. "Madam?"

She repeated her question.

"Ah, there is no one renting that house for quite some time."

"I see. Does it have something wrong with it?"

The man shook his head. "I am thinking it is just an unhappy house."

"I don't suppose you know the family who used to live there?"

"No, sorry, madam, I am not knowing the family."

Adele nodded, feeling she had exhausted the questions she could decently ask without attracting attention to herself. She was just pushing the door open when the man called out to her.

"Madam? The little boy, he used to be coming here. He was coming here a lot."

She turned back. "Do you remember his name by any chance?"

"No, madam. But he was liking football very much."

"Thank you." She nodded and walked out. Well, that narrowed it down.

*

ADELE MADE HERSELF some cheese on toast and a cup of tea and sat down to her laptop. She should have thought of doing this in the first place. There would be something online about what happened.

Her searches brought up stories on several missing children over the years, far too many, all of whom were either last seen on the heath, or who lived nearby. It took a few clicks to find the right one, and even though she half expected it, it still made her gasp with recognition. Pictured was Charlie Falk, *her* Charlie Falk, holding a soccer ball, looking straight at the camera, as cheeky as you like.

Adele sat back in her chair and swallowed convulsively, her heart thudding painfully against her ribs, dread seeping into her nerves. She gripped her hands together in her lap to stop them shaking, but the loose volatile feeling spread to her arms and up her shoulders. She swallowed again and pulled her glasses off, trying to focus on the manual task of giving them a vigorous clean with the corner of her shirt. There had to be some mistake, or an explanation that she was just too dumb to see.

She read through the short piece and looked for more. The articles confirmed what Stephen had told her. Charlie had last been seen at the after-school game in the park on the eighth of December, which coincided with their last week of frantic activity prior to vacating the house and the country. Not a time when she would have paid much attention to media and news reports, even when the subject was so close to home. She had been truly hunkered down by that stage just trying to drag herself to the finishing line.

Further articles featured an interview with one of the football fathers, Sam Norton, who was at that last game and recalled seeing Charlie walking up the slope to where he normally caught the bus. This was followed by a picture of an unhappy-looking Stephen carrying his sport bag. One article even attempted to link

Charlie's disappearance with two others that had occurred over the previous two years, both where the boys concerned played soccer on the heath, although they were from different schools.

Towards Christmas the pleas became more desperate with the parents interviewed and pictured. Someone had come forward to say they'd seen Stephen hanging around the heath after dark, and there were reports of him being taken in for further questioning. Adele was chewing her finger by this time, worrying a rag nail.

By January, the articles were thinning out and pretty much recycling the same information with nothing new to add. Sniffer dogs had done the rounds of the heath and nearby locations known to be on Charlie's walking route to school and the heath. Any trails picked up had gone cold near the Vale of Health, leading nowhere. There was even a quote from the Indian shop owner, Mr Bopanna, saying how Charlie would drop in every day on his way home from school—"he was being very keen on collecting football cards"—but not on the day he went missing.

The only other article she found with anything new, distressingly, was about a search warrant issued for Stephen's home. Nothing was found, but it noted how he'd had to take "stress leave" from work, and some parents were expressing concern about teacher screenings and police checks.

After a long gap in time, she found one final piece dated last November, around the two-year anniversary, bringing together those two other missing children. While the report postulated a theory that they might be linked, it also noted there had been no similar disappearances since, which could mean the perpetrator had lost his nerve, been apprehended, or moved on. The journalist had interviewed the local police and been informed that the search for the perpetrator was ongoing and for anyone with any information to come forward etc.

Adele glugged her cold tea and fetched a band-aid for her now-bleeding finger. She returned to one of the articles with Charlie's picture. How could this *be*? Her computer said *nooo*. Any explanations she could cobble together involved twin brothers and impersonating tricksters and were too laughable to be taken seriously. Even the possibility of her simply hallucinating begged the question of why him, when she wouldn't have known him from a bar of soap before this? The only real explanation was that he was still alive and no one knew. Had he cooperated in his own kidnapping? And why had no one else reported seeing him when he was running around in broad daylight?

Adele's temple throbbed as her ideas became more radical and far-fetched. There had to be some key fact missing that would join everything together so it made sense.

Her thoughts returned to Stephen and how caring and sad he'd been after Toby's death. To be then dragged through all *this*. It surely must have played a part in his marriage break-up, and if not, it certainly twisted the knife. It was a wonder he was still able to hold it together, poor man; he had a lot to be bitter about. Perhaps she should give him a call. Suggest another catch-up...just to talk.

Adele looked at her watch. It was *that* time of the day already. She'd had a walk already, and a *run* come to that, but her thoughts were so jumbled and anxious she was in no state to concentrate on work, and sitting around the house would probably result in multiple pantry raids and the decimation of what was supposed to be a week's supply of biscuits.

She grabbed her coat off the back of the sofa where she had thrown it earlier, and thrust her arm through a sleeve, having a strong sense of taking up some kind of gauntlet. She wrapped her scarf around her neck and cinched her belt tight round her waist, pausing, with her hands on her hips, to stare at the dark glass panel in her front door. Her reflection stared back at her, her mouth a hard, defiant line.

"Okay then. Bring it on."

Chapter Ten

Exoplasm

Def. 1. The outer layer of cytoplasm 2. Exteriorised spiritual energy

THIS WAS STUPID. She was stupid. It was *all* stupid. Her thoughts were on an unhelpful unending loop as she trudged along, hands deep in her pockets. Was she trying to prove that she wasn't mad? Or that she was?

She stumped up the grass bank, noting it was now getting long enough to blow over in the breeze. She paused at the top and closed her eyes, allowing the wind to hit her full in the face and blow all the loose tendrils of her hair back. She took a deep breath and walked forward. It would all be an anticlimax. What on earth was she expecting?

But no. Her heart constricted painfully. There he was.

"Hello, Mrs Soames."

You cheeky little bugger. She walked carefully up to the bench as if he was a skittish colt to be scared off at the least noise. She took a seat and pulled the flanks of her coat over her knees. She turned and gave him a direct look.

"Hello, Charlie."

What *was* it with those brown bananas? And that awful scab that refused to heal? Clearly, he was a picker. And that tribal banging on the bench rung...

"You led me a merry chase today, young man. What were you doing in the church?"

"My mum cleans the church. I meet her there sometimes."

Adele frowned. "There was no one there, Charlie. Anyway, you left alone." A further thought occurred to her. "Why weren't you at school?"

His cheeks were bulging with banana and it seemed for a moment that he wasn't going to answer her. His throat moved up and down convulsively. He licked his lips as he screwed up his paper bag. "I'd forgotten something."

"Charlie, where are you living? Your parents are so worried about you. What are you doing here?"

Charlie's mouth fell slightly opened and he looked frightened. "I—I'm getting extra coaching. To improve my kicking...he said it would be okay. He'd tell Mum…"

Charlie pushed himself off the bench, and panic rose in her chest.

"But Charlie, you can't—"

"I've got to go." He ran over to the bin and lobbed his rubbish in. He stopped suddenly and turned back to her, as if he'd forgotten something. "Mrs Soames?" He gave her an agonised, searching look. "Toby says he misses you. He said to tell you he's okay."

He banged the side of the bin with the flat of his hand and raced off.

*

SHE WAS STILL there on the bench, like Lot's wife, an hour later. Her face felt burnt where the sharp wind had repeatedly dried the wetness on her cheeks, pulling the skin tight. She continued to stare out over the playing fields, seeing nothing, only dimly aware of the fading light. A crow flew down and perched on the bench rail next to her. She turned to look at it, and it cocked its head to one side, its yellow eye piercing and curious.

She watched as it took off, a lithe black spirit, disappearing into the sky. Gradually, an awareness of a sore bum and stiff joints came to her, and she stretched her legs out straight in front of her.

Oh Toby, Toby, Toby. Why send an emissary? Why not come yourself?

She stood and slowly turned to go home. All her movements

were stiff and laboured, as if she was pushing her way through half-set jelly. Somehow she found herself at her front door, her mind still thick with fog, fumbling for her house keys in her pocket.

The door squeaked open, and she squinted into the gloom, wondering if Toby might be there to greet her. Without turning the light on, she sat on the sofa, as if the solution was to sit still and wait, that if she waited long enough, and focused hard enough, he would come. After a while, she heaved herself up and got a scented candle in a glass jar, still in its box on the dresser. She lit both its wicks and placed it on the coffee table in front of her. She sat and focused on the twin flames, blanking her mind.

If only she could empty her mind, there might be room for something else to come in.

*

HER EYES OPENED. At least it felt like they had opened. She blinked and stared into the dark, seeing nothing. There was the smell of acrid smoke. As her eyes adjusted, she became aware of a pale grey square of light: the street lights still glowing through her front door. She groped her way to a standing position and found the switch on the lamp behind the sofa—a soft golden illumination rather than the sterile blaring glare of the downlights in the ceiling. A tendril of smoke still wafted to the ceiling from the expired candle.

Her neck felt stiff and her head was heavy, but she felt

somehow peaceful, as if there was nothing more to do or hope for. What was, was. What wasn't, wasn't.

Mercifully, she still had her trench coat on, and she pulled it tight around her now, all the chill and bleakness of 5.00 a.m. coming on her in a rush. There didn't seem any point in going to bed now, so she went to the kitchen and put the kettle on. Her mouth felt dry and horrible. She was gagging for a tea.

She jiggled her teabag and splashed some milk into the mug, a routine she had performed thousands of times in her life. Instead of returning to the sofa, she took a seat at the breakfast bar, the seat next to the one Toby had last sat in. She imagined him there, sitting next to her, calmly watching her as she sipped her tea. Where was he now? Where was Charlie? Was Toby also somehow condemned to relive his last routines over and over like Charlie? Was he also in turn appearing to some random other person rather than to a significant loved one? Would he visit Roof and not her? Her heart ached at the thought.

Adele did not believe in an all-powerful male god visiting inequity on a believing and non-believing population. It was all a lot of political hogwash built up over time to support the superiority of one tribe (or sex) over another. The origin of spirit and what it was all about at the most basic level seemed lost to modern civilisation with its multitude of agendas. There was an energy source out there. It was what she felt when she sat in St Bart's; it was what she felt in the quiet richness of a forest. And she sensed that Toby and Charlie were now part of that surrounding energy. The only difference was, Charlie had somehow manifested. An image of Lockwood dragging Cathy's wrists over broken glass flashed into her mind as she recalled the stony chill of Charlie's small hands as she had tried to warm them. The memory sent sharp prickles through her nerves.

She didn't pretend to understand it; there was no point trying. She knew what she had experienced. She just had to go with it and see what it meant. Maybe Charlie would bring Toby to her.

One thought taking shape in her mind was that she needed to share these ideas, needed to get this off her chest somehow, to someone who would be open to receiving such concepts.

She hopped off her stool and searched for her phone. She soon found the number for the support group at St Bart's. It was nearly 6.00 a.m., so she would have to wait till business hours to hear back. She texted a brief request for Joanne to call her. Would she have any time to see her today for a private chat, a spiritual consultation?

Adele had just placed the phone on the counter, when to her embarrassment, it rang.

"Oh, Joanne, I'm so sorry. I thought you'd collect my message later."

"That's okay, Adele. I'm an early riser. I do some meditation usually, followed by a walk to get my brain going. Requests for spiritual consultations at odd hours should be acted on immediately, I think."

"Oh dear. It's very good of you. Could I...could I take you for breakfast perhaps?"

"Why don't you head over now and we'll do a walk together. At this time of the morning, the canal paths are reasonably private. By the time we're coming back some cafes will be open, and we can grab something then, if you still feel like it."

Adele hung up, but not before receiving a firm injunction to "rug up".

She pulled up near St Bart's within the quarter hour. The front door was ajar, and she crept in. Joanne was already striding down the aisle, rubbing her hands together.

"Excellent. Let us depart."

They crossed the street and walked under the bridge to the canal path. Joanne turned right, towards Regent's Park. Even colder air seemed to emanate from the water, and the mist hovering above it resembled exoplasmic shapes extending fingers and hands toward the canal banks.

They walked in silence through the pools of light issuing from street level and house gardens. Adele pulled her scarf down from over her mouth and felt the sharp wet air enter her lungs.

"Thank you for seeing me at short notice like this."

"I had a feeling you would be in touch at some point. I've been waiting."

Adele turned to look at her. "What gave you that idea?"

"It's like I said when I saw you the other day. I sense there's a struggle going on within you. I knew it would out somehow, and

I hoped you would come to me when you needed help."

"Well, you were right."

They walked on in silence, their mutual attention caught by a boat gliding in the opposite direction, back under the bridge.

"Joanne, in your support group, did you ever encounter the parents of a boy called Charlie Falk? This would have been a few years back."

"Hmm. As I've told you, I'm great with faces, not so good with names...although Falk. That name does sound familiar."

"Apparently his mother used to clean the church?"

"Oh! Yes, of course. Sylvia! Yes, she did clean the church, but she didn't come to the group. I invited her, though, a few times. She and her husband weren't coping at all well after the disappearance of their son, as you would expect. They soon decided to leave the area altogether. I'm not sure where they are now. Why do you ask?"

Adele took a deep breath. "Because Charlie has been coming to see me."

"What?" Joanne stopped walking and turned to face her. "Their son Charlie?"

Adele nodded. "Yes."

Joanne's eyes narrowed. "What do you mean he's been 'coming to see you'? You know he's been missing for a long time now?"

Adele reached over and threaded her arm through Joanne's; a gesture she probably wouldn't have made with even her closest girlfriend, yet it felt natural with Joanne, inevitable, even.

"Let's keep walking," she said quietly.

After they'd walked on for a few minutes, she continued.

"I go to the playing fields on the heath every so often just to sit and spend time with my son, because it was a place where he was very happy. Also the place he spent his last afternoon alive." Joanne squeezed her arm around Adele's and patted her hand. "And Charlie sits with me and keeps me company."

Joanne said nothing. She simply raised her chin and stared directly ahead as they continued walking. Eventually she spoke.

"I counsel many people who visit psychics and charlatans desperately trying to contact their loved ones. Occasionally you hear stories that feel genuine, but I do wonder. It's easy to deceive someone vulnerable, willing something to be true. But I have no doubt we are surrounded by spirits and angels." She paused to look sideways at Adele, a sad expression in her eyes. "I wish Sylvia could know this, poor woman. Does he speak to you?"

"Yesterday, he said that Toby had told him to pass on the message that he misses me, and that he's okay."

Joanne's eyes closed briefly, and her pace slowed. "Blessed child. Of course he's okay. He's in the arms of the great loving spirit." She turned to Adele. "How did that make you feel?"

"More whole. More at peace. I just wish he'd come to tell me himself."

"Oh dear." Joanne leaned into her and gave her a grim smile. "We humans...we can't help it. Whatever we get, we always want that bit more. So many grieving people would give their right arm just to have the confirmation you've received."

Adele nodded but couldn't speak. They walked on in silence, each with their own thoughts, but connected through their inter-linked arms, the warmth of which Adele felt along the whole left side of her body.

"And what of poor Charlie? His soul must be restless. They never found him, you know."

"That is… That's what I wanted to talk to you about." Adele described how she had followed him to 37 Putney Street.

"Yes, yes. That was their home. The owners have struggled to rent it, for some reason."

Adele stopped dead, pulling Joanne back in her stride.

"Sorry, I just—" Adele's hand went up to her mouth. "I just thought…"

Joanne waited, a concerned look on her face. "Thought what?"

"Charlie said—has said more than once—that he's there 'wait-ing for someone'." Adele looked fearfully at Joanne. "You don't think it's…"

"The last person who saw him alive? His…abductor?"

"Oh my god." Adele's breath came in ragged pants, fog puff-ing out of her mouth in the icy morning air. She leaned over and placed her hands on her knees, her head hurting with the thought that had just hit her.

She felt Joanne's hand on her back. "Adele, are you okay?"

She levered herself up, aware of how contorted her face must look when it felt frozen in horror. She tried to speak, but her voice came out only as a choked whisper.

"Joanne, oh my god, *Joanne.* He said he was waiting for his *coach.*"

Chapter Eleven

Expresso

Def: Coffee brewed by forcing hot water through finely ground darkly roasted coffee beans.

JOANNE HAD INSISTED, at the end of their walk—prematurely cut short when she had led a shaken Adele back to her office for a cup of tea and some privacy—that Adele come to the next counselling session. When she objected out of hand, Joanne had been clearer.

"There's someone in the group it would be good for you to meet. I think she will want to meet you, too."

Joanne had not elaborated further, except to say that maybe the two of them, once introduced, could grab a coffee after the meeting. It was two days since their walk, and Adele now found herself loitering in the vestibule of St Bart's, reading about the upcoming spring jumble sale on the community noticeboard.

The last two days had been awful: trying to work, trying to sleep, and achieving little in either department. The thought of walking to the heath now filled her with dread. Her brain whirred away non-stop, going over and over scraps of remembered dialogue with both Charlie and Stephen, googling fruitlessly about what had happened to Charlie and coming up with nothing more than the first time she had searched. But Charlie telling her that he was waiting for his coach had to be significant—how could it not be if it was one of the last things he did?

But *Stephen*? It seemed fantastically impossible...but her mind kept returning to how he had revealed himself to be different to what she had been led to believe once horizontal compared to vertical... Not unusual, she reminded herself: everybody had their secret selves. Perhaps it was just the disappointment of finding it wasn't what she had hoped for—she had extrapolated to a fantasy man only to find someone more faulty and human.

And then, she mused, thinking of Rufus, beyond the secret self we show our intimates, there exists an even deeper, hidden layer, that we show no one at all...and perhaps are only dimly aware of ourselves...

Adele let out a gusty sigh and looked up from the pamphlets she was idly rifling through on the table beneath the noticeboard. She didn't know why she was here. A support group wasn't what she needed. She wanted something more practical: some advice, some *answers*. But where from? A clairvoyant? She rolled her eyes at herself and walked into the church.

The meeting was in a small anteroom out the back, used for church and committee meetings. She could hear murmurings and the clank of metal. Joanne had said the group was small, and when she entered the room three women were unstacking chairs and arranging them in a circle. Joanne looked up and gave her a welcoming smile.

"Ah. Here's Adele." Joanne walked over and gave her upper arm a light rub. "Thank you for coming," she said in a lower tone. "Come over and meet Sally and Rachel."

Polite hellos exchanged, she was invited to sit in one of the six chairs while they waited for the last two group members. Adele folded her hands in her lap and looked around the room. An abundance of natural light came from a pair of tall windows in the wall, but also from a skylight directly above, giving the room, and the circle of chairs at its centre, an almost holy or celestial feeling. The floor was coir matting and the greenish-straw smell emanating from it put her in mind of a stable, which brought an ironic smile to her lips.

Joanne was coming and going from the room, and the other two ladies had taken their seats and were quietly chatting. Of course, the group members, or at least some of them, must know each other quite well...secrets shared, confidences made, not to be revealed outside.

Footsteps sounded behind and another woman entered the room, and with her the energy level perceptibly shifted. She strode up to Joanne, in what seemed like rather a business-like fashion, and started talking to her in an undertone. The conversation couldn't have been too serious, as Joanne let out a throaty chuckle and gave the woman's arm a squeeze, directing her to take a seat. She sat opposite Adele, nodding politely at the other two, then turned to give her a smile. Her face seemed animated and friendly, even though she spoke not a word. Perhaps this was the person Joanne wanted her to meet, as the other two women had taken little notice of her. Before she had time to consider this further, a young man rushed in, his hands flapping around.

"Sorry. *Sorry*! I'm always last, aren't I. You haven't started yet? Oh, good." He sat in the last remaining chair, dropping his knapsack to the floor. He leaned over to scrabble around in it, finally producing a bottle of water.

Joanne had taken her seat and was flicking through some papers on her lap. Finding what she was after, she extracted a sheet and laid it on top of her pile. She looked around the circle and gave them one of her warming smiles.

"Hello, everyone. And please welcome Adele to our gathering. I thought we might keep the structure fairly loose today and just see what happens. I see some of you have brought your journals. We'll do some sharing from those in our week-in-review section at the end, but to get us started, I have something to kick us off."

The young man next to Adele reached down to scrabble in his bag again.

"We've talked a lot about symbolism, story, and parable, and how we can use more abstract thinking to give ourselves comfort. I have a story here from Anglo Saxon times, from the Venerable Bede, that I'd like to read to you.

"King Edwin of Northumberland was on the verge of converting to Christianity, but he thought to gather his council of elders to consider what the missionary bishop Paulinus had to say first.

"One of the thanes spoke in response. He compared the present life of man on earth with that time of which we have no knowledge. He described our time on earth as that of the flight of a sparrow through a banqueting hall. In the hall's midst, there is a comforting, warming fire; outside, the winter storms rage with rain and snow. This sparrow flies swiftly in through one door at the end of the hall, and out through another. While he is inside, he is safe from the elements; but after a few moments of comfort, he vanishes from sight into the wintry world from which he came. Even so, man appears on earth for a little while; but of what went before this life or of what follows, we know nothing. Therefore, the thane said, if this new teaching has brought any more certain knowledge, it seems only right we should follow it."

Joanne laid her paper on her lap and looked around at the group. "So, what do you think? Are we just sparrows flying through a well-lit barn? Some of us flying the full length of the building, but others perhaps don't fly so straight. They escape out of a hole in the roof, or a gap in the wall, which cuts that short journey to an even briefer one."

Sally and Rachel both had things to say, and the young latecomer, Aaron, also made some observations. Adele was happy just to listen, and she noticed that the woman opposite kept her peace as well, although her intelligent eyes followed the conversation. Adele found her mind wandering, imagining Toby as a wayward sparrow, flying off at an angle, through a broken slat, while she and Roof kept flying straight, the large opening at the end of the hall in their sights. Would he fly around to the end of the barn and meet them both at the end? Was it only a matter of time? In the larger scheme of things, only a tiny amount of time, really. It was just the light and activity that made it seem larger than the dark.

Adele's thoughts drifted, visualising large halls full of merriment, bearded Viking types raising tankards and eating hunks of meat with their hands, grease running down their chins; music perhaps, with dancing and carousing. While above their heads there flowed a continuous stream of sparrows, dipping and swaying on the air currents, some perching and stopping for a short rest, others, like Toby, making premature exits; but all ultimately leaving the barn for the great unknown. Adele smiled. Or perhaps you circled the barn only to fly another circuit, perhaps as a sparrow, maybe next time as a raven. She looked up, having heard Joanne speak her name.

"What are you smiling at there, Adele?"

Caught off guard, she laughed. "Oh, I was just thinking about reincarnation and perhaps we fly through that barn as numerous kinds of birds over time."

"Oh. I like that idea," said Aaron.

Adele had felt warmth flush up her neck when she spoke, feeling guilty for her lack of engagement. She had been aware of the eyes of the woman opposite on her, observing her closely, as if trying to read between the lines of what Adele was saying.

Adele stared at her hands in her lap. She couldn't help extending the metaphor: what about birds out in the dark, prematurely finished or looping around for a new journey, peering inside at all the activity? And how maybe some birds inside caught glimpses of them through the cracks...

The group then pulled out their journals and read some excerpts of how their weeks had gone, and any new thoughts or experiences that had a bearing on their grief and how they were feeling.

Adele watched each person as they read, but her thoughts were elsewhere. She now knew that the woman opposite was Sandra. It appeared from her week that she had some kind of role counselling or working with grieving parents herself. She found herself observing Sandra when she had her head turned to whomever was reading. She was a solid-looking female: strong-looking arms and capable hands, her trousered legs crossed at the ankles in front of her. Fit. But in contrast, she had a pert nose and light blonde hair in a feathery pixie cut with a fade at the back and sides.

Tough with pretty edges. Adele wondered why Joanne was so keen to bring them together.

The hour came to an end with Joanne suggesting some exercises for the following week, offering everyone a chance to talk with her if the session had brought anything up for them, or to arrange something if they wanted to chat in private later in the week. Adele couldn't help thinking that Joanne must be incredibly busy with so many people wanting her time, but she supposed that was what she had signed up for. She was so obviously a people person.

Adele felt awkward hanging back with no apparent reason to do so. Aaron was chatting with Joanne as she and Sandra returned the chairs to their stacks at the edge of the room. Adele pretended to be interested in some prints on the wall: watercolours of the nearby canals from the nineteenth century.

Aaron could talk, that was for sure. She was beginning to wonder how much longer she could feasibly feign interest in such bland pictures, when she heard Aaron yell his goodbyes as he rushed off to catch his bus. When she turned around, she found Sandra watching her and grinning. Joanne also allowed herself a wry smile.

"Sorry about that, girls. Thanks for being so patient. Adele, I'd like you to meet a friend of mine, Detective Sergeant Alexandra Bentley, although she prefers Xandra, with an X."

Xandra moved towards Adele, her hand extended. When they shook, it was a firm, friendly grasp.

Adele's throat locked up. A detective? This woman? She gave Joanne a look of consternation, aware at the same time of a memory flash of seeing that exact spelling in writing...

"Xandra's been coming to my groups for a while now. In a personal capacity."

Adele's gaze shifted back to Xandra, who returned her look in a forthright manner.

"I work on child abduction and murder cases, some involving sexual abuse. It all takes its toll. Work referred me for some counselling after a particularly rough patch...gosh, how long ago now? Seems like years." She flashed a grin at Joanne. "I've kept it up, even when I haven't got any investigations going. I find it really helps."

A tremor of panic caused Adele's eyes to dart between Joanne and Xandra. "Joanne, I thought our conversation was private? I don't want to make some official—I can't possibly..."

Joanne held both her hands up. "Adele, Adele, it's fine. Please. I haven't repeated any of our conversation." She exchanged a look of concern with the detective. "As I said, Xandra comes to my groups in a private capacity. The reason I've asked you here to meet her is because you have some areas of...overlapping interest, shall we say. I thought that bringing your different perspectives and concerns together could be of mutual benefit. I'm prepared to be wrong, of course, but I find talking about things is always ultimately better than not talking about them." She looked to Xandra, who nodded.

"Don't be upset with Jo. All she said to me was she had recently met someone who had been impacted by Charlie Falk's disappearance, and who might benefit from a chat. That maybe I could give you some background on the investigation...or just talk about more general stuff."

"But I—" Adele fell short, not knowing how to continue. She took her cue from Joanne's reassuring expression and faltered on. "So, you...worked on his...disappearance?" Suddenly, the memory flash made sense. She'd come across Xandra's name in one of the articles she'd read only yesterday.

Xandra nodded. "Yes. It's considered a cold case now, but it's not cold in *my* mind. And I don't believe Charlie's disappearance was isolated. I'm just waiting for the right piece of information to link it to some*thing* or some*one* else."

"I see." Adele found herself staring at the chairs stacked up behind the two women, with a sense that something was expected of her. A few moments passed before the silence was broken.

"So, what do you think?" Joanne put it to her gently. "Would another time suit you better?"

Adele looked up to see two kind and reassuring faces. "I'm sorry, Xandra. You must think me a bit rude. I don't know who I thought Joanne was intending me to meet. Another grieving mother, I suppose. I hadn't really thought about it."

"Will you let me buy you a coffee? We can talk about Charlie, or we can talk about whatever you like. Please don't feel under any pressure."

Seeing Adele's face relax, Joanne said, "That's the way. Maybe Tony's just past the bridge? He does nice pastries." Joanne had gathered up her papers and was turning towards the vestry. "I'll have to leave you both to it, I'm afraid. I'm already running late for a phone call I promised." She raised her hand in a wave and disappeared through the door.

Xandra grabbed her jacket and started putting it on, still looking at the doorway Joanne had passed through. She shook her head ruefully. "She never stops, that one."

They passed out onto the street together and by mutual agreement headed towards Tony's Expresso, a tiny stand-up bar with only a few high stools under a shelf facing the street. A young barista was wiping down the milk steamer on the machine when they entered, and there was a man standing with his back to them, hunched over a ciabatta roll, his cheeks bulging, while he read from his tablet on the counter.

Xandra ordered a macchiato and a biscotti for herself and turned to Adele with an expectant expression.

"Just a latte...and a snail, please."

Instead of turning to close the order, Xandra was giving Adele what could only be described as a Benny Hill look. The barista laughed and leaned forward to point under the glass. "I think she means a swirl."

Adele laughed too as Xandra's features transformed from comical consternation to wry acceptance. Adele grinned at the barista. "Bloody Australians."

Leaving them to the paperwork, she hoisted herself up onto one of the stools and waited for Xandra to join her. She stared out at the passing traffic and the people walking up and down and recalled that less than a week ago she had pursued Charlie past this strip of shops. Xandra came and sat facing her, her hands clasped between her knees angled outward.

"Nice little part of the world here near the canal, isn't it?"

"Yes. Do you live nearby?"

"Oh no." Xandra laughed. "Out of my budget. I'm in Kentish Town, over that way." She gestured with her hand down the street.

"But you're not from here originally, are you?" Adele had noticed a soft burring undercurrent and lilt in Xandra's speech, but not quite enough to identify it.

"Y'nut sayin' I've an ucksent now are ye, lassie?" A broad grin replaced the feigned look of horror. Xandra leaned back as their coffees and pastries were placed on the ledge between them. "I'm from up near Glasgow. Paisley, if you've heard of it. A stone's throw from where Robert the Bruce's sister Margery died after falling off her horse. My father's family are Londoners, though."

Xandra picked up her biscotti and broke it in two, prior to dipping one of the halves in her tiny drink. She munched her biscuit and sucked the crumbs off her fingers, aware that Adele was watching her. She licked her lips and smiled.

"So. What can I tell you about Charlie that might be of help?"

"I—I don't know. I hadn't really thought about questions to ask. What about his parents? What happened to them?"

"They're still in London. At least, she is. The husband died last year. We keep in touch with the wife still. Returned to her family in Laos for a while, but she's back now. Bit like you." Xandra ate the second half of her biscuit and wiped her fingers on a serviette. "There was some suspicion of the husband for a while, but we soon eliminated him as a suspect, partly through alibi, but also just the circumstances and their personal stories. I don't believe either parent had anything to do with it. They were shattered, both of them. We also spent a lot of time following up some near-relatives and the like. Funny business with kids so often comes from known quarters, but everything seemed to check out. We were left with person or persons unknown."

Adele tore a piece off her snail. "Oh. I heard the coach was under a cloud of suspicion."

"So, you do know something about what happened."

"I, uh, happen to know Stephen. He coached my son as well...back in the day. Although Toby didn't get any special coaching."

Xandra's eyes immediately flashed into an alert state. "'Special coaching'? What are you referring to?"

Adele immediately regretted her big mouth. The only place she'd heard about it was from Charlie. "I'm sorry, I don't know much about it at all. As I said, Toby wasn't in receipt of any. I just heard that some other boys maybe..."

She commenced tearing pieces off her snail, hoping not to have to say anything more. Xandra said nothing, but her intent gaze fell on Adele's busy fingers, which made Adele stop abruptly and grab a serviette and screw it up tightly in her lap.

"Do you know if Charlie received this 'special coaching'?

"I—I really don't know. I didn't really know him. I did hear that the parents had to give permission for it, though, as it took extra time, of course."

Xandra paused before upending her coffee for the last sip. "That's very interesting. It could give me a new line of enquiry, especially in terms of matching details with those other cases."

She slowly returned the cup to its saucer and placed it with deliberation on the shelf, as if needing to ensure it stayed put. When she spoke, it was in a musing tone, almost to herself.

"Lane had an alibi from his wife for most of the time in question, but there was a gap immediately after the game: probably not enough time for this extra coaching, but a gap, just the same. I wasn't convinced she was telling the truth, back then, and I'm still not convinced now. Expand that gap of unvouched-for time and you have a real possibility, but without a body and time of death, it was hard to make anything stick."

"Charlie's body was never found?"

"No." Xandra looked at Adele's plate where the snail lay in torn strips. She raised her fingers and pinched her lower lip thoughtfully. "How about you tell me why you're interested in this case?"

Adele explained how she had lived in the area around the time of Charlie's disappearance but hadn't been fully cognisant of it until now. She was aware of Xandra's steady regard while she swirled the dregs of her latte around in the bottom of her glass, considering. She took a breath and continued.

"I had reason to learn recently that Charlie was the boy who kicked the ball that hit my son, the impact that triggered his brain haemorrhage."

"Oh god. That was *your* son? I'm so sorry."

Adele pushed her glass and plate away. "Yes. The school wasn't keen to tell us at the time, although I think my husband must have found out due to his helping out with the games as he did. I'm glad he didn't tell me. It wouldn't have helped. Maybe would have made things even worse."

Xandra nodded but said nothing.

"It sounds like Stephen has had a terrible time...living under suspicion that he has no power to dispel."

Xandra glanced out of the window. "Mmm, yes, well, he had the misfortune to also have connections to two other missing boys that we are running files on. Both were members of school teams that played in the same area. Lane was even known personally by one of the child's parents."

Adele's mouth went dry. "But nothing was proven."

"No. Again, Lane's wife was able to provide alibis for the timeframes we think were about right."

"Were the other children...recovered?"

"No. The incidents adhered to a similar pattern, which is why I'm sure they're linked. Both went missing following their after-school games at the same time of year. Both were of a similar age."

"And his wife has left him now."

"Oh yes. Don't think I didn't have another go at her statements after that, but she was solid on what she said—very little deviance from her original stories. If she's lying, she's still happy to support him, married or not."

"He's still the father of her child."

"Indeed. And the payer of her child support."

Adele bit her lip. There was no way she was going to tell this woman what she had heard from Charlie's own lips about waiting for his coach. She'd already said too much. It provided no further evidence on what was already available; all it did was compound suspicion. Worried her face must be somehow giving her away, she steeled herself to change the subject.

"It seems you've known Joanne quite some time then?"

"Yes, we go back a long way. It was Jo who suggested I come along to her group when I was following up on my referrals from work. She knew I was going through a really bad time: not sleeping, stress-related eating, health problems; all that sort of thing. Apart from the support group, she recommended some health professionals and other programmes, and between her and my doctor, I was put on a path of slow improvement. She's been bloody brilliant."

"I can't imagine how you do it. My brother was already living in Heaton Chapel at the time Jamie Bulger went missing, so we were following the case closely back home. The details that came out about what those little boys did to him will be with me forever. I'm surprised his parents can go on living knowing all that."

"That was a case that really got me fired up in my uni days—helped determine my career path. It was a landmark case in a lot of ways: the struggle for people to accept that two young boys could have been so deliberately evil, just for starters."

"Yes. It was truly horrible. It must be tough, doing a job where you have to be the strong one all the time. The one who has to face the music so others can be protected. I can see why you come to Jo's group."

"I love my job, though. It's a chance to step in and help those who can't help themselves. I felt so powerless to change things when I was growing up, and now I have a job that helps at a societal level. It's what Jo does, too, but she's more behind the scenes I think, at the building-block level."

"She works hard, like you say. I sent her a text in the wee hours, and she responded straight away. I felt terrible."

Xandra smiled. "That's Jo, all right." She sat up straight and rubbed her palms up and down her thighs, looking back towards the counter. She lowered her voice, "I think they're wanting to close up now."

The barista had been cleaning the coffee machine while they'd been talking and had just turned away a customer asking for a coffee. Adele saw his retreating back as she turned to grab her bag and had a brief sense of déjà vu, but quickly dismissed it in order to focus on dismounting from her stool. Xandra held up her hand in thanks as they headed out the door.

"Thank you for the coffee. I can't help feeling that I've wasted your time. It was very kind of you."

"Dinna fash yersel' hen." Xandra grinned. "The least I could do for Jo. She has a good eye for people in need. Maybe the time isn't right yet. Will I see you at the next meeting?"

Adele hesitated. She had no intention of joining the group but didn't want to sound ungrateful. "I'm not sure that it's my thing. I go and sit in the church sometimes, and I do experience some benefit from that. And Jo *is* wonderful to talk to. You just feel...*enriched*...like you've been hooked up to thorough goodness for a little while and received a top-up."

Xandra put her head on one side but didn't say anything for a moment. Then she smiled. "I think you'll be back."

Chapter Twelve

Excitation

Def. 1. The act of exciting or putting in motion 2. The application of energy to something

XANDRA JOGGED UP the front steps of the yellow brick building and nodded to the officer on duty. Moments later, she was planted in front of her laptop, staring at her screen over clasped hands. In front of her were her case notes relating to the disappearance of Charlie Falk, but she wasn't taking them in.

When Jo told her there would be someone coming to the group with a connection to the Charlie Falk case, she had tried to rein in her excitement. She'd lost count of the hours she'd spent poring over the notes for his and similar cases, willing something to present itself in a new light. Her boss said she was like a dog with a rotting carcass, but then he'd laughed, saying it must have been why he'd recommended her for promotion last autumn.

After Charlie's disappearance, they had interviewed as many people connected to the boy's school and family as possible. This woman had been outside their radar range, and by her own admission, she would have been of little assistance at the time in any case. Sometimes facts took time to settle and link up.

Xandra rubbed her fingers over her lips and redirected her gaze to the window where the afternoon light bent glowing bars down the wall onto her desk. The background buzz of conversation and keyboard tapping provided a conducive aural blur for her thoughts to float on.

Special coaching. Presumably extracurricular and on a one-on-one basis. Why had this not been mentioned before? She brought up her files and did some word searches. Nothing.

On its own, it was a slim lead, but asking the question could jog some memories, shine a new light on an old fact. One thing was clear: she would need to talk to Stephen Lane again. All roads seemed to lead back to him.

Forty minutes and several phone calls later, her schedule for the next day was mapped out with interviews booked with teaching staff at Pilgrims Way, New End, and Fleet Primary. It was a good start. The parents of the missing children she could speak to more informally.

She laid down her phone and fell to musing again. The parents. This woman had also lost her son. Charlie Falk kicking that fateful ball seemed like too much of an amazing coincidence. She brought up her case notes again and searched for "Soames". Xandra blinked at the screen. Ah, yes. Jo had mentioned a husband left in Australia. She had interviewed him. Rufus Soames was on her list of parents who helped out with the team. She'd caught him on his last day in the office, as well as the country, and his answers to her questions, while helpful, had been distracted. Was it through Rufus that Adele had learned of this "special coaching" or had her son perhaps mentioned it in passing?

An image of Adele's face came into her mind. She had seemed a bit dowdy at first, her small body wrapped up in her coat, blinking behind her glasses, but over coffee, Xandra had been drawn in by the sadness hiding behind those light-brown eyes and the way her nimble fingers had minced that pastry.

One thing was certain: Adele had regretted mentioning the special coaching. There was definitely more to learn there, but she would need to put in some spade work and gain her trust. It was an exciting prospect. She was one or two conversations away from learning a key piece of information, she felt sure of it.

A knock on her desk made her swing her head around to see Detective Constable Guy Fenwick, his pen poised over a pad of Post-it notes. "Doing a coffee round. You in?"

Things were definitely looking up.

Chapter Thirteen

Excavation

Def. To dig out and remove; to expose to view by digging

ADELE WOKE UP in the dark with a sense that it was the middle of the night but, on rolling over to look at her clock, found it was 6.20 a.m. She turned to face the ceiling, rubbing the heel of her hand into her forehead. She felt like there was a third eye there burning a hole in her head. Already, her thoughts were grinding into gear and taking off. She had read till late to try to keep her mind from wearing gutters in her synapses, but the quick take-off was the same as accidentally jiggling your mouse to bring your computer out of sleep mode. God knows what processes had been running in the background overnight.

Except she did know. Charlie waiting for Stephen Lane to come and give him some "special coaching". Over. And over. And over again. She wondered if she could even approach Stephen about it, whether it was even advisable. The thought had crossed her mind that maybe this had actually occurred innocently enough, and maybe whatever had happened was afterwards, and Stephen had been too afraid to say anything for fear of not being believed. And maybe therein lay further clues as to what had really taken place? Tossing these arguments back and forth had become ferocious and exhausting.

She slid her legs from under the bedcovers and padded down the stairs. As the kettle rumbled into life, she heard various neighbours' cars likewise rumbling down the street. For the umpteenth time, she gave thanks that her work could be done at home so she didn't have to join the rat race on the bus and tube routes into town every day.

The editing was going well. She was into the second half of her first round and had already sent some sample chapters back to the author to get a sense of how her feedback would be received. It was enough for her to justify hitting the pause button till she heard back. She stood on the bin pedal and dropped her teabag in. If she wasn't going to work today, she needed to use her time productively, if only to keep her thoughts off a pointless hamster wheel.

On the third step from the landing, she paused. The noticeboard from St Bart's had flashed into her mind's eye, recalling her to the upcoming jumble sale. Yes. Now *there* was an example of background processing being of sterling use.

The house itself was clear and tidy, but like unfinished business, she was aware of items piled up in the attic that were probably creating bad feng shui of some description, literally hanging over her head. Mostly they consisted of things belonging or connected to Toby that could be left behind, but at the same time couldn't, at that time at least, be disposed of. Maybe enough time had passed for her to be able to face it.

Curled up in bed with her tea and her novel resting on her raised knees, she tried to read, but her mind kept straying to the attic. The timing was good. Jeremy had messaged her earlier in the week and had suggested coming down for the weekend. She would enlist his help in moving some of the bigger items downstairs. She already had the foosball table on her hit list. As to the rest, she would have to go up and remind herself what was there. In her imagination, it was an amorphous pile of battered suitcases and Chinese laundry bags full of clothing and old toys. It would be hard going through the memories, but it was an emotional clearing she needed.

After a boiled egg and some toast, she put on leggings and an old jumper. The stick with its hook on the end was there, faithfully at attention, in the cupboard at the end of the hall. She hooked it into the ring in the ceiling and gave a deft pull. And another. It gave, and a mote of dust sprinkled her face, and with it came a waft of stale attic-smell. The steps unfolded to the floor. The plan was to go through everything up there and drop bags down for the sale or for throwing out, leaving the space empty.

The aluminium steps creaked and flexed as she cautiously made her way upward. It wasn't a trip she wanted to repeat too many times and she prayed the foosball table would come apart in manageable chunks. She poked her head through the hole and was soon hoisting herself up onto her knees.

The air felt close and heavy, yet chilly. Hands on hips, she surveyed the space: plastic crates and cardboard boxes stacked against the wall; laundry bags and smaller plastic bags with loose bits and pieces sticking out. The foosball table had already been dismantled, thank god, and flat slabs of it leaned against the end wall. Roof must have done that in those last days of packing; why, she wasn't sure. Maybe it had felt right to dismantle something before he left.

Already feeling the weight of despair at so much to go through, so many containers full of items, each loaded with individual memories and associations, she almost turned tail. But no. She ground her thumbs into the sides of her index fingers as her eyes swept over the piles and stacks, trying to find an "in". Finally, she stepped forward and commenced dragging the smaller plastic bags into the centre of the room where there was a scrap of remnant carpet. There were five bags all up, so she sat down cross-legged and started to go through them.

It took over an hour. Every second item gave her pause as memories flooded in. The Thomas the Tank Engine that had been

Toby's bathtime companion for over a year; beautiful wooden train tracks that fit together like jigsaw pieces that had gone through hundreds of permutations on his bedroom floor; Meccano, LEGO of all descriptions—the reason she and Roof had no longer dared to go barefoot in their own home—and at the bottom of the last bag, Ellie Phant, as her son had christened her, a furry grey creature with a long appendage hanging from its face. "Ellie's Phallus", Roof had called her in private. Adele clutched the musty thing to her chest and buried her nose in its soft head, picturing her son doing the same. After a moment, she held Ellie at arms' length for a better look. Maybe, if she survived a run through the washing machine, she would keep Ellie. No self-respecting child would pick her off a jumble stall, and she couldn't bear to think of her on a rubbish heap.

She pushed all the bags to the other side of the room. It was breaking her heart, but they had to go. Some child would benefit from them. Their time of dispensing joy was not yet over, and she took some comfort from that.

The laundry bags were easier. Mainly just old bedspreads and linen that could go straight to the charity bins.

Down to plastic crates and boxes now, she peered in the tops: a box full of board games and jigsaws went straight to the sale pile. Other boxes contained ornaments like christening paraphernalia, booties, first teeth, and little snipped locks of red hair...no. That all had to stay. And another box full of framed photos and albums, likewise, but she couldn't bear to look at them now or she'd be stuck up here till next week.

She was pretty much done and only two boxes had survived. A far better ratio than she had dared hope for. She unfolded her stiff legs and eased herself to a standing position, shaking out her pins and needles while she considered what was left. She wandered over to the pieces of foosball table to see how big a challenge it would be. The front slab was green, marked out in white lines. She tipped it toward her to judge its heft: fairly light, actually, but her attention was caught by the sound of something falling to the floor against the wall. She pulled forward the other panels stacked behind, peering to the floor where the metal rods and men were bundled up. The sound had been of a piece of card or papers, maybe the assembly instructions... Stretching her arm to its fullest extent over the panels, she managed to grab the corner of a protruding Manila folder jammed at the back, its corner creased over with loose papers sticking out. It slid out grittily.

She opened it and went to stand closer to the window to investigate. Sketches. Some of Roof's design work in rough form. A series of kettles, a matching line of toasters. A few aborted rough-outs of biscuit packets. She flicked the pages towards her, gently pulling apart pages stuck by random blobs of paint, the dust bringing on three sneezes. More kettle designs...then her heart clunked in her chest. A soft pencil drawing of her son in the bathtub.

Entranced, she returned to the floor and laid the folder flat to examine the sketches more closely. It wasn't often Roof deployed his talent for drawing into more pleasurable pursuits. He did enough of it for work, he said, but on several occasions, she had seen him on bathing duty, sitting on a stool, with his pad on his lap, drawing their son as he tipped water from one vessel to another. One or two he'd even allowed her to frame. But these were pictures she hadn't seen before.

She couldn't help tracing her fingertips over the soft outline of Toby's back, the bumps of his spine visible like knots, his hair in wet kiss-curls on his neck. There were several more sheets and her hand trembled, hoping not to be disappointed with more kitchenware. A smaller piece of card showed Toby's face in profile, probably at the age of six or seven; another A4 sheet showed several small roughs of parts of his body: his hands gripping toys, a back view of his bottom and thighs, a foot and ankle, his benign stumpy genitals.

Adele swallowed as she placed each page carefully on top of the last, each of varying paper quality and thickness. Nothing frameable, but all to be treasured. She wondered why Roof hadn't. Maybe he had taken the best and these were the rejects, or judging by the condition of the folder, perhaps it had accidentally slipped into oblivion and been forgotten.

She smiled. The morning had been worthwhile if only to find these. She moved all the bags and boxes as close as possible to the manhole. They would make quick work of them soon after Jem arrived, then it would be done. Apparently, there was a church van available for pick-ups of larger donations, so she would call Jo-anne and book that in for next week.

Adele lowered herself to all fours and carefully extended her leg out of the hole to a ladder rung, the Manila folder clutched to her chest.

Chapter Fourteen

Exertion

Def. Physical or mental effort

XANDRA THREW HER gym bag down and slumped onto her sofa. A shite day with nothing to show for her efforts. She rubbed her eyes and reached for the TV remote.

Of course, her job was full of days like this, but this one impacted more than most. Not a single teacher or principal knew anything about any extracurricular arrangements associated with the schools' football activities, and Stephen Lane had verged on hostile. Back at the office, she'd been able to contact the parents of the missing children, none of whom could offer anything further. And it wasn't for want of trying, she thought sadly. One woman had been unwilling to let her finish the call, as if she thought by sheer force of will she would think of something to help.

Xandra sighed and leaned her head against the back of the sofa to stare at the ceiling. Whatever she was after, she was convinced, was locked in Adele Soames's head. She glanced down at her phone. It was tempting to call her, but she had to go about this carefully if she was to get anywhere. She glanced at her watch before dialling another number.

"I thought it would be you. Just a minute."

Xandra got up and wandered over to the fridge while she waited for Jo to find a quieter place than her living room to talk. She was separating a clammy piece of pizza away from its last fellow when Jo came back on the line.

"How did it go, then?"

Xandra went through her conversation with Adele and the fruitless efforts of her day.

"I'm sorry to hear that. No sense of anything different from Stephen?"

"No. He got quite worked up, accusing me of making stuff up in order to frame him. He was barely controlling himself, which of course makes it easier to imagine him departing from his respectable image of trusted teacher and coach."

"Mmm."

Xandra waited. "I was hoping to get more from you than just

'Mmm'. There's more to Adele's story than just this 'special coaching', isn't there."

"You're putting me in an awkward position, Xandra."

"Yes, and I'll make it even more awkward if I think something's being covered up to hinder this investigation."

There was a lengthy pause, during which Xandra muted her TV.

"What I think is…you have to be patient. Adele is struggling with a lot right now. She's grieving not only for her son, but for her marriage. She's transplanted herself back here and she feels isolated. She needs support and people around her she can trust."

"Well, you saw how her trust evaporated when she realised what my job was."

"I think you could get around that. She needs a friend right now."

"Jo, it's not my job to be her friend."

"No…but I was thinking…"

"What?"

"That maybe *you* could do with a friend, too, since—"

"No. Just stop. Stop right there. I know you mean well, but it's inappropriate."

"Oh, Xandra."

"Don't you 'Oh, Xandra' me. I need to know what she's hiding. I've just wasted a day of my time following up a lead that apparently wasn't there."

Xandra heard an extended creaking sound which meant Jo

was changing position in her antiquated office chair. Possibly shifting to find something on her desk or access her laptop, maybe just running her fingers through her hair, something she only did out of hours when it was free of its usual constraints.

"I can only recommend patience and persistence. Adele's still processing what she knows, trying to figure out what it means. And there could be more to come, if I understand her correctly. If we can maintain a connection through the weekly meetings, I think she will come to us when she's ready."

"Sitting on my dot, passively twiddling my thumbs, is not my style."

"I know that, but you've waited this long, a little longer to get a result will be worth it. And right now, there is no Option B."

Chapter Fifteen

Expression

Def. 1. The action of making known thoughts or feelings 2. A look on someone's face

ADELE DROVE DOWN to Belsize Park tube when she got Jem's text. He wouldn't have much luggage, but it was a bit of a walk. Luckily, he was waiting out the front, so it was a quick stop and go. She had been wrong about the luggage.

"You are just staying the weekend, aren't you?"

"Yeah, course. But I had to bring all my gear...and two outfits, just in case."

"A girl has to be prepared." She shot him a sideways grin. "All your own things or have you raided your sisters' wardrobes?"

"Clarr let me have a pair of shoes, and Con has some nice hair accessories and earrings. Apart from that, the rest is mine."

"Franny and I used to wear each other's stuff all the time. I couldn't tell you how many fights we had when we planned a big night out only to find the outfit we wanted was in the dirty clothes." Adele stifled a guffaw. "I can't imagine what it would have been like to have your father raiding our dresses when we weren't looking!"

Jem gave her a wry look. "No, Aunty Del, I can't, either."

Adele grinned out into the traffic. "And just as well. He doesn't have the legs for it anyway."

They pulled up and got Jem's bags into the house. Adele couldn't help wanting to be a fly on the wall when Mrs Henderson across the road flicked her curtain back tomorrow night to check out her visitors.

"So, how many did you say are coming again? Three, wasn't it?"

"Yep. My friends Seb and Roger, and Roger's flatmate Letitia."

"What, a girl? Does she dress as a guy?"

"No."

"Oh. I was thinking I should wear a pantsuit for the occasion. What do you think?"

"Can if you like."

"Better than being outdone by you boys. No point in competing."

Over some coffee and biscuits, they sketched out a menu plan for the following evening. Adele didn't want to ruin her nephew's fun, but she did have to keep reining in his elaborate choices, otherwise she could see what was going to happen: she would spend all her time preparing and cooking while Jem fussed with his hair upstairs. In the end, they settled on palmiers with cream cheese and sun-dried tomatoes for hors d'oeuvres, a first course of pesto gnocchi, to be followed by honey roasted chicken and vegetables. Dessert would be a simple pavlova.

"We can go shopping in the morning and start with the prep after lunch. You don't want to be cooking when your friends arrive."

"I'll need plenty of prep time myself, too."

Adele lifted an eyebrow at her nephew. "All the more reason to get in early so we're not stressing at the last minute. Oh, and that reminds me. I have some things up in the attic I need to get down here for a jumble sale pick-up on Monday. I could really do with your help if I'm not going to fall helter-skelter down that ladder."

Jem nodded. "That's cool. Oh, and Seb and Rog said they'd bring a bottle of gin. How about we make some gin cocktails?"

"What did you have in mind?"

Jem shrugged and lifted his hands palms up. "I don't know. I just had this vision of pink gin in fancy glasses…"

Adele smiled. "Okay, we'll google some recipes and pick up a few mixers and some fruit. I've got some nice glasses in the cabinet over there."

Jem went over to the glass-fronted doors and bent over to inspect what was on offer. "Oh, I like these. They look like something out of a black-and-white movie."

Adele peered over his shoulder. "Your grandmother's Marie Antoinettes. Nice choice."

Jem looked back at her warily. "Marie Antoinettes? Are they valuable? I'd freak out if we broke anything."

Adele laughed. "No, it's the style. They're a champagne coupe supposedly modelled on her breasts."

"What?" He leaned in for another look, angling his head for different views. "Bit flat-chested, was she?"

By mutual agreement, they opted for a quiet night of pizza and movies. While Jem was in the shower, Adele rang her favourite pizzeria with their order and got the plates and cutlery sorted. With no time for much else, she grabbed a magazine and slumped into a corner of the sofa to enjoy some mindless page flicking. She was casting around for her Sudoku book when the shower finally terminated. She'd just located her pen when she heard a tentative, "Aunty Del?"

"Yes, sweetie, what's up?"

"I need your opinion on something."

Flattered to think she wasn't yet too old or daggy for her nephew to value what she thought, she dumped her book and skipped up the stairs. On making it to the doorway of Jem's bedroom, she stopped short. An open bag was on the bed and there were clothes strewn everywhere. Jem stood over it, clutching the top of a shiny green sheath of a dress up to the level of his chest, while he tossed things aside looking for something.

"Wow, um, you might want to hang some of those up so they don't get creased. There should be enough coat hangers for you."

"I've already left my phone charger at home, and now I can't find my falsies. Oh well. Could you please…?"

He turned his back on her and slipped his arms through the long sleeves. She stepped forward and zipped him up. The dress fitted him like a second skin. Oh, to be so svelte!

Jem turned, eyeing himself critically in the wardrobe mirror, smoothing his hands down his front. He met her admiring gaze in the reflection. "It will be filled out a bit more once I find my bra"—he cupped his hands on his chest and jiggled them up and down—"but what do you think?"

"Très élégant. That's a daring shade of green, but with your dark colouring, you get away with it."

Jem turned this way and that. "Do you think?"

"You said you had two outfits. What's the other one?"

"Unzip me and I'll show you."

She did so and awkwardly turned her back. He wasn't the little boy who used to share baths with Toby any more. Jem sniggered. "It's okay. I've got pants on."

When she turned around, he was shimmying a black jersey number down over his corrugated ribs. Of course, her nephew had no curves to fill the dress out, but then, so many androgynous-looking supermodels these days didn't, either.

He put his hands on his hips and swung this way and that. "It looks better with shoes on."

"Yes, they always do." She looked him up and down. "It's criminal. You look better in that dress than most girls would." She reached over and appreciatively rubbed the dress's material between a thumb and forefinger. "You must be going through some money kitting yourself out."

"These are both charity shop buys, would you believe? Recycled fashion. I get some great buys that way. Con and I go together sometimes, although it causes fights as we like the same things."

"That's good though: you can share."

Jem raised a diabolical eyebrow. "Some things you don't want to share."

Adele squashed a laugh and gave him an affectionate smile. "Well, you wanted my opinion. Both dresses are lovely. The green makes a real statement, but the black is a safer bet if you were going somewhere and weren't sure what the standard would be like. What sort of frocks will your mates be wearing?"

"I think they're going to go all out. Glitter and glitz, falsies and frills."

"Well, there's your answer. Definitely the green." She turned to leave him to get changed but then stopped to lean in the doorway. "So, um, what's this Letitia going to wear? I'm getting worried I'm going to be the ugly stepsister tomorrow night."

"Not sure. Just a nice dress, I s'pose. She's not as into it as we are."

"I'm still thinking the pantsuit is the go. I might slick my hair down and make a false moustache to glue on as well..." She managed to duck just before the pillow hit the doorframe.

*

ADELE ENJOYED THE next day immensely. She and Jem seemed to be on a similar wavelength on so many things, but on top of that, he was such a decent, well-mannered kid. It was hard not to wonder, at various times throughout the morning, whether Toby would have matured the same way, or whether he would have taken a more nerdy path, or worse, become a football hooligan.

Every time she turned from selecting an item off the supermarket shelves, she looked at the boy leaning negligently on the trolley expecting, or wanting, to see her son. No doubt the trolley would have been full of multiple cartons of milk and breakfast cereals in order to get him through a single week, not to mention all the snacks and meat...

Given she had been surviving largely on cheese on toast and eggs, the bill at the register was a shock to the system. Still, it wasn't like she spent a lot on going out or drinking at the pub. It would be worth it to see Jem express his true self a little, and no doubt his friends would also put on a show. She was looking forward to meeting them.

They stopped at Dominique's for coffee, and she ordered the red velvet cheesecake. "Not quite The Flag Pole." She grinned at him over the rim of her latte glass.

He smiled as he popped a marshmallow into his mouth. "Great hot chocolate, though."

As soon as they got home, Adele deployed Jem in the kitchen to chop vegetables and fruit, while she made the palmiers and arranged them on baking trays.

After scraping all the chopped berries into a bowl, Jem looked up to squint at the clock. "Oh wow, it's three already. I'll need to start getting ready in a bit."

"But your friends aren't coming till six?"

Jem flipped his wrist at her. "Daarling, I've got legs to shave, nails to paint, skin to buff...and that's all before I've done my make-up and hair!"

"Oh dear. Of course. Silly *me*." She laughed. "Just as well I bought a pre-baked pavlova shell then, isn't it. I'll just whip some cream, and we'll be close to done. All that we'll need to do then will be to boil a saucepan of water and shove things in the oven. Then I can have *my* shower. Just make sure you don't completely clog the drain up with all that leg hair, okay?"

Once the food was prepared as far as possible, she busied herself with some general tidying up. Jem could set the table, and she'd let his friends select the music they wanted to accompany dinner. After she'd introduced Jem to *Priscilla, Queen of the Desert* last night, unable to believe he'd never seen it before, she suggested they have a little miming/singing entertainment after dinner, as she also had the soundtrack to the film.

"Classic drag queen anthems you need to learn if you're

going to be serious," she'd said, wagging her finger at him.

Adele looked around the room and plumped the sofa cushions a second time. It was as good as it was going to get. She gazed up the stairs where the sound of Jem singing "I Will Survive" in the shower drifted down intermittently. She looked at her watch and raised her eyebrows. May as well get that Sudoku out again…

*

MADE UP, SUITED, and aproned, Adele initiated the next-to-last stages of dinner. It was just as well she'd kept it simple, as Jem was currently sitting in front of her dressing table in his stretchy pants, his hair rolled up in curlers, layering more make-up on then she used in a month.

She glanced up at the clock. In half an hour, their guests could be here, although if they were anything like Jem, perhaps she shouldn't get too excited about serving dinner on time. She went to the fridge and pulled out the Adelaide Hills pinot grigio she had placed there earlier. Glass in hand, she made herself comfy on the sofa and went back to her Sudoku. She'd filled in three numbers when a plaintive call from upstairs made her sigh and put her pen in the book and throw it back on the coffee table.

"My hair's not going right," Jem moaned. "Please help me. It needs more shaping at the back—some more height."

"I'm not much of a hairdresser, sweetie, but I'll try. Hand me that fat brush."

Jem watched her in the mirror as she did her best imitation

of her hairdresser. "How did *you* get so lucky with all the curls, anyway?"

She gave him an indulgent smile. "Don't worry. They're the bane of my life, never doing what I want them to do. Everyone wants what they don't have."

Jem frowned into the mirror. "Rog and Seb have wigs and hair pieces, but good ones are really expensive. I've got to get better at doing it myself."

Adele rolled up a long tress of hair and applied the hair dryer. "How about we coil it up and pin it like this..." After a lot of fiddling and bobby pin sticking, she sprayed a mist of hair lacquer to fix everything in place.

"Come on, let's get you zipped up and you can come downstairs. They'll be here in a sec." While doing his hair, she had also been admiring his makeup. Flawless porcelain foundation with perfectly applied thick eyeliner. The transformation was incredible. He was reminding her of a less drug-hardened version of Amy Winehouse.

Jem was pointing his toes into his black patent heels. "I was thinking I might make an entrance down the stairs once they're here."

"Oh, I see. Well—" Both their heads turned at the sound of the front doorbell. "Thank goodness for that. I was beginning to wonder when I could put the chicken on."

On opening the door, Adele was confronted with a sandy-haired girl with a fresh-faced smile. A strappy dress was visible under her long coat. Adele held out her hand. "You must be Letitia?"

"Letty's fine, Adele, and I have with me here…" She turned her head and gestured with impatience at the hedge to her right, "Siobhan and Trixie."

Two long slender creatures tottered out from behind the hedge, not quite confident on their stilettos on the uneven flagstone path but flashing nervous lipsticked smiles. Adele ushered them in, pausing behind them to look over her shoulder at Mrs Henderson's curtains.

Letty handed her a brown paper bag containing some pink Beefeater and a bottle of hock. Trixie dropped her handbag—sequined turquoise to match her dress—on the sofa and paraded around the room, her hands floating around. "What a *lovely* home you have."

Siobhan was still standing in front of the door, her hands clasped in front of her. Adele was about to compliment her on her dress when Siobhan looked over Adele's head, up the stairs, her face lighting up. "Oh, *Cry*stal! You look di-*viiine*."

Adele turned to see her once-was nephew draped sexily against the banister in a pose straight out of a movie. Letty was looking at Jem with admiration also, but then she turned to grin at Adele. It was a look of conspiracy and fun, and Adele immediately warmed to her.

Letty came into the kitchen to help Adele while the girls cooed and fussed over each other. Adele pulled the tray of palmiers out of the oven and placed them on the stove top. Throwing the oven mitts aside, she said close to the girl's ear, "Tell me. How is it when they decide they want to be girls, it's still us doing all the work in the kitchen?"

"Don't worry," she murmured back in Adele's ear. "I make sure Roger does his share of the housework."

Thanks to the simplicity of the menu, it all went to plan with nothing burned or left to go cold. The pink gin had all disappeared along with Adele's pinot grigio, and now she cast a watchful eye on Crystal as she tottered and swayed back to the table bearing the hock.

Adele was enjoying the raucous laughter and play-acting, but one part of her remained the watchful adult. Once the pav had been decimated—oh, I'm on a diet, but go *on* then—they migrated to the sofa and the girls took turns to "sing" and mime extravagantly. When Letty got up to have a go, she surprised Adele by not only actually singing, but in full throaty voice.

When the energy lowered a few notches, Adele got up and put the kettle on and spooned some coffee into the plunger. As much as she was enjoying herself, and enjoying the kids enjoying themselves, she was planning to make sure they went home at a decent hour and in a respectable state; particularly Siobhan, who still lived at home. She brought a tray to the table with the coffee and cups and let them serve themselves.

They were a little more settled in their positions around the sofa now, although quite tiddly. Adele tried not to look as Trixie yet again placed her hand on Crystal's knee.

"It's now the time of the evening to play some parlour games," Trixie said, rubbing Crystal's knee for emphasis.

Oh no.

Crystal giggled. "What, like spin the bottle?"

"No, no. We're going to play at Challenges. Someone challenges the group to a question, and when each person gives their answer, the rest of us have to figure out whether they're lying or not."

"What's the point of that? We'll all just lie," said Letty, leaning over to pour milk in her mug.

"Well...okay. The idea's supposed to be that you drink if the group votes that you're lying, but as we've finished the wine, it will just have to be a slap on the bum...or something."

"But what if you really are telling the truth?" Siobhan sent a look of appeal to Adele.

"Oh, come on, you party poopers. It'll be fun. I'll start us off. My question is, how old were you when you first kissed a boy?"

"What sort of kiss?"

"Doesn't matter. Come on, Letty, you start."

"Why me?"

"Because someone has to be first. Come on."

Letty placed her mug on the table and stared at the floor a moment. "Er...ahh...fifteen."

"All in favour raise your hand?"

All raised their hand except Trixie, who jabbed a finger at

Letty. "Liar. You kissed *me* in Year Three."

Letty laughed. "Did I? Oh well, it clearly didn't make an impression."

The questions were kept to a good-natured level, but Adele sensed Trixie had some kind of agenda and she couldn't help feeling wary. Everyone was laughing and enjoying themselves, though, so she made an effort to turn off her censoring brain and just go with the flow. And she did, until it was Trixie's turn again.

"Okay, so now I want to know how old you were when you had your first sexual experience."

"Please define."

"Something involving an orgasm—wet or dry. With someone else."

Crystal gave an exaggerated slap on the thigh to Trixie. "You realise my *aunt's* in the room?"

"Adele's cool. Come on. You first."

Crystal cast a look of mock despair at Adele. "Okay then. Eight."

Adele couldn't help her mouth dropping open, but she heard Letty snicker, and quickly realised Jem was fudging it to get it over quickly. The only vote for the truth was Trixie. Crystal looked at her complacently. "Too bad, too sad. Next."

Trixie looked like she was about to object, but Adele quickly jumped in with, "Okay. Twelve for me." Over the laughter and "no ways", Adele continued to watch Trixie out of the corner of her eye. She was still frowning at Crystal.

Adele was glad when they got tired of the game and Letty, who had assumed the role of group mother, got up and said it was time they headed off. Shoes were hunted for and squeezed back on, handbags were searched for and found.

Letty helped Adele bring the coffee things back to the kitchen. "I'm sorry we're leaving you with such a mess."

"Oh, that's okay. That's what dishwashers are for. I'll set Jem to work on the rest in the morning."

Letty laughed. "Good luck with that. He's looking a bit the worse for wear."

Crystal was busy exchanging hugs and kisses in the living room while Adele walked to the front door with Letty. "It's been lovely, Adele, it was so nice of you to do this for the girls. It's been great fun." Before Adele could answer, Letty leaned in and gave her an affectionate embrace.

"My pleasure," she responded softly.

There was a round of hand shaking and kisses from the girls before they staggered out into the night. Adele watched them zig-zagging down the street, giggling and talking, wondering if Mrs Henderson was still up to take note. She closed the door and found Jem curled up on the sofa.

"Are you sure they'll be okay getting home at this hour...dressed like that?"

"Oh, yeah." Jem waved his hand carelessly. "If they've missed the bus, they'll share a cab. Letty'll make sure they're okay."

Adele eased herself down near Jem's bare feet. "I really liked your friend Letty. She's a lovely girl."

Jem let out a prolonged yawn. "Yeah, she's okay." He went to run his hand through his hair, and found due to the lacquer, he couldn't. "Oh, wow. I should probably have a shower. But I'm too drunk."

"At least take off your make-oop. I'll never get it off the linen, otherwise."

Her nephew gave her a tired smile and patted her knee. "Yes, Aunty." He unfolded his legs to the floor.

It wasn't the right time to raise sticky subjects, as tempted as she was, so she simply said, "Did you have a nice time tonight?"

"I had an *awesome* time. Made me feel very grown up hosting a party."

Adele smiled fondly at her nephew. "You're growing up way too quick, as it is."

They stood up together, and Jem looked around for his heels. She watched as he headed up the stairs, his shoes suspended from two fingers. On the third stair, he paused and turned around.

"Aunty Del?"

"Yes, sweetie?"

"Thank you for taking us seriously."

She kissed her fingers and blew it up to him.

He answered her by catching it and pressing it to his cheek. Then he twiddled his fingers in a wave and trod heavily up to bed.

*

IT WAS TEN o'clock, but she let him sleep. She'd just been removing her own make-up prior to going to bed when she heard heaving in the bathroom at the end of the passage. She hurried out to find her nephew hugging the toilet bowl. She gently lifted his hair out of the way, and when he was done, made him drink a large glass of water.

Jem wiped his mouth and groaned. "Seriously, Aunty Del. I really didn't drink that much."

Adele nodded sagely. "Must have been the mixing."

"Maybe. Sorry. I think I got it all in."

"Been there, done that. You know someone really cares about you when they hold your hair out of the toilet bowl."

She unloaded last night's dishwasher effort and put in what was left while she waited for the kettle to boil. She took her tea and placed it on the coffee table with a sigh of satisfaction. She could finally finish that dratted Sudoku. She was in that last stretch of filling in the remaining easy numbers when she heard the toilet flush, followed by padding down the stairs. Without looking up, she said, "How's the head?"

"All right, thanks."

"No more talking to Hughie during the night?"

"What?"

Adele looked over the back of the sofa. "Talking to Hugh*eeee* on the porcelain phone."

Jem laughed. "No, just a headache, but a coffee will see me right."

"And some water."

"Yes, Mum."

He made himself a coffee and joined her on the sofa, elegantly tucking his feet up under himself. Adele watched him for a moment as he commenced flicking through the magazine she'd left on the shelf under the table. She debated with herself for a while before speaking.

"Can I ask you a nosey question?"

Jem's mouth quirked to the side as he threw the magazine on the table. "As long as I have the right not to answer."

"I wanted to ask you about your answer to one of those questions last night."

Jem sighed. "Here we go. Bloody Trixie loves making my life difficult."

"Whatever you say stays between us, of course." She shifted on the sofa in order to face him more squarely. "You weren't joking about your first sexual experience being at the age of eight, were you."

He reached over for his mug and took a gulp of coffee. He placed it back on the table before answering; even then he looked at her for a while, as if he were weighing things up.

"No, I wasn't joking."

Adele's breath caught in her throat. "Oh, Jem. Please tell me it was playing doctors with some other child or—"

The look on Jem's face stopped her.

"Jem?" Her voice was barely above a whisper as she reached

over and placed her hand on his, all sort of terrible possibilities tumbling into her head. "Did some adult...do something...to you?"

"It's okay, Aunty Del," he said, patting her hand. "It's not like you're thinking."

"Then tell me."

He took his mug up again, but let it rest on his knee. "It was a family friend who used to come by—"

"Oh my god—"

"He used to be bit touchy-feely with me and I remember liking it. He was gentle and nice to me. One day when we were alone, I experienced this delicious wave of sensation... So, of course I wanted more." Jem wasn't meeting her eye but staring into his mug as he swirled the contents around. Eventually he looked up at her and spoke quietly. "Please don't be upset, Aunty Del. It was like he was the only person who understood me. I learned a lot from him over the time."

"Learned a lot? Bloody hell, Jem! He could have gone to gaol for what he did. Who *was* this?"

"It's not important. He's moved on now. But I used to really look forward to his visits. It was the most exciting thing in my little life." He laughed to himself. "Maybe it still is. I suppose it was my first crush."

The contents of Adele's stomach were swirling around, making her feel physically ill. What if this had been Toby, and some trusted friend had been touching up her infant son behind her back? Bad enough her nephew. There was absolutely no question of her ever repeating this to her brother, yet she felt dreadful *not* telling him, knowing how she would feel if something like this had been kept from *her*.

Her face must have revealed her quandary, as Jem reached out to pat her hand again, speaking in an almost fatherly tone. "Aunty Del, there's nothing to be upset about. I wasn't abused or perverted. There was no pain involved."

"You were little more than a *baby*, Jem! This person was *grooming* you."

He withdrew his hand. "I don't see it like that."

"Did he—" The revolting words stuck in her mouth, but she needed to know how serious this was. "Did he make you do things or did he..." She couldn't even put her worst fears into words.

"He just...played with me. It's just that the touching was more intimate...more personal. He made me feel like I was the only person in the world."

Adele's breath was coming in short pants as she stared at the coffee table.

"Aunty Del? It's nothing for you to worry about. It's in the past now. *Please.* I'm not damaged by it, it isn't what 'made me gay', and it hasn't given me any complexes. I'm okay with what happened."

Okay? My god! "The girls said you've been seeing a counsellor. Have you talked about this with them?"

Jem grunted and refolded his legs around his other side. "The counsellor is a joke. I just entertain myself making shit up. If

Dad wants to waste his money, let him."

"You could get yourself into trouble doing that. Who knows what they will conclude and tell your parents?"

"It can't be worse than what Dad imagines, can it? Some of the shit he comes out with is ridiculously homophobic. He actually called me a poofter the other day. You can't half tell he's Australian."

"Oh, Jem."

Jem glugged the last of his drink and eased himself off the sofa. "Anyway, I think it's time we got off this subject. I wish I hadn't told you if all you're going to do is build it up into some kind of childhood tragedy."

She bit her lip and watched him stride into the kitchen and open the fridge. It was hard to believe there could be no psychic or emotional damage from such an experience. His innocence stolen by a knowing, manipulative adult. Surely he was just burying it or somehow blocking the worst of it out of his mind? If that's what he'd managed to do, she supposed that was something to be grateful for.

"I'm going to finish this fruit off. Is that okay?"

*

BEFORE JEM SHOWERED, she got him to help her with the depopulation of the attic. Once emptied, she gave it a good sweep, knowing she need not come up here again.

"It's a shame about getting rid of some of these," Jem said, lifting a box out of the board game bag. "I remember playing them with him."

"I know, sweetie, but you just can't keep everything…and sometimes holding on to the past stops you from moving on."

Jem carefully returned the box and looked at her. "I miss him, Aunty Del."

The quiet simplicity of the statement hung in the air. She looked away as the tears welled in her eyes.

"I know," she breathed. She wiped her cheek with the back of her wrist. "Hey, I've got something to show you. You know those sketches of Uncle Roof's that your mother framed? I found some more that he'd made of Toby. Here, I'll get them."

She went over to the dresser and pulled out the drawer. She handed him the Manila folder. She looked over his shoulder as he rested it on his outstretched arm, flipping over the leaves.

"Toasters…kettles…Ah." Some of the pages were sticking together so he put them down on the dining table, freeing both hands to examine them more carefully. "This is similar to the series he did of me."

"Yes, except yours are more finished. I don't know whether he did more that he kept or whether these just got mislaid some- how."

Jem continued turning them over thoughtfully, a small crease between his brows. "Oh, this is nice. You could frame this one." He held up the small square card with Toby's profile.

"Maybe."

He held up the thick A4 sheet with the disembodied studies. "Reminds me of those anatomical studies you see of Leonardo da Vinci's."

"Yes, they do a bit, don't they?"

Jem held the sheet up and started flicking at the edge with a fingernail. Before she could ask what he was doing, there was a small tear and a pop and he'd pulled the paper open to be twice the size.

"Oh! You've got good eyes. Are there any more?"

"Yes, seems so…"

Adele's eyes flew over the paper, more body parts, some profiles, what—

She snatched the paper and ran over to the window pretending to look closer. Her breath had stopped and her hands were shaking. She quickly folded the paper back in half, pressing it tight between her fingers as if doing so would erase what she had just seen.

Jem stared at her, a look of real concern on his face. "Are you okay, Aunty Del?"

"Yes…I'm fine. Just. It's—seeing these upsets me sometimes. You never know when a certain expression will just—look, we'd better get your stuff into the car. Time's getting away if we're going to get you a phone charger for your trip."

Chapter Sixteen

Explosion

Def. 1. A violent shattering or blowing apart 2. A sudden outburst

JEM GAVE UP trying to engage her on the trip to the electronics shop and later to the tube station. When he hopped out to get his bags, she got out with him to say goodbye.

"I'm sorry about those pictures upsetting you so much, Aunty Del. I guess it's something we're never going to get over as a family."

"Oh, Jem." She gave him a prolonged hug. "I'm so lucky to have you guys. I loved every moment of my time with you and the girls this last trip, and the last couple of years with Harry and

Rosie. You're all such great kids…but I'm always seeing an empty chair wondering where Toby would have fitted in."

"Of course. And being all on your own doesn't help. You should come up and live near us."

"You're sounding like your father now."

"No way! That's a nice insult to part company on." He laughed and slung his bags into one hand so he could wave over his head and swipe his card at the turnstile.

On the way back home, she immediately jumped back onto the merry-go-round of thinking Jem had temporarily pulled her off. *What the hell? What the hell?*

When she walked in the front door, she deliberately ignored the folder of sketches screaming at her from the table. She had to block that last drawing out of her sight. Couldn't process it…couldn't… She put some washing on and got the ironing board out. She put on her favourite high-energy ironing music: Stevie Nicks's *Timespace*. She sang along at the top of her voice, shouting down her thoughts, and it helped.

But even as she yodelled like a frantic goat, what she had seen was silently howling, open-mouthed, at the back of her mind like Cathy's spirit at the window beseeching Lockwood to let her in. The thoughts slipping through the cracks were frightening her enough that she started planning the rest of her evening in terms of distractions. Like jumping from one melting block of ice to another, so long as she kept moving…

She rang her parents, and they had a long conversation. She

rang her sister afterwards. She was tempted to ring Joanne about the jumble sale pick-up, but resisted because she was the one person to whom Adele would probably talk about what was really bothering her, and she still hadn't got her head around her own thoughts yet, let alone felt able to articulate them out loud in any sensible form.

It was all too dangerous to touch, but like with Stephen, there would be a logical explanation. There had to be.

*

ADELE WOKE UP with a start. She looked around, temporarily disorientated. She was sitting up in bed. Her second movie on the laptop had finished, doing the work that was intended of sending her to sleep. So, what was that noise? She didn't have long to wait to hear it again: aggressive rapping on her front door.

What the hell?

She slipped out from under the covers and tiptoed into her office to see if she could see who it was. There was adequate light from the street lamps, and she was grateful she hadn't watched her movies downstairs with a light on to give her away. As it was, she could pretend not to be awake, or at home.

She leaned forward but couldn't see anything. The knocking stopped.

"I know you're in there, you bitch! Answer the door!"

Adele fell back from the window, her hand covering her mouth. It was Stephen. Patently drunk.

"I saw you, Adele. I saw you with that dyke detective having your cosy little tête-à-tête. In ten minutes, she was on my fucking tail again. What the bleeding fuck did you say to her? You haven't a clue what you've done! Stirring up shit that you know fuck-all about."

There was a break of quiet and she prayed he'd gone away. But then, to ratchet up her alarm even further, the banging started at the back door. "Come down here and face me, you vindictive cunt. You lousy fuck…"

Adele's whole body was flushed and hot and her pyjamas were sticking under her arms and in her groin. Hardly daring to breathe, she crept downstairs and found her phone. He wouldn't have heard anything over the hammering and yelling anyway. Oh god…the neighbours…

Safely back upstairs, she dialled Xandra's number and prayed she didn't turn her phone off at night.

A tired voice answered, "DS Ben—"

"Xandra, I need your help."

Xandra's tone immediately changed. "What's happening?"

"I've got Stephen Lane pounding on my door raising hell. He's drunk. And now he's in my garden attacking the back door. Says you've been making more enquiries and he's put two and two together because he saw us together the other day."

"Shit. I'll call the station for backup. I'll be there in ten minutes. Keep your head down and under no circumstances answer the door."

As *if.* Adele pulled her knees up to her face and wrapped her arms around her legs, hunkering into the smallest shape possible, willing the banging and abuse to stop. No doubt houselights were flickering on the length of the street by now. There were hardly any understandable words linking the terms of abuse together as Stephen became increasingly incoherent.

What the hell had Xandra *said*? Adele tried to think back to their conversation, trying to piece together how things had resulted in her being in this appalling situation.

The "special coaching". That was it. Xandra hadn't known about it. Jesus.

Adele raised her head. It wasn't her imagination. A distant siren was getting louder but then seemed to cut out at the end of her street. Then she heard the car itself as it screeched to a halt.

"Called your girlfriend now, have you? That cunt won't be happy till she's totally destroyed me—fucking man-haters the lot of you."

Car doors slammed and there were quick footsteps. This was followed by another man's voice now, deep and calm, issuing instructions to Stephen. She crept into the office again but didn't dare stick her head over the parapet for fear of being seen.

To her horror, Stephen broke down crying. Despite her earlier panic, all she felt now was shame and pity. His abject sobs tore at her heart. She could hear his stress and pain, and yes, his *fear.*

She braved a look, and was in time to see them pushing

him into the back of the police car, its lights alternating Mrs Henderson's front windows from blue to red. And yes, also the two goggle-eyed faces peering around the thrust-back curtain.

Giving Mrs Henderson the razz would never be funny again. She could hear it now: how she was dragging the neighbourhood down with her vulgar Australian ways. Adele had never liked her after that first conversation when she'd moved in. She was used to Brits bringing up the word "class" all the time—not a word you heard much in Australia in this rigid context—but Mrs Henderson seemed to relish it more than most.

"So surprised when we heard Rufus married an *Australian* woman." Delivered with a saccharine smile. "We all thought he'd marry one of the Inglis girls. His family have known them forever you know; same class, so much history..." Blah blah blah. "Oh yes, we know it's so different in Orr-stray-lee-ah. That dreadful show *Neighbours*..."

If she was tossing up whether to sell the house or not, tonight had just about decided her. At the minimum, she could no longer live here.

She heard the car drive off and her shoulders sagged. But they quickly shot up to her ears again with more knocking at the door. Fuck. Not the neighbours—then her phone rang.

"Hi, it's me. Let me in?"

Adele scooted to the door and opened it. Xandra held up a bottle of brandy. "I didn't know what your liquor cabinet was like, so I took precautions." She strode in. "Where's your kitchen and

I'll put some tea on."

Adele stood by, folding her arms tight around her chest, locking her hands in to stop them shaking, while Xandra filled the kettle and put it on. She said nothing to help Xandra, just watched as she opened cupboard doors looking for mugs and glasses. Seeing it was all under control, she went and collapsed on the sofa.

"Here, start on this." Xandra put down a tumbler in front of her with an inch of tan liquid in it. Adele lifted it to her lips, willing her trembling not to jolt it out of the glass, grateful for the burn as she took a gulp. She didn't even like brandy.

Then came the tea, and Xandra's weight sinking reassuringly next to her.

Adele dropped the rest of her drink into her tea mug and suppressed the impulse to dive under Xandra's arm and cling to her solid form.

"Seems I owe you an apology." Xandra cradled her own brandy in her cupped palms and brought it up for a meditative sip. "When you said you knew Stephen, I hadn't thought he would make any connection between my investigations and you. Of course, he may still not have, if he hadn't seen us together."

"No. I've been racking my brains over that. There was a guy who came in while we were having coffee, when it was too late to order anything. I saw his back turn and had a passing thought that he looked familiar, but I was too busy thinking of other things so it dropped out of my mind. I'll bet that was him—Tony's is between his school and the football field."

"Right. Not good. Sorry."

"I should probably tell you something else, just so you're clear. We also had a date a few weeks ago where we talked about some of this stuff...followed by a rather unsuccessful attempt at sleeping together. Not something I was intending on revisiting."

Xandra let out a gusty breath and grimaced. "Oi-oi-*oi*."

"Yeah. Well."

"So, I really dropped you in it. Sorry. But I had to follow up on what you told me. It's not like I went in there all guns blazing. They were just formal follow-up questions due to some new information coming in. Source not revealed, of course. I also spoke to Mrs Falk and the other families."

"What did they say?"

"None of them knew about any extracurricular coaching. Tania Lane also claimed ignorance. If there was anything going on, it was between 'the coach' and the children directly."

"But didn't the parents question their children coming home later than expected?"

"We don't even know if the other kids actually got these extra sessions at this stage. Maybe they just got one before they disappeared."

"Oh. I see." Adele clutched her mug and sipped her tea with great concentration. She rested her drink in her lap and returned Xandra's concerned gaze. "He said some really awful things about you tonight. 'That fucking dyke detective'."

Xandra laughed. "Yeah, they always go for the personal

angle. Somehow it justifies their anger and invalidates me doing my job."

So, you are a lesbian, then. This should have made no difference at all to Adele; in fact, if she'd considered things, she would have figured it out herself, perhaps. But it changed how she looked at the woman next to her. It made her seem tougher, yet more caring, all at once. A lightning bolt struck her from left field.

"Is Jo gay as well?"

Xandra leaned back in to the sofa and let out a guffaw of laughter. "Oh my. Who's the detective now?"

"Wow, so she is?"

"Yes and no. She was married for a long while. Long enough to have three children. Then she found her calling and it didn't gel for her husband that he'd suddenly been supplanted by God, as he saw it. They separated.

"Jo studied theology at nights and became heavily involved in church administration and politics—the business end of things. She was finally—controversially—awarded her own parish."

"Controversially? Because she was gay?"

"No, because she was a woman. And a separated one, at that."

"Oh yes, of course."

"I met her around that time. Someone I was interviewing was in her flock, so I came to services to meet with them. Anyway, Jo being Jo, she wanted to know who I was and all about me. I was honest with her. She's not a person to bullshit with."

Adele laughed. "No."

"We started a clandestine relationship. Jo couldn't afford anyone to know, so we were extremely careful. I think I was her first female lover and I gather it was something she had wanted for a long time, but had suppressed, as so many women do, so they can be 'normal' and have kids."

"So, you're a couple?" Adele thought back to that greeting, Jo squeezing Xandra's arm; that throaty intimate chuckle.

"No, sadly." Xandra tossed off the last of her brandy and poured herself another finger. "I couldn't stand the subterfuge. It put a lot of pressure on both of us. All I want, Adele, is to have a happy home life with a partner, out in the open, where I don't have to lie about my life. Apart from not wanting to be vulnerable to blackmail, it's just me wanting what everyone else has. I was never going to have that with Jo."

"Oh, that's so sad. But you're still friends?"

"Yes. I can't stop loving her. Jo is Jo. She's full of love and compassion for everybody. No malice in her. She's a special person to have in my life, and I couldn't lose that. She understood my decision, though, while also making her own priorities clear."

"So, you may be her only experience ever, then?"

"I doubt it; she's pretty red-blooded." Adele thrilled to see a shiver of memory momentarily light up Xandra's face. "If she's found someone more aligned with her goals, she'd keep it quiet, I think. It's just too risky for her."

"Well, it's not me, just so you know."

Xandra gave her a curious smile. "The thought did cross my mind."

They sat in silence sipping their drinks, each with their own thoughts.

Adele broke the quiet first. "Where did they take Stephen? Will he be in a cell overnight or something? Or just get let off with a warning?"

"Not sure. His being drunk and breaking down were all in his favour. He'll get a drunk and disorderly or a breach of the peace, most likely. Especially in a posh street like this."

"Yeah...a street I won't be able to raise my head in tomorrow."

Xandra gave her a look of comic despair. "Whoops." She raised her glass in mock salute. "You seem like a tough chick under that cute fem exterior. I'm sure you'll work it out."

"Wow. Do you think?"

"That you're cute or that you'll work it out?"

Adele felt her face suffuse with blood. "I wasn't fishing, I—"

Xandra let out a throaty laugh. She was clearly enjoying herself.

"It's okay. I'm only teasing you, to lighten the mood. I was worried when you opened the door and I was greeted by a shaking mess on the other side. You seem a lot calmer and together now."

"I don't feel it. I don't think I'll sleep tonight now, at all. I had enough buzzing around in my head already before this."

Xandra looked at her for a moment. "Well, he can't return,

and he'll most likely get a restraining order put on him so that he can't come back any time at all, so don't go worrying about that."

"I'm more worried about what it all *means*."

"If it makes you feel any better, I don't know that he would have exposed himself like this tonight if he really was guilty. No person in their right mind would want to draw that kind of attention to themselves. Unless he's a consummately clever actor...and I don't think Lane is that clever."

"Or consummate." Adele giggled, surprised at herself.

She took in Xandra's mock shock, and they both burst out laughing. "Like that, was it?"

"Sort of. I hadn't had sex in a long time, and I was gagging for it, not to put too fine a point on it. Too keen to wait or exercise any caution and...the train jumped the tracks, I guess you could say. Anyway, it's done now, and I won't be trying again in a hurry."

"That's a shame. Don't let one man burn you."

"No, it took two. My husband had a starring role in destroying my sexual confidence."

"Ahhh. *Men*."

"A problem you avoid."

"In my bed, but you can't get away from them everywhere else."

"True." Adele glanced at Xandra's empty glass. "You can't be okay to drive after two glasses. Please stay. I have a spare bed all made up—my son's old room, if that's not too icky for you. I'd appreciate knowing someone was here after that experience."

"I could easily cab home. I thought I'd do that and come back and check on you in the morning when I returned for my car. But I can stay, no problem."

Adele relaxed even further. "*Thank* you. I'll make you one of my famous omelettes for breakfast."

"As long as the coffee's strong, I'm good, me."

Adele led her guest up to Toby's room and showed her where everything was. She turned to leave her, but on impulse, turned back and squeezed her arm.

"I'm so relieved you're staying," she breathed, making an abrupt dash for her own room before Xandra could respond.

Chapter Seventeen

Ex Gratia

Def. As a favour or from a sense of moral obligation

XANDRA SAT ON the single bed and checked her messages. Stephen had been put in a cell overnight and they'd read him the riot act in the morning. She placed her phone on the bedside table and lay back on the bed, fully clothed.

She stared up into the dark, trying to fight the creeping feeling of hopelessness. She couldn't exonerate Lane purely on tonight's pathetic performance, but he was certainly looking less likely. Unless Adele revealed something new, she was left with widening her search for this "special coach". That could be anyone with some connection to the schools or sporting teams—or not, if they were a smooth enough talker.

Xandra raised her arms to clasp her hands behind her head. There had to be something in common across the three boys who disappeared in the three-year period from the three different schools. If they really were separate events, the possibilities were endless.

Xandra pressed her eyes shut briefly, weariness now catching up with her. She'd left her laptop at home and she couldn't leave now she'd promised Adele she'd stay.

A smile tugged at her lips as she recalled the frightened woman who had met her at the door. Minus her glasses and with her dishevelled hair, Adele had looked like a vulnerable young girl. And the cold-hardened nipples noticeable through her T-shirt had pushed the word dowdy well out of Xandra's mind. She gave herself a mental shake.

And this house. Adele had certainly married into some kind of privilege. She didn't seem the gold-digging type though...and "privileged" was probably not how she'd describe herself after losing her son and her marriage. She was the sort of woman Xandra would be curious to know better—*damn you and your matchmaking, Dysart*—under different circumstances, although she had to draw the line at friendship. Too many reasons to keep her distance.

Sighing in resignation, she sat up and reached for her phone. It was 3.00 a.m., and although the back of her eyes burned with tiredness, she despaired of getting any sleep now. She tended to avoid social media, but emails and catching up on news would keep her going till morning, and failing those, she could indulge in silly videos if she kept the sound down.

As her thumb scrolled and words and pictures flew by, she couldn't help the nagging hope that Adele might tell her something useful over breakfast, and if not then, very soon.

Chapter Eighteen

Ex Cathedra

Def. With the full authority of office

XANDRA HAD STAYED long enough to have a coffee with her before heading off home to get ready for work. Now Adele sat at the kitchen table contemplating the hollowed-out shell of her boiled egg. Life was tumbling in on her and she barely knew where to turn. Xandra's cheery face sweeping out the door had carried Adele's last vestige of positivity with it.

She glanced over to the counter where she had left the folder of sketches. The thought of looking at them again was making the eggy taste in her mouth vomit-inducing. She walked over to the fridge and poured herself some cold water to freshen her mouth and mind. She placed the half-drunk glass on the table and fetched the folder. She sat down and placed it in front of her, contemplating its neutral, inoffensive colour, its creased and dirty corner. Such a common object.

She opened the cover and flipped through the leaves until she came to the page she had assumed was simply a thicker A4 sheet. If it hadn't been for Jem, she may never have seen the hidden extras contained within the folded piece of A3 paper. Her hand trembled as she unfolded the sheet again, still sticking and needing to be plucked apart anew, wondering if her mind had exaggerated what she had only quickly taken in, but no. Among more small studies of body parts, there was another face in half profile. A nicely drawn portrait, only to be layered over with fangs at the corner of the mouth and the eyebrows more heavily done over, changing the face from innocent to evil.

She reached blindly for her glass of water, unable to take her eyes off the face. The freckles, the stringy fringe, the cheeky grin. She couldn't wring any sense out of her frightened and exhausted brain. What the hell was Roof doing sketching Charlie Falk?

*

THERE WAS NO point pretending she was fit for anything today. She needed to find things out, to *think*. Within half an hour she was rugged up and trudging up the hill to the heath. It was the wrong time of day for soccer games, but she didn't have to worry about bumping into Stephen Lane in any case, thank god.

She made a short run towards the bank to get up enough momentum to breach the top. Panting, she looked over to the bench. He wasn't there. She unwound her scarf and stuffed it in her pocket. She would just sit for a while and focus on his presence. Surely he would come; it was his spot as much as hers.

The field below was empty, the only moving figure in the whole scene was a man with a large black dog. She thought once again about Charlie's message that Toby was okay, and that he missed her.

"I miss you, too, Toby. Please come and see me."

"Mrs Soames?"

Adele jumped. He was there as if he'd always been there.

"*Charlie*. You scared me."

"Sorry, Mrs Soames." She watched as he pulled his brown banana out of his paper bag and proceeded to peel it.

"Charlie, why does your mother give you those squashy old bananas to eat?"

He looked at her uncomprehendingly, his cheeks bulging. He finally swallowed a mouthful and said, "I like them when they're mushy and sweet. They're my favourite."

Oh. She couldn't help smiling. Cursed for eternity to eat his favourite fruit, then; not reject rubbish after all. That was something, at least. She gazed out sadly over the playing fields, wondering if she would ever be able to share that fact with Sylvia Falk.

She took a steadying breath. "Charlie, I have some questions for you. Do you think you could tell me some things?"

"I don't know." He gave her a wary look. "I'm not very good at maths. Or spelling, either."

"That's okay." Adele plucked at the corner of her coat laying just over her knee, wondering how to ask what she didn't want an answer to. She decided to sidestep and ask something else that had been eating at her.

"So, tell me. When you spoke to Toby last, where did you see him?"

"We have a special place we hang out together. It's dark and leafy. Very quiet and peaceful."

"Quiet and peaceful?"

"Yes. No one much goes there. Just us."

"Just you and Toby? No other...boys?"

"Just us."

"Is this place...near here?"

"Yes. Just over the way." He waved his hand towards the other side of the heath.

Adele nodded. "I *see*. Yes. I think I know where you mean. It *is* very peaceful over there, isn't it."

Charlie had stuffed his banana skin into his bag and was screwing it up into a ball, signalling his imminent departure.

"One more question, Charlie, before you go? H-how's the special coaching going?"

"I don't know. This is my first session."

Adele sucked her lips inwards and bit them together hard.

"It's—it's nice..." Adele felt her breath shortening. "...*good* of Mr Lane to give you some extra help..."

Charlie paused in the act of lobbing his rubbish in the bin. He grinned back at her as if she was having a joke with him. "Not *him*. He's too busy!" He lowered his voice with a conspiratorial look on his face. "But you can't tell anyone or the other boys will be jealous. Mr Soames said we have to keep it a secret."

Chapter Nineteen

Extirpation

Def. To pull up by the root; wipe out

ADELE BACKED OUT of the bushes on her hands and knees. Like a wounded animal she had half staggered, half fallen into the undergrowth to regurgitate egg over the grass.

Still on all fours, all she could do was groan, unable to get up. The black ugly thoughts she had been keeping at bay since she had seen that little sketched face had burst into life and flooded her mind with incomprehensible horror.

It just wasn't possible. It wasn't. How could it be? Her own husband?

She edged away from her spray of egg to a cleaner patch of ground. She focused on the blades of grass in front of her, the different thicknesses and types. Stray dead strands, sticks, the odd leaf fallen or blown from elsewhere; her attention caught by an ant, then another, traversing the major obstacles in their paths. She hung her head as another wave of nausea swirled in her stomach. When nothing eventuated, she collapsed and rolled onto her back to stare at the sky.

Still half under the bushes she had crawled into, their branches and reaching bare twigs formed the top edge of her view. The sky was like gruel, with no blue to ease or refresh; just varying textures of white on grey. A study by Whistler copying Monet.

It all became a blur as she cast her mind back to that time, trying to place some retrospective order on events. That first week. The trip to the hospital. The stress and stasis following. She tried to remember, to line things up. Where had Roof been? There was a memorial gathering at the local football club... Roof had been away up north to close off a project... The packing, the endless phone calls. Functioning like an automaton. Then they were gone, dragging suitcases to Heathrow.

In this amorphous lump of time Charlie had gone missing. According to what she had read online, it was towards the end of their last week. Possibly after the service—was he there? And Roof's trip north: she was sure that was also after the service. Maybe he wasn't even here when it happened? A twinge of hope allowed her to take a deeper breath, but this was quickly squashed.

She had it on Charlie's authority whom he was waiting for. Was it possible someone else had come? But why would Roof impress him with secrecy?

Adele placed her hands on her stomach and gently moved them around, testing. She focused on drawing deep slow breaths, monitoring the slightest movement in the clouds. When a bird shot like a black dart over the corner of her screen, she involuntarily sat up.

She swallowed convulsively, which hurt, as her throat and mouth were dry and raw. Another, different memory struck her. Roof had been adamant about knowing who had kicked that ball into his son's head. Was that what this was about?

She felt old and heavy. It was an effort to get to standing. She was about to stagger back to the bench but thought better of it: she needed privacy. Her house was the natural place to run to, but already her feelings towards the home she had made and shared with Rufus were dramatically changing. But as of right now, it was all she had.

She wiped her mouth with the back of her hand and pulled her coat tight around her. She hunched her shoulders, casting furtive looks on either side, emerging like some evil presentiment from the undergrowth.

*

SHE WAS EQUALLY drawn and repelled by the house as she stood on the street, looking up at its higher windows peeking out through the sprouting tree branches. Adele took a few steps toward the front door, but then, obeying some visceral instinct, made a sharp right and headed down the side path to the back garden. The path Stephen had taken to her back door, stomping on some of her budding crocuses.

Adele stopped. Those crocuses. An irrational flood of anger and resentment washed into her chest, lapping up to the backs of her eyes. Roof's darling fucking flowers.

She got to the end of the path, already frantically tearing off her coat. She threw it on the grass and followed the paving stones to the back shed, an outbuilding she had rarely visited, as it was the domain of Rufus and the hired gardening help.

Not even computing what she was doing, she reached for the first tools to hand: a gardening fork and a small spade. With one in each hand like an avenging Kali, she hurried back to the strip of plants between the side hedge and the path and threw herself down on her knees. She took the fork in both fists and started hacking at the hard ground and the new green leaves. Dirt spat back at her face and the fork chinged and scratched against small stones and leafage. She was barely breathing as she imitated a sewing machine, stabbing and shredding every single plant to ruins.

The fork grabbed in the ground and she paused, leaning on it to catch her ragged breath. She threw it to one side and took up the spade. It wasn't enough that the plants were slashed to death, she required full extirpation. She hacked at the loosened ground and jammed her spade in to reveal the naked bulbs themselves.

The bulbs Rufus had so assiduously planted and cultivated.

Adele levered and chopped, and when that wasn't enough, dug her bare hands in to yank and pull. Her nails were packed tight with dirt and her hands were scratched and bleeding, but she tore and ripped like a madwoman. Her hair had fallen all around her face and she was sniffling as her body heat caused condensation in her nose.

The smashed brown bulbs were piling up like Pol Pot's skulls, and it still wasn't enough. She wanted every last vestige of the plants removed, excised and expunged.

Her shoulders were stiff and aching, but she extended her attack to the second adjoining flower bed to cleanse the earth of its poison. She was gasping and crying now, hysteria taking over. She had raised her hand to pull hair out of her mouth and had been revolted at the mucky black claw that had appeared in front of her face.

She leaned on the ground and looked into the jagged maw of earth in front of her, and its resemblance to an open grave made her stop. Her lips spread in an open-mouthed grimace as she gave way to the ugliest crying she had ever allowed herself. Her voice came out as a hoarse, guttural growl.

"You evil, *evil* bastard! Where did you put him? *Where?*"

Her elbows trembled under her weight, and she tipped forward. Both her hands landed in the shallow gutter, and she weakly pounded her fists into the hard ground, oblivious to the cracking and scraping of her knuckles against the shards of rock and chalk she had chipped and exposed. Exhaustion made her keel over entirely, and she allowed herself to tumble onto her side into the open wound of dirt, not caring if she ever got up again.

*

ADELE CAME TO awareness as something jolted her shoulder.

"Adele, Adele! Good lord, what's happened here? What have you done to yourself?"

Adele turned her face slightly and squinted upwards into an unfamiliar face. She held up a hand protectively and screwed her eyes shut as fragments of dirt dropped into them, and she had to blink feverishly to see anything at all.

"Oh, my goodness. Your hands! Let's get you off this damp ground, you'll catch a chill..."

It was all background noise as she dumbly submitted to strong hands pushing and dragging her to a sitting position. The face now registered in her database of known visages. What had made it strange was the foreign expression of horror and despair it had held as it hovered over her. The raised and worried voice also was out of its ordinary range.

She allowed Jo to ease her up to a standing position.

"Are you okay to walk?"

"Yes—no—I... Oh, Jo, I *can't*... It's too terrible—"

She staggered and collapsed against Jo's solid body, a torrent of crying released from a sense of having reached comfort and safety.

She was unsure how much time had passed, but eventually she felt Jo push her away slightly and mutter, "Come on, girl. We need to get you inside." Jo's voice sounded more kindly and together now, having established that Adele was at least physically functional.

Adele sat despondently at the dining table, watching as Jo busied herself in the kitchen. She soon apprehended the sound of water accumulating in the sink.

"Bring those hands of yours over here, and we'll start by soaking the worst of that muck off."

Adele came over to stand beside her. Jo was vigorously pumping a soap pack into the gushing water, creating a pile of foam. Then she grabbed each of Adele's forearms and pushed up her sleeves, releasing a shower of dirt crumbs.

Despite the stinging cuts, it was lovely to have her hands in warm water, feeling them uncurl from their contorted claw shapes, and the dirt soften and fall away. But it wasn't just that. Jo's mere presence was having a calming soporific effect on her heart and mind. Everything would be okay now Jo was here.

Jo, meanwhile, had flicked the kettle on and searched out mugs to place next to it on the counter. Adele watched this wonderful woman busily rub her hands together and look around.

"Have you got a nail brush somewhere?"

"Yes. Bathroom at the top of the stairs."

As she listened to Jo thump up the stairs on her mission, Adele gazed out of the window at her newly blasted open cut mine. It reflected how she felt: eviscerated, with the shell of her insides scored and bleeding, the nerves all torn out, leaving her feeling numb and dead. There was no sense of either regret or accomplishment at what she had done. It just was.

Jo was beside her again, placing a comforting hand on her hunched and aching shoulders as she leaned into the sink, weeping uncontrollably.

"Come on, girl," she murmured, fishing for a hand in the sink. Adele watched as if from afar as Jo gently massaged the soaped-up bristles over her cuticles and into the creases of her knuckles. A vague sense of comfort and bath times with her mother as a little girl came to her.

As Jo got her to swap hands, a thought struck her. "Why are you here?"

"Why?" Jo paused in her scrubbing to look at her in comic despair. "Goodness, girl. You *asked* me to come. The jumble sale pick-up. Remember?"

Adele dipped her head. "I'm sorry," she mumbled.

"Come on," Jo murmured more to herself than Adele. "Let's get these rinsed and dry, then we can have a hot drink."

Jo patted her hands dry with the towel she had brought down with her. "And rub this in." She squeezed some hand cream out of a tube onto Adele's raw skin.

She was sitting on the sofa, still kneading the cream in, when Jo deposited two mugs on the coffee table.

Jo sat catty-corner to her, sipping her tea, observing her

without comment. Adele reached for her cup but found its heat was too much for her sensitised hands. She took it by the handle and used the coaster underneath to lift it with her other hand. She took a mouthful and enjoyed the heat going down her throat. She stared into the middle distance, trying to ignore the weight in the air of Jo's unasked questions. Where to begin?

Jo must have read her troubled expression. She placed her mug firmly on the table and leaned forward, clasping her hands together. "Adele, I can't leave here until I understand what's going on for you. It's like you've had an enormous shock or trauma of some description. What's happened?"

The words, spoken so gently, evoked more warm streams down her face. She sniffed and looked beseechingly at the ceiling. "Oh, *Jo*."

Shakily, she got up and walked over to the dresser where the folder lay. She extracted the sketch, came back to sit beside Jo, and placed it in her hands.

Jo held it for a moment in silence before giving her a questioning look. "I don't understand. This looks like Sylvia's son?"

"Yes."

"But this...?" She traced the outline of the brows and the fangs with a fingernail. "You found this here? In the house?"

Adele nodded quickly, feeling another onset of tears.

"And...it's by...your husband?"

"My ex-husband, Jo. My ex!"

"Shh-shh. It's okay." Jo placed her hand on Adele's arm,

while she continued to gaze at the drawing.

Not removing her hand from Adele's arm, she placed the drawing carefully on the table and swivelled to face her. She reached over and took both Adele's hands in hers.

"This doesn't have to mean anything. It's just an idle doodle. Maybe it's just an emotional reaction to him finding out—"

"No, Jo, there's more."

Jo tightened her hold on Adele's hands. "Go on."

"I needed to find out myself, needed to ask. I went—" She gulped and panted, dropping her head for a moment. Licking her lips, she raised her head again and continued, "—I went to see Charlie. I asked *him*."

Jo's eyes widened. "Asked him what?"

"Who he was waiting for. God help me, Jo! I even tried to get him to confirm it was Stephen, because I knew, I *knew*..." Her head fell forward. She was crying again, unable to speak. She pinched her nose, hot breath wetting her hand; she wiped tears and snot away, verging on hyperventilating.

"Adele, you need to take a slow breath and calm down. Are you going to tell me it was Rufus he was waiting for?"

"Yes."

Jo leaned back and stared at the ceiling, then briefly closed her eyes.

"I see," she said softly.

"No, you don't *see*! I've been living with a *murderer*! Anyone who could do anything to a child is beyond evil, Jo! Beyond redemption! The lowest—" Adele grabbed her stomach and groaned like a wounded animal.

"You can't know that for sure, Adele. This picture alone doesn't prove anything. You could be jumping to wild conclusions. There could easily be a logical explanation. It's a serious accusation." She moved more side-on to Adele and put her arms around her. "You don't think, possibly, that this pain spewing out of your heart is partly the result of bottled-up resentment at your lost marriage? The reasons for rejection and failure you've been searching for?"

Adele sat bolt upright, wiping her face. "*No!* No, I—"

Jo reached up and pushed some hair out of Adele's face and stroked her cheek. They sat in silence a moment, looking at each other.

"Do you really think Rufus was the kind of man who could hurt a child?"

Adele's face crumpled as she turned towards the side window. "I don't *know*. I spent the last few years of my marriage wondering who it was I was sharing a house with, as I hardly recognised him anymore. And the more I think about it, Jo, the more I realise it wasn't all down to losing Toby. There were signs even before that. I just became good at rationalising and making excuses for him."

Jo said nothing, allowing her to catch her breath and wipe her face with the back of her hand. "He—he'd become more introverted, secluding himself away from me. Less social. So many excuses..."

Adele spun more of the same threads of thought. So much computer time, trips for work. The only things he had made time for were work, his son, and helping out with the football team. And once they had gone to Australia, there was only work left.

"Well, you know what I'm going to suggest, don't you." Jo stood up and took their mugs to the kitchen.

Adele watched Jo's back warily as she stood at the sink rinsing out their mugs. She set them upside down on the draining board and turned around. "You need to speak to Xandra."

"Jo, I can't make this official. I'd look like some hysterical—"

"Xandra would know how to handle this, Adele. You forget that she's been on this case for a long time now. She's interviewed people, pooled evidence and leads, sorted through alibis. She might already have information that clears Rufus or adds support to what you think...or what you tell her may give her a whole new path of enquiry she didn't know was there to follow."

Adele was quiet for a moment considering this. "Did she say anything about Rufus at the time? We left not long after it happened, but he used to help out at the football games after school sometimes."

"I don't recall. This is why you need to speak with her."

Adele sank back into the sofa cushions. She wanted to, but she also didn't want to. Once set in motion, it might be the most horrible Pandora's Box ever opened.

"Do you think I should try and speak to Rufus?"

"No. Absolutely not. You don't want to be implicated in this.

Let it be handled through formal processes. And in the event he has something to hide, you don't want to put him on his guard."

Jo's certainty and being told she didn't have to fix things herself, even if that were possible, was a relief.

"Shall I give Xandra a call?"

Adele's head shot up. "No. Please. I need to think about this overnight or for a day or so. I—I think you're right. I will. I'm just not ready...yet. I need to be careful what I say to her...plan it out."

Jo walked back over to the sofa and held out her hand, inviting her to stand up. "Okay, I understand, although I would rest easier knowing you had some company tonight. You seem more yourself now, but promise you'll call me if you get wound up again?"

Adele smiled and nodded. "You're the best, Jo." She leaned forward and gave her a hug.

Jo looked at her watch and gave her a rueful smile. "I'm not, actually. I'm running late on my jumble sale pick-ups, so I'd better get going. Where's this gear of yours?"

A few in-and-out trips later, and the van was loaded. Adele already felt a little lighter watching the door slide shut on all that stuff, knowing the attic space above her head was empty and clear.

She walked Jo to the driver's side of the van and gave her a parting hug. "I'm sorry I've made you late. I seem to be taking up a lot of your time lately. You've been a good friend to me, Jo."

Jo squeezed both of her upper arms and gave her a satisfied smile. "Always my pleasure. I'll call tomorrow to check in and see how you are. I hope you see your way to talking things over with Xandra. I sense it's the only way you are going to find release, one way or the other."

Adele nodded and folded her arms over her chest. She lifted one hand to wave as the van chugged off down the street.

"Yes," she muttered to herself. "One way or the other."

Chapter Twenty

Expedition

Def. 1. A journey undertaken 2. Promptness or speed in doing something

AS SOON AS Adele came back inside, she fixed herself a glass of whiskey with a single ice cube. It had never been her drink of choice until she met Roof. In those early days when they'd started going out together, it became a habit to crown the evening with a little nightcap of the amber fluid. Given that she now associated it with Roof drinking too much and flare-ups of bad temper, it was surprising that she still enjoyed a glass, but she did. And now she really needed some forgetfulness.

Glass in hand, she wandered up the stairs, needing to get away from the day's drama downstairs. She thought about sitting in the easy chair in her office but, instead, opted for her son's room. She plumped up the pillows and turned on the bedside lamp for a softer, more forgiving light. Propped up, with her legs crossed at the ankles, she rested her drink on her thigh and stared into space.

Jo was right. She needed to talk with Xandra. Lock down dates and facts and get things straight. Could he or couldn't he, did he or didn't he? Worrying and supposing would turn her into a mental case—surely whatever she was imagining was worse than the reality?

And Jo was right about not calling him. What fit of madness was she in when she proposed *that*? As if she could coax some confiding conversation from him on any subject at all, let alone something so dangerously personal and accusatory.

Letting her gaze wander around her son's room, it made her wonder what *he* thought about all this. *He* already knew the truth. He must. Had he witnessed what happened to Charlie? Did they talk about it? Is that what drew them together?

Adele took a thoughtful sip of her drink. Charlie had said they weren't in the same team; not even in the same class. So, they probably hadn't known each other that well, if at all. But they hung out together now. She strained her memory. What was it Charlie had said? They hung out in a peaceful place. Yes, that was it. She had assumed he meant where Toby was buried. That would make sense. And it *was* a peaceful place. Highgate Cemetery was riddled with paths winding through trees, almost undergrowth, with vines creeping over headstones and up trees, absorbing any noise, and, perhaps, any pain.

The place where Toby was buried was predetermined. The Soames's family plot was away from any main path and under a large ash tree. Roof's parents had purchased it long ago for themselves, with remaining space for their son and his future spouse. Relieved to have one less thing to decide, they had buried Toby next to his grandparents. It had all been so rushed, the choosing of things, but she had been pleased with the baby angel that now sat in front of his headstone.

She had been negligent in not visiting. How strange that she somehow felt closer to her son on the heath watching football games than sitting near his actual resting place. But perhaps it wasn't so strange: on the playing fields he was still running around, wild and free, happy with his hair flying, playing the game he loved. Being near his grave made his death more real, a limiting thing: there he was, locked in, horizontal, six feet down in a wooden box.

But perhaps, oh just perhaps, if she went there, he might come. Yes, that's what she would do tomorrow. She would visit Toby, and consult with him, be with him. See what *he* thought about this situation.

She tossed off the last of her whiskey and stood up. Yes, she had a plan. It was a forestalling kind of plan, but it was the best she could do.

*

EVEN THOUGH SHE must have dozed at some point, Adele felt like she'd been awake all night. When she couldn't stand it any longer, she went downstairs and made a tea to bring back to bed. There was no point rushing as the cemetery didn't open until 10.00 a.m.

There had been some rain through the night, and the ground would be wet. She had her trench coat, but she also grabbed a waterproof picnic rug to take with her. She drove round to Dominique's and joined the morning queue for coffee. Eyeing the pastries off, her conscience pricked her when she was reminded of the shredded snail left ungraciously on her plate that time with Xandra. She ordered one now, and a pain au chocolat, because that was Toby's favourite.

The traffic wasn't too bad, and she was soon looking for a park. She carried the rug, her coffee, and the bag of pastries down Swains Lane, showed her pass at the gate for the east side, and headed into the deep foliage of the cemetery. It was a pleasant walk, and already there were a few tourists milling about, even on a chill day in late February. It was hard to believe it would officially be spring next week.

Walking down an avenue of evergreen trees, it seemed to grow even dimmer. She hoped the sky wasn't about to open with more rain. Finally, she found the graves that marked her departure point from the path. She weaved her way between slabs of stone and crosses to a row farther back, under the bough of an ash tree. Adele paused. The angel was sitting there, a little grimier, but still guarding Toby's place after all this time.

She approached carefully, looking around for any movement. She put down her food and spread the picnic rug half over the stone slab, up to the toes of the angel. Pulling her coat tight around her, she lowered herself down and curled her legs underneath her. Finally, she could pull the lid off her coffee. She took a generous mouthful and looked around her. Still no rain, but the new sprouting leaves fluttered softly in the breeze as if in anticipation of it. Adele turned to her paper bags, pulling out the pastries and arranging them on the paper as if she was laying places at a table.

"I brought one for you, darling. I know how you love your chocolate croissants."

She tore a strip off her snail and this time enjoyed its damp, papery sweetness with her coffee. She sipped and chewed but kept a sharp eye out for any movement in the foliage, still hopeful that he might come.

"If you don't come soon, Toby-my-lad, I'll have to eat your pastry as well, and I'm sure you wouldn't like that, now." She looked around and deliberately tore the pain au chocolat in half: nothing. She ate half of it: nobody. She sighed and finished it, followed by the last of her drink. She screwed up the paper, stuffed it into the empty cup, and jammed the lid back on. An act now indelibly linked to Charlie. Even he was staying away today. Maybe she asked too much.

She sat for a moment more, contemplating Toby's headstone. *Dearly beloved son of Rufus and Adele. Taken too soon.* "Taken too soon, indeed, my beautiful boy," she murmured.

She reached over and stroked the head of the angel. The text in the headstone still read sharp and clear and required no cleaning. She got up and folded her blanket. It was only then, standing up, she noted the green shoots of daffodils behind the headstone in the remaining part of the plot: more bulbs that Rufus had insisted on planting. "Better than leaving rotting vegetation in dirty jars," he said. She fought the urge to pull these out as well. Everything he'd touched now felt tainted and infected.

She hung the blanket over her arm and strolled around the tree, aimlessly reaching out to touch its bark. She shuffled her boots through the wet ground cover and mulch, careful not to get entangled. Overhead a bird cawed, causing some leaves to shiver in its wake. It was a lonely, desolate sound that echoed in her heart.

She closed her eyes for a moment and breathed in the cool, green, earthy air. Instead of walking back to the path, she continued further into the wooded area in front of a short embanked slope leading up to the wall bordering the cemetery. She glanced casually behind her, and there he was.

"Hello, Mrs Soames."

"Charlie. I didn't think I'd be seeing you today."

"I'm always here."

"Is—is Toby...around?"

"Oh sure. Somewhere." He waved his arm vaguely in the

direction of Toby's grave.

"I didn't see him. Do you think you could pass on a message for me?" Charlie looked at her, waiting. "Please tell him I love him and I miss him. Every day."

Charlie smiled. "He already knows that, Mrs Soames."

"And Charlie? What about your mother? Can I tell her anything for you?"

The boy's smile wavered. "Mum is very sad. She's always unhappy when I see her. I wish she would smile more. Dad's worried about her, too."

Adele nodded, tears welling in her eyes. She burrowed in her pocket for a tissue. "I will do that for you, Charlie."

She looked around as she blew her nose, then back to where he sat crouched on the bank. "So, this...this is where you like to hang out?"

"Yes. Down there with Toby. We both like the daffodils."

"Yes, they'll be so pretty when they..." She looked around and stopped. From where she stood, new green shoots dotted the empty rectangular space and crept down either side of the slab in front of Toby's headstone.

Her breath suddenly felt sharp in her lungs and she heard her own pulse drumming in her ears. "Oh god. My *god*. Charlie, of course," she breathed.

Adele turned back around to say something more to him, but he was gone.

Chapter Twenty-One

Expertise

Def. Expert skill or knowledge in a particular field

THE TIMING OF Adele's call had been good, even if Xandra was on the other side of London. After spending the morning in the Coroner's Office at Croydon, she had finally been able to grab her first sustenance of the day for the journey back north. DC Fenwick was driving, so she was in charge of the serviettes and sausage rolls. She was in the act of squeezing tomato sauce onto her roll when Adele's name came up on her phone.

Hastily sucking her fingers, she answered.

"I'm sorry to bother you when you're busy, but it is a work call."

"Okay, I'm listening."

"It's about...what we've been talking about. I—I've learned something... It might be...important."

Xandra's breath caught in her throat. After trying not to think about it all week, this could be it. The wariness in Adele's voice was a good portent.

"Right. I'll have to make some calls and rearrange things." She glanced at Fenwick who was busy negotiating an intersection. "I'm currently in South London, so it's going to be a while before I can get there. Is there any urgency? Do you feel safe where you are?"

"No, no. I'm fine. It's just important that I speak to you as soon as possible."

It was just after two when Adele's front door opened to reveal a tired and anxious-looking face. She had sounded nervous and cagey on the phone, giving the impression she couldn't speak privately, but now Xandra was pleased to hear relief in Adele's voice as she welcomed her inside.

"I'm sorry for razzing up your day. I'm so grateful you could come."

"Don't be sorry. The fact that you felt you couldn't wait was enough to make me drop everything." She strode in and placed her laptop bag on the dining table. "I told you I've been waiting for that missing piece of the jigsaw. I'm excited to think this could be it."

She sat down and unpacked her computer, snatching glances at Adele's face as she did so. It was less than a week ago when she had seen her last, and she noted the subtle changes. Her eyes had lost their sparkle and her face was lined with worry.

Adele moved to hover next to her, clutching her fingers together as Xandra tapped in her password.

She looked up and smiled. "Don't look so worried. I've brought my laptop so I have my case notes to hand in the event I need to cross-check anything. How about you put the kettle on and we can have a more relaxed chat over some coffee?"

Adele nodded and headed to the sink.

"And biscuits? Do you have any? Brunch was a rush job, sorry."

"That's no way to look after yourself."

As she focused on bringing up the right files, Xandra could hear the sound of plastic rustling and biscuits tinkling onto porcelain behind her. A mug of coffee and a plate with cheese and crackers landed next to her laptop.

"Here you go. Better than a pile of sugar."

Xandra gave her an amused glance. "Thanks, Mum."

Adele slid into the chair opposite and watched while she wolfed down three cheese-laden crackers in quick succession.

"Mmm. Thanks for this. That'll keep the worm happy for a wee while." She leaned down to her bag and pulled out a small spiral-backed notebook with a pen hooked on the cover. "Right. I'm ready. Any time now's good."

Adele placed her fingers over the edge of the table as if she was about to push herself away and stand up. She studied her nails for a long moment before looking up at Xandra.

"There are two things," she spoke quietly. "They may be connected, but I don't know. One of them is going to be really hard to tell you, and I'm not even sure if I can, yet."

Xandra sighed inwardly. *Here we go.* She frowned and dug her chin into her palm, her eyes trained on Adele's face.

"There's a reasonable chance that I know where Charlie is buried."

"What?" Xandra's head jerked up and she slapped her hand down on the table. "Explain yourself."

"It—it might be a wild goose chase. I can't tell you how I found out. You wouldn't take me seriously... Can you just say you're following up an anonymous tip-off? That way if he's not where I say, it can just be...dismissed."

Xandra narrowed her eyes. Adele was struggling to maintain eye contact with her, and it didn't bode well.

"What. It came to you in a dream, or something?" She instantly regretted her tone of voice when Adele's face creased up in misery.

"No..." She paused, biting her bottom lip. "I can take you there. Maybe when you see the place, you'll agree that it's a highly feasible spot."

"So, where are we talking?"

"Highgate Cemetery."

Xandra let out a low whistle. "Close to the heath, but far enough away...but how—"

"And it closes at 4.00 p.m. in the winter months, not long after the time Charlie was last seen."

"Assuming he died not long after that. And assuming he was buried shortly afterwards."

"Well, yes, of course..." Adele clasped both hands around her mug.

"And the second thing?"

Adele's grip on her mug tightened. She opened her mouth, but nothing came out.

Xandra reached over and placed a hand over hers that was gripping the mug. "You're worrying me, Adele. You look frightened."

"I—I am."

"Are you feeling threatened in any way?"

"No, it's not that. I'm scared of unleashing something that could get out of control. And what if I'm wrong?"

"Just give me the facts and I'll do the work to follow up. Either they can be corroborated or not."

"But your 'follow up' impacts on people's lives. Look at poor Stephen."

"My enquiries and investigations will be kept as confidential as possible. Snooping media is something I wish I could control, but..."

Adele licked her lips, her glance flickering over the table's surface. Xandra could almost hear Adele's thoughts jangling against one another. Whatever was going on, the conflict was playing out on Adele's face… Who was she trying to protect?

Adele stood up and shakily pushed out her chair behind her. She walked over to a dresser in the living room and picked up a folder that lay on it. She extracted a page, returning with it held tightly in both hands in front of her. Once seated, hands shaking, she passed it like an offering, over the table. Xandra said nothing and solemnly took it from her with both of her own hands, like a Japanese businessman accepting a proffered card. She placed it in front of her but retained eye contact with Adele.

"Where did this come from?"

"I found it. Here in the house," she whispered. She motioned with shaking fingers. "You need to—to unfold it…here…"

Xandra chewed the inside of her lip. Using both hands she gently separated the halves of the page, unfolding it to A3 size. She was aware of Adele's eyes locked on her face and her own breath suddenly stalled in her chest. Infinite time passed as Xandra just stared at the familiar face with its heavily lined desecrations. The facts zinging around in her mind were starting to reassemble into a new shape. Finally, she spoke.

"Drawn by your then-husband, Rufus Soames?"

Adele simply nodded, her eyes fearful and pleading.

Xandra's fingertips pressed her top lip into her teeth. "I see."

"But what do you see, Xandra? It doesn't prove anything on its own."

"No, it doesn't. You're right. But it's a direct connection. More direct than we were previously aware of."

Xandra's mind was already trying to dredge up the details of her conversation with Soames, wondering what she had missed. Had the clues been there all along? She had been all too ready to accept that his frenetic state was due to the recent trauma in his own life and flying out to Australia the following day. To escape…

"It casts new light on old evidence and provides a new line of enquiry."

She could see Rufus Soames fussing around his office. She had already been briefed on the recent loss of his own son, but she had nonetheless been struck by his nervous energy, observing that here was a man under stress. He had not sat still for the interview but had insisted that he continue with his packing and sorting while they spoke, providing his answers while peering into boxes and files. It occurred to her now that he had known exactly what he was doing.

Xandra turned the paper over to look more closely at the drawings of random body parts. "Were there pictures of any other boys?"

Adele quickly shook her head. "Just Toby."

"I'll need to take the whole file away, if you don't mind."

While Adele was fetching it, Xandra said, "So you found something among Rufus's things to indicate the burial location?"

"No. I still can't tell you more about that, I'm sorry."

Xandra pursed her lips in frustration. "Well, I feel a bit more confident chasing up your hunch, if that's what it is, if you're saying your ex-husband might be involved in this."

"Tell me more about that time, Xandra. I was hardly aware of any of this back then. I may have heard something in passing, but I was too deep in my own grief and moving deadlines to be aware of anything except my own heartbeat. I'm not even sure Roof knew anything about it—and if he did, perhaps he was trying to shield me from more upset."

"He certainly did know, because I interviewed him. I met him at his office in town." Xandra tapped a few keys and brought the document up. "His name was on the list of parents connected to the after-school game activities. I interviewed them all myself." She hit her down arrow a couple of times and peered at her screen. "When questioned about his movements that day he said he'd gone into work that morning but had left around three to catch a train down to Manchester Piccadilly. He was able to show me his booking information, and...yes, we verified that he checked into the Holiday Inn near the station that evening. He was also able to produce a work colleague to confirm they'd had dinner and drinks together before he checked in."

Adele leaned forward, her face eager. "So, it can't have been Roof then, can it?"

"Prima facie, no. But we can't say for sure yet. At the time, his alibi was accepted at face value. But after seeing this"—she tapped the sketch with her finger—"I'd like to see if it stands up to further scrutiny."

Adele had sat back again in her chair and a frown had gathered on her face. She was examining the table in front of her, drawing loops with her finger.

"What's the matter?"

"Oh n-nothing, really, I suppose. Just that he usually stayed with my brother's family when he had trips north. Maybe with everything going on he just wanted some privacy."

Xandra scribbled a note in her pad then continued scrolling down her screen. "That's all I have. The focus was really on Stephen Lane after that, and of course, you both left for Australia the very next day."

"I wish I could map my movements during that period more clearly. Of all the times it would have been handy to have kept a diary…"

"Do you post on social media? What about your emails over that time? All of those things brought together could remind you of what you were doing those days."

"I wouldn't have been posting anything—I was in hiding, Xandra. I was barely existing. There might be emails, though, that's a good idea. Not sure if the phone company would give me information on calls going back that far…"

"They'll give them to me."

Adele blushed. "Yes, of course."

Xandra turned to her laptop screen pretending to scroll and read, when in reality her brain was frantically pulling apart old data and reassembling it to make new patterns. While Rufus and other parents had been on her radar due to their direct connection to the team, spouses and other family members had not been, especially if the alibis held. She was beginning to wonder if this had been a mistake.

Adele might be able to verify her then-husband's movements at that time, but could she verify her own? What was she hiding? Who was she trying to protect? A distant alarm bell was jagging in the back of Xandra's mind and emanating from its source was a tremor of unease.

"So, here's what I want you to do: go through everything you have available and construct a timeline for me of that period of both of your movements, referring to any supporting documents, physical or electronic. Note any contacts with people who might be able to verify what you say." She wanted to add more, but the look on Adele's face said she was already scaring the horses.

She folded her laptop shut, keeping her eye on Adele's face. "Are you okay?"

"I'm having this irrational feeling that this is somehow all my fault. Something I should have known about and stopped. Or that the world is about to crash on Roof's head, and that will definitely be my fault."

"I can make a lot of enquiries and do data-matching behind the scenes. If we get some interesting or inconsistent results, it will be worth questioning him again. Your name doesn't have to come up anywhere...except as the erstwhile spouse of a potential suspect." Xandra cut another wedge of brie and placed it on a biscuit.

"And let me tell you something for nothing, sister. If your ex did anything to that little boy, he deserves the whole world to come down on his head."

Adele drew a shaky breath at the prospect. "How soon before you can start looking for Charlie?"

"Well, I trust you can come with me now to show me where ground zero is? Good, okay. Then as soon as I get back to the office, I'll be setting the wheels in motion. Before the end of the week, depending on how the teams are booked."

"It's a public place. The media will find out pretty quickly."

"We'll see. I can't imagine the trust managing the cemetery will want any publicity, either, so I'm sure they will be as accommodating as possible." Xandra was packing up as they spoke and she now rested her laptop case in the seat she had been using. "I trust you've already been speaking with Jo."

"She didn't say—"

"No, no. Calm down. Anything you say to Jo is in the privacy of the confessional as far as she is concerned. I just figured you would have confided in her first."

They were at the front door now and Adele was pulling her coat from the hook.

There was something vulnerable about her as she pulled the large coat around her small frame. For a brief moment, her round-eyed stare and loose curls reminded Xandra of a porcelain doll. She smiled and reached over to give an errant curl a playful tug.

"I just have to figure out how to inspire you with enough confidence to share your secrets with me, too."

Chapter Twenty-Two

Excogitation

Def. To think out; to devise

AS SOON AS Adele came back home, she shut the door behind her and leaned against it, her palms flat to the panels. She swallowed, fighting the nausea rising in her throat. It was done.

She had watched as Xandra walked slowly around the patch of ground behind Toby's headstone. Among the lush green leaves shooting skyward, one near the edge sported a long yellow bud angled down like a micro lamp.

It was absurd, but she found herself grieving the loss of the green shoots and their imminent joyful display for the boys' sake.

But if she was right about Charlie being there, they had been used to draw a blind over something truly evil. She would never be able to enjoy the sight of daffodils ever again.

She reminded herself that Roof had an alibi, although her relief from earlier had dissipated to almost nothing.

If Charlie really was there under those flowers, had someone taken advantage of the situation? Not only taking over the agreed appointment when Roof couldn't make it, but also the fresh burial place itself? A long list of people had visited Toby's grave, and an even longer list knew where it was. It could just as easily be someone connected to Roof's work. Or what if some random murderer scoped out new burials in Highgate? She didn't envy Xandra her job at all.

She pushed herself away from the door and headed for the drinks cabinet. She took out her half empty bottle of Kilmartin Glen and poured a generous splash. She threw back a gulp before she'd even screwed the lid back on, grimacing at her sorry reflection in the glass panels of the cabinet, realising she could so easily follow Roof's alcoholic path to oblivion.

She put the bottle away and leaned heavily on the dresser. No amount of whiskey was going to stop her mind rattling the cage of facts she had discovered, the events that had accumulated over these last few weeks and what they seemed to be adding up to: Roof guilty of an incredible crime.

She took her drink up to the study and, without switching on the light, sat in the easy chair in the corner. She put her feet up on the footstool and lay back staring into the new foliage of the birch tree outside the house, the unfurling leaves like shimmering reflectors as they turned and fluttered in the light wind. The street lights filtered through the tree branches into the small room, the bright shards picking out items and surfaces from the subfusc shadows.

Was it possible that the last few years, or even more, of her marriage had been a lie? That the joint life she thought they had built together, and that she had tried to salvage, was just her constructed version of a façade that had a very different flipside? A flipside Roof lived alone in, while allowing her to potter along in her own fantasy world?

Yes, "poor old Addle", as he often called her. Affectionately to start with, condescendingly later on, and near the end, with contempt. She rubbed the rim of her glass over her bottom lip, deep in thought. Poor old Addle had had no idea. Wishful, determined thinking. If you believed the best of people, they would feel the love and try to live up to it.

Adele let her mind go back to that awful day, burned in her mind: the eighteenth of November. A Friday. How grateful and relieved she had been when Roof had happened to call. How quickly he had assimilated and dealt with her cry for help. Then, that night in the hospital, he had alternated between being the caring husband with his arms around her and the father fighting for information and answers about his son. He had been her strength then. She had meekly followed where he led and did what he instructed.

They had become an enclosed unit of two.

The following days had been spent bunkered down in their house, long hours on the phone with relatives, breaking the news, explaining what had happened, reliving it over and over again; somehow hoping that in the repeated telling it would become less real and the ending of the story would miraculously change.

Peter and Sim had come to stay for a few days. Sim had taken over the kitchen and shopping, and Peter had sat up long hours into the night with Roof, drinking scotch side by side with him on the sofa, catatonically watching football, murmuring short sentences to each other.

Sim had sat with her on Toby's bed, leafing through photo albums comparing their memories of events they had both attended, comparing the growth of their sons. She had always liked Sim. They'd never been close, but in those days she had been like an older sister, alternating quiet care with mild bossiness.

Peter and Sim had also acted as both hosts and buffers for the endless stream of people who wanted to show their respects. Often it was Peter who entertained the visitors while Roof sat in dark silence, seeking out answers in the bottom of his scotch glass.

After extending their stay a few days, Sim had spoken to her over breakfast while Peter was out getting the papers and Roof was still in bed.

"I'm so sorry, loove, of course we'll return for the service, but we really have to get back. The kids have got things on at school and—"

"Oh, Sim. Please. Of course you have to go. You've both been wonderful."

Sim gave her a crumpled smile. "But I don't feel comfortable leaving you. Is Roof—"

Adele took Sim's hand. "We'll be fine. We...have to be."

"This talk of leaving. Is Roof serious? He'd just pack up and leave this house?"

"I think so. I'm also feeling it's for the best. Moping around here looking at all the reminders of our life with Toby will slowly kill us."

"If you say so. I'm sure it will be good for you to be near your family." Sim had squeezed her hand. "And it might give Roof some different...routines. Give him a fresh start."

Both Peter and Sim had refrained from mentioning Roof's drinking. While imbibing copious amounts of beer at the pub was taken as read by most Brits, getting into a lot of neat spirits tended to attract a little more notice. The bottle had always been Roof's friend; Adele had put it down to Roof's feeling socially exposed. She had managed, over the years, to piece together a combined picture of an abusive father and severe bullying at school. Because of that, and their deteriorating relationship, Adele had turned a blind eye to Roof's increased drinking over the last few years because up until Toby's death he'd managed to camouflage it as social. After Toby's death, all pretence was dropped. Peter had joined him for some of those sessions, as he often did when Roof stayed with them, but more often than not, Peter sat on one glass sipping, while Roof downed several in succession. Most evenings ended with Peter tucking Roof up on the sofa with a blanket or slinging Roof's arm over his shoulder as he helped him upstairs to Toby's bed.

And Roof's drinking did not lessen in Australia, it just became more private.

Adele tried to cast her mind back to those days following Peter and Sim's departure. It had been a countdown to Toby's funeral, delayed due to the autopsy report.

They had both been touched and awed by the number of people who had turned up for the service held at the school chapel. Neither of them had a large circle of friends, and in the case of Adele, no relatives, barring the Walmsleys, but the chapel had overflowed to the courtyard outside with children and their parents. Adele had not been able to stop herself searching their faces, looking for the one that was missing. Apart from the children singing, the one abiding memory of the service had been the pressure of Jeremy's hand holding hers throughout. Roof had invited him to sit between them, oddly enough, but it had helped: feeling the missing place between them filled, if only temporarily.

It was in the days after the funeral that Roof had gone off for long periods during the day, ostensibly to "check on their work" at Highgate, then to plant the bulbs behind Toby's headstone. She had been relieved; not only to have him out of the house, but because gardening always put Roof in a better temper. Adele had gone to the gravesite only once on her own, in the last days before they left, to say goodbye. The carved stone was all clean and sharp-edged, but in contrast, the surrounding earth was loose and recently turned over where Roof had been gardening. Someone, presumably her husband, had laid some long strands of ivy over the stone slab in front of the angel.

It was after the funeral that Adele's sense of time became dim and compressed. Between the funeral and their leaving the country had been less than three weeks. What with the lead-up to the holiday break for Christmas, it had been a struggle to get last-minute flights, but the date had finally been set at the fourteenth of December. That much she remembered.

So, what had happened in that blur of time? The one event she could lock in was the day that Charlie was last seen, Thursday the eighth, only six days before they flew out. She got up and placed her glass next to her mouse and turned her computer on.

Looking over her monitor down into the street, waiting for her computer to fire up, she noted the leaves flickering in the trees and the comparative stillness everywhere else. Due to the rain that had fallen earlier, the tar of the road glistened in patches where the light fell brightest.

She took a seat and logged in. It had been a smart suggestion of Xandra's to check her email trail. Maybe something would jog her memory. She picked up the thread during Peter and Sim's stay.

Adele had a vague memory of Roof hanging around the house after they'd left, pottering in the garden and in his shed out the back, while she emailed and made Skype calls with her family in Australia. It had also been left to her to start searching for a possible rental property. Franny and Nick had stepped in to help, which had led to several check-in calls and emails about possibilities. There was also the planning for a memorial service for Australian family and friends.

According to her emails, an Australian girlfriend who happened to be in London had dropped in to see her on the Sunday. Roof had made himself scarce. The pub, she seemed to recall.

She continued scrolling. Those days following the funeral when Roof had been at Highgate had been spent in her office wading through the mass of emails that had built up. The messages of condolence just kept coming in from Roof's friends as well as her own, as it seemed they expected her to correspond on his behalf as well. Or in the case of one old school friend, he had messaged her when his email to Roof remained unanswered. The more urgent correspondence was about trying to close off their old life and start up the new. It was only when Roof left the house that she had felt free to think about other things. His presence had become a dead weight that stopped her feeling agile or responsive.

Roof had insisted on going back to work on the Thursday, and she had agreed with relief. She had ordered in boxes and commenced packing up their possessions into tea chests to be shipped to Australia.

On the Friday afternoon, she had caught the train to Stockport for one last visit with the Walmsleys, returning on the

Monday. She had emailed Roof Sunday night to advise him of her train home, telling him what she'd been up to with the family, but the update wasn't reciprocated.

Adele sat with her chin in her palm, rolling her mouse wheel back and forth. She had scribbled a few notes on a pad to try to line up events more clearly, but there wasn't much to go on.

The week following her return showed little contact with her husband. He had continued working, claiming he had a lot to tie up, and clients who wanted to take him out for lunches and dinners before he left. She ate alone in the evenings and her husband came home the worse for wear much later, crashing in Toby's bed. Some mornings, she awoke not confident that he had even been home at all. She had no memory of actually seeing him that whole week; in fact, the email trail showed that she had had to resort to messaging him to get basic answers to questions regarding the rental property she needed to commit them to. He proved largely uninterested, and said whatever she chose would be fine, so long as it had four bedrooms.

The Thursday of that week was the day Charlie went missing. She had a one-line email from Roof that morning saying he'd be overnighting up in Manchester at the Holiday Inn and there would be no time to see the Walmsleys.

She had no knowledge of Roof's temperament, nor could she even vouch for his movements. And no one had asked. All she could see from the emails was that work had given him a farewell party that Friday night. It seemed she wasn't invited, and she recalled him playing the whole thing down. She hadn't wanted to go to such an event and be forced to smile and be jolly, but she had been put out to not even be asked, nonetheless. She had been to previous work events with Roof and knew enough of his colleagues that to not be invited seemed a bit dismissive. Of course, it was highly likely that he simply hadn't wanted her to go.

Her own afternoon that day had been taken up with attending her first meeting at St Bart's. Rereading Jo's short welcoming email made her smile; it hadn't at the time, merely adding to her stress levels. It was only now, recalling how worked up she had felt after the session, that she remembered spontaneously following up on the invitation from a work colleague. Initially, she had refused the offer of dinner and a drink, but after all the discussion and exposure scraped her raw, she was desperate for a distraction and unable to face going home to be alone in her own head.

It wasn't until the early hours of Saturday morning that she'd finally heard the back door creak open.

That last weekend, Roof had spent packing up his office. He had insisted on doing it himself, and it had made her nervous to see it left till the last minute. In between the sound of papers being torn up by hand and the shredding machine chugging and munching on thicker wodges of documents, there had been the screech of packing tape being pulled off the roll. Adele had left him to it, and on the Sunday, she had visited Toby for the last time.

On coming home, she did have a memory of their bins being on the street and her peering into one before going in the front door. It had been three-quarters full of shredded paper and torn shards of Manila folders. She now wondered if any of these had come from the attic, with that one fateful file slipping away from notice.

She pushed back in her chair, sighing. In retrospect, it all painted a picture of a marriage falling apart. Even worse, she couldn't account for Roof's movements the night Charlie went missing, or the next day or night. According to Xandra, it was the Monday she had gone to see him in at his office, catching him as he was packing up some last items for shipment.

Adele shut down her computer and stood up. She upended her glass, but there was only a drop left. She made a last sweeping survey of the street. All the same as before, except a small moving shadow caught her eye. She leaned towards the window. The shadowy blob paused, then sped up, and she recognised Mrs Henderson's Russian Blue, Wilberforce. Adele's lips set in a grim line. She had caught him stalking birds in her garden more than once, and she had no fondness for the creature as a result.

"I wonder what mischief you've been up to that your mother doesn't know about." Memories surfaced of Mrs Henderson protesting that *her* Wilby wouldn't attack birds. He had a bell around his neck, after all.

She kept an eye on him as he slunk up to Mrs Henderson's front hedge and slithered under the front gate. Adele grunted.

"Yes. Back where you belong, you little shit."

Chapter Twenty-Three

Exhumation

Def. The action of digging up something buried

AFTER A CALL with her boss, the phlegmatic DI Alan Turner, to advise him of the latest development in the Falk case and to request an allocation of team resources for follow-up, Xandra had spent the evening putting together a task list. She had already made an appointment to meet with the Highgate Cemetery Registrar the next morning to make the necessary access arrangements.

The bulk of the work revolved around substantiating the movements of Rufus Soames on the relevant days. Work that had to be done, thanks to the discovery of that drawing, whether they found the body or not.

The list of interviewees grew as Xandra checked her case notes. A fuller list of Soames's old work colleagues would be required, with more details about that farewell party. To her relief, Turner, known as The Screw when it came to budget allocation, had agreed to reassign DC Guy Fenwick and extra officer support for some of the grunt work; she would get Fenwick onto running the interviews with the work colleagues. The trip to Manchester she would make herself.

She had also started jotting down any ideas that popped into her head so they wouldn't be lost. So many more permutations and combinations now seemed possible after what she had learned this afternoon. How Soames, or anybody for that matter, could have smuggled a body into Highgate Cemetery was a fascinating point. It wasn't like you could just walk in there among the tourists with a body to bury, and out of hours the place was locked up.

Staring at her dots and arrows and circled words for a moment, Xandra turned over a fresh page and wrote *The Wife*. It was eating at her that Adele wouldn't reveal the source of her knowledge. The answer had to be that she was somehow implicated. If she knew from Soames directly, had she found out by accident or because she was an accessory? And why reveal all now? Divorce-fuelled revenge? Or a far more diabolical scenario: what if Adele had somehow pulled off this crime herself and it was time to pin it on her husband?

Xandra drew some triangular doodles, joining them up and

running over each line until it broke through the paper. It was perfectly feasible Adele had been in on the whole thing; it defied belief that she could have pulled it off on her own. Not to mention the incredible front to be maintained. And what of the other boys? An image of Fred and Rosemary West rose up in Xandra's mind, triggering a shudder of revulsion.

She threw her pen on the table and shook her hand out. Pages of scribbled ideas and questions she would corral into some kind of logic on her computer and add to her plan of attack.

She got up and headed to the fridge. The last slice of pizza was now a piece of slate. Even nuking it wasn't going to lead to much improvement. She couldn't help a wry smile, imagining Adele tut-tutting, as she waited for the microwave to ding. How sweet to have a partner like her to come home to; someone who cared about such things.

As she returned to the sofa, chewing her wet cardboard, a random image of climbing under the duvet in a lamp-lit bedroom popped into her head. Adele would already be snuggled up with a book on her raised knees, fully focused, but after Xandra shifted her curls to one side and kissed her on the forehead, she would look up and smile, pushing her glasses up her nose with her index finger.

Xandra paused mid-chew and angrily shook her head at herself.

*

WHILE THE TEAM unloaded their equipment and prepared to light the site, Xandra took Fenwick on a walk around the cemetery's perimeter to assess possible ingress points. It was a question she had already put to the woman in charge of organising access.

"If you were asking about a period before 2007, I would have said there were several possibilities, but since then we've expended significant funds to restore the walls in the eastern section of the cemetery. Anyone attempting a break-in now would risk attracting attention to themselves and possible bodily harm."

They turned down Swains Lane from the main gate. The boundary wall varied in height as it stepped down the hill, with spiked iron railings mounted on a solid brick base. Fenwick reached up to the top of the nearest spike.

"You'd need a good ladder to clear that," he commented. He swayed his torch around as he peered through the railings. "And then you'd have a nice drop on the other side into the dark."

"And leave the ladder outside? Seems unlikely. Even less so if you were carrying a body."

At the bottom of the hill, they turned left at Chester Road, with the same style of fence continuing until they reached Chester Road Gate. The road then split away from the cemetery's boundary.

"So where does this go?" Fenwick approached a traffic barrier mounted across Stoneleigh Terrace.

"Not sure, but it's still bordering the cemetery. Let's take a look."

The spiked railing had been replaced by a solid wall topped with round iron loops, continuing up behind what appeared to be a block of flats. Fenwick stood on his toes peering left and right over the wall as he moved his torchlight back and forth.

"Not too big a distance just here, but the ground on the other side drops away towards you."

Xandra had walked up ahead to inspect some coloured bins against the wall. There were large green rubbish bins on wheels at intervals, and next to these were squat yellow salt grit bins. "You wouldn't need a ladder with these ready-made steps."

"Yeah, you would, but you could then drop it over for the other side. Then you could get out the same way."

Xandra consulted her map. "We're not too far from the grave site, either."

Fenwick stood with his hands on his hips looking up at the building behind them. "Might have been seen, though, eh? It's not exactly private. Can't see any CCTV, though, more's the pity."

"No, I already asked the question. Not much help there. I think we're better continuing our inspection from—" Xandra stopped and answered her phone. "We'll be there in five minutes."

She sucked in a large breath of air, and it was all she could do not to let it out in a loud whoop, but with Fenwick's enquiring gaze upon her she restrained herself to a broad grin.

"They've found something."

Chapter Twenty-Four

Expiscation

Def. To fish out; to find by investigation

THE REST OF the week became unexpectedly busy. Adele's author had returned the section of his novel she had reviewed with his own comments and rewrites. He had largely accepted her cuts and recommendations, barring one or two lengthily argued refusals, which meant she could now proceed with confidence. She emailed Carol over the weekend to let her know that the goal of cutting the word count to below one-twenty was looking realistic, and she might even get it down further on a second run-through. Carol responded by asking whether a shorter deadline might be possible:

she'd been forced to substantially change the work schedule due to a cancelled contract.

It was with a sense of relief and renewed enthusiasm that she returned to her office with a pot of coffee to get back to work. Perversely, a tighter deadline was exactly what she needed to focus her mind. It wasn't until Monday afternoon, when she was deep in a tense dialogue between the main characters in a café in Vancouver, that Xandra's name came up on her phone.

Feeling like she'd been rudely lifted out of another world and plonked back in her office chair, she took the call.

"Sorry it's taken a while; I've put off calling you till I knew for certain. I have some news."

Adele gripped the phone tighter. "Yes or no?"

"Yes. They found the body of a young boy on Wednesday night. I've just had confirmation from our forensics people. It's Charlie, all right."

Adele closed her eyes, aware of her short shallow breathing.

"You still there?"

"Yes. I—I'm horrified, but I'm also relieved. I was worried it might be a wild goose chase."

"We're going to have to talk more about how you knew, Adele. I don't care how crazy or farfetched you think it is. There might be more to it than you think. Something important."

Adele bit her lip. "Have you contacted his mother?"

"Yes. We're working with Sylvia Falk at the moment preparing a statement for the media."

Adele swallowed and shifted her phone to her other ear. "That poor woman. Have you told Jo? Sylvia's going to need some support."

"Yes, and so will you. This is not going to be pretty, Adele."

Adele could hear background noises of a busy office and briefly wondered what it must be like there. She forced herself to focus on what Xandra was saying.

"—the Trust is keen to keep the exact location out of the media. The site has been tidied up, they even saved a lot of the bulbs, but any enterprising journalist worth their salt would be able to make some educated guesses about a newly disturbed plot and connect it to back to you and Rufus. I'm hoping not, but it's best you're prepared."

Adele's voice sounded small, even to her own ears. "You still don't know if it was Roof." She scratched at a small mark on the desk in front of her.

"Which brings me to the other reason I called. I need to bring the team round to your place as soon as possible."

"To my place? Why?" Her voice had gone up an octave, sounding like she'd just been poked awake.

"I want them to check out that garden shed of yours. If Rufus had anything to do with this, he would have used his own tools, in which case soil forensics might be able to do some matching. He may even have kept the body there for a short time."

"Oh god, Xandra..." She rubbed her knuckles hard into her forehead. "But...we've had tenants, it's been more than two years..."

"You'd be surprised what can be picked up."

"Well, if that's the case, you are almost guaranteed to find soil matches, but it won't prove anything." Adele explained Roof's gardening activities around Toby's grave in their last few weeks.

"So, he was in the vicinity in broad daylight, with gardening tools, digging the exact spot with impunity?"

"Yes."

Xandra didn't speak for a moment, but Adele could hear furious tapping on a keyboard.

"Would tomorrow morning be okay for us to pop around? We'll keep it low key with unmarked cars and plain clothes."

Adele groaned inwardly, imagining the forensics team continuing with the botanical holocaust she'd already started. "Thank you. Mrs Henderson has had enough excitement for the time being. Will I... Do I need to do anything?"

"No. Just provide us with access to the shed. The team may also want a bit of a snoop around the rest of the garden space, but it shouldn't involve making a mess, I hope."

"That's okay, it's not looking so tidy at the moment anyway."

*

ADELE WAS STILL in the office long after ending the call with Xandra, staring out of the window as the light grew ever dimmer. It was hard to believe this was happening to her. And to someone she knew. More than just *knew*. What would Roof be doing right now? She glanced at her watch—it was very early tomorrow morning for him. He wouldn't even be out of bed. Maybe sleeping off last night's bender. Unaware that an even bigger headache was about to split his head wide open.

She drummed her fingers on the edge of the desk. It was like she should be doing something, making plans, *anything*, but she didn't know what. Sitting like a rabbit waiting for the headlights to turn into a massacring truck didn't feel like a great option. Before she could progress that thought, her phone rang. It was Sim.

"I'm sorry to bother you, Adele, but we might have an issue to manage."

The fuzziness immediately left her head. "What's the matter?"

Sim let out a pained sigh. "I don't suppose you've heard from Jem?"

"No?"

"Peter and Jeremy have had a bit of a set-to. It got a bit out of hand with stupid threats on both sides. It ended with Jeremy running out of the door with a packed bag saying he wasn't coming back."

"Oh, shit. And you think he'll come to me."

"That's what I'm hoping."

"Surely he's got friends that are a lot nearer?"

"He does, but he'll be needing somewhere to stay, and he loves you, Del. He was on top of the world after that weekend you spent together. And of course, it's me hoping, as well. I need to know he'll be somewhere safe where we can keep a remote eye on him."

"Do you want me to give him a call?

"No, it will put him on guard, and he might change course. Let's just see what happens. He left here around three. He might have gone to friends; he might have gone straight to the train station. I'm just putting you on alert in case you had plans."

"Wow. Okay." *No. No plans, just a police search of my backyard and a potential interrogation…apart from that, perfectly free to accommodate a random, curious visitor.*

"I take it Peter's not adjusting as fast as Jem would like, then."

"Oh, Adele, it's not so much that. Jem's results at school are really suffering, and Pete is attributing it to his 'wayward' friends and his 'social' activities."

"Mmm. It's a good stick to beat him with."

"And it's somewhat justified…but of course Jem doesn't see it that way."

"Of course not. Let's see if I hear from him or whether he just shows up. If not, I can try calling him in the next day or so?"

Adele ended the call and put her phone back on the desk.

Great. Just what she needed.

*

THE EVENING PASSED with no word from Jem, much to Adele's relief. He'd probably gone to friends, and once he'd cooled off, he'd head home. A storm in a teacup.

Xandra's team arrived at ten the next morning and consisted of three people: an older man and two younger officers, a guy and a girl. They gave her serious professional nods as Xandra introduced them and were polite to Adele as she showed them to the shed. Xandra followed Adele back inside and sat at the dining table, pulling out her laptop.

"I'd like to go over the timelines with you as a way of cross-checking what we already know. Did you get a chance to look at your emails like we discussed?"

"I did, but I'm afraid they won't be of much use."

Adele had preprepared a coffee tray and switched the kettle on when they arrived. She placed a mug in front of Xandra and handed her a page of handwritten notes.

"Roof had gone back to work the previous week, and he was either working late or out every night of the week. I hardly saw him at all. And he'd been drinking a lot.

"The weekend prior I'd spent up in Stockport with my brother's family, leaving Roof alone in the house over that time. I came home on the Monday and apart from maybe hearing him come in late or seeing his bedroom door closed, I don't think I saw much of him at all that whole week."

"Not even at breakfast?"

"Maybe I heard him in the shower, then he'd be straight off. He didn't hang around to eat. It was like he was deliberately avoiding me. In some ways, I didn't mind, as he wasn't good to be around at that time, but in other ways, I resented his neglect. There was a farewell party for him at work on the last Friday night, for example, but I didn't even get an invite...or if I did, he didn't see fit to pass it on."

Xandra took a sip of her coffee and frowned at her laptop screen. "So how did you even know there *was* a work farewell party?"

"We communicated via email. He wasn't even answering my calls by then. He'd respond to my voicemails by email."

Xandra grunted. "Not even text? Nice."

"I was pretty occupied with packing up, closing UK accounts, opening Australian ones, and getting us a rental property in Sydney. And when I wasn't frenetically busy, I was talking to family on the phone and doing my own moping and crying."

Xandra had paused in her notetaking and was simply looking at her. "He wasn't much of a husband to you, was he?"

Adele returned her gaze as she raised her mug to her lips. "No. He wasn't. Nor was he much of a friend or lover, either. I made a lot of excuses for him then, as anyone would, with what we were going through, but what I've come to realise is that the distancing and neglect had actually started much earlier, and this whole situation just accelerated it. It was starkly obvious once we were in Australia. I wanted him to seek help, but he refused. That was when I realised he didn't *want* us to come back together in any kind of way."

"That must have hurt."

"I think all the love had been beaten out of me by that stage. It was more about having to face letting go of the only person who had gone through the same pain and loss as I had, as well as the shame of admitting defeat on my marriage."

"So, let's go back to the end of that last week. On the Thursday Charlie disappeared, Rufus said he caught the 3.30 p.m. train from Euston, which arrived at Manchester Piccadilly at 5.37 p.m. He then met a colleague for dinner, one Andrew Ford, and checked into his hotel afterwards at 8.09 p.m." Xandra cast her a sideways look from her screen, then returned her eyes to what she was reading. "I'm reserving judgement on that till I speak with Ford in person, but that's what we have as of right now." She continued tapping her down arrow. "Then he returned to the London office straight off the train the next day. It then sounds like you're saying Rufus went straight from work to this farewell party?"

"Yes. If he went anywhere in the gap, it wasn't to come home. Those days just all blended together, really, but I'm pretty sure I was here all afternoon."

Xandra responded to her apologetic smile with a severe look. "Can anyone vouch for *your* whereabouts? And what about the previous day?"

Adele's mouth went dry. Xandra's immobile expression told her everything. How naïve she'd been to think this was just about Roof. It had never occurred to her that her own motives and actions could be called into question. Adele's breath started coming in short gasps as it dawned on her that, from Xandra's perspective,

Adele might be just as easily capable of an unhinged revenge quest as Roof. She gripped the table. *Oh my god. I could be framing my husband.*

She pressed her fingertips to her forehead. Her throat constricted painfully with nothing to swallow. She was vaguely aware of a seat being pushed back, followed by the sound of the kitchen tap running. Xandra placed a glass of water in front of her. She remained standing with her arms folded, looking down at her.

Adele reached for the glass and sipped. "Thank you." Her voice was barely above a whisper. She raised her eyes fearfully to Xandra. "I've just realised how bad things look. For *me*."

Xandra returned to her seat. "Take me through your own Thursday afternoon and the next day. Can you do that?"

Adele nodded vigorously. "Yes, yes, I can, thank god. I went to Jo's support group! I think it started around four...there's an email...but I went there a little earlier to just sit in the church and get my head in the right place. Maybe Jo might remember something...and I don't have anything in writing, but I called a friend, a work colleague, actually, and went for a drink and dinner after that. I guess phone records..."

Xandra nodded slowly, to Adele's relief. "Funny to think you were with Jo that afternoon. Okay. I'll check in with her, and if you could just give me the details of this work colleague, I'll take it from there." Xandra's eyes strayed back to her laptop screen. "So, you can't say for certain that Roof didn't come home in that gap between returning from Manchester and showing up at his office.

When did you next see him?"

"They must have really tied one on at that after-work party. I heard him creep in at some early hour Saturday morning."

Xandra glanced at Adele as her fingers flashed over the keyboard, making a note.

"But when did you actually *see* him?"

Adele looked at her own scribbled notes. "Lunchtime, maybe, when he emerged from Toby's room? He spent the weekend clearing his office out. Mainly with the door shut. But I heard the shredder going constantly and lots of paper tearing."

"Then your tea chests were picked up on the Monday, the day I interviewed Rufus in his office, and you flew out the next day."

"Yes."

Xandra folded down her laptop screen. She paused and thoughtfully drummed her fingers over her closed lips. "Even with what he was going through, his behaviour seems strange. Almost as if he was covering up an affair. Do you know if he was seeing anyone else?"

"If he was, it's never come to light, and then of course we left."

"Wasn't it Rufus who decided you had to abruptly pick up sticks and leave for Australia? Maybe his amour was going there too...or already lived there?"

Adele's lips opened in surprise. "I hadn't thought of that. I guess it's possible..."

"Believe me, I'm looking at all possibilities now." Xandra ticked off some items on a list in her notebook and ran her line through another. "And on that note, I need you to run through this same exercise for two more dates. I want a similar timeline of what you were both doing the weeks commencing 30 November 2009 and 13 December 2010."

"But that's years before...what—" Adele stopped short.

"I haven't given up on Charlie's disappearance being linked to those of Will Moore and Abbi Singh. I can't see any record on file about Roof being connected or questioned in relation to those disappearances, so if he can be eliminated as a possibility there, it would be a good loose end to tie up."

Dear god. Could it get any worse? Adele's chest twinged sharply as she took a deep breath and nodded her assent.

Xandra stood up and indicated the back door with a wave of her hand. "I'll just go out and see how they're getting on."

Adele cleared away their coffee things and put the kettle on again. She mulled over the possibility of Rufus seeing someone else. She shook her head. For anyone else to even bear his company, let alone have an affair, it presupposed Roof was undergoing an amazing transformation for this new person...either that, or they were some kind of masochistic saint taking on a problem case. She sighed. Or could she really have been married to a two-faced psychopath all these years? Her life had become such a crazy nightmare it now seemed anything could be possible.

While she was rinsing the mugs her phone dinged. She dried

her hands, went back to the dining table, and opened her messages. Jem.

I'm in town. Can I come and see you?

She sighed. It was as good a time as any. She told him she'd be home all afternoon and to let her know when he was on his way. Then she texted Sim.

The backdoor closed, and she looked up from her phone.

"I think we're all good, Adele. They're pretty keen to get back to the lab, so we'll head off now."

"Did they find anything?"

"They won't know till they've done the analyses. They've bagged up some of the tools and some other bits and pieces as samples, but you'll get them back."

"Maybe I won't want them back." She turned round to look out of the window over the sink. The female of the team was making her way past the open cut mine carrying some garbage bags.

"And while we're on the subject of samples…" Xandra was leaning over her bag, extracting something. "If you're okay to provide one now, Adele, it will help speed things up."

Her eyes widened. "Of course! Absolutely." It was all she could do not to snatch it out of Xandra's hand.

The swab test completed and sealed, Adele watched with a mixture of foreboding and relief as it was packed away in the depths of Xandra's bag.

"Frank was asking what happened there at the side of the house?"

"Oh...I decided I didn't want crocuses there any more. Sorry. It's a bit of a mess."

Xandra looked at her a moment before slinging her laptop bag over her shoulder. She came over to place a reassuring hand on Adele's arm. "I don't know what to say to you, lass. This is a really tough situation."

"It's bloody surreal."

"That, too, aye. I'll be in touch over the next few days. I've got a lot of phone calls to make and loose threads to pull in. And a bit of travelling. A few things are starting to stick together, though, and that always spurs me on."

"Please let me know if anything comes of all this, although I have to hope Roof's alibi will stack up." She cast a rueful glance at Xandra. "Although *that* would create a whole new set of problems for you, wouldn't it, and the media could still get a hold of things and twist them into a headline. I haven't even thought about what I'm going to tell my family. Hopefully there will be nothing *to* tell."

"You've got to remember this isn't about you. It's about him."

"Anything that might have happened was right under my nose, Xandra. That's how people would see it. How could I not have known?"

Xandra paused with her hand on the front doorknob. "You should give Jo a call. She said she'll be seeing Sylvia Falk—she's staying with family in town for a bit—she wanted you to meet her."

Chapter Twenty-Five

Excuss

Def. 1. To examine, to decipher 2. To shake off or out; to investigate as if by shaking out 3. To proceed against

XANDRA SWIPED HER card and exited the platform into the main concourse of Manchester Piccadilly station. She swapped her overnight bag from one hand to the other and adjusted the strap of her laptop bag on her shoulder. The train had been delayed but she still had plenty of time. The Holiday Inn was situated on the canal, five minutes' walk from the station.

After checking in herself, she met with the manager who took her through the booking and check-in records for the evening of

8 December 2011. Xandra ran her finger down the computer printout and reverified the 8.09 p.m. check-in time, noting the signature and ID.

From there she walked past reception into the café and bar area. She paused to survey the brightly coloured furniture, all of which looked designed for style rather than comfort. In the end, she opted for a small table near the window with two houndstooth armchairs.

She was halfway through typing an email when a tall blond man with his hands in his pockets walked up to reception. After leaning in to enquire, he turned his head in her direction and, identifying her, raised his hand in greeting. Xandra stood up as he approached, noting his jaunty step and stylish suit. As he reached out to clasp her hand, her gaydar gave a brief tingle.

Andrew Ford's large blue eyes flickered around the space as he made pleasant small talk and fiddled with a coaster from the table.

"I was surprised to get your call. I haven't heard from Rufus since he left for Australia. As I told you on the phone, I no longer work for Magnus Design... I hope there's nothing wrong?"

"You only knew him as a colleague then?"

"Sure. We worked on some of the same accounts, so we'd catch up when he was in town."

"I understand that he normally stayed with family in Heaton Chapel, is that right?"

"Sure. I think that's where they were. On the train line, at any rate."

"But not on this occasion?"

"No. Maybe they were away or something? He didn't say and I didn't ask."

"Soames initiated this meet-up, am I right?"

"Yes, he wanted to say goodbye to colleagues here...before he left, you know."

"But it was only the two of you that evening?"

"Sure. It was a bit last minute. He called me to see if I was free for dinner. I was having some drinks with a client after work, so it was easy to pop across."

"That makes you a bit special?"

Ford inspected the coaster as he slowly spun it between an index finger and thumb. He gave a short laugh. "Oh, not really. It was more opportunistic, I think."

Xandra gave a little laugh as well. "Because Soames was an opportunistic kind of guy?"

Ford glanced up uneasily. "I suppose you could say that."

"Can you confirm the time you met up?"

Ford started flicking the coaster with his fingernail. Without looking up, he said, "It was definitely after work. So, probably after six?"

Xandra narrowed her eyes.

"Can you give me the name of your client? I'd like to speak with them to cross check. I'd also like to see your credit card records for the evening to check the time of any purchases. At the prior interview, you were informed that this was in relation to a missing persons enquiry. I need to tell you this has now been upgraded to homicide, so it's important you think hard about your answers." She reached over, deftly took the coaster from him, and snapped it down on the table like a trump card.

Ford looked up, startled, his large eyes reminding Xandra of a landed fish. "Homicide? What? Is Roof...?" He swallowed and took a deep breath.

"It could be relevant to our inquiries. Take your time."

"I had no idea... Sure, um. Look, he mentioned having a bit of trouble with his wife about a—a friend he'd been spending time with. Said she was getting really funny about stuff, checking up on him and the like."

"Not without justification, it seems. So, he asked you to say you met earlier?"

"Not in so many words...but he mentioned having arrived by an earlier train so he could meet this other friend... I didn't want to be the one to get him in trouble for the sake of a routine enquiry... So, okay, it might have been later than seven by the time we met. Maybe closer to eight.

"I met him at the Maison Grill over the road. He came in with his bag straight from his other appointment. That much I remember."

"And you were together, how long?"

"More than an hour, maybe two."

"How did he seem to you?"

Ford shifted in his chair. "He wasn't in the best of spirits. He'd recently lost his son, you know? But he seemed chipper enough under the circumstances."

"Who paid for dinner?"

"Now that I do remember clearly. I put my card on the table, but Roof insisted he pay. I felt the need to insist again. A farewell from me, you know? But he snatched the docket off me and laid cash on the table, not even waiting for a receipt. This was before I'd even finished my drink."

"So, on his own account then, not the company's."

"Maybe. I was a bit put out by his manner, but he'd had a few whiskeys by then, and well, you have to make allowances, don't you."

"So, he was a bit under the weather. Where did you leave him?"

"I saw him back to his hotel. He was a bit slurry by then. I wanted to see the lift door close on him, to be sure, like."

"Right, but he still had to check in, didn't he?"

"Oh, uh. I don't recall…"

"What time was this?"

"I honestly couldn't…"

"Did you go straight home? Taxi? Train?"

"Train. But I had a bit of a wait. The bill reminded me I was low on cash, so I stopped at an ATM. Just enough time to miss my train and add twenty minutes to my trip."

Chapter Twenty-Six

Excrement

Def. Waste matter discharged from the body

JEM TURNED UP with just one canvas bag. He had walked from the train station, not wanting to trouble Adele with the drive. He dumped his things in Toby's room and came back down to join her on the sofa. He threw himself down with a big sigh.

"Merde."

"Merde?"

He opened his eyes to look at her. "It's French for excrement."

She couldn't help a derogatory sniff. "Mercy buckets, Jezza," she drawled, dragging her vowels out flat. "In Uh-*stray*-ya, we use good old Anglo-Saxon words like shit."

Jem let out a dry puff of laughter. "However you want to dress it up, it's the same thing."

She was about to ask what the argument was about but bit her tongue just in time. All she supposedly knew was that he was here. Surprise!

"So, what brings you here? What kind of poo has hit the fan?"

"I just can't live with Dad's homophobia any more."

"Is it really homophobia or is that just how his worrying about you has manifested?"

Jem sat up straighter to look at her more sharply. "Oh, come on, Aunty Del, you're not going to defend him, are you?"

"I'm trying to point out to you that there are always two sides to an argument. Tell me what happened."

"I was heading out the door for a night with friends and Dad started in at me about whether my school work was done. I told him there was nothing to worry about, but he started bringing up old shit to try and prove his point."

"Okay." Adele nodded. "So, tell me, *is* all your schoolwork up to date and going well? Does he have a point or not?"

"*My* point is, if he approved of my friends, he wouldn't be making such an issue over it."

"Wouldn't he? Don't most parents go through this with their kids? Your sisters did happen to mention your grades weren't doing so well, so maybe he has reason to be concerned?"

"Oh, don't *you* start." He slumped back and folded his arms.

"Okay, we'll leave the conversation there. But clearly you need to have a long hard look at what your future plans are going to be, Jeremy. If you aren't going to make an effort with your studies and you say you can't live with your father, then you need money to live. I'm guessing a job waiting at the Flag Pole isn't going to keep you in the manner to which you've become accustomed."

"No, it isn't."

His belligerent tone didn't bode well, but she kept going. Maybe if she played bad cop, his dad wouldn't seem so bad. "You can stay here for a week, but by the end of that week I want to hear what your plan is."

"I could turn a few tricks on the side. Some of my friends make good money that way."

Adele resisted the howl of protest that rose in her throat. "Sounds like pulling the plug on your life so you can shoot down the drain all the faster, if you ask me. Running away from the real issue isn't going to help you."

"Well, you'd know all about that, wouldn't you? Running away to Australia, then running away from Uncle Roof. You're pretty good at running away yourself."

A cold shaft of anger flashed in her heart. "Don't you *dare* accuse me of things you know nothing about."

"Ditto!"

Before she could respond, he'd launched himself off the sofa and was running up the stairs.

*

SHE WAS JUST opening her front gate, returning from a walk to the shops, when she heard a car door slam and running footsteps. She glanced over her shoulder to see a young man in a smart coat hurrying in her direction. He raised his hand to arrest her progress through the gate.

"Adele Soames?" Any thought of him being a friend of Jem's evaporated, and she quickly shut the gate as a barrier between them.

It didn't act as any kind of deterrent.

"I was just wondering if you have anything to say about the desecration of your—"

"No comment," she gritted out, fumbling for her key in her pocket.

"Mrs Soames, do you think it's a coincidence—"

She slammed the door, breathing hard.

*

THE NEXT FEW days passed uncomfortably with Jem either staying in his room or venturing out with no explanation. It was like her time with Rufus repeating itself. Maybe she had this effect on men? During one of his prolonged absences, she called Sim.

"Has he been in touch with you?"

"Not with me, but Connie admitted she'd had a response to a text. Asking for money."

"Oh." Adele closed her eyes momentarily. At least that

implied he wasn't earning it how he'd threatened...yet. It also showed he wasn't game to ask her for any after their argument the other day.

"I'm sorry he's being a pain, Delly, but I'm just so grateful knowing he's with you."

"Except he's not most of the time, but sure. He's got a roof over his head, and I can assure you food in my fridge is disappearing. Which reminds me: I'd better go and do a shop."

"We can send you some money."

"Don't be ridiculous. He's family. Not to mention what you guys have done for me in the past."

"Oh, Delly..." Sounds of Sim sobbing issued down the line. Adele didn't interrupt her. Sometimes it was better just to let someone's misery play out. "I should probably send you some anyway, as—as a kind of contingency fund. In case he needs it for his train fare home..."

"Shh. We can sort that out as and when."

"You said you've given him a deadline of a week? What if he just disappears after that?"

"I'm hoping reality might have set in for him by then, and he'll be prepared to have a more rational conversation. He's a sensible kid when all's said and done. He just needs space to let off some steam."

Adele had spent a wakeful night agonising over whether to mention anything about the discovery at Highgate to the Walmsleys. Apart from not wanting to add to Sim's worries, a quick google showed that there was only one mention of the body being found in an "empty plot" in the eastern side of the cemetery. But that journalist's questions proved she was on borrowed time. She decided to err on the side of caution. It was still possible that Roof had nothing to do with it, so why raise a false alarm?

After the call with Sim, Adele had intended to get some tasks completed for work. Her study wasn't a bad place to be as she had a view of the street and might see Jem coming before he got to her front door. She checked her phone. No messages or missed calls.

Apart from the dramas with her nephew, it had been easier to settle to work these last few days, just knowing that Roof had a possible alibi. His not even being in London was the best news she had had in weeks. It all pointed to a random stranger taking advantage of an opportunity.

The fact that Charlie may have been waiting for Roof meant nothing. Work had dumped something on him at the last minute, and he'd had to rush up north to deal with it; regardless of what he might or might not have promised Charlie. It was even possible Charlie had mistaken something kind or vague Roof had said as a concrete promise. Charlie's hanging around in the fading light, all on his own, had put him in the way of an evil or unhinged person ready to act on a temptation dropped in their lap.

Of course, there was nothing concrete to exonerate Stephen in Xandra's mind yet, and of course, *he* could even be the random person who turned up...but no. It made her stomach twinge to recall Stephen's radical accusations and tears; she was no psychology expert, but to her, Stephen just didn't seem a likely possibility any more.

As her thoughts were running over this unproductive ground, she remembered Xandra's request. She flipped open her notebook. No wonder Xandra thought the disappearance of the other two boys might be linked. All three disappearance dates were in the weeks leading up to Christmas, a year separating each one. *Please, no.* Adele bit her lip and placed her notebook to one side as she fired up her computer.

She opened her email archive for that period, starting her search at the beginning of December 2009. As she scanned the subject lines, names of people that she hadn't heard from in ages floated up the screen. The name of her travel agent appeared a few times in succession. Of course. She'd taken Toby home to spend Christmas in Australia with her family that year.

Adele frowned as the memories returned. Roof was supposed to have come but had pulled out at the last minute. Work commitments. Some conference or other and urgent deadlines for Christmas advertising, or some darned thing. There'd been an argument, and she had a visceral memory of how pissed off with Roof she'd been. She'd made him tell Toby himself, although their son's disappointment was short-lived when Roof had countered with a promise to buy him the long-wished-for foosball table. She sighed. The upshot was she hadn't been here to know what Roof had been up to. Shit.

Adele cursored through a few more days of correspondence

till she came to the relevant date. There were emails from Roof with attachments. On opening them, she saw that in response to her pictures of Toby at the beach with his cousins, and various other outing updates she'd sent, Roof had responded with some photos of pre-Christmas parties and shenanigans at work. It looked like at least one of them might have been on the day or evening in question.

She dragged her sidebar down to emails dated the following December. Closer to Christmas this time. Lots of emails from Carol marked as urgent. Ahh. Yes, the stress of that time came back to her. Toby was already staying with the Walmsleys. Roof had taken him there on a business trip the week before, so that she and Roof could focus on clearing the decks and getting some Christmas shopping done.

He'd returned by train, she seemed to recall. She opened an email from Roof dated the sixteenth, the critical day.

> *Hello Addle, back to London this afternoon. Don't wait up, I've got Brewsters' Christmas party tonight. Had to step in for the boss last minute. Soz.*

She checked her sent mail. Yep. She'd been mightily annoyed. It was the only night they'd both had available to shop for Toby's gift together. As it was, she'd had to carry several large boxes back from Hamleys on a packed tube on her own.

She made some notes on the dates and events, concerned that she had nothing to the point for either of the key dates, although it looked like Roof was covered for the second date, at least.

Adele stared at her dot points for several minutes. She hated to admit it, but these emails only seemed to prove that their lack of "togetherness" was apparent even before they lost Toby. She pushed her notebook to one side and opened up her work file. She wondered if Magnus Design's appointment diaries would be of any more help. People couldn't be expected to remember minute detail of where they were, or who was around, after five years had passed. Especially in the blur leading up to Christmas. Again, she found herself musing on how tough Xandra's job was.

At 6.00 p.m., she shut down her computer. Her first-round edits of the manuscript were complete now, and she would soon be able to organise a meeting with her author for a more in-depth discussion. She was in the laundry grabbing her shopping bags when she heard ringing upstairs.

She raced to the office and snatched her phone up from the desk. It was a request for a video call on the new app Xandra had asked her to install.

"You sound puffed. Have I caught you out walking?"

Her shoulders relaxed at the sound of Xandra's friendly tone. She quickly took a seat and leaned her phone back against her monitor.

"No, just had to run up the stairs. I thought you were my nephew. He's staying for a bit." She peered closer at the image on her phone. "Are you in bed already?"

"Ha. I wish. No, I've had a long day of interviews and travelling to Manchester and I'm finishing up with some calls and emails with my feet up at the hotel I'm staying at.

"Look, I've got another phone appointment coming up, but I wanted to run something by you and get your reaction.

"On cross examination, it turns out this chiel Andrew Ford, the colleague Rufus had dinner with, wasn't quite so certain as to when they ate after all. It seems he felt obliged to help him avoid unnecessary unpleasantness."

"What do you mean?"

Xandra scratched her cheek. "Tell me, Adele, we talked about the possibility of Rufus having an affair... Had you ever considered the possibility of his being attracted to men?"

Adele blinked at Xandra's image on the screen.

"No! Of course not..." She let out a ragged breath, her stomach lurching. "But gosh... I suppose it could explain some of his behaviour..."

"So, you never had any reason to hassle him out about his seeing someone on the side...even if it was only a 'friend'?"

"No, we had arguments of course, but nothing like that." Adele frowned. "Where's this coming from?"

"Ford implied that he had to protect Rufus from his paranoid wife. According to him, you were always checking up on him."

"Rubbish."

"He also strongly implied this friend was male...and I was able to ascertain through casual conversation with his erstwhile

Magnus Design colleagues that Ford is himself gay, which could explain his being in the know about such a thing, and his being singled out for a private catch-up as the person most likely to show sympathy and close ranks for Rufus.

"When I told him the missing persons enquiry had since been upgraded to a homicide investigation, he became a bit rattled, and was subsequently more forthcoming. It turns out he *did* recall some more details from their meeting. Rufus refused to let him pay; he insisted, almost to the point of rudeness, on laying down cash on the table and getting up to leave before Ford had even finished his drink."

"I'm not following you."

"This was a work colleague, and it wasn't just for coffee: the bill was over eighty quid. Why didn't he put it on his card to claim the expense? Was it so there'd be no record of the time they ate?"

"Seems a long bow, Xandra. Maybe it was just so Andrew didn't get the chance to slip in his own card."

"Perhaps, but it doesn't matter. It reminded Ford that he was short of cash, and after saying goodbye to Rufus, he stopped at an ATM and withdrew some money."

"So, you have been able to fix a time after all."

"Yes. Ford's withdrawal occurred at 9.47 p.m."

"I'm sorry if I'm being a bit slow, but so what?"

"It proves that Rufus checked in *before* they went for dinner—8.09 p.m. to be precise—not after, like he said. So, he has unaccounted for time between arriving and checking in.

"We could go with Ford's version that he had some kind of secret assignation in that gap, but it is also entirely possible that Rufus bought a second ticket and arrived at Manchester Piccadilly as late as 7.45 p.m., which means the train he caught from Euston may have been as late as the 5.40. Not the 3.30 as claimed. That would leave the two-plus hours unaccounted for at the London end."

Adele suddenly felt exhausted.

*

ADELE HUNG UP and sat with her head bowed and her hands pressed together between her thighs. She had been sitting like this for a short moment before a sound made her spin round in her chair, only to lock eyes with Jeremy, standing in the doorway.

Her nephew's eyes were round and fearful. Before she could think of anything to say, he spoke.

"Is Uncle Roof in trouble?"

Whatever she had planned to say by way of cover-up was clearly pointless. She decided to err on the side of bluster.

"I'm not in a position to talk about it, Jem. I'm sorry. If I'd known you were home, I would have ensured the conversation was more private."

"Aunty Del! It sounded like you were talking to the police?"

Gone was the arrogance and bravado of that first afternoon. Now she was seeing her nephew's face stripped down to vulnerability and fear.

"Jem, I can't—"

He was almost in tears. "Oh, come *on,* Aunty Del. I'm sorry about what I said the other day. Okay, okay, you're right. I don't understand why you left Uncle Roof. No one told me anything... please. What's going *on*?"

Tears had started in her own eyes. She got up from her chair and took the few steps necessary to embrace him. He returned her hug impatiently, then struggled away to look her in the face. "Aunty Del?"

She let out a sigh that caught on the teeth of an invisible hacksaw. "Come on downstairs and we'll talk."

The trip down the stairs allowed her to hurriedly pull her thoughts together. There really was very little she could tell him. The investigation was still going on, and nothing had been proven one way or the other. To start telling Jeremy things would be to risk potentially slanderous and hurtful rumours breaking out, and to frighten him unnecessarily.

As they both sat down on the sofa, her mind was still churning through the facts to see if there was anything at all she could safely talk about, enough to satisfy him until more was known. Her eyes landed on the dresser shelf where the folder of sketches had lived before Xandra took it away, and she thought of Charlie's defaced visage. In the time it took for her to open her mouth to speak, her brain had ripped through a chain of connections and she almost choked on her words.

"Are you okay?" Jem started patting her on the back as she

leaned forward.

Adele sat up, almost gasping for breath. "No, I—yes, *yes*, just get me a glass of water, would you?"

He placed a glass in front of her, his face full of concern. He watched her closely but said nothing as she reached out a shaking hand for the glass. She placed it back on the table after gulping a few hasty mouthfuls.

"Jeremy, *I* have a question for *you*. You freaked me out when you were last here, telling me someone had...had *touched* you...inappropriately when you were young. You said it was a family friend, someone who was 'out of the picture' now."

Jem started to recoil into the corner of the sofa as if he was planning an escape.

"I want the truth, Jem." She reached over to clutch his hand, looking him hard in the eye. "It was Roof, wasn't it."

Jem stared at her, speechless.

She gripped his hand tighter and shook it. "Answer me, Jem."

Jem tore his hand from hers, his face fracturing like Picasso's *Weeping Woman* as his head fell forward into his palms. His shoulders shook with raking sobs. It was all she could do to bite back her own tears.

Adele now stood on the rim of an ever-widening black pit. One false move and it would swallow her whole.

Chapter Twenty-Seven

Exchange

Def. To give or take in return for

XANDRA HAD TRAVELLED back earlier that day and gone straight to work. She now sat across from Guy Fenwick in a meeting room in the imposing yellow brick building that was Kentish Town Police Station. Their table was directly under one of the tall front windows, and the late afternoon sun stretched the shadows made by the muntins across the table.

Xandra had already updated Fenwick about some of the key points from her interviews from her hotel room in Manchester, in the event they had any bearing on his own interviews at Magnus

Design's London office. Apart from the possibilities opened up by Andrew Ford's evidence, Soames's former work colleagues in Manchester had added little to their store of knowledge.

"Did you get anywhere with the seat bookings?"

Fenwick nodded and flipped open his spiral notebook. "Yes and no. We did track down twenty-four-year-old Melissa Ashby, who had booked the seat next to Soames on the 3.30 p.m. train. She got on at Milton Keynes. She makes the trip regularly, and she wears headphones the whole time. She had no recollection of her seat mate for this particular trip and wasn't able to pick Soames's picture out of the selection offered."

"Better than if she had."

"True."

"CCTV at the station?"

Fenwick turned a page and winked at her. "Better luck here. IT put in a top effort on this. We went through footage from all the station and platform entry point cameras from 3.00 p.m. till 5.30 p.m. I've got some frames in for closer analysis: we have someone who resembles Soames hurrying down some stairs, and then from another angle diving into the first carriage of the 5.19 p.m., due to pull in at Manchester at 7.34 p.m. We're waiting for confirmation at the other end to see the footage of him getting off."

"Excellent. Have you got any stills?"

Fenwick swivelled his laptop around and brought up some grainy images. He indicated with his pen where Xandra should look on one of them. A slim man with shaggy curls and a Van Dyke beard was stepping up to a train carriage. He wore jeans and running shoes and carried an overnight bag.

"Yep, that's looking good. No other possible matches?" Xandra looked at the image a little longer and couldn't help musing aloud: "I wonder how many times he had to change his clothes that afternoon?"

She sat back and smiled. "Good work."

Fenwick ducked his head and riffled more pages in his notebook. "Mostly Chen and Seaton from IT. I just watched." He continued, "To go with that, the interviews with his work colleagues weren't very fruitful. It was an irregular week for Soames, so there were no office meetings or appointments in his diary, as he had little scheduled work on and was racing around packing and popping out for spontaneous drinks and coffees with colleagues and clients. It seems like he was in his office, though, up to at least 2.30 p.m. on the Thursday, and one of the girls recalls he had his door shut making some phone calls. Nothing of value after that." He cocked his head to one side and looked at her.

"Might be worth another run round to see if anyone remembers what he was wearing?"

"Maybe."

"And the farewell party? Did you find out if Soames's wife was invited?"

"Yes, she was, but she wasn't up for socialising, was what Soames put around. No one questioned that under the circumstances. He'd arrived back at the office straight off the train from

Manchester after 3.00 p.m. More mixing and farewelling and off they all went to the Duke of Albany round the corner from the office, ten minutes from Angel tube."

"What was his behaviour like? Did he tie one on?"

"Quite a few noted that he had a whiskey in his hand at all times, laughing uproariously and flirting away—" He held up his hand as Xandra opened her mouth. "Yes, I'm getting to it, Bentley: consensus seems to be that he left after ten, possibly later, but certainly before 10.30."

Xandra closed her mouth, then reopened it. "Wasn't seen leaving with anyone?"

"Nope. But nothing to stop him picking someone up on the way home."

"No. And his wife has no idea what crow of the cock it was when he came in, so we have a lot of time to fill."

Xandra drummed her fingers against her top lip. The criticality for a follow-up interview with Soames was building, and she was damned if she was going to leave it to someone else. She had to nail this piece of shit; leave no wriggle room for a wily defence lawyer or a fickle jury. Get the comfort of that "warm runny feeling inside", as The Screw relished saying. She'd already put it to him, calling him straight after her interview with Ford.

"We've found the body right where he was known to be digging that same week. He went out of his way to set up a false alibi in advance. Then there's his sketch of the victim. I'm applying for an international warrant, sir. Get him on suspicion and then grill him for a confession. You've got to let me at him. I'm the one for the job. You know it."

Turner sighed. "Bentley, you're letting your emotions take over. We have perfectly able colleagues in Australia."

"Do you want to take that risk? I'm the one who knows this case backwards. You've already got the media on your tail, not to mention the local schools and community groups. It's high profile. Exceptions are made in such cases. We might even get other solves out of it. If we can bring him home for trial, it could be massive."

Turner sighed again and leaned back in his chair, making it squeal in protest. "It's big dosh, Bentley. Let me see what more you can get on him, and I'll push it up the line."

Once they had the CCTV from Manchester Piccadilly, and the final report from forensics, she'd put together her brief of evidence and make the formal business case for the trip. The growing political pressure surrounding the case was all to her advantage. Her eyes wandered back to her own scrawled dot points.

"Did you get any more from the parents on Soames?"

Fenwick had taken the opportunity of a break in Xandra's barrage of questions to check his incoming messages. "Yep, yep, yep. Getting to it, getting to it."

"Sorry, after years of dead ends on these cases, I feel like we're finally on the edge of something."

"Could be, could be," Fenwick muttered as he scanned his notes. He stopped abruptly. "Ah. Here we are. I started with Stephen Lane."

Xandra couldn't help a grimace. "How was he?"

Fenwick cocked an eyebrow at her. He'd been the one to interview Lane the day after his little escapade. "Not great, but his demeanour changed considerably when I started asking about the movements of other people." He flipped a page. "Let's see...

"There were three regulars who came at different times apart from Soames. Chris Rutherford, Allan Tenning, and Sam Norton. Depending on their availability they helped with away games and comps. None of them did any 'special coaching' as far as Lane is aware."

"And I've already asked around at the other schools if they knew of any special coaching done by their own people or outsiders. I did some further interrogation on the alibi of Sam Norton, too. He's the only other one, apart from Lane, who ticked the proximity boxes."

Fenwick looked up from scanning his notes. "Yeah, I saw that in the notes. I threw a few suggestive questions at him when we got bantering about football, but he didn't put a foot wrong, so to speak. His movements were clean."

Xandra nodded resignedly. "At least you got to take your Cheltenham chat outside of the office for a change."

He gave a short laugh. "Well, it does come in handy sometimes. What I got was mainly more colour on Soames and the boys: all three men were at the funeral and were devastated by Toby's death; Rutherford commented that Charlie was a 'pugnacious player', but it could just as easily have been another kid who kicked that ball."

"He was there on that day?"

"Yes. Said Toby had stood up, shaken his head a bit and given them all a big grin, and ran back to his position.

"Allan Tenning said he really liked Charlie. Described him as a cheeky kid who'd talk to anyone. He seemed to think that might have played a part in his abduction."

Xandra looked up. "They were his words?"

Fenwick met her eye. "Not sure that's a problem. The word's been bandied around a bit, hasn't it?"

Her shoulders sunk back to starting position. "Aye, go on."

"Sam Norton was the only father on duty on the eighth of December, and as such, he's been interviewed at length already, plus your further verifications. He confirms that he doesn't recall whether he saw Charlie or not during the game. He assumes he must have done but can't remember anything specific. He thinks he caught sight of him walking up the slope to catch his bus after the game when Norton hung back to exchange some words with Lane. Then he took his own son for some food on the way home to their family. At the time, a shopkeeper was able to recall him dropping by.

"The other two have solid alibis. Rutherford was at a work function and Tenning was at his local gym. Lane was the only one whose story looked rubbery."

"Mmm." Xandra was doodling faces on her pad. She'd started drawing fangs from their smiley mouths. She looked up abruptly, realising Fenwick was waiting for a response.

"I know this is covering old ground, but did you check whether any of the Pilgrim Way parents have any connection to the other schools or teams where Will Moore and Abbi Singh went missing? Especially Rufus Soames."

"Nothing obvious that we could find, but it wouldn't be hard to stop and watch a game and get talking to other parents, would it? We spoke to the coaches of those teams, but it was asking a bit for them to recall people who'd just dropped by during games. And the coaches themselves all had strong alibis for where they were that entire afternoon and evening. The only one who stands out is Stephen Lane. He seems to be well known around the area and has a lot of involvement in the game outside of the school he works at."

"Yes, those are all avenues of enquiry I've worn flat already."

They sat for a moment, consulting their own notes and thoughts. Ambient noise filtered in from outside their room, making them aware of hard leather heels clomping up and down corridors, the trill of incoming calls and slamming doors.

"What I don't understand," Fenwick mused as he flicked and rolled his pen in a circle around his hand, "is if Charlie went missing on the afternoon of the eighth, and Soames only has two hours unaccounted for, it's not enough time to have done the business and bury the body after the cemetery shuts at 4.00 p.m., which was barely dark, and still make the 5.17 p.m. train to Manchester Piccadilly. And if he didn't bury him till the next night—"

Xandra's phone was set to vibrate and they both watched as it burred and twitched next to her notebook. She lifted it and glanced at the screen. "I need to take this.

"Frank. I've got Fenwick here. Can I put you on speaker?" She put the phone down between them. "Tell me, tell me."

"Irene's report should have hit your inbox by now. Cause of death strangulation, no signs of sexual abuse as far as she can tell; but she'll take you through the detail herself. We've got about as far as we can following up on our findings. As we discussed earlier, the soil samples in the shed matched with those of the site."

"You know what I'm after, Frank. Put me out of my misery. Please."

Frank cleared his throat. "Yes, well. As we noted that night, the body was buried in a plastic garbage bag, and that has retarded the normal rate of decomposition."

Xandra glared at Fenwick's wrist where he was busy tapping a pen. He stopped.

"With anything foreign hopefully kept in situ."

"Yes. Unfortunately, it was all pretty clean; there were indications gloves were used—none were found in the shed, you recall—no traces of rope or other similar fibrous material, no foreign matter under the nails that produced anything...no broken skin at time of death. We've analysed a lot of samples, which has consumed a great deal of our time. The biggest possibilities were three discrete sections of hair caught in the fibres of his jumper that didn't match his own. We've been in contact with the mother, and two of the samples have proven to be hers."

Xandra darted a quick look at Fenwick. "And the other one?"

"So far, unmatched."

Xandra's eyebrows lifted and she stretched back in her chair. "Maybe a classmate he sat next to that day...someone on the bus...or his killer. Get me that data, Frank. If the gods are smiling on me and I can get a match—"

A noise like a snuffle came down the line. "Mumm is my tipple of choice, Bentley."

"Nice try." Xandra grinned at Fenwick and tossed the phone back onto her notebook. "It's building up nicely, but if we could get a DNA match on that hair, it would be the final coup de grâce, thank-you-for-coming." Xandra sighed. She covered her mouth with her hand and stared out of the window.

Fenwick leaned back and rubbed both hands back and forth over his head until his hair stood on end. "Yeah...so back to what I was saying. I guess it all comes down to proving Soames buried him. The logistics of how he pulled it off aren't relevant if we can prove that."

Xandra nodded. "Yep, the trail died in the Vale of Health... and nothing from the people at the caravan park nearby. I'd hoped the shed would tell a story, but no. My guess is the body found an overnight home in the boot of his car, but that's long gone."

Xandra had had high hopes for tracing that car. It was amazing what could be found now with the latest forensics techniques, but it wasn't to be. Soames had sold his 2002 Volvo to a scrap dealer in the days before they left. The paperwork noted it had been towed in, having come into contact with a tree on a country road just south of Leatherhead.

"Ballsy to take those kinds of risks. Someone exiting the heath carrying a heavily loaded garbage bag the size of a body would have been noticed."

"I don't know. From the Vale of Health to the caravan park is no distance, and it was probably an hour after sunset. And he's definitely ballsy. I've just got to get this prick one-to-one," Xandra muttered to herself, cracking her knuckles.

Fenwick winced. "One thing all this does tell us is, it couldn't have been spontaneous. There's a lot of pre-planning gone into this little caper." He pushed his chair out, closed his notebook, and slipped it into his laptop case. "I don't know about you, but I'm feeling good about this. It's taking shape. We just need the missing piece."

"Yes, and that piece is currently over ten thousand miles away in another hemisphere."

"Be positive. It could be that hair fragment. Besides, media and community interest is running hot now we've found a body, and The Screw's been in and out of high-level meetings all this week, getting crankier and crankier, so your luck could be in. Especially if you start getting feisty on him." Fenwick grinned at her. "Don't forget to pack your thongs."

Xandra's mouth dropped open, and he burst out laughing.

"You'll need to get with the programme, Bentley, if you're

going Down Under. That's what they call flip flops."

He zipped his bag and stood up, pausing to rest it on the table, his grin having progressed to a teasing smirk.

"But I'm sure it'll be warm enough for you to parade around in your thong as well. Just make sure you're at the beach."

Chapter Twenty-Eight

Expostulate

Def. To remonstrate with

THEY HAD SAT crying on the sofa together for some time, mostly with Adele comforting Jeremy. She had quickly got the sense that the racking sobs issuing from her nephew were about far more than whatever had happened with Roof all those years ago. All she could do was hold him tight and let him spill it all out.

She didn't attempt to ask him anything else or even to speak—her question had been answered. The whys and wherefores weren't going to change what had happened or its wider implications, but it had sent her thoughts racing off to other frantic conclusions. She held his drooping head to her breast and stroked his hair, rocking him gently, her eyes closed as she tortured herself.

Unable to bear it any longer, she stared at the furniture around her, not knowing how to think about things any more. Everything in the room had some connotation to her life with Roof; everything she looked at now was anathema. She would have to sell this place, with everything in it, and soon. She wasn't even sure staying in the UK was a good idea...but going home? She was beginning to hate him. Every place he'd been, or they had gone to together, was now tarnished in her eyes. All those memories just left a rancid stink over anywhere she thought of to run to. Where could she go for a fresh start? New Zealand? It was like she would never clean herself of this taint. But Lady Macbeth she was not, so why did she feel so inveigled?

Jem's emotions were subsiding, but he seemed happy to just be held. After some time, he sat up and dug the heels of his hands into his eyes.

They sat there together, side by side, crouched over their knees, Adele's hand on Jem's back. The room was getting dim, and the odd car that passed now had its headlights on. Jeremy sat back in the sofa and let out a deep, exhausted breath. He wiped a hand over his mouth and gave her a sad look.

"So, Uncle Roof's got himself into trouble, then?"

"I can't say for sure, Jem, but it's starting to look like it."

Jem looked up from contemplating his wrestling fingers.

"You won't say anything about what I've told you?"

"Obviously I'd rather not, but if stuff comes out, do you think your parents will be able to look at those sketches he did of you ever again? Do you think they won't want to ask you some searching questions?"

"It's none of their business."

"The *hell* it's none of their business, Jeremy! You were their *child* living under *their* roof and *their* responsibility. Can you even imagine what I'm going through right now wondering whether Rufus abused his *own* son? I will never know, and I will have to live with that torture forever!"

Jeremy shrank back into the corner of the sofa at her tirade, which ended with her gasping into her palm.

He reached out a quavering hand to her. "Aunty Del," he whispered. "He wasn't a violent man. He was always loving and kind..."

Adele shook him off and slapped her hand on her thigh. "So loving and kind he's suspected of murder." She had spat it out before she thought, and now saw her mistake in Jeremy's eyes.

"What are you talking about?"

Adele swallowed hard. In for a penny, in for a pound. It would all be out soon, anyway.

"Nothing has been proven, but there's already damning evidence coming to light. A young boy from Toby's school went missing in the days before we flew out to Australia. They found his body last week—in the reserved plot next to Toby—and there are possible links to Rufus."

"Next to Toby's grave? You're joking! What does Uncle Roof have to say?"

"I don't *know,* Jeremy! Your uncle has barely spoken to me in two years. The police are handling the enquiries. What you heard was a courtesy update because I asked to be prepared if anything was likely to hit the media."

"The media! Aunty Del..." He groaned. "This is serious shit," he whispered.

"It's beyond shit, my love. And you cannot, *must not,* say a word."

*

JEM HAD GONE up to his room, leaving Adele with her own rampant thoughts. After pacing up and down the room, putting things away and wiping down all the surfaces in the kitchen, she had found herself in front of the drinks cabinet. She poured herself a whiskey, and before long she was on her second.

It was like her innards were spiralling down, down, down and she was being sucked into an endless black tunnel. She considered watching some TV, but the prospect of enduring the superficial goings-on of made-up people, or worse, the made-up goings-on of superficial people, sent a wave of revulsion through her stomach.

She pressed the heel of her palm to her forehead to quell another spate of gasping tears. She was so sick of crying all the time.

She needed help. She needed to get away...from this. From thoughts of Roof...her marriage, her whole history with him. Something to block out the horror. Something—she took another gulp of whiskey—practical. Strong and decisive. Protective and shielding. A warm mothering image of Jo presented itself, but it was quickly supplanted by Xandra, striding around her kitchen, her strong arms and capable hands depositing bags and pouring drinks; her mind clear and analytical, her manner forthright and kind. Her soft-lipped smile and even teeth. Adele reached for her phone.

"Hey, how are things?"

"Not good."

"Talk to me."

"Xandra, I can't handle this, I need to escape my *life*. I don't want to be me any more! I'm just—" She broke into sobs.

"Oh, hush. Do you want me to come round?"

"No, I have Jem here. It's all too... Could I come to you? I promise I won't stay long."

There was a pause—was that a sigh of resignation?—while Adele waited for a response, dimly aware through a numbing veil of alcohol that she was imposing too far on such a new relationship...and an official one at that, but her anxiety was riding too high and her feelings too intense to want to dwell on it.

"Are you fit to drive?"

"I'll get a taxi."

"Okay. If you think I can help." She gave Adele an address in

Kentish Town.

Less than thirty minutes later, she was stepping out of her cab halfway down Rhyl Street in front of a three-storey block of flats. She blinked to focus on the numbers of the intercom and pressed number five. The door clicked open and she was admitted into a tiled hallway with junk mail scattered on a side table. Xandra waited for her at the top of the first flight of stairs. The sight of her looking relaxed in a long-sleeved T-shirt and loose-fitting tracksuit pants had an immediate effect on Adele's tightly knotted stomach: a feeling of coming home. She would be safe here.

"Come in, I've just boiled a kettle."

Adele paused one step from the top and sheepishly extracted a bottle from under her coat. "I figured I owed you one."

Xandra raised an eyebrow and led her inside. Adele peeled her coat off and followed her to a small alcove kitchen where two mugs were already lined up next to the kettle. Xandra opened a cupboard and extracted two chunky tumblers. She gestured over the counter with one.

"Make yourself comfortable."

The room was small but functional. A narrow dining table with two chairs stood under a window looking down onto the street, and an old sofa covered in a faded geometric pattern faced a coffee table and a TV mounted on the opposite wall. Adele's eyes searched for something more personal: photos, books or magazines, knick-knacks, but the room gave nothing away.

"Very Spartan."

Xandra nodded and sat down next to her. "I don't tend to spend a lot of time here."

"Do you have things…elsewhere?"

"No, I just don't like to get weighed down with stuff."

"But you would have made an exception for Jo."

Xandra's face expressed surprise. "Jo was never a weight."

"But you were prepared to take on all the issues…and she has three children?"

Xandra took a swig of her drink. Settling the glass into her upturned palm, she gave Adele a thoughtful look. "She does. Alternate weeks with her ex. But why do you ask?"

"I—I'm just curious. I've come to the conclusion I have no idea how other people live. What goes on below the surface."

The side of Xandra's mouth tilted upward as she laughed softly through her nose. "In most cases, you don't need to know."

"But I'd like to understand. My nephew has just come out, you see."

"Ah. Is he okay? How has his family taken it?"

"His sisters are fine—it's almost a non-event for them. His mother is rolling with it, or pretending to, but my brother is struggling."

"Right." Xandra drank the last of her whiskey and placed the glass carefully on the table. "There are worse places to start."

Adele turned side-on to face her on the sofa. "So, where did *you* start?"

"Oh, it's about me now, is it?"

"I'm sorry. Do you mind me asking?"

Xandra gave her a sardonic look. She pushed herself back into the corner of the sofa and folded her arms. Her eyes flitted over Adele's face, showing a hint of scepticism, and for a moment Adele thought she had overstepped, but then Xandra ruffled her hand through her hair as if shuffling her thoughts. She frowned briefly before speaking.

"I've always found women's bodies beautiful. I was certainly more exposed to them from a young age: my mother's and my sister's. Dad left us when Cathy and I were very young, so men and their bodies were a mystery to me. A mystery I wasn't interested in solving, as it turned out."

She paused and laughed under her breath. She turned to glance at Adele to share the joke. "I remember seeing a picture of the statue of David, in kindergarten it must have been. I turned to the girl next to me and pointed between his legs. 'What's that slug doing on his leg?'

"She just giggled and whispered, 'That's his knob.'

"I wanted to ask if it opened something, but I was afraid she'd laugh at me. Anyway, knobs didn't interest me any more than slugs did. I used to get cosy with my best friend when we had sleepovers…all fairly innocent stuff, mind you, but I remember the last time, when we were twelve. We'd not long started high school. We usually slept wrapped around each other, but when I went to kiss her goodnight, she pushed me away, saying, 'We can't do that any more if we're to get boyfriends.'"

Adele could see the buried hurt in the brief twitch of Xandra's mouth, followed by an exhale through her nose.

"Did you ever try to like boys?"

"Ironically, as I got older, playing a lot of sport, I acquired more male friends—friends, mind you—and lost my female ones. It wasn't till I joined the police that I had my first proper girlfriend, and by then I'd learned the hard way to be careful whom I trusted."

Adele set her empty glass on the coffee table a little harder than she meant to. She sloshed some more whiskey into her glass.

"You sure you're okay?"

"If a bit of oblivion's good enough for Roof, surely it's good enough for me."

Xandra leaned over and gently extracted the glass from Adele's hand. She placed it out of reach on the floor behind her side of the sofa. She hooked her leg up underneath her to sit sideways and extended her arm across the back of the sofa towards Adele.

"So, talk to me. You're under a lot of pressure right now, I understand that. Is your nephew staying bringing it all home to you in some way or is it something else?"

Adele didn't want to talk about the Jeremy-Rufus thing. It was too painful; too ugly. Their conversation would become an aggressive interrogation, and she couldn't go there. Facing Xandra, she pressed her cheek into the back of the sofa just below Xandra's draped hand.

"This whole situation has left me feeling betrayed and alone. I was thinking about it on the way over here. I've had a few rock-bottom moments this last month, and either you or Jo have been there to pull me out. You've both quickly become people I can tap into for emotional support, but it's more than that. You both make me feel *safe*."

Xandra smiled and rubbed a forefinger back and forth over her lips. "Well, given one of us is a minister of the Lord and the other a minister of the law, I'd rather hope so."

Adele frowned. "Please don't make light of what I'm saying. It feels like more than that. It's some inner circle. Like...like..."

Xandra propped her temple up with a finger, an amused expression on her face, waiting for Adele to speak.

Adele glanced longingly at the whiskey bottle. She addressed it instead of Xandra. "That first day I saw how intimate and warm you and Jo were with each other, I felt what I later interpreted as jealousy, but have come to recognise as emptiness. Like it triggered a deep longing that's been asleep, an unaddressed need. Like I've been missing out on something important. Always trying, but never getting. Not even knowing what it was I was trying to get.

"If I had to put words around it now, I'd list things like kindness, softness, intimacy...the need to feel *nurtured*, if you like. *Known*, at a deep level. I'd never had that with Roof or any other man. I think... I guess it's not what men do."

Adele stared glumly at the label on the whiskey bottle, absorbing Xandra's silence. "I think...I just think...I'd feel...safer with a woman." She drew a quick in breath. "They're more giving"—she stole a quick glance at Xandra—"and more beautiful, if it comes to that."

Xandra smiled kindly. "They can also be more bitchy, more emotionally complicated, more deceptive, and crueller, too. Take it from me." She laughed. "I think I'm diagnosing a case of grass is greener, Adele, not that I want to tell you how to feel, but you're in a vulnerable state right now. Maybe not the best time to be making decisions on a new romantic direction."

"But...you don't think I should try it?"

"By all means, but no relationship should be contemplated when you're feeling vulnerable and needy. That's a recipe for disaster. Not to mention you attract the wrong people."

Xandra was in the act of raising her glass to her lips when she stopped and gave Adele a penetrating stare. "Is that what brought you here tonight?"

Adele's eyes bulged and heat rushed up her neck. "If you don't give me my glass back, I'll drink straight from the bottle."

Xandra sighed and reached down for Adele's drink. Adele took it from her and upended its contents down her throat. "I'm just not an attractive prospect, am I."

"Oh, for god's sake, stop with the self-pity already. If there's one thing a lesbian hates it's the idea that we're here to be experimented on by bisexual, or worse, straight women. And then dropped for a man when their curiosity's been satisfied."

"But I didn't—I—I'm so sorry, I... God, I'm so embarrassed..." Tears of humiliation slid down her face. She moved around trying to fish a tissue out of her pocket. She paused in her actions when she felt Xandra's palm on her cheek. Her lip quivered as Xandra's thumb stroked her jawline.

"Don't be sorry and don't be sad; and there's no need to be embarrassed. You're going through a tougher time than most people ever experience, and you're holding it together fine so far. Jo would love you to keep up the support group, and I think that's a good idea. You need to stay connected to good people."

Adele lowered her chin, nodding.

"In the meantime, I think we'd better get you a cab so you can go home and get some sleep. And yes, maybe leave the whiskey here."

Adele stole a pained smile at her, just in time to see Xandra leaning in to kiss her. Just a gentle pressure on her lips, then she was removing her hand and getting up off the sofa. Adele's hand came up to her cheek to quell the loss of Xandra's warm contact. She watched her in silence as she picked up her phone from the coffee table and rang for a taxi. She rose unsteadily from the sofa, and Xandra pointed her in the direction of the bathroom.

She took her time splashing water on her face and bemoaning her predicament to her sorry face in the mirror. She was snapped out of it by Xandra calling for her to get a move on, the taxi was downstairs.

Xandra walked her down to the front door. "Promise me you'll drink a goodly amount of water before you go to bed."

"Yes, Mum," she mumbled.

Xandra took the lapels of Adele's coat and pulled them in tighter around her.

"Everything's going to be fine, lass. Just make sure you take care of you."

Adele tottered out into the cold night air and clambered into the back of the waiting cab, the fuggy odour of sweat and stale fart that hit her stimulating a wave of nausea. She quickly wound down the window and rested her head back in the seat, sadly aware there would be no one to hold *her* hair away from her face when she got home.

Chapter Twenty-Nine

Exeat

Def. Formal leave of absence granted

IT WAS 7.45 a.m. and Xandra was flicking through the *Daily Mail*, waiting for her coffee to be called out, when The Screw's name lit up on her phone.

"Where are you?"

"Andy's."

"I've got a call coming in from the NSW Police."

"On my way."

*

XANDRA TAPPED ON The Screw's open door and poked her head in. He waved her in to the seat next to him at the meeting table beside his desk. His monitor was angled to take them both in, and, when she was in position, she saw a uniformed officer with a face full of freckles.

"Senior Constable Phil Barber, this is Detective Sergeant Xandra Bentley."

"Officer Barber is responding to our recent enquiry. I'll ask you to repeat what you've just told me, Barber." The Screw turned to look at her. "You're going to love this."

Xandra turned her full attention to the screen. If it wasn't for his serious demeanour, Barber's wedge of ginger hair and dark eyes would have rendered him a cartoon character.

Barber nodded. "Your request for assistance in setting up an interview with one Rufus Tobias Soames of 4 Lily Crescent, Annandale has been passed to me. I'm based at our head office in Parramatta in the Child Exploitation Unit."

Xandra tried to keep her face under control, but she was aware of an immediate doubling of her heart rate.

When she refrained from comment, Barber continued, "We are familiar with your Mr Soames. We've been keeping an eye on his activities for some time now."

Xandra exchanged a wide-eyed look with The Screw. "So, what's he been up to?"

"So far, nothing we can act on. He's been popping into some online chatrooms we monitor. Talking with children."

"I'm surprised he would expose himself like that."

"He's posing as a kid."

Xandra let out a gusty breath, raising her eyes to the ceiling. *"Right."*

"So, we're naturally concerned to hear that he's a suspect in a child homicide case. I'm keen to work with you on this. We don't want him replicating any nasty tricks here." He paused, rubbing his cheek. "Your boss tells me you're organising a warrant. You'll be seeking extradition?"

Turner cleared his throat. "That would be ideal. But so would a confession."

"Okay. First things first. I think we need to hurry up and move before he gets wind of what's been happening over there. We'll lose the advantage of surprise if we muck around."

"Agreed."

Barber rubbed his cheek again in thought, then slid his hand around to cover his chin. "Look, I'm going to run this by my own boss and see if we can speed things up at this end. Our raison d'être is about protecting children, not just acting after the fact. Leave it with me and I'll be in touch."

The call ended with Barber saying he'd send through some of the chatroom transcripts for her to have a look at. Xandra blew out her cheeks. She looked at her boss, who was scraping his knuckles on the tabletop. "So, what do you think?"

Turner sat back in his chair and folded his arms. "I backed you for this last promotion, Bentley, because you're good at what you do. You're a safe pair of hands. And you know there's mounting pressure to put this one to bed. I wouldn't send just anyone halfway round the world if I didn't—"

Xandra bit her lip to stop herself from smiling. "I won't let you down."

*

XANDRA HAD THOUGHT it best to give Adele some space after her late-night visit, but the investigation was now progressing apace. After the call with Sydney, she'd texted Adele to make time for a video call that evening.

"Sorry I haven't been in touch these last few days. Things are starting to heat up."

"Oh dear. I was hoping no news might have been good news."

Xandra watched Adele's face closely. She seemed subdued and downcast. "Are you two managing to hold it together there?"

"Jem's been keeping to the house pretty much, and I've been trying to work."

"Good. I'm glad you've got an outside focus to keep you busy. Listen, I'm calling to let you know I'll be on a flight to Sydney tomorrow evening. We had a call with our counterparts in the NSW Police this morning, and things are moving quickly."

Adele's expression immediately became anxious. "What's moving quickly?"

"My enquiries have caused a bit of excitement down under. It turns out your ex-husband has been a 'person of interest' for some time."

"What the hell does that mean?"

"They've been monitoring his activities online. In chat-rooms."

"But why? Is he talking to criminals or something? Is he part of—"

"Adele, he's talking to children. He's been posing as a child online."

"Whhh—"

Xandra filled the silence with even, business-like tones, explaining the situation.

"But if he's done nothing wrong...it doesn't prove—"

"Adele, you have to admit this isn't normal adult behaviour. You said yourself he was spending an inordinate amount of time locked away on his computer at night when you were still together. Even before you left the UK, if I recall. And his interacting under false pretences with young children—all boys, as it happens—provides dangerous signposts."

Adele sat gaping at the desk in front of her, her lips quivering as if she was preparing to throw up. "My *god*, Xandra. When will this fucking end?"

Xandra could hear the desperation in her voice. It was hurting her heart to bring reality crashing down on the poor girl's head.

"Adele, listen to me. I'm taking a big risk revealing this sensitive information to you. You asked me to give you warning of anything going public and I'm trying to prepare you, god help me. They'll be watching him more closely now, and it's possible he might withdraw if he hears of the body being discovered. They're going to want to move on this sooner rather than later. He's done me a favour, though; this news helped remove any last quibbles on the paperwork I need to get out there and work with the Australian authorities on bringing him in."

"For—for questioning?"

"Adele, I have enough to arrest him on suspicion. I just need to get at him to take it the rest of the way. He needs to be locked up where he can't destroy or damage any more children."

Adele removed her glasses and rubbed her eyes. "How long will you be gone for?" Her voice was now tired and resigned.

"I really don't know. At this stage, I'm allowing a week."

"My...my sister's family live in the same suburb as Roof..."

"Annandale?"

"Yes." Adele replaced her glasses and blinked. "If things go badly...I don't want to say anything to alarm them yet, but..."

"I think you need to get in there first, Adele, but I can go and speak to them if you think that would help? Are they still in touch with him?"

Adele gave her a grateful look. "No. Mum sends him Christmas cards. She still makes excuses for him, hoping he'll have some kind of epiphany, God love her. He's never responded."

She pressed her fingers to her forehead and let her head droop forward. She looked up bleakly. "What am I going to do,

Xandra? I should be warning my family before it blows up, but I can't tell them. I just can't. I've brought this person into their homes. Exposed their children to him."

"Adele, I've already told you. This is about him. Not you. You are not responsible for another adult's errant behaviour. You didn't know you were living with Dr Jekyll."

"Some people would question how I could *not* have known." Her head drooped again; her breath was ragged.

Xandra wanted nothing more than to reach out and touch her. She watched her raise her head and lift her glasses to wipe her eyes. It was a gesture she was starting to identify with Adele.

"I'll ring you as often as I can, okay? I'll let you know if anything major happens."

"Don't worry what time it is here. Just call." Adele tried to smile and failed. "Oh, Xandra. I'm feeling wobbly just knowing you won't be here."

"You'll have Jo. She's the best."

Adele dictated contact details for her parents and sister. When Xandra had finished scribbling, she looked up and gave Adele what she hoped was a reassuring smile.

"I'll do my best for you, lass."

"And for the Falks, Xandra. Do it for Charlie."

Chapter Thirty

Execute

Def. 1. To perform; to carry out a task to the end 2. To carry out a sentence of death

SYDNEY WAS FAMILIAR, but not. From the moment Xandra emerged into the arrivals hall, she was aware of a certain spaciousness; a room to move. A feeling that wasn't necessarily supported by the evidence of her own eyes in the hustle of the airport precincts.

Feeling more human after a shower, she wandered over to the window of her hotel room still wrapped in a towel. Everywhere she looked, tall irregular buildings blocked her view, and the roads were full of traffic. The hotel map showed she was a few kilometres south of the famous harbour.

It had just gone nine o'clock, so even a power nap was out of the question. She padded over to the bar and put a pod in the coffee machine. As the machine whirred into action, she pulled clothes out of her bag. SC Barber had invited Xandra to meet his boss and some members of his team in Parramatta, west of the city. There would be a briefing over sandwiches.

She paused to sip her coffee and allowed her eyes to fall shut. It would be 10.00 p.m. at home. She'd already fired off an email to Jo during her stopover at KL airport, giving her instructions to keep a close eye on Adele. It was only a matter of time before the media harassment started, and she feared for the girl's ability to cope under any more stress. Especially if it got ugly. Xandra sniffed. It was the British press. Of course it was going to get ugly.

Within half an hour, she was in a taxi, driving past the nondescript buildings of Parramatta Road. As they crawled up to yet another set of traffic lights, her eyes were refreshed by a stretch of green.

"Snotta park, love, that's Sydney Uni," said the taxi driver in response to her question. He then pounded the accelerator and abruptly switched lanes, causing her to catch her breath.

Uh-huh. The university. That gave her some bearings. According to the map she'd studied, Annandale, where Rufus and the Sanders lived, wasn't far from here. "So, that's Glebe on our right?"

"Yep. Fulla lezzos," her driver grunted. He turned to glance at her, a new thought occurring to him. "You Sco'ish? Och aye the noo and all that, eh?"

Xandra raised her eyebrows and gave him a grim smile. "Yes. Something like that."

The drive was about as scenic as trawling through the outer suburbs of London, and about as drawn out, but mercifully Fangio limited any further conversation to muttering at the surrounding traffic, allowing her to muse in silence.

By eleven, she was walking into the glass mouth of 1 Charles Street and asking for SC Barber at the front desk. As he approached with his hand held out, her chin rose sharply to take him in. She had to smile; videos could still leave room for surprises. He also proved to be a lot more relaxed away from the setting of the formal conference call. Happily making small talk, he led her to some nearby escalators where, on the step ahead of him, she could briefly be at his eye level.

"You're looking pretty good for someone who's just jumped off a long haul. I hate 'em. Never enough leg room."

"Coffee is my friend."

"All sorted. We'll put an order in for some to go with the sangers. And speaking of sorted, Soames is in custody as we speak. We got him last night."

"That's excellent news." Xandra paused and offered her hand to Barber.

"Thanks, but there's a lot of work ahead of us yet."

Xandra was keen to interrogate him on the spot, but he forestalled her.

"I'll leave the details for our formal update session. You'll be meeting two other Senior Constables, Tracey Donovan and Tom Best. Boss Browne is in another meeting, but she's hoping to pop her head in." Barber's freckled face creased up in another easy grin. "There's a lot of Bs in the team, so you'll fit right in."

Startled, Xandra didn't know what to say, but then she laughed, realising he only meant their names. The Screw had exchanged some emails with DS Rose Browne, the head of the unit, but Xandra was yet to make contact. With a name like that, she was being sucked into imagining a girly type, similar to Adele, but taller.

Barber showed her into a room with a long table and a projector screen at one end. Tom Best walked around the table to shake her hand and Tracey Donovan stood up from tinkering with the projector to give her a wave.

By the time Donovan had finished running through a short orientation slide show on the NSW police and their sphere of operations, Xandra was ready to chew her own fingers off. Barber finally took over and reported on what had been happening while she'd been suspended in the air.

Based on the new information she'd provided, they'd moved in with a covert sting operation. They baited the line with a specialist officer posing as a child, and Soames had grabbed it; soon after, finding himself apprehended and remanded in custody, his computer confiscated. It would take a week or two for Data Forensics to comb through all his computer files, but they'd already found enough to incriminate him on several counts and press charges. He would be transferred to Long Bay that evening.

Barber flipped through some pages in front of him. "And now you're here, we can get our interview strategy worked out."

Xandra then presented her report to date on the Falk file.

Barber leaned back in his chair, both palms rubbing the back of his shorn scalp. "So, is it fair to say Soames is still unaware the body has been found?"

"Looks like it, or he would have dived underground before we could get to him." Donovan looked up from scratching a note on the pad in front of her.

Xandra nodded. "We've managed to keep the details fairly tight, but the other thing you've got to remember is how isolated Soames has become. He's broken contact with his ex-wife's side of the family, and he's the only child of dead parents. Our interviews with work colleagues and other associates have shown no close relationships, or if there were any before, they were discontinued when he left Magnus Design and the country."

"Next to his own son's grave." Best shook his head. "I suppose after two years he must have been feeling pretty safe. Only would've been discovered once he was buried there himself. Jesus."

As Best spoke, there was a knock on the door and a woman of middle height entered the room. Xandra walked over to meet her. DS Browne had a plain face devoid of make-up, her hair scraped back into a tight bun, reminding Xandra of her senior school hockey coach. She smiled briefly as she took Xandra's hand. *Hard face, soft hands.*

Rose Browne now braced those hands on the back of a chair, leaning over the table. "We've booked an interview with Soames tomorrow. At this point, we've said the questions will relate to his chatroom activities and his interactions with children in real time. We need to allow forensics more time with his computer, but that should give us a second bite at the cherry, based on what we've seen so far. Phil, I'd like you to lead off the questioning, with DS Bentley coming in halfway for the surprise element. Tom and Tracey can act as observers next door." She sent a small smile in Xandra's direction. "His reactions to Bentley's questions should be interesting, to say the least."

"He'll be reacting well before that when he recognises me."

Best rubbed his hands together. "That could be well worth the price of admission alone."

Browne turned back to face Xandra. "I should warn you that Soames's solicitor has already requested an assessment to see if his client is fit for interviewing. From what we have on Soames to date, we should be okay to proceed, but we'll know by close of business if that's going to pose a problem."

Xandra nodded. "There's certainly a lot of evidence to suggest mental instability. Adele Soames has described a history of strange and volatile behaviours in the latter years of their marriage, starting even before the death of their son."

"Which may have been what pushed him over the edge?"

Xandra turned to Donovan and shrugged. "It's possible. I'm curious to hear from forensics about these porn downloads. If any activity dates back prior to his son's death, that could tell us something." She tapped her fingers on the desk in front of her. "Speaking of forensics, how did your guys get on matching that hair data we sent over?"

Barber answered her. "Sorry, mate, no dice."

Dammit to hell. She rubbed her hand over her mouth in an effort to hide her frustration. Of course, it had been a long shot. She had no right to be too disappointed. At least it also hadn't matched the sample Adele had provided.

After the briefing, the team had interviews scheduled with Soames's Australian clients to see if they could pick up any behavioural clues or other indications. Xandra excused herself to make a call to Adele to give her an urgent update on Roof's arrest. She'd already warned her it was imminent, but this was even earlier than she'd expected.

The call was brief, but it caused a spiky little ache to flare up in her chest. She swallowed it down with an effort as she made her way to Rose Browne's desk for their post-briefing meeting.

"When I last spoke to your superior, he said you'll be seeking extradition orders for Soames to stand trial in the UK?"

"That's what I'm here for, yes."

"Well, you've got time while he's cooling his heels, but from what I understand, you've only got enough to arrest him on suspicion." There was a pause, and Xandra found herself being directly appraised by Browne's intelligent gaze. "Your boss says you're planning to ride him pretty hard and see what you can get out of him. Says you're not one for taking any chances."

Xandra exhaled through her nose, the memory of that last conversation with The Screw, before he finally relented and signed off on her travel, fresh in her mind.

"I've been chasing this case for too long. The more I can get to convince a jury, the better I'll feel."

Browne studied Xandra's face for a disconcerting moment before speaking. "It's hard not to let some of these cases get under our skin." She gave her a wry look. "Par for the course in this line of work, though."

Xandra nodded as Browne slid some folders toward herself and opened the top one.

"There's a few ways this could go, and often it can come down to a judge's discretion. The usual situation is the felon is tried locally for crimes committed here, and that could add any amount of time to getting him back. But if you can get your ducks in a row and crack this homicide case open, it would be unlikely they'd oppose extradition."

Browne tapped a fingernail on the document in front of her, her high forehead creasing slightly in thought. "And that would be my preference, to be frank. Soames has gone top drawer getting Will Ramsay on his case. He's likely to get him off with a reduced sentence or maybe even just a warning for a first offence, if the online stuff is all we can pin on him. I'd rather he go home and face the real music."

"Like death metal, perhaps?"

Browne gave another one of those small smiles that Xandra was quickly warming to.

"Well, there's a thought. My vision was more about a fat lady singing."

Browne took her through some other local steps and procedures, giving her some reading material. She glanced at her watch.

"That should be enough to ensure you sleep okay. Your jet lag must be kicking in hard by now. I'm surprised you've stayed sharp this long."

"Glad you've been fooled. I'm fast approaching the sharpness of jelly. I hope there's a good night's sleep between here and my interview with Soames. I'm going to need it."

Chapter Thirty-One

Excruciate

Def. To rack or torment; to inflict the severest pain

JEREMY HAD STOPPED going out. He could be found on the sofa, on his phone or with a book, or up in Toby's room. Once, she saw him out in the garden inspecting the damage she still hadn't cleaned up.

"I'll sort it out for you. It will give me something to do. Just fill it in and smooth it over?"

It had been that afternoon, when she'd been watching him work from the kitchen sink window, when the phone rang.

"Oh, Jo, I'm sorry. I should have called you before this.

Xandra—"

"It's all good. Don't worry. She emailed me during her stop-over. She said the flight was tiring, but she managed to get some sleep. She'll be staying in some serviced apartments near Central Station. I assume you know where that is. And I'm under strict instructions to keep an eye on you."

"No new news?"

"Not yet."

"I'm sorry I missed your jumble sale. I realised it was this last weekend gone. How did you do?"

"A little over one hundred and eighty-seven pounds. The cake stalls usually get us over the line, and they were fabulous this year."

"Oh dear." Adele laughed weakly. "Perhaps it's as well I didn't go."

"Anyway, I didn't call to discuss church finances. Xandra said she told you Sylvia Falk is in town. I thought it would be a mercy if you met with her and shared some of your experiences. She has a Family Liaison Officer assigned to her, but I'm providing her with some extra support. I've been spending time with her since they found Charlie, and I'm of the thinking that she would take great comfort from anything you could tell her."

Adele was watching her nephew as Jo spoke. His hair was tied back in the ubiquitous man-bun and his strong forearms strained as he used a spade to transfer the dirt from her pile back to the gutter of torn earth. It was the most manly she'd ever seen him look, and the sight gave her a kind of comfort.

"Jo, how would Sylvia feel knowing she could be speaking to the then-wife of her son's murderer?"

"She doesn't know yet, and I won't be saying anything of the kind to her. It's all supposition until they can prove it. But even so, there is great power in being able to confront those you think are responsible, and even though that's not you, it could be a proxy for her to deal with her grief if anything does come out."

"Sounds traumatic for all concerned."

"It doesn't have to be. Handled well, it could be a comforting and potentially healing experience. Can you trust me?"

"I would like to meet her. She's been in my thoughts. And Charlie and I did talk about her."

"Ohh. Yes. That's exactly what she needs, Adele. Just to talk about her son, express her grief, her sadness and loss. To someone who not only understands, but who can relate to her situation. I think it will help you, too."

Adele rang off with an agreement to meet the next morning.

It was nearly midnight when her phone rang again. She put her book aside and picked it up from the bedside table.

"Sorry for the late hour. Must be nearly twelve there, right?"

"It's okay. I can't sleep anyway. What's happening?"

"A lot. I've just nipped out of a briefing to call you. He's under arrest."

The groan that sprang from her throat sounded like a wounded animal, even to her own ears.

"His computer's now with Data Forensics, and he's in custody with bail opposed. I'll be interviewing him tomorrow. They've managed to keep it out of the news so far, but journalists are already sniffing around. You don't have much time left if you want to prepare your family."

"But Xandra! You said he hadn't done anything?"

"Things have ramped up since my involvement. They put a specialist officer, posing as a child, into one of the chat rooms Roof's been in. The conversation went to places that triggered the ability to act."

"You mean they tricked him?"

"He thought he was talking to a child who he could manipulate into meeting him, Adele. And I'm sorry, but there's more."

Adele's body tensed, waiting for the blow.

"He's been downloading child porn."

Christ! Adele screwed her eyes up tight. "I don't need to hear any more."

"I'm so sorry, lass. I'm trying to prepare you as best I can."

There was a space of quiet where Adele couldn't think of anything more to say. These last blows seemed so final.

Xandra spoke again, almost in a whisper. "I understand how bloody hard this is for you. And it's going to get worse before it gets better. I wish I could be there with you. Please, please get in touch with Jo. She's the best help you have right now."

Adele nodded against her phone, unable to speak.

"I do care about you, you know."

Before Adele could pry her mouth open, Xandra had hung up.

*

ADELE ARRIVED EARLIER than the agreed time. She just wanted to sit for a while. She took up her usual spot at the back and enjoyed the quiet. With all the news and disruption, she hadn't visited St Bart's since she'd chased Charlie out the door. It occurred to her now that, despite having gone to her bench and Highgate since recent events, she had not seen Charlie since. Perhaps she had served her purpose. Gladness gave way to loss when she realised she might no longer have any way of communicating with Toby.

Part of her was already regretting agreeing to see Sylvia Falk. How could it possibly go well? It would be down to Jo to finesse the situation. She knew Sylvia, after all, so must have known what she was about setting up the meeting.

Adele had been sitting there for a good while when she heard footsteps in the foyer followed by distant voices in the vestry. She picked up her bag and headed out to the room where they had the group meetings. The space was empty, so she busied herself setting up three chairs. She was just taking a seat when she heard Jo's voice speaking in low tones.

Next to Jo, the woman at her side looked almost like a child, slightly hunched and clasping her hands in front of her. Sylvia Falk's dark eyes flashed when they saw Adele.

Adele stood up awkwardly. That brief contact had caught her off guard. She now found herself shaking a small, fine-boned hand, a featherless baby bird, and looking into Charlie's eyes in a woman's face. Adele was barely aware of Jo speaking.

The woman took a seat opposite. Her posture was that of a cowering animal, timid in its actions, but hungry in the eyes. Adele made an effort to tune into what Jo was saying.

"...with her sister. She'll be staying in town for a week after the funeral. The police have asked that she delay her return."

"You must be under a great deal of strain right now."

Sylvia leaned forward eagerly. "Yes! First it was the not knowing, but now...*now* they tell me they still not know. Why they not take this man Lane? The papers say—"

Jo placed a calming hand on the woman's arm. "Let's not talk about that right now. There's no new information, and it will just get you all worked up. Adele has been kind enough to come at my invitation today. She has something wonderful to tell you. About Charlie."

Those black eyes centred on Adele's face again, scrutinising her, weighing her up. "You knew my son?"

Adele glanced at Jo, who nodded her encouragement.

"Sylvia, just before my own son Toby died—"

The woman let out a whimper, extending her hand towards Adele. "Mrs Soames—"

"Adele, *please*... I—I'm not married any more." Again, she glanced at Jo for reassurance. "Our—our sons used to play in opposing teams in the after-school football games."

Sylvia nodded, her eyes creased in a mixture of sympathy and concentration.

"I never knew your son...until recently. In January, I returned after being away for a long time. I like to sit on a bench on the heath to—to watch the boys play football. Oh, Sylvia, I don't know how to say this the right way, but your son...your son's *spirit*, would come and sit with me."

"My—my *son*?" Sylvia shot a look at Jo. "But they found my son, he's—what are you saying?"

As she watched the woman in front of her become more and more agitated, Adele tried to explain how she had slowly realised Charlie was not real, but a ghost.

"A spirit of his former self," put in Jo, smiling.

"But why? *Why?*" Sylvia's eyes switched back and forth between her face and Jo's.

"Sylvia, we can't begin to—"

Sylvia leaped out of her chair, hitting her chest with her fist. "Why he come to *you*? Why not to *me*? His own mother!"

Adele watched helplessly as Sylvia broke down in the most abject crying.

Jo got her back in her chair, but it took some time before her near-hysterical litany of "why-why-why" subsided to mere tears.

"Sylvia, I understand how hard this is for you. I want to know the same thing. Why did *your* boy come to me and not my own son?"

This question had the effect of stilling Sylvia's moaning and recrimination. "Oh, Mrs Soames—"

"Sylvia, please call me Adele. I have divorced my husband."

"You no longer a wife?" She wiped her eyes with her handkerchief. "Me, also. I am no longer. My husband, he die before Christmas." She pounded her chest again. "From grief!"

"Oh, Sylvia, I'm so sorry… I—I wanted to tell you about your son. How he loves brown bananas—"

"I gave him good bananas! Always! He let them go bad in his bag. So careless…"

"He said that's how he likes them. Very sweet."

She shook her head. "He just say that to cover up his forgetting."

"Charlie passed me a message from my son. Toby told him to tell me he was okay… I waited and hoped he would come, but only Charlie. I asked Charlie if he visited you and he said he did."

"He came? When?"

"Yes. He said he sits with you, but you are always so sad. He asked me to say you need to smile more." Adele swallowed hard, recalling something more. "He—he also said, 'Dad's worried about her, too'." Adele reached over to squeeze Sylvia's agitated fingers. "So at least you know they're together," she whispered.

It was painful to watch Sylvia's agony. Adele could feel her intense longing and grief as if it were her own; and of course, it was her own. She wanted to tell her as much as possible. About him waiting for someone, about finding him, but realised it was unlikely to stay a secret long if she did. She'd overloaded the poor woman as it was.

"You take me to see him? Can we go now?"

Adele shot Jo a panic-stricken look. "Sylvia, since they found Charlie's body, he hasn't come any more. I haven't seen him. I think...I think his purpose in seeing me is finished. He can rest in peace now."

"Rest in peace? No! How can he rest in peace? Who did this to my boy? The police must find him and kill him! This evil should—"

Jo took over, putting an arm around Sylvia, speaking to her in low comforting tones. She glanced at Adele. "Would you put the kettle on in my office and make some tea, please?"

Grateful to get away from the tense atmosphere for a moment, she almost ran to Jo's office. By the time she was balancing a tray of tea ware in front of her, things had calmed down somewhat.

Jo had placed a fourth chair between them, and Adele laid the tray on it. As she went to straighten up, Sylvia clutched at her hand.

"Thank you...Adele. You have made me so happy...and so sad...all together."

Adele gave her a crumpled smile and nodded. "I understand."

When they had finished their tea, Jo offered to see Adele out, saying she wanted to speak with Sylvia alone. Out on the front step, Adele felt like she could breathe again.

"I honestly don't feel like I've helped her at all, Jo. If anything, I've just stirred things up. And when she hears—"

"No. Dear Adele. Don't think like that. This has been a long and painful struggle for Sylvia. What you've shared with her today will take a while to sink in, but it will all help with her healing. To know her son comes to her; that he is saying he is okay where he is. All of this helps, painful though it is."

Adele turned to look down the street, taking a big breath. "Yes, I suppose you are right. I'm still worried how she will take any further news." Then a new thought occurred to her and she clutched Jo's arm. "She can't be repeating any of this to anybody, Jo. If the media—"

"Yes, I understand. I'll be spending time with her over the next week, and I'll reinforce that message. I'll prepare her as best I can for whatever comes up. She also has a Family Liaison Officer working with her to provide the support she needs, so don't worry."

Jo laid both hands warmly on Adele's arm. "I'm sorry there hasn't been any time to see how *you* are. Xandra expressed concern about you. Shall I come and see you?"

"No, it's okay. I know how busy you are right now. I have my nephew staying with me at the moment. We're looking out for each other."

Jo gave her a searching look. "You only have to call me, you know."

"I know." She leaned in and gave Jo a kiss on the cheek, then quickly took off down the steps to the street.

Chapter Thirty-Two

Expugn

Def. To take by storm, to overcome

XANDRA'S FIRST WAKING thought was of Adele and how, or even whether, she was managing any hard conversations with her family yet. She rolled over and grabbed her phone. She'd been dead to the world since 7.00 p.m. so there were plenty of messages. She zeroed in on one from Rose Browne after 10.00 p.m.

Soames arrest on news.

Shit.

Xandra lurched out of bed and switched the television on.

She started scrolling on her phone and with her free hand she groped for a pod for the coffee machine. While she was reading single paragraph announcements about the arrest of an English paedophile, a short clip of footage ran on the television of a clearly recognisable Soames being guided into a waiting police car.

Xandra dialled Adele's number. No answer. She texted: *Roof's on the news. Call me.* And there would be more to tell her after the interview, but by then, it would be the middle of the night for her.

Two hours later, Xandra was staring out of a car window, wondering why she hadn't heard back from Adele. Long Bay Correctional Centre was located south of the city, on a peninsula near Botany Bay. Tom Best was driving and enjoying playing tour guide.

"This is Moore Park you can see on either side of us. That's the Sydney Cricket Ground and Centennial Park off to our left. If you enjoy a walk"—he turned to give Xandra a cursory glance—"or a run, it's a great place to unwind and blow the cobwebs out. There's bike hire, too. And coming up here on the left is Randwick Racecourse..."

Xandra was finding the greenery restful after all the urban sprawl, but she was only half tuned in to Best. Most of her mental resources were running over how she was going to approach Soames. After the shock of seeing her had sunk in, it would be a challenge to get more out of him, especially with his lawyer there. She had one ace up her sleeve, and possibly a king, and she had to be careful how she played them.

They turned off Anzac Parade and entered the grounds of the prison. Xandra noted the odd palm tree with an ironic smile as they drove around and through a maze of buildings until they pulled up in an area where there were some other police vehicles. They were met by Donovan and Barber at reception.

The interview rooms were up a level and down a long corridor. Between gaps in the buildings Xandra glimpsed flashes of water as they passed each window. They were shown into a room on the right.

"We'll be in here." Best pointed to an adjoining door where he and Donovan would view proceedings via a one-way window. Xandra would be with them until the time came to make her entrance.

Xandra took a seat next to Best in front of the window connecting them to the interview room, placing her notes in front of her. They watched Barber set himself up at the table. He glanced at the attendant who'd shown him into the room and nodded.

Soames, looking like he'd just rolled off the sofa after a two-day TV binge, was escorted in with his expensively suited solicitor striding ahead of him. After Browne's comments, Xandra had done some homework online. Will Ramsay was a high-profile defender of celebrity cases, and he was adept at winning sympathy for his clients. Soames wasn't leaving anything to chance, either.

After fixing her thoughts on him for so long, Xandra was now having to reconcile her imagined Soames with the real one now in front of her. Already, he seemed small and fuzzy around the edges compared to his tall, sharp-edged legal rep. Soames had allowed his already shaggy hair to grow long enough to be tied back, although his Van Dyke remained trim and neat. His face looked grey and tired, and he had heavy pouches under his eyes. He took a seat, avoiding eye contact with Barber, leaving the greetings to his solicitor. Soames's eyes were locked on his hands clasped in front of him.

Barber initiated the recording process, formally identifying himself and those in attendance. He opened the interview with the standard identification questions and cautions. Then he asked what had brought Soames to leave the UK and other details about his life in his new country.

Soames provided minimal answers. "My son's death…only in-laws…divorce was amicable…grown apart. No further contact. She's now in the UK."

"Have you continued your involvement with children's sporting groups? We understand you helped out with the school soccer team at home."

Soames's lip curled. "My son's death ended all that. The only *football* I watch now is on the television."

Barber checked his notes and nodded. "There are some other matters we'd like to speak with you about in connection with your previous interactions with children. I have a colleague who will be joining us for some further questioning on matters potentially relevant to this case."

Xandra walked in, but Soames continued to stare at his hands.

"I'll pass you over to my colleague, Detective Sergeant Bentley, representing the London Metropolitan Police. She'd like to question you about your life back in the UK in connection with another matter that you may be able to assist us with and that may also have some bearing on this current matter."

For the first time, Soames lifted his head. A crease gathered between his eyes as he focused on Xandra's face. A tic near his right eye twitched.

"You may recall, Mr Soames, our brief interview before you left the UK two years ago."

Soames's reaction to her voice was immediate. His pupils dilated and his shoulders visibly stiffened.

Ramsay's glance flicked sideways at this client. He cleared his throat. "If this is unrelated to the current charges…"

"We believe there is relevance, especially in establishing past history and behavioural patterns." Xandra looked poignantly at Soames then Ramsay. "So, I'll proceed.

"Mr Soames, have you maintained any connections with the local schools or sporting teams back home since you've been living in Australia?"

"No."

"You will recall—"

"I actually have very little recollection of our conversation that day, Ms—"

"Detective Sergeant Bentley."

"—Detective *Sergeant* Bentley. *You* may recall I'd recently lost my son. My wife and I were racing against the clock to be ready for our flight the next day."

"So, you recall the day, at least." Xandra looked down at her notes. "At the time you assisted us with our enquiries, Mr Soames, we were investigating the recent disappearance of Charlie Falk, a young boy who played in the school football games that you and your son were associated with."

"You're wasting your time. I don't recall the name, and I'd be hard pressed to even pick him out of a team photo. He wasn't a friend of my son's; Toby never mentioned him. It doesn't sound like he was much of a player. That I might have noticed."

"Hmm." Xandra idly turned some pages in her notes back and forth. "I was under the impression you *had* noticed he wasn't much of a player. Why else would you have arranged to provide him with some 'special coaching'?"

Soames glared at her. "I made no such arrangement. I never provided any child with 'special coaching'."

"I see." Xandra frowned and jabbed her pen at one of her dot points. "What exactly *was* your connection to Charlie Falk, then?"

"I've told you. I didn't know him from a bar of soap."

"I'm prepared to believe you didn't know much about Charlie Falk before the eighteenth of November 2011. But after that date you made it your top priority to find out, after he kicked that fateful ball into your son's head."

A gasp from Soames.

"Dragging the death of my client's son into this—"

"Is highly relevant if you will let me expand on my questions." Xandra turned a fixed stare on Soames. "And because you weren't present, you showed up at the school and made numerous vigorous efforts to find out who had sent that ball on its way."

"And the bastards wouldn't tell me!"

"Would. They. Not."

Xandra watched with steely eyes as Ramsay laid a hand firmly on Soames's shoulder and Soames extended his own shaking hand towards the glass of water in front of him.

"As it happens, Rufus, I now have confirmation that you *did* know. That you created a rather ugly scene at the school, making threats to some of the staff."

He put down his empty glass and cast his eyes around. "I need some more water."

"Why was it so important for you to know which poor hapless kid happened to kick that ball? What did you plan on doing with that information, exactly?"

"I just wanted to *know*! Jesus Christ. I had a right to know the cause of my son's death."

"I imagine you and Sylvia Falk could have an interesting conversation together about parents' rights. For two years, she hasn't even known whether her son was alive or dead."

Xandra had to take a deep breath. Her disgust for the man in front of her was beginning to rise in her throat like bile. It was important she keep the upper hand and control her emotions.

"So, let me ask you a different question." Xandra opened a folder to her right. She placed a page in front of Soames. "Do you recognise these sketches?"

Soames glanced at the page. "Where did this come from?"

"Please answer the question."

Soames licked his lips. "They could be drawings I've done for work...at Magnus Design."

"Could be? You're not sure? What about these? They're from the same folder. The Breville contract you worked on in the last months of 2011, prior to leaving the UK, I believe?" She put a further page in front of him.

"Yes, yes." Rufus waved an impatient hand. "I suppose they must be mine."

"And this one?" Xandra deftly flipped the page over.

She had the pleasure of seeing Soames's eyes start.

He sat back in his chair abruptly. "It's not mine." He cast a furtive glance at Ramsay. "Easily forged. You can't prove it."

"Oh, but I think it is yours, Rufus. Furthermore, I should inform you that I've already gone to the trouble of having some independent experts appraise these drawings. Your work colleagues have also been consulted.

"So it appears we've now established, contrary to what you've been saying, that you were *very* familiar with what Charlie Falk looked like." Xandra watched as Soames shifted uneasily in his chair. Perspiration beaded on his brow.

"Okay, let's come at things from a different angle, shall we? You must be wondering why I'm following all of this up with you two years down the track."

Xandra pretended to wait for his answer as he stared at his hands, now gripped, rather than clasped, in front of him.

"Poor Sylvia Falk has been living in agony for two years now, desperately hoping for word of her son, Rufus." Xandra paused. "I can now confirm that Charlie Falk has recently been found."

The only sound was the crackle of Soames's swallowing as his Adam's apple rose and fell in his throat. He withdrew his trembling hands and thrust them under the table.

Xandra allowed the silence to stretch out as she simply stared at him, aware also of Ramsay's eyes likewise boring into her. When she finally spoke, it was with a studied lightness.

"Well. You do astonish me, Rufus. I would have thought as a fellow parent who has lost a child, you would be relieved and pleased for Mrs Falk."

Xandra pretended to go through some pages of her notes, letting him stew. After turning a final page, she spoke in a measured tone, implying she had all the time in the world.

"In the light of new information we've obtained, I was hoping to ask you some further questions about your connection to Charlie and the team, and your movements that day."

"I told you—" Soames's voice had gone thin and high, and he broke into a fit of coughing. Ramsay poured him some more water, and they watched while he drank. He placed the glass unsteadily in front of him and cleared his throat. "I told you. I can barely recall after all this time. Whatever I told you then—"

"What you told us then, was that on the afternoon of Charlie's disappearance you had caught the 3.30 p.m. train to Manchester Piccadilly, which was around the time Charlie was last seen. You then met a colleague, Andrew Ford, for drinks and dinner straight off the train, checking in to your hotel afterwards at 8.09 p.m." Xandra flipped over a page of her notes, deliberately drawing out the moment. "When pressed, your colleague had some interesting additions to make to his initial statement." She looked up at him. "I'll cut to the chase, Rufus. We now know you actually left London on the 5.17 p.m. train. You therefore have more than two hours of your time unaccounted for that afternoon."

"How is this relevant—"

"Mr Ramsey, given the current charges, if we establish that your client has prior involvement in the disappearance of a child, I can assure you it is highly relevant."

Ramsey closed his file and pulled it towards him. "I must speak to my client in private. Mr Soames needs time to consider these questions. Two years—"

"It was unfortunate, Rufus—" Xandra narrowed her eyes, watching him as he pushed his seat back. "It was *most* unfortunate about the daffodils. As to the wider damage…"

Soames's head snapped up, his eyes suddenly alive with hatred. An inarticulate sound choked from this throat as he lurched forward over the table out of his lawyer's reach.

"*Damage?* You pigs! How dare you touch my—"

*

RAMSAY QUICKLY SHUT down his client and strong-armed him away from the table. They were both escorted to an adjoining room. As soon as the door closed behind them, Xandra took a deep breath and allowed her shoulders to slump.

Barber emitted a low whistle. "Way-hey. Nice-lee done. You've really rattled his cage. Ramsay will be taking him apart right now for that pants-dropping effort. He's not accustomed to being on the back foot."

Xandra nodded, indicating that she wanted to use the time to go over her notes.

"No worries. I'll see about some more water."

Ramsay and Soames were gone for a full quarter of an hour. When they re-entered the room, Ramsay led the way, his face grim and determined, or was he just royally pissed off, Xandra wondered.

She took a moment to study a seemingly chastened Soames, who was once again staring at his hands clasped in front of him.

"So, Rufus, you've just made it pretty clear that not only did you already know Charlie was no longer alive, but that you even had prior knowledge of where he's been buried for the last two years."

"I got confused. I didn't know what I was saying."

"Too late for back-pedalling now, Soames. It's time to come clean."

He stared down at the table, casting a sideways look at the tabletop in front of his solicitor. "I have no further comment to make."

"Let's just do a little recap of where we're up to on this, shall we? You seem to need convincing of the deepness of the shit you are now in."

Xandra tapped her papers into alignment before slotting them into the folder that she placed to one side. She then clasped her own hands, leaning conversationally towards Soames.

"After the death of your son Toby, you made every effort to find out who kicked the ball into his head, and when you found out, you started planning your revenge. That drawing is very revealing of your state of mind at the time.

"In the days leading up to Charlie's disappearance, you were at the burial site preparing the ground in the vacant plot next to your son's. You had knowledge of the victim's movements. You arranged to meet Charlie after the game that day on the pretext of providing special coaching—"

"You can't prove—"

"You left your workplace after 2.30 p.m., which allowed you enough time to commit the crime. My guess is you hid the bagged body overnight either in the undergrowth in the Vale of Health or in your car boot, prior to catching your train at 5.17 p.m., having earlier purchased a ticket for the 3.30 p.m. train. You inveigled your colleague Andrew Ford into providing a misleading alibi, which has now been—"

"I didn't ask him to do anything. He obviously misremembered. Anyone could do that. We'd been drinking."

"—which has now been broken, and further, you lied to us about your train trip and whereabouts at the key times—"

"I got delayed and missed the first train. It was a busy and stressful week. It's hardly surprising I got it wrong when asked."

"Convenient then, that you could produce the ticket documentation for the first trip and not the second. I'm not buying it, and I'm pretty sure a jury won't buy it, either."

Soames remained silent.

"We've had Data Forensics go over your back shed, and we've collected samples from the bag the body was found in, which are being tested against your DNA as we speak."

A vein was pulsing visibly in Soames's jaw and he spoke between gritted teeth.

"No. *Comment.*"

"That's fine, Rufus. I think you've given us quite enough for one day." Xandra sat back in her chair. "Rufus Tobias Soames, I hereby charge you with the abduction and murder of Charlie Falk, committed on Hampstead Heath in London, England, shortly after 3.30 p.m. on the eighth of November 2011."

Xandra picked up her folder and stood up.

"See you back in the UK, Rufus."

Chapter Thirty-Three

Extradite

Def. Formally removing someone from one jurisdiction to another to face legal proceedings or consequences

THEY HAD SHARED a tub of gourmet chocolate ice cream and now sat boggle-eyed, high on sugar in the dark, bingeing on episodes of *Breaking Bad*. When the phone rang, Adele didn't think much of it until Jem's face, ghostly with flickering television reflections, glanced toward the kitchen and said, "Must be Australia."

Reality stampeded over the anodyne lulling of fantastic storytelling as she scrabbled in her handbag on the kitchen bench. Finally reefing her phone out, she realised it seemed even shriller because Jem had hit the mute button on their show.

She signalled for him to keep watching as she hurried towards the stairs. It had to be Xandra, and she needed privacy. She paused at the bottom stair only long enough to answer the call and to see that it wasn't Xandra.

"Adele! Oh my god, Mum just called. She was just watching the news, waiting for her show to come on, and—"

Adele gripped the railing on the landing, forgetting her run for privacy. "Wh—what time is it there?"

"Adele! Listen to me! There was some story about a man being investigated for child pornography or something, and they showed the police escorting him somewhere, and Mum got the shock of her life. She screamed out that Rufus was on television. By the time Dad rushed in, it was over. He just thought Mum had made a mistake, but she was adamant, and called me. I looked it up online—Adele, it's true! What's—"

"I know."

Her quiet interruption was enough to create a shocked pause in Fran's verbal hurtling.

"What do you mean, you know? Is this why you left? Did you—"

By now, Adele was in her office. She'd closed the door and sunk to the floor with her back against it. "Please, Franny, I... Life has gone completely to shit."

She gave her sister a thin outline of events so far, minus her chats with Charlie, placing more emphasis on the sketch she'd discovered.

"Fuckity *fuck*! So, it's even worse than just...but..."

Adele made no attempt to break the long silence as Fran processed her thoughts.

"So...so...he's been holed up in his office all this time tracking down kids and kiddie porn? And they think he's done something to this missing boy? Christ, Adele, that's disgusting...beyond... I never would have... You think you know someone... Unbelievable..."

"I'm sorry you had to find out by accident. I hadn't developed a plan for breaking the news yet, stupidly thinking I still had time or that things could still turn out okay. The detective as good as told me... Poor Mum... I should have—" Adele gave in to crying, the shame choking her.

"Oh, sweetheart, *I'm* sorry, I had no idea... Does Pete know?"

"No! There wasn't much evidence until five minutes ago, anyway. And even now there is, how can I possibly tell people? Especially *them* with all those sketches he'd done of Jem on the walls."

"Oh shit," Fran whispered. "I forgot about those. Like the ones—"

"*Yes*. Just like the ones of our own son."

"Oh no. No, no, *no*, Adele...don't go there. Don't torture yourself. He couldn't have...wouldn't have."

Adele pulled off her glasses and wiped her palm over her clammy face. When she finally spoke, her voice sounded miserably small to her own ears.

"Fran, I just don't know anything anymore."

*

THE CALL HAD ended with Fran saying that she would phone Peter and break the news herself. The thought of her two older siblings talking it over without her there was both horrifying and comforting. But it wouldn't take long for the Walmsleys to make the connection to those sketches of Jem, then they would have the same horrid visions in their mind as she had.

It was now getting on for 11.00 p.m., and she could see them both sitting up anxiously in bed listening to Fran with open mouths. Jem would soon receive his marching orders...

It wasn't till she got off the phone that she saw the missed call and message from Xandra almost four hours earlier, probably when she'd decided to take a de-stressing bath followed by zoning out with Jem on the sofa. She had sat on her frightened hands too long, and now it had come to this.

As if on cue, there was a gentle tap on the door directly above where her head rested. She moved enough for Jem to slip through the open door. He joined her in her huddled position on the floor as she told him what had happened.

"So, she's talking to Dad right now?" His voice broke on its way up to the next octave.

"Yes. I'm so grateful you're not there, sweetheart. Gives you some time—"

Jem sunk down next to her, clutching his hair with frantic hands, straining his head backwards. "Foock, foock, *foock!* They'll be ringing here any minute. I don't want to talk to either of them. Please, Aunty Del, not now, I can't."

"It's okay, it's late and you're in bed." She took his forearms and pulled his hands down. "Shh. It will be okay. Our families love us, Jem. That's what counts in the end. Come downstairs and sit with me for a bit. I need a drink."

Jem sat hugging himself at the table, watching her pour a measure of whiskey into a tumbler. She gestured the bottle at him, but he smiled and shook his head. She set the glass down and pulled a chair out for herself.

"On second thought." Jem grabbed her glass and took a mouthful. She smiled grimly and turned back to take the bottle off the counter and place it between them.

"Seems I'm no better than your uncle when it comes to being a corrupting influence."

Jem's eyes flashed. "Uncle Roof did not 'corrupt' me, Aunty Del. Can you please just get that thought out of your head?"

"Didn't he? It felt normal to you to have an adult male make sexual advances to you? *Really?*"

"You don't understand."

"Explain it to me, Jem, I need to understand."

Jem rolled his tongue around in his cheek, controlling his anger, marshalling his thoughts. He pushed his chair out and paced to the counter and back.

"He made me feel...special. Loved."

"What, your own parents didn't make you feel loved? Come on, Jem. That's bullshit and you know it."

"Aunty Del, I had a crush on Uncle Roof. He understood me. As I got older, I began to realise I wasn't like...I was expected to be. And that my feelings weren't something to share with my parents. It was like a burden, a secret I couldn't tell anyone, until Uncle Roof."

"You told him you fancied boys?"

"No, not in so many words. He just got me. I accepted that and felt lucky. Dad's always judging me and criticising. I've always had to live up to his expectations being the only son."

Adele opened her mouth to contradict him but found that she couldn't. It was true Peter had always had a brisk manner with his son. Always worried that the baby of the family was being made too much of by all the women in the house, feeling that he had to be the counterbalance to their forgiving softness. And it hadn't helped that the girls had both been high achievers at school and Jem had been a bit slower off the mark.

"Be that as it may," she began cautiously, "it's no different to older men zeroing in on young women. Sensing a weakness or vulnerability and taking advantage of it. As a child, you wouldn't have seen that, perhaps still don't see it. He groomed you into what he wanted you to be."

Jem let out an impatient sigh as he collapsed back into his seat, slumping his chin on folded arms on the table. "Have it your own way, but I don't see how any of that suddenly makes him a murderer of children."

"Fear of being found out, maybe? A need to up the ante?" She slid her tumbler around in a circle on the table, watching the remaining liquid swirl. "And there's another thing. There was something unique about this particular boy."

Jem looked up from under his dark brows, a new wariness in his eyes.

"This was the boy who kicked the ball into Toby's head."

Jem recoiled in his chair. "You *knew* who did it?"

"*I* didn't. But Roof made it his business to find out. I know that now."

Jem laughed incredulously. "What, a revenge killing, Aunty Del? That just sounds ridiculous."

"To someone sane and rational, sure."

"Are you saying Uncle Roof was off his trolley?"

She was about to answer when a message beeped on her phone. It was Xandra.

Call me if you're still awake.

Her fingertip touched the call button without hesitation. It was too late to hide anything from Jem now.

"Sorry if I woke you. I know it's late."

"Not possible to sleep when I have family in Australia calling with frantic questions."

"Things moved too fast for me to get in touch with your

family like you asked, Adele, but I did say we couldn't keep it under wraps much longer. It was a done deal when they walked in with the search warrant. They've already found enough on his computer to press several charges. The footage on the news was his transfer to a higher security prison."

"Is he considered so dangerous?"

"For his *own* safety, Adele."

Adele's eyes met Jem's.

"So, what happens now?"

"We'll be talking to the media at 6.00 p.m. Your 5.00 a.m. To quote my Australian colleague, he 'dropped his pants' in the interview this morning; not quite a confession, but more than enough to press charges. We've initiated the process for an extradition order." There was a brief pause on the line. "Adele, we've got him."

Chapter Thirty-Four

Exposé

Def. A full account; the act or an instance of bringing a scandal, crime, etc., to public notice

IN THE FOLLOWING week, Adele had watched and listened as members of her family had progressed from shock and disbelief, through horror and shame, to arrive at a point fluctuating between grief and anger, with some occasional resentment thrown in.

Roof's limited family connections meant that the media had zeroed in on Adele. In fact, some stories barely fell short of implying she must have covered up for her husband if she wasn't an outright accessory. How could a wife living in the same home not have known, or at least suspected, something wasn't right? How could she indeed. Adele was sick of excoriating herself over it. And to have journalists probing her grief over the loss of her son only poured gall and salt in her open wounds.

Apart from a short, crafted statement that Xandra had helped her with, she had avoided any further engagement, locking herself away in the house at Holly Grove.

Adele had insisted on decamping from Hampstead Hill Gardens first thing the next morning after Xandra's warning about the impending press conference. She wasn't going to sit like a rabbit in the headlights waiting for the media to start banging on her door. Jeremy had taken some convincing as he had no desire to be extradited, but Adele said she would have his back with Peter as much as she could.

They had already agreed not to reveal what had happened between Jeremy and Roof—putting that knowledge in peoples' heads would only cause further unnecessary pain and suffering for all concerned. Nothing could be done to change what happened, and it was looking like Roof was going to be dragged through enough hot coals without pouring more on his head.

At a comfort stop just outside Coventry, Adele called Jo to let her know what had happened and what she was doing.

"I think that's for the best, Adele. You need your family right now and they need you. I'm afraid the media will still be here when you get back, but by then, Xandra might be here to deflect some of the heat."

"Have you spoken to her? How is she?"

"Grimly triumphant, I'd say. This is what she's been working towards for a long time now...but she's not happy about how her success is impacting on you."

"Oh well, there's nothing to be done about that, is there." Adele watched as Jem wolfed down a jam donut, his eyes glued to his phone on the table in front of him. Then, as another thought occurred to her, she stood up from the table. As she pushed the door open that led to the carpark, she said, "Jo, has anything been said about those other missing boys? Please tell me they're unrelated to all of this."

"Nothing so far. First things first, I suppose."

Adele hung up and rubbed her stomach. A huge slice of cheesecake had seemed like a good idea at the time... She thought about the other two boys. Xandra had said they were from two other primary schools and sporting teams in the area. Teams Charlie and Toby might have played against. Part of her wondered what difference it would make if Roof was responsible there, too, he'd already sunk so far—although of course it would make a world of difference to the boys' parents—but the other part of her prayed that Charlie was an isolated grief-maddened case, or perhaps that the arranged meeting, initially not ill-intentioned, had somehow gone wrong and ended badly. She pressed her eyes closed for a moment. *The straws we clutch at.*

Adele leaned against the car and rubbed her forehead in despair. What the fuck difference did it make anyway? Charlie was dead and Roof was online trying to entice kids to play with him.

A hand landed on her shoulder, and she screamed.

"Whoa, Aunty Del, it's only me. Are you okay?"

She nodded feebly, and they got back in the car.

A couple of hours later, they parked in a spot across the street from the house in Holly Grove. Adele switched the ignition off and turned to face her nephew. "Everything is going to be just fine. Just remember that they love you."

Jem's teeth were tearing at his bottom lip, and she feared it was to stop the tears. "I have to live my life."

She reached for his hand and squeezed it hard. "This too shall pass," she whispered. "In a few years, we'll look back on this and share some wry laughs."

"I can't see us ever laughing about Uncle Roof."

"God, no. I meant you. This...other...might help you slip under the radar as a relative non-event."

"Or be a constant reminder if things go wrong." He leaned towards her, crying now. "Aunty Del, I'm so glad you're here. I couldn't do it..."

Adele held him and thought of how the fourteen-year-old Jem had held her hand through the whole of Toby's funeral. Roof's hand as well, if it came to that. Such a brave boy he'd been to try to absorb their adult pain.

In the event, they were ushered into the Walmsleys' front hall with hugs and pats on the back, their bags taken from them. The girls were out but would both be in for dinner.

Adele was impressed that Jem didn't take the teenager option of retreating to his room, instead sitting down with the adults around the dining table for drinks and discussion. Peter manned the coffee machine and Sim busied herself with brewing a pot of tea while Adele and Jeremy opened the assault on the plate of Hobnobs.

"I hope you brought enough clothes with you. I wouldn't be going back for a few weeks at least."

"Pete, I can't even think beyond a few days right now—"

"Just stay as long as you need, loove. I'd hate you to be on your own with all this going on. I still can't believe it." Sim shook her head, staring into her mug.

Peter looked at each of them in turn. "Can someone please explain how we got to this point? It seems finding this missing boy has directly implicated Rufus, but how the hell did the police know they'd find him next to Toby?"

Adele took a gulp of coffee and set her mug down. "I can't go into all the details, but I found some sketches of Roof's when I was cleaning up in the attic. Most were just the usual kind of thing he drew for work or leisure...but there was this other one. Of the missing boy."

"Is *that* what you saw when I pulled the paper apart? I was wondering what had made you shut up like a clam."

Adele placed her hand on Jem's arm.

"I still don't see—"

"I'm sorry, Pete. I really don't want to go into all the ins and outs of things. It's all too ugly. Please just accept that I've been talking with Detective Sergeant Xandra Bentley who's been following Charlie's case since we left the UK...and on comparing notes, we began to realise things weren't adding up with Roof's movements the day Charlie Falk went missing. When Xandra initiated the process to interview him again in Australia, she found he was already on the radar of the local police due to his activities in some online chatrooms. Things just escalated from there." She gave a helpless look of appeal to Sim and Peter.

"I can't believe this of someone who was part of our family. Someone we knew and loved for so long. What in god's name happened to him?" Sim wiped a tear from her cheek, and Peter reached over to hold her hand. Nothing was said for a minute or two while they each mulled over their thoughts. Eventually, Peter looked up at the clock on the wall.

"The news will be on shortly. Shall we face the music?"

Adele had last checked her phone for news at their comfort stop almost four hours ago. A British national was under arrest in Australia for charges relating to downloading child pornography and consorting with children online, and this had led to his being charged with the murder of a Charlie Falk in London, missing since 2011. At least Roof's name had not been released yet, which had allowed her to breathe easy for a little while longer.

They moved over to the sofas while Jeremy grabbed the TV remote. He came back and sat next to Adele. They didn't have to wait long. To Adele's horror, it was the opening news item, and this time Rufus was named. The footage of his transfer to the higher security prison was played again with commentary on why he had been apprehended. The segment then switched to a clip of a press conference in Australia where a Detective Inspector Paul Knott noted they were working with the London Metropolitan Police due to Soames's alleged involvement in the two-year-old case of a missing child whose body had recently been found. Then Adele's breath caught in her throat. Xandra's face filled the screen. Adele was too busy studying her to even focus on what she was saying.

Just as quickly, the screen switched to scenes from the winter Paralympics in Russia and the family let out their collective breath and all started talking at once.

"Thank god you're here with us, loove."

"Is that who you were talking to the other night?"

"This is unbelievable."

Then, simultaneously the landline rang, Adele's mobile joined in, and Sim and Peter's mobiles both pinged several times. Nobody made a move to answer any of them.

*

BY THE FOLLOWING morning, the house in Holly Grove was besieged by journalists wanting the family's reaction to the news. Adele was grateful to have her big brother answer the door with his own terse "no comment", and her phone was now switched to silent, meaning she had to remember to look at it periodically in case there was anything from Xandra. No doubt the Sanders were copping it as well.

Neither Peter nor Sim had said anything to put Jeremy on the spot as yet, but Adele had already noticed that the small square framed sketches of him that ascended the wall next to the stairs had been taken down. She had quietly led Jem over after breakfast and indicated with her eyes the empty spaces. He'd sighed heavily and whispered, "Yep. Saw that last night."

Peter arranged a family Skype call with the Sanders with everyone taking turns to crowd into his office. Franny had their parents staying with her for a few days to minimise the media hassling they were all getting. Pat Walmsley had been quite shaken when a woman who approached her in the supermarket pretending to know her turned out to be a reporter from Sky News, and Harry had been followed home on his bicycle by a car from Channel Nine.

Adele's morning routine revolved around calls with Xandra. Now the worst of the news was in play, the routine check-ins were more incremental updates on the steps in the extradition process and the boxes that had to be ticked.

The clocks had gone forward for daylight savings now, making ten in the morning Xandra's 8.00 p.m., so while Adele sipped her mid-morning coffee, Xandra would be eating a takeaway dinner out of a plastic container. Tonight was chilli basil chicken stir fry.

"I hope you're going to take the weekend off."

Xandra nodded, her mouth full. She swallowed. "Well, sort of."

"What does that mean?"

"I've been using the police gym facilities with Tracey in the mornings. She's offered to take me to the Blue Mountains on Sunday."

"Oh, I...really? That's nice... Is she um, will it be just her, or..."

Xandra paused, her fork hovering in front of her, trailing a slimy strand of bok choy. A grin slowly spread over her face. "Aww, lassie. Are you jealous?" She chuckled when Adele's response was to bury her nose in her mug and glug her tea. "I think she's bringing her boyfriend if you must know; he works in the force behind the scenes, but that probably won't be enough to stop us talking shop the whole time."

Adele nodded, wishing she were better at hiding her feelings. "It is lovely up there. I've always wanted to have a cottage in Leura or Blackheath to run to on weekends." She drank her last mouthful of tea. "What about Saturday?"

"Tom suggested Centennial Park as a good place to chill out and get some exercise. I thought I might hire a bike."

"You're not a beach person?"

"I grew up in Scotland, lass, what do *you* think? Anyway, Fenwick put me off good and proper telling me everyone would be parading around in their thongs."

While they were laughing over some of Xandra's other

cultural experiences, Xandra got up to put a pod in the coffee machine.

"It's not good to be having coffee this late at night. You won't sleep well."

Xandra paused in pulling some milk out of the bar fridge. "Are you lecturing me, girlfriend?"

Adele gave her a mutinous look. "Yes, I am. Actually. It seems if I don't, no one else will look out for you. You might go to the gym and have an amazing body to show for it, but you disrespect that body with the things you put into it."

Adele enjoyed the smug smile that crept over Xandra's lips as she poured milk into her mug. Xandra looked back at her screen and wiggled her eyebrows in an exaggerated way.

"Well, thank you for the compliment. I have to say the quality of food I've been eating has risen since I've been here, if that makes you feel any better. As for the coffee, I have a pile of admin to get through, followed by more calls to the UK, so don't think it's a movie and beddy-byes for me when I get off the phone with you."

"That's not good." Adele sighed. "Has there been anything new at all? Based on our last few chats there's either nothing happening or you're not telling me everything."

Xandra sipped her brew and returned to the table where she had her laptop set up. "Since that first interview, we've had some follow-ups going through his movements with a fine-tooth comb. His lawyer's already getting a bunch of psychiatric reports and assessments in anticipation of the trial."

"Will they get him off, do you think?"

"I don't know at this stage, a lot will depend on how he pleads, but I've already got from you that he's someone with multiple issues exacerbated by trauma with no help sought to manage them."

"Yes." Adele chewed her finger, reluctant to ask, but needing to know. "So, tell me, do you still think he's connected to these other cases you've been trying to link up?"

"No direct indications have come to light so far, but I haven't given up. I do understand that it would be a relief for you and your family if there's nothing. One child is bad enough, but three would be a whole different order of magnitude, especially in terms of the psychological implications. We've initiated some psychological profiling with what we have so far, to see if that gets us anywhere.

"The team back home have been trying to reconstruct his movements around those key dates—your email about the Brewster party for 2010 was a good lead—but peoples' memories are foggy after that amount of time and it's slow going. For the earlier dates in 2009 it looks like he might have driven to Bristol to stay overnight for another client Christmas party, but we're still digging into the detail, keeping in mind the train ticket subterfuge he set up for the Falk murder. But unless something comes up out of the blue, or we find more bodies, pinning anything on him is going to be difficult."

Adele exhaled. She had often complained about how much time Roof spent travelling for work, but it seemed like a blessing in disguise now. "I know how keen you were to tie those cases up, but I am relieved."

"Yeah, well, it might give more weight to his psychiatric assessments if they point to a one-off incident of losing control of himself triggered by emotional trauma and stress. They still have to deal with all his meticulous pre-planning, though. Either way, they'll have a tougher time explaining away his online activities."

Xandra drained the last of her coffee and placed the mug in front of her. "I'm sorry, hen, I've got to get back to work while I've still got some zing left."

"Yes, I know. Have you booked your return flight?"

"Not yet, but very soon, as I've got The Screw breathing budget numbers down my neck. And you? You should really stay with your brother as long as possible."

"I know, I know. But I want to be home when you return. I'll come and get you at the airport."

Xandra gave her an amused look. "Oh, will you now?"

Chapter Thirty-Five

Exordium

Def. The beginning of something; a prelude

AFTER A WEEK of barely leaving the house, Adele was ready to go back to London. When she raised the prospect at dinner, her brother had taken her aside afterwards and said, "Let's you and I have dinner out tomorrow night before you head off."

While part of her always enjoyed the rare occasions when she had her brother to herself, the other, larger part was worried about where the conversation would go.

Usually, they would walk over to The Elizabethan for some pub grub or the excellent Italian up the road, but neither of them were keen to be caught out in the open by a keen-bean journo. Instead, they drove to a small Lebanese restaurant in Levenshulme. The dips and starters had just been placed between them when Peter fired his opening salvo.

"Right. It's just us now and I expect you to be frank with me. I appreciate you sparing Sim and the kids what you've been calling the 'ugly stuff', but I need to know."

Adele's mouth went dry and suddenly the mounds of hummus and baba ganoush all looked insurmountable. The granite-like set of Peter's features reminded her of how insistent Rufus had been on knowing who had kicked that fatal ball, and she said so.

"I don't think it's unreasonable to ask what's been going on around my family—my *children*—under my very nose. Things that might still be playing out." He paused to give her a stern look. "And you know exactly what I'm talking about."

Adele looked helplessly at the table in front of her, then reached blindly for her water glass. She gulped a few mouthfuls and let out a breath, trying to buy some thinking time under her brother's unswerving gaze.

"I'll help you out a bit. It's all shaping up to look like Roof has been indulging in some kiddie-fiddling. When do we think this all started?"

"I honestly don't know, Pete. Roof would never talk much about his childhood, although I know for a fact he was bullied relentlessly at his posh school. He told me stories about how severe his father was with him, too... Now I'm imagining worse things than the occasional beating. It could explain a lot. His solicitor is already preparing psych reports, presumably to demonstrate that Toby's death was what finally pushed Roof's cheese off his biscuit."

Peter took up a piece of flatbread and ripped it in half, his lips set in a hard line. "I'm asking what *you* think, Adele. You were with him for fourteen years. You seemed happy to me for a lot of that time. Was it all a front?" He paused in dabbing his bread in some yoghurt, acknowledging her wince. "I'm sorry, Addie. I know these are personal questions. It's why I wanted to talk to you alone."

"I thought we were happy. But you can imagine I'm re-assessing every single thing that ever happened between us now, and it's pushing me to the edge of insanity." She took another shaky mouthful of water. "I hadn't...you know...had a lot of boyfriends before Roof, and I was young. And you make allowances for things when you're in love. Everyone has their own quirks."

Peter raised an eyebrow. "Quirks?"

"I didn't mean that to sound sinister. I just meant..." She desperately scratched around the floor of her brain wondering what she *did* mean.

"I'm going to ask you a blunt question. How was your love life?"

A small gasp escaped her lips as she gripped her hands together under the table. "F-fun...at first. Based on reports from some of my girlfriends, I'd say we weren't terribly active, but compared to others, maybe not so different. I…I would have liked more affection from him. Toby coming along changed our relationship. All our pent-up love was poured on him."

Peter nodded grimly. His eyes searched hers intently, and he appeared to be about to say something, but closed his mouth abruptly, seeming to make a decision. He paused to sip his beer before he spoke, and when he did, it was in a heavier, more thoughtful tone.

"It's not uncommon. I feel blessed that it hasn't been my own experience. Sim used to say in the thick of us wrangling three kids under six that we should run away together and leave them to someone else."

Adele smiled. "Yes. You have been lucky. And so has Franny."

Peter gave her a sad look so full of love that she picked up her serviette in case she embarrassed herself.

"So, tell me. Do you think he's been in the closet all this time? I always thought he was a bit too charming and suave for his own good."

"No. Well, not as a gay man, at least. I've had some conversations with Xandra about this. A lot of people seem to think being gay and molesting children go together. The psychology as well as the statistics don't bear this out. Having sexual feelings for a child is nothing like a mature attraction to an adult. And most convicted paedophiles have a history of heterosexuality, in any case."

Finally, Adele reached for some bread. She paused in the act of dipping it. "It's beginning to look as though Roof may have allowed some people to think he swung both ways, though, as a screen perhaps."

Peter grunted. "From *when*, is my question."

Adele braced herself. "Do you have reason to think his interactions with your own children weren't above board?"

"Well, you know about Jem."

"Meaning...?"

"I think he's hiding something. He was always very close to Roof. There were times when I felt..."

"Jealous?"

Peter gave her a mutinous look, but it crumbled under her compassionate gaze and he sighed in defeat. "Yes."

Two plates of grilled meat arrived and the dip plate was shifted to accommodate them, creating a heavy pause in the conversation. This was the time to tell Peter what had happened, but she couldn't. And the subterfuge was making her feel ill.

"I think..." she began, feeling her way, "that whatever may or may not have happened in the past is for Jem to bring up with his counsellor. But all in all, he seems balanced and well-adjusted to me."

"Balanced and well-adjusted? Come off it, Adele."

"Is he depressed? No. Is he suicidal? Definitely not. Does he have normal friendships and get along with his family? Yes. Is he generally a happy kid? Yes. Does he behave like an annoying, rebellious, narcissistic teenager? He certainly has his moments."

Peter dipped his head and glared at his plate. When he spoke, it was barely above a whisper. "Addie, I don't want him to be gay. It will make his life so difficult."

Adele exhaled and reached her hand over to cover his. "It isn't for you to decide, Peter." She squeezed his hand and withdrew her own, murmuring, "And an unsupportive father is making his life much harder than it needs to be."

Peter looked up, and his eyes were red. "I love my son, Adele."

"I know you do, Pete, but letting Jem know it too would really help right now."

Having reached an unsteady détente, they began their meal in earnest and tried to speak of other things, such as her future plans. To her relief, the removed sketches were not mentioned.

"So, you will sell up, after all."

"Yes. I'll start calling some agents as soon as I get home. I need to offload everything and start fresh."

"Mrs Henderson will miss you."

Adele rolled her eyes. "Truly."

"Should we start looking around here for you?"

"No. I'll stay in London for the time being. I've got some good...support there, and I need to see how some things play out."

She was aware of Peter scrutinising her closely. "You've met someone?"

Adele cursed inwardly. It seemed that everyone could read her like a cheap detective novel. Except there would be no novel if *she* was the murderer, as she'd be caught in the first chapter.

She met her brother's eyes and made a decision. "Yes, actually, I have. And perhaps I should warn you. It's a she."

Peter dropped his hands to the table and made a show of staring around the room. "Am I on *Candid Camera*? Is this a conspiracy?"

Adele laughed nervously.

"But seriously, Addie, this isn't some violent overreaction? In some ways, I'd understand if it was, but—"

"I'll tell you what I want, Peter. I've had a lot of time to think about it." She raised her hand and counted on her fingers. "Kindness. A cosy home life. A bit of sparkle in the bedroom. Someone who needs me. And someone who makes me feel safe; who can be my rock."

Peter wiped his mouth with his serviette and slowly nodded. "I'm guessing Roof didn't score highly on many of those points, if any. But why a woman?"

"I've met someone who just feels right. She turned up and started to fill gaps that I hadn't even realised were there. Someone who opens up all sorts of possibilities in my mind." Adele reached for her untouched wine. "I just have to convince her."

*

"I DON'T WANT to rain on your parade, hen, but your meeting me in the arrivals hall can't happen. It's best if we text and arrange to meet somewhere. Even then, if there's the least sign of a camera or microphone you are to disappear immediately, and I'll catch a taxi."

It was their last call, and Xandra was packing her bag, listening to Adele describe how her first Sunday back was going to be. The programme included slow-cooked lamb at Adele's place, accompanied by a good red wine, after Xandra had been allowed a power nap. She needed to stay awake till evening in order to adjust to London time and give herself the best chance of sleeping through the night.

"Listen to you, Ms Bossy Boots."

"I'm not a waffly flake all the time, you know. I'm more than capable of taking care of someone else, as well as myself. And I think you definitely need a bit of taking care of."

Xandra had signed off with a mock salute and a "Yes ma'am", but for all her wary amusement, she spent a good deal of the flight home thinking about this person who had stepped into her life and where it was all going. Despite all the energy Xandra had put into suppressing her growing feelings, Adele was beginning to feel like the Real Thing. If anything came of it, Jo would be delighted, of course, but Xandra couldn't completely shut off the need to keep a metaphorical foot on the floor. Unguarded lust had taught her some tough lessons early in life, and she'd spent a lot of time beating herself up about it since.

And if the normal hurdles to a relationship weren't enough, what if Adele changed her mind when the novelty wore off? After what she'd been through this last year or so, it was natural for her to make a run for something, or someone, completely different. She had admitted that she was desperate to feel safe, but how could she have that if she lived with someone who went through this emotional grinding mill regularly for a job? Xandra sensed Adele was probably a lot tougher than she looked, but could she do that to her?

And overriding all these considerations was something far bigger. Allowing herself to become involved with a key witness in Soames's trial would jeopardise the very outcome she had worked so hard to bring about, not to mention destroy her professional credibility and kill her career stone dead.

The flight was long and tiring, and Xandra spent most of it awake, arguing the case for her love life and sanity over her obsessive need to see the job done.

Obsessive being the operative word, Jo would say. Now there was a woman who had shown her how rewarding a loyal and loving relationship could be; all the good things that were possible. Adele held out the promise of all of that plus a future...but not yet. The question was, how much longer was Xandra prepared to wait? And even if she could tough it out, could Adele? Soames's trial could drag out over years, not months, and Xandra wanted to be there to support Adele in every way possible. Ways not open to her now in her professional position.

Xandra's head was aching with fatigue and too much caffeine. It was time to lasso her thoughts so she could put them in order. She pulled her laptop out from under the seat in front of her and started a list of dot points under the headings *Pros* and *Cons*. By the time the blinds were going up and the smell of hot food was permeating the aisles, Xandra had got her head around the conversations she needed to have.

Xandra folded her laptop shut and placed her palms on its warm surface. She had broken the back of the case and brought Soames to book. She could hand over the loose ends. She could; that's all they were. When she got back to the office, she would ask The Screw to take her off the case. She could claim exhaustion, but she owed Alan more honesty than that. Rose Browne's words came back to her: she had allowed this case to get under her skin and she needed to take a step back. It didn't mean giving up any of her achievements, it was about acknowledging there was more to do elsewhere. If she could solve the cold case of Charlie Falk, then she could do the same for Abi Singh and Will Moore.

Masticating some chicken sausage and some rubbery scrambled egg, she tried to distract herself by watching the London tourism reel, which only served to remind her she'd hardly seen any of the things they were promoting. By the time she was holding her cup up like a begging bowl to the hostess with the coffee pot, the funky techno intro to the BBC news was playing. *Here we go.* She took a hot gulp of coffee and braced herself, but to her surprise, Roof did not lead off the segment. In the early hours of this morning, the Minister for Education had been found dead in a hotel room in Leicester. Xandra sniffed. She wondered if his rent boy had been able to sneak out before the shit hit the fan. She couldn't help feeling sorry for his wife who may not be on top of her husband's double life, but it occurred to her that this new shiny thing may have just saved her bacon by distracting the media, even if only for a moment. The news on Roof told her nothing she didn't already know, so that was also good.

After going for a wander to splash some water on her face in the loo, Xandra was feeling slightly more alive. The decision to take herself off the case was the right one. Already, her shoulders felt looser. The biggest wild card now was Adele herself.

*

XANDRA'S BONES CLICKED as she yanked her bag off the carousel. A text had already popped through telling her where Adele was parked. The realisation that she was not returning to an empty flat and an even emptier Sunday was enough to give her a spurt of energy to push her trolley through the crowds to the exit. The frisson of knowing someone was on the outside waiting for her—for *her*—was enough to lift her out of a heavy fug of tiredness.

Keeping her head down, her face partly shielded by the visor of a cap she'd bought at Sydney Airport, she did the stop-start dance guiding her luggage around the people loitering with their signs for hire cars and Mr Watanabe and Miss Creighton. Xandra held her breath, expecting any moment to have some pushy journalist launch at her through the congestion of hugging couples and bags, but after she shadowed a family group through some sliding doors out of the main area, she began to relax, looking for signs for the carpark.

The lift doors parted, and she was assailed by exhaust fumes and the echo of squealing tyres negotiating tight corners. She bit her lip as she waited for two elderly ladies to exit ahead of her. *Just calm down, will you. Don't be too keen. It never ends well.*

Surrounded by concrete beams and pillars, Xandra paused to scan up and down the rows of boots and bonnets searching for a short person with big curls and an even bigger smile.

Deciding a call would be quicker, Xandra dug in her pocket. As she raised her phone to her ear, a figure emerged from behind the pay station to her left. A set of familiar glasses perched above a quivering smile. Before she could walk around her trolley to greet her, Adele had pulled out her own A4 piece of paper. Her smile broke into a silly grin as she brandished it and executed some little jumps.

Pick me! Pick me!

*

XANDRA HAD PAUSED in front of her, an unreadable expression on her face. To Adele's relief, it dissipated when she simply shook her head and laughed. But then she had stopped laughing and slipped her hand under the back of Adele's head, gripping her curls, to swoop in for a lush, open-mouthed kiss that left her shocked and breathless.

Adele tried to conduct normal conversation as they made their way to her car, but knew she was gabbling rubbish. In one kiss, Xandra had electrified her nervous system to an on-state it had never experienced before.

With her mind approaching the state of melted butter, she wondered if she'd be okay to drive. Apparently sensing her hesitation, Xandra paused to watch Adele as she closed the boot on her bag.

"You okay, lass?"

Adele gave her a mock furious look. She reached out and in one deft movement yanked Xandra's shirt out of her pants and placed a hot palm on her bare stomach.

"How dare you even ask, after that...that—"

Xandra locked eyes with her and leaned forward to murmur near her ear. "Just get in the car."

An unfathomable amount of time passed with them in the back seat, grappling with clothing and having the delirious sensation that she was devouring, and being devoured by, Xandra's mouth. In the fray, Xandra's hand squeezed its way down the front of her pants and within what seemed like moments, Adele's body had unleashed an enormous tremor of energy, leaving her gasping and weeping.

The sound of a car door slamming close by whipped away the steamy curtain. Xandra laughed breathlessly against her cheek before pulling away from her. She made a mesmerising show of sucking each one of her fingers before delivering a small kiss to the tip of Adele's nose.

"Time to go home."

Chapter Thirty-Six

Expurgate

Def. To cleanse, to purify, to purge

THE MONTH FOLLOWING Xandra's return had been tough, and if it hadn't been for the promise of their budding relationship, Adele may have just given up and abandoned everything. After that first exhilarating week, Xandra had been the pragmatic one, providing the balancing doses of reality to Adele's fluctuating emotions.

Adele had been shocked when Xandra told her she'd requested to be taken off the case. Then shock had given way to awe when she realised why Xandra had done it, and what it meant for them as a couple, for their future together.

Their first week together was intense to the point where in the early hours of the second morning in Xandra's deep-sheltering embrace, Adele had broken down.

"I've wasted so much of my life trying to make the wrong person love me."

"That wrong person also gave you great joy with your son. Ten years of wonder and love. Nothing wasted there."

They'd spent their nights at Xandra's as Adele was less and less able to tolerate being in Roof's house, as she now thought of it. And she still had to be constantly on her guard for loitering media.

As well as packing things in boxes, at every visit, she brought items to Xandra's flat under the guise of needing them for cooking their evening meal or so she didn't have to keep fetching and carrying. After every meal was tidied away, the items all found new homes on Xandra's empty shelves.

At the end of their second working week together, Xandra leaned against the fridge sipping a whiskey, watching Adele lay out the constituents of their meal along with a whole set of freshly unpacked pasta bowls and serving plates.

"I hate to tell you, hen, but you really are a stereotype."

Adele paused in her busy-ness to give Xandra an anxious look. "How so?"

"There's this joke about lesbians...it goes, 'What do lesbians bring on a second date?'" She grinned, anticipating Adele's reaction. "The removal van."

Adele's shoulders slumped, and she gave the counter a sweeping crestfallen glance. "Am I that bad?"

Xandra placed her glass on the bench and came up behind to wrap her arms around her shoulders. "Yep." Adele felt Xandra's hot breath as she chuckled into her hair. "And I'm good with it. If you overstep any lines, I'm more than capable of speaking up. But I have to say, it's lovely to see you so bright and happy." Xandra's warm lips pressed to her temple as Adele made no attempt to end the embrace. "And if I haven't made it obvious by now, you make me happy, too."

Over dinner, however, the conversation became more business-like.

"Adele, we're going to have to be careful about how we see each other for the next while. In fact, we may need to stop altogether for a period when things really heat up. Even though I'm now officially off the case, the media would still have a field day making up salacious stories about our connection, and I don't want anything to prejudice our ability to commit Rufus for trial."

Adele focused on twirling spaghetti around her fork as Xandra spoke, nodding glumly. "I know you're right, but it makes me angry that my life—*our* lives—have to be put on hold because of *him*. I've lost enough—"

"Hey." Xandra reached over and took her free hand, giving it a small shake. "Here's a more positive way to look at it: Rufus has gifted us this chance to be together." She reached down to place an open-mouthed kiss in Adele's palm.

Adele sighed, more at the kiss than the thought. "I suppose so…yes. Trust me to look at it from the negative standpoint."

Xandra continued. "It's going to be a tough road, and a long one too: due process in Australia, getting him back here, waiting for a trial date. It can be a long and tedious business, and there'll be a lot of media attention. You need to be prepared. It's going to get worse."

"It makes me want to run away to a little hut in the woods in Canada. The thought of even being in the same country as him is giving me the heebie-jeebies."

"One day at a time, lass, that's all we can do. This could make us or break us. We'll just have to see which one."

*

AS THE WEATHER warmed up, Adele had kept busy with finalising the manuscript she was working on and, at Xandra's insistence, committed to two more. She had met with a few real estate agents discussing sales strategies for the house and was on the verge of choosing one. In the meantime, she was occupied with handymen doing minor fixes around the place and selling some of her larger items of furniture at auction houses or online.

One day after school, Jo had come round with the van to pick up some smaller items for her jumble sale, accompanied by her son Felix. Adele had already met Jo's children when she and Xandra were invited over for dinner. Felix was the oldest, followed by two younger sisters, Cecily and Mira.

"Hey, this is really nice." Felix flopped down onto the leather sofa, spreading his skinny arms out looking like he intended staying there. He was fourteen but looked older. He had Jo's dark colouring and some endearingly large jug ears. His oversized red T-shirt only managed to emphasise his thin frame.

"Don't get too comfy there. I think we'd best start with the biggest items first if we're going to fit everything in, and that doesn't include the sofa. Adele's sending that to Hamilton's."

Felix groaned and rubbed his palms in an exaggeratedly sensual manner over the leather. "But it's so *niiice*, Mum. Why don't *we* buy it? We could save Adele the trouble *and* she wouldn't have to pay moving fees or any commission!"

"Our suite is perfectly comfortable."

Adele laughed as Felix made a big show of loving the sofa cushions. "Seriously, Jo, if you'd like it, it's yours. My gift to you, for all you've done for me."

"See, Mum? Ask and ye shall receive!"

Jo gave her a mock stern look. "Adele, that's wonderfully generous of you, but you can't just give it away. It would bring a handy amount of money in, I'm sure."

Adele walked over to a gleeful Felix and shook his hand. "Sorry, Jo, it's a done deal. As long as your son does the majority of the lifting."

"Dear Adele." Jo smiled ruefully. "I suppose we could sell ours instead. That will be a nice surprise for the girls."

Between the three of them, they managed to stack the sofa

components into the van like Tetris pieces. After that went the buffet cabinet and Toby's wooden toy trunk.

Standing next to the driver's side of the van, Adele prepared to wave them off. Jo paused in the act of winding up her window. "I forgot to ask. How's it going with Delia?"

Jo and Xandra had ganged up on her and insisted she seek out extra independent support. "It's just as much about preparing you for what is coming, as what you are already trying to digest," Jo had said.

Adele smiled. "So far so good."

Current discussions with Delia Hubbard, the counsellor Jo had found for her, were focused on how Adele could best achieve emotional closure. Adele had still not shared her worst fears with Xandra or Jo on the question of Roof's relations with Jeremy and his own son, but she had talked openly about it with Delia, who had proven to be a good source of impartial advice and support.

"Once his trial is over, you could request a private interview with Rufus, if you thought you were up to it," Xandra had suggested. "A lot could depend on the final verdict, of course."

"I can't see Roof agreeing to that."

Jo had expressed a different view. "You don't know what head space Roof's in now. He's had a lot of time to think about things, knowing that you and your family will be wearing the impact of everything. He may feel a need to get some things off his chest; ask your forgiveness, even."

Adele had stared at Jo when she had said this, wondering

whether she should even try to believe it possible. Assuming she could even go through with it. The mere thought made her skin crawl, but her growing need for answers was beginning to tip the balance. Answers that would not be forthcoming in his trial.

On the many nights she was alone, Adele lay awake running imaginary conversations on a loop, winding herself up over Roof's possible answers or non-answers. She had even gone so far as to write out the questions she wanted him to answer.

So much damage had been done, so much healing needed to happen, if it ever could. Not just for her, but for Sylvia Falk, Stephen Lane, her immediate family, and for the wider community of schoolchildren and parents. Delia was pleased with the progress she was making, largely due to disconnecting from the house and its memories, but also her blossoming under Xandra's attentive care. But underneath her healing surface, the questions about her own son bubbled away like corrosive acid.

Delia pointed out that if she discovered the worst, it could be highly damaging. Adele agreed, but living with the possibility unconfirmed could play out for the rest of her life also, just in a different way. Even if it was the worst, like Rufus needing to know which boy kicked that ball, she had to know. Only then could she learn how to move forward with whatever she could salvage from the wreckage.

Adele watched the van move off, then pause, prior to turning onto Pond Street. Whatever happened, at least she knew now she wouldn't have to face it alone.

*

THE HOUSE SOLD in the last week of spring. Adele now booked extended stays in Airbnbs in the area, rather than have a fixed address. Apart from a few sentimental items she had taken to Xandra's, she had offloaded everything. She was free.

Due to her agreement with Xandra about carefully regulating their time together, Adele spent most of her evenings wherever she was staying, either working or in calls to her family. There was no news yet on Roof's extradition, and Adele's longing to see her Australian family members was growing.

The Friday night following the sale, Adele invited Xandra out for dinner to celebrate. Conversational topics on everyday subjects were expanding between them, so it wasn't until after the entrée when Xandra was in the act of refilling their wine glasses that Adele steered them back to future planning.

"No updates from Australia?"

Xandra shook her head. "Not yet. The waiting's hard, I know, but you may as well get used to it. And there will be a lot more waiting ahead as well, even once we get him back."

Adele sighed, tracing circles on the table in front of her. "I've been going over things with Delia. I—I think it would best if I could speak to Rufus before he comes back. Before all the real hoo-ha starts. Catch him in this period of...abeyance." She lifted her glass and took a big sip, meeting Xandra's steady gaze. "I also want to see my family. It would help get me through this limbo period of not being able to see you much and waiting for the house settlement to go through."

Xandra said nothing for a moment. She braced her elbows on the table and leaned her mouth into her clasped hands. Finally, she disengaged her hands and took up her glass.

"Do you think you're ready? Wouldn't it be best to wait until it's all over?"

"I'm as ready as I'll ever be. I'm also thinking he might be more receptive to talking to me before he's hauled over the coals in public. The trial is likely to bring up ugly and confronting things—I'm not sure I could face him when all that's out in the open."

Xandra drummed her fingers against her closed lips for a moment. "I would suggest making a formal request first. It will probably have to go through his solicitor as well. Rufus won't be able to talk about the case with you, you know that, don't you?"

"Of course." Adele frowned, shifting in her seat. "I need to clear up some more...personal matters. Get some closure, as Delia calls it."

"I feel like I should be going with you for this, but I can't."

Adele reached across the table and took Xandra's hand. "I'll have my family. It's okay." Then she smiled. "It will make the waiting pass more quickly and reduce the risk of us being linked together. I don't want to be the reason the trial or your career are jeopardised."

"Oh, hen. How long are you thinking?"

"A month? Probably best if I'm back in time for the house settlement."

Xandra groaned. She raised Adele's hand to her lips, closed her eyes, and kissed it. "It's so typical that after being given a taste of heaven, it should be torn away from me so quickly." She opened her eyes and gave Adele's fingers a slow lascivious lick. "I'm glad you'll be sharing my bed tonight. It will help me forget for just a little bit longer how much I'm going to miss you."

*

IT ALL CAME together surprisingly quickly. Before Adele knew it, she was in a different time zone, experiencing brighter light and a more relaxed vibe.

Nick met her at the airport and on the drive home, gave her his views on how the family was taking things. Adele had always felt comfortable with her brother-in-law, and getting his perspective, one step removed as it were, was helpful.

"The press attention has settled down, thank god. Pat and Terry are back home, as you know, which is a relief, but we're all sharply attuned to the news now, expecting any moment to hear Roof's name."

Adele stared out of the window as terrace house on terrace house slipped by. That name was also her name and hearing it in connection with Rufus on the radio or television caused her stomach to twinge painfully.

"I'm so sorry, Nick. It's so huge and I can't—"

"Yeah, I know. No one's blaming you. We just have to stick together and get through it as a family." He reached over and patted her hand, turning briefly to smile at her. "You've made Fran so happy, coming out. She's been so worried about you."

*

BY THE END of the week, Adele received the promised phone call setting up a time to see Rufus. She booked an Uber and arrived twenty minutes early.

After the signing-in process, she was shown to the visiting room, an area filled with tables of people talking. It was almost two months since Rufus had been arrested and charged with all his offences. She was still struggling to comprehend the reality of it all.

While she waited at the designated table, she looked around at people with heads bent together in conversation, murmured snatches coming to her over the general hum. Roof had agreed to see her, and she had felt strong enough to come alone, but that didn't mean she was feeling confident. Far from it.

She caught sight of him moving towards her from a doorway at the back. He was looking thin and drawn in the face, much as he had on the television screen, the only difference now was his cheeks were rough with stubble and he sported a man-bun. He nodded at her and pulled out the seat facing her.

Adele's hands were clasped tightly together in her lap under the table. "Thank you for agreeing to see me."

He nodded again. His eyes focused on her but seemed devoid of light.

"Are—are they treating you okay?"

He shrugged. "Did you bring the pictures?"

"Yes. Yes, of course." She reached down to her bag on the floor and extracted a plastic sleeve. Roof's only request had been that she bring him some recent pictures of Toby's grave. She pushed them across the table and watched his face as he slid them from the folder. There were three in all. The uprooted daffodils had not been replaced and what remained was just a neatly trimmed rectangle of grass.

"I'm planning on leaving London, so I won't be there to maintain it, and to be honest, I can't stand the sight of daffodils any more. Clean and neat is best."

Roof scrutinised each picture, nodding impassively. Adele watched as he slid the photos back into the sleeve, unable to help noticing the tremor in his hands. Maybe it was nervousness, but her more cynical side suspected the impacts of a forced detox.

He paused in his actions to look up at her sharply. "You're leaving London?"

"Yes."

"What—will you leave the house empty? Rent it out again?"

Roof's eyes had sharpened in focus, as if a veil had lifted.

Adele briefly considered lying but thought better of it. "I've already sold it."

Roof stared at the table as if something had lodged in his throat. "I—I gave it to you, because I thought you'd keep it. F-for Toby. I entrusted you—"

A thousand responses leapt to her tongue, and it was by sheer force of will that she controlled her anger. "Given what you did while living under the roof of that house, I think you expect too much."

She now knew, thanks to Xandra, that the forensic analysis of Roof's computer files showed his downloading of child pornography had predated Toby's death by several years. This sickening revelation had been the final decisive factor in her deciding to sell the house.

Adele tried not to think of any of that now. This could be her only chance to air the question nagging and burning at her sanity, and it was the hardest of all to approach because most of her didn't want to hear the answer.

She gripped the metal frame under the table once more and literally braced herself. Her voice sounded hard and grim as she said, "Jeremy sends his love."

Roof raised his face and openly stared at her. He said nothing for quite some time as Adele held his searching gaze, her mouth set in a hard line.

"Is he okay?"

"He's upset, naturally, but I should warn you, he and I have been having some confronting conversations."

A ripple of tension tremored through Roof's body. "What has he said to you?"

"Everything."

Roof was now breathing hard, and his eyes had come to life.

"What does that mean?"

"It means that you're damned lucky you weren't charged with a whole new round of child abuse charges. For various reasons I won't go into, Jeremy and I agreed that it would cause more pain than good revealing the extent of it to his parents and the rest of the family."

Roof's mouth was opening and closing and his eyes flickered unseeing over the surface of the table between them. "But I never... *Jeremy*..." he whispered, his face frozen.

"You've broken us all, Roof, but Jeremy has suffered particularly badly."

"Adele," he choked out her name, "*Addle*, I never hurt him. I *loved* him. I still do. You must believe me. I wouldn't hurt a hair on that beautiful boy's head."

"You've hurt his heart, Roof, and how you've distorted his emotional and mental development can only be guessed at. But that's not what I came here to talk about."

Roof sniffed and rubbed the heels of his palms into his eyes, muttering, "It's not true." He ended by scratching the stubble on both cheeks in an agitated manner.

Adele took a deep breath, surprised to find herself with the upper hand over Roof after all these years. "I want to know about our son."

"Our *son*? What are you talking about?" Roof stared at her, his eyes glassy and bloodshot.

"We've all seen the sketches of Toby naked in the bath, Roof;

just like the ones you did of Jeremy. *You* tell *me*." Adele paused and her last words were ground out between clenched teeth. "And god help you if you even think of lying to me, you bastard."

Roof was now physically shaking and looking around the room as if seeking help. "I never... *Jesus,* Adele! How could you even... Toby! Never... Oh *Christ,* how could you... *Noooo.*" He clutched his face in both hands and slumped over the table, groaning and shuddering.

People from other tables were glancing over, others turning bodily away, not wanting to witness a prisoner melting down in their midst.

An officer was making her way over, and Adele took that as her cue to stand up. She took one last look at the top of Roof's head, quivering in his clawing hands.

She had received her answer, which she was determined to accept, but it would be some time before she would feel any better for it.

Chapter Thirty-Seven

Experientia Docet

Def. Experience teaches

THE ENGLISH SUMMER was in full swing by the time Adele returned to London. While she and Xandra cautiously picked up where they had left off, contact during the week was still limited to calls and texts, with Adele showing up at Xandra's on Friday evening and leaving late Sunday evening.

Adele had returned to find Xandra working harder than ever, and still obsessing about finding a connection between Charlie's murder and those of the other two boys. After listening to Xandra describe her latest efforts following up on leads and rechecking old files and data over dinner, Adele said, "What will you do if you don't find any connection? I'm getting worried about how this is impacting on you."

Xandra frowned. "I'm sorry. I shouldn't be downloading all of this on you anyway."

"Darling, I'm not saying I mind. I'd rather you tell me what's bothering you than not. I've just been through years of being with someone who hid everything from me, and look how that turned out. I'm just speculating on where it might go for you...or not."

Xandra let out a gusty sigh as if to clear her head. She rubbed her palm on the tabletop, then she curled her fingers and tapped the surface as if coming to a conclusion.

"Okay, but before we change the subject, there *is* something I need to follow up with you. A rather serious loose end."

Adele quailed at Xandra's sudden change in tone.

"When you revealed to me that you thought you knew where Charlie was buried, I said I would need to know more about how you knew. You fobbed me off at the time, and I let it go, considering I had bigger concerns at the time, but this isn't going to go away, Adele. When Rufus goes to trial, it will come up, and if you can't explain yourself to the court's satisfaction, it could raise all sorts of nasty questions."

Adele's face quivered on the verge of collapse.

Xandra continued. "*I* also need to know, as your answer might give me this elusive connection to those other boys."

"Oh, Xandra..." she whispered.

Xandra's gaze was relentless. "Don't 'Oh, Xandra' me, Adele. You have to put some trust in me here. I'm trying to save you from being dragged through the Spanish Inquisition, or even worse, having something ugly stick to you."

Adele stared helplessly at the remains of their meal. She then looked up to the window, a golden square of late summer evening light. The light decided her.

"Let's go for a walk. Maybe I can tell you more easily in the right place."

They donned caps and sunglasses and walked the two kilometres to the heath. When they passed Hampstead Heath railway station, Adele started to tell Xandra the story from the time she came back to London. She took Xandra to her bench and invited her to sit down while she described what she had experienced and what Charlie had told her. Intermittently through the telling, she pulled her gaze from the distant playing fields and glanced at Xandra, which felt viscerally odd, when she was so inured to seeing Charlie sit in that exact spot.

When she got to the part where Charlie said he was "waiting for Mr Soames", Adele paused and waited for Xandra's reaction.

It took Xandra a while to register that Adele had stopped speaking. She shook her head and let out a laugh of frustrated despair.

"Jesus, Adele. This won't wash in court."

"I know that. Why do you think I didn't want to tell you?"

They sat in grim silence for an extended period, Adele not

wanting to aggravate things further.

Xandra was deep in thought, and Adele couldn't stand the silence. "You think I'm crazy, don't you?"

Xandra slowly turned her face towards her and spoke quietly.

"No, hen, I don't. I've been going to Jo's group too long to disparage spiritual people or those who have any kind of second sight. It just doesn't make for good evidence in court."

She turned her face back to the expanse of playing fields in front of them and got up to shake her legs out. She put her hands on her hips and looked up at the sky, stretching her back. After a long moment she shook her head and laughed mirthlessly before sitting back down.

"Bloody hell. I can't believe I'm going to say this. We'll just have to come up with something else. Some hint from the past that triggered your thinking, something Roof said that connected to another memory. *Anything* but what you've told me just now."

"Okay." Adele's voice was small.

Xandra sighed and moved closer to her, putting an arm around her. "I'm sorry to put you through the wringer over this, but it's nothing to what you'll face from Roof's defence lawyers." She leaned toward Adele and kissed her temple.

As they walked down the slope to cross the playing fields, Xandra paused and looked back at the bench.

"You said you haven't seen Charlie since the body was found?"

Adele shook her head.

Xandra gave a sigh, and her shoulders slumped. "Dammit, Adele, if only you could have asked him about the other boys."

*

THE SIGHT OF St Michael's high upon the hill in Highgate brought up some sweet memories for Adele. As they turned back down the slope, she described to Xandra how Toby used to stare out of his window in the late summer evenings, with her lying in bed beside him, making up stories about what happened on the heath and how the church spire was always the ruling centre, whether as a castle, a tower prison, or a wizard's lair. No matter that he had no view of it from his room.

Xandra smiled. "Sometimes actually seeing something you've always imagined can ruin it for you. Like when you watch the movie of your favourite book. Nothing's as big as what's in your own head."

Adele's smile faded. "And that can be a huge relief, when it comes to bad things."

They paused, waiting for traffic to pass so they could cross a road. Xandra broke their "in public" rules and clasped Adele's hand for a quick squeeze. She leaned sideways to murmur in her ear.

"Your son sounds like a wonderful kid, Adele. I'm so sorry for your loss, and that I'll never get to meet him. It's become my loss, too, now."

As they strolled past Keats' House, a thought occurred to Adele.

"Hey, listen, the house sale settles this Tuesday and the new owners are doing their final inspection on Monday. Do you mind if we just pop by to make sure everything looks okay?"

Xandra squeezed her hand again. "Fine with me. All this summer evening walking's got me thinking of ice cream, though. Shall we drop into Silvio's on the way home?"

They cut across to Downshire Hill and were soon turning into Hampstead Hill Gardens. The birch tree at the front of the house was now in full leaf and shielded the top windows from view.

Xandra paused to look in the lower windows as Adele pulled a wodge of junk mail out of the mailbox and transferred it to the recycling bin.

"You've given up your key, haven't you?"

"Yes. If anything's shorted or the boiler's blown, there's not much I can do now. I just wanted to make sure the garden was tidy. No fallen branches, no nasty little presents from Mrs Henderson's darling Wilby."

Xandra chuckled and gave Adele's ponytail a tug as she followed her down the side path. "You're a funny wee thing. I'm sure it wouldn't matter."

Adele turned to give her a look. "It matters to *me*."

Xandra strolled around the back of the house, looking in the windows as Adele paced around the trees and peered behind the hedges. Xandra then walked along the opposite side fence to the garden shed. She tapped on the door, above the padlocked latch.

"Nothing left in here?"

"No, all cleared out. Your team took care of most of the stuff in there."

Xandra nodded, returning to where the path down the side of the house ended. As Adele pottered around picking up windfall from the trees, she watched with amusement as Xandra leaned in to squint through a hole in the fence at the neighbours' garden.

Adele threw her pile of leaves and sticks into the compost bin and headed back to where Xandra paced back and forth where the side path ended.

"That open gutter filled in nicely."

"Yes. Yes, it did. Jeremy took care of that for me. We laid some new turf over it. All back to neat now."

Xandra ran a speculative toe over the grass, frowning. "Jo made some reference to your frantic gardening the other day. Something about crocuses. What was that about?"

Adele blushed, momentarily cursing Jo and Xandra's close relationship.

"Oh nothing. It was no big deal."

Xandra glanced up at her abruptly, giving her that narrow-eyed look Adele had come to recognise. Adele shifted her weight uneasily and sighed.

"If you *must* know, when Charlie told me it was actually Roof he was waiting for, I had a bit of a meltdown. A major meltdown, actually. The enormity of *my own husband* being capable of such evil just overwhelmed me. When I came home and saw those crocuses all shooting up...I just...lost it. More of Roof's loving handiwork. He had a thing for bulbs: daffs, tulips, crocuses. I got it into my head that they just had to be rooted out. *He* had to be rooted out."

She sighed again, putting her hands on her hips. "Anyway, it doesn't matter now. Jem filled it back in when he was here, and I got him to throw the bulbs away." She gave Xandra a rueful smile. "A tragic waste, I know, but I've rather gone off bulbs. So, keep that in mind when Valentine's Day comes round." She reached over and poked Xandra in the ribs.

To Adele's disappointment, Xandra didn't laugh; in fact, she didn't even react. She just continued staring down at her feet, her mouth in a tight line. The smile fell from Adele's face as she followed Xandra's gaze down to the strip of new turf.

"What's the matter?"

When Xandra spoke, it was like she was far away, her eyes unseeing. "When did Roof plant those bulbs?"

"Oh, years ago. He made out they were for me, his way of saying sorry after a disagreement, but really, they were for him."

Xandra frowned. "What was he saying sorry for?"

"I don't remember now—" But suddenly she did. The bed closest to the kitchen was all neatly laid out and sprouting by the time she came back from her extended Christmas in Australia, the trip Roof had pulled out of. Toby had got the foosball table, she, supposedly, got the crocuses...and the other—

"Oh, Xandra..." Adele swayed towards her, clutching at Xandra's arm, her knees suddenly weak.

She felt a strong hand under her elbow. Xandra's voice was in her ear, low and urgent.

"Tell me, Adele. What have you remembered?"

"No. It can't be right. I need to think about it...check..."

"Adele. Tell me *now*." Xandra turned Adele towards her, and the fierce expression on Xandra's face made Adele quail even further.

Xandra gave her a shake to prompt her.

"They were Christmas presents...sort of," she whispered.

"When?"

Adele swallowed hard as Xandra came in close, their noses almost touching.

"It was 2009 and...the following year, 2010."

Xandra let her go abruptly and pulled her phone out of her pocket. Adele watched in round-eyed terror as Xandra quickly dialled a number and held the phone to her ear. She heard a man's gruff voice answer.

"Frank? I've got an urgent job. If you can get the team to Hampstead Hill Gardens tonight, there's a case of Mumm in it for you."

Chapter Thirty-Eight

Exode

Def. Conclusion of a drama

IT WAS A Wednesday evening at the flat, late in September, when Adele finally heard Xandra's key in the door. She interrupted setting the table for their late supper and collided with Xandra on the other side of the sofa for a long and frantic hug.

"God, I've missed you so much," Adele moaned.

Xandra dragged her mouth around the side of Adele's face, and they kissed hungrily for a long moment. The last time they'd been in touching distance was the night they unearthed the two boys.

"Sorry I'm so late," Xandra murmured into her hair. "There was a delay in getting the determination sent through."

Xandra had warned her she could be late. Fenwick had said he would let her know unofficially as soon as it came in, but she had wanted to get the news first hand, which Adele totally understood.

"So, what's happening?"

"Your Attorney-General has signed off on Roof's surrender. The wheels can now start turning on the logistics. The how and the when and who'll escort him. HMP Stafford looks like being his new home. He'll be on trial before you know it."

The irony was Adele felt like she had been on trial herself ever since Roof had been arrested. The finding of Abbi Singh and Will Moore where the crocus beds had been at the side of the house had tightened the ratchet even further. If her world had fallen apart at the discovery of Charlie Falk, what was left had detonated into smithereens.

The press had gone ballistic, touting Rufus as the worst serial killer since Peter Tobin. Before the first day was out, Stephen Lane was in the firing line again, his face filling Adele's television screen. She was in lockdown at her Airbnb in St John's Wood, glued to the TV news loops watching his sad face on repeat, microphones jostling for position, as he expressed his relief that the boys had all been found and at his own effective exoneration.

"I've lived under a cloud of suspicion for so long now, the relief is just…immense." His fingers swiped at his cheek. "The police have shown a dogged persistence in solving this crime, and there were times when they made my life a living hell, but I realise that if they had let the whole thing drop, my name would never have been cleared." He swallowed and gathered himself. "My heart goes out to those families, the Singhs, the Moores, and of course Sylvia Falk. I just hope this can deliver them some kind of closure."

Stephen glanced to the side at some inaudible question, and his mouth tightened. "I'd rather not comment. Just let me say, I knew the family. I can't begin to imagine what they are going through right now."

She had been grateful for the group pronoun, that he hadn't singled her out. The clearing of Stephen's name had been something positive to cling to, even though his nightmare ending meant hers gathering pace.

And on a more practical level, the sale of the house had fallen through. Her best hope now was to rent it at a discount once the media's Eye of Sauron had moved on. But that truly was the least of her worries.

The furore in the media had meant that Xandra and Adele had stopped seeing each other in real time, increasing her isolation and reducing her available support, but due to tonight's pending communication, they'd decided to take the risk. Adele would be back at her accommodation ensconced in siege mode before the sun rose and well before the news from Australia filtered through. This interval of humming abeyance would be over in several hours, and it was their last chance to connect before the deluge.

Adele took a deep breath, letting Xandra's news sink in. Her involvement to date had been limited to a written statement to the court in Australia on her husband's behavioural patterns prior to their formal separation and her moving out of their Annandale home. She would not get off so lightly this time.

Xandra pulled back, and Adele raised her chin to take in her lover's face. Adele could see her own misery reflected there.

"We have to stay strong until Roof's trial is over."

Adele nodded, clutching Xandra tighter and biting her lip. "Stafford. That's just north of Birmingham, isn't it?"

Xandra nodded, her hands moving up and down Adele's back. Adele closed her eyes, enjoying the immense comfort of her lover's touch. If it hadn't been for Xandra's calming presence on nightly video calls, and Jo and Delia's constant support, and now a therapist to boot, she would have descended into madness. Nightmarish scenarios of watching the boys rise out of their graves from the kitchen window or her digging up the still-living children with her bare hands meant she could no longer sleep unassisted. And on top of all that, she now had a full shopping list of medications to manage anxiety and depression.

Xandra had begged her to leave the site before Frank and co had turned up, but Adele had insisted on being there. The vision of the forensics team working under their strong lights, and the little she had glimpsed between amorphous figures in jumpsuits and plastic sheeting, had been nothing compared to her rollercoaster imaginings. Xandra had been occupied in deep conversation with Fenwick and her replacement when Adele had retreated behind the shed to vomit.

And now Roof was coming home.

She felt Xandra's lips on her closed lids.

"I just want this ordeal to be over. I dream of us being spat out of this horrible machine all fresh and new." She opened her eyes. "You said once that all you wanted was to have an open, loving relationship where you could have what everyone else has." Adele's face started to crumble. "It seems you picked the wrong girl."

"No, no, *no*. Stop thinking like that, lass. I picked the *right* girl. I just have to be patient. *We* have to be patient. What you are to me is so worth waiting for, and we are going to be so much stronger for getting through this horror. Believe me. Believe *in* me."

Adele reached up with both hands and pulled Xandra's face down for a kiss as Xandra started gently walking her backwards towards the bedroom.

"You're here now, love, for a brief and exciting moment, with the door locked fast and safe behind you. Prepare to be ravished to exhaustion."

Epilogue

Exeunt

Def. They go out (stage direction)
January 2016

"THAT'S THE LAST one." Xandra levers herself off the floor and pushes the taped-up box across the carpet next to its fellows.

"I'm just about done here, too." Adele throws the last few scrunched-up wads of paper towel into the plastic rubbish bag and ties it up. "I'm so looking forward to just shutting the door behind us and having a quiet night with Jo and the kids."

Xandra walks around the kitchen counter to stand behind Adele and wrap her arms around her. Adele lets out a sigh, allowing her eyes to drift shut as she relaxes against Xandra's chest. After Roof's sentencing in the autumn of the previous year and once the media caravanserai had moved on, Xandra had joined her at the Airbnbs and left her flat a glorified storage unit while they decided what to do. The relentless hype and attention had also taken a toll on Xandra, and Adele had insisted on spiriting her lover off to a cottage in a Greek fishing village for the month of December where they focused on rest, healing, and each other.

Life had become so comfortable and simple living with Xandra. No second-guessing, no stressing, no doubt. Just being happy.

After locking up, they go their separate ways from Kentish Town to run last-minute errands in the remaining hours of the afternoon. Adele's errand takes her up to the heath. She parks in Downshire Hill near the Freemasons Arms and walks the old familiar route until she arrives at her favourite bench.

She sits with her hands clasped in her lap staring down the slope seeing but not seeing the walkers, the picnickers, and various children running around. She has already said her farewells to Toby, making sure his headstone and grave are clean and tidy. This quiet pause is just a time to contemplate and reflect on how far she's come, and all the new things in her life she has to be grateful for.

A woman with a pram stops briefly to sit next to her, and Adele is aware of a dog and its owner passing behind where she sits. A father and son run around in the stiffening breeze attempting to launch a kite. The light gradually fades, and the number of people thins.

Reluctantly, she rises to leave, wondering when she will next be able to return to this spot that holds so much meaning for her. She stands for one last extended moment, gazing down the slope where some children are still running around, until two, closer to the woods' edge, catch her eye. They are running hard with a ball coursing ahead of them and the taller one has bright-red hair.

Adele watches and waits. The game stops when they crash into each other and the smaller boy picks up the ball. He pokes his friend and points up towards her. Both turn and wave before racing into the shadows between the trees, Adele's blown kisses disappearing in the wind.

Acknowledgements

Coming out as a writer of books has engendered so much support and interest from those around me, which is exactly what you need in such a lonely occupation, but it does make ensuring you've acknowledged everyone quite a task, especially when your support stretches over continents.

Ex had early readers in Denis Corke, Dale Johnson, Lynda King, Dianne Munt, Diane Prior, and Trudy Whitcombe. All gave their time, support, and encouragement. Especial thanks and deep gratitude must go to my amazing beta readers Vivien Wright, Kate Noble, and Jason Harvey who all provided insightful comment, critique, and chewy discussion, helping me to make Ex a better book.

Crime writers have to work harder these days to stay abreast of the latest techniques and developments, not to mention their knowledgeable readers. With Ex stretching across both UK and Australian jurisdictions, it was necessary to consult widely on a broad number of matters. People who provided input of a more technical/factual nature include Richard Bailey, Scott McCosker, Debra O'Keeffe, Helen Orrell, Peter Romeis, and Lorraine Saxon. I owe particular thanks for advice on police procedural matters to Jack Roney in Australia and Paula Benson in the UK.

I must also express my thanks to the staff of Highgate Cemetery who did not, after all, report me for asking suspicious questions.

Having said that, I hope this book is only the beginning of my asking such questions. Ex marks my bid for entry into the wonderful community that is Australian crime writers. A fun and fascinating bunch of people who are generous with their time and encouragement to other writers, actual and wannabe. In particular I express my awed thanks to Matthew Spencer and Hayley Scrivenor, two Australian crime writers at the top of their game, for their endorsements. Two excellent role models right there.

The editing and pre-production experience has been rendered smooth for me, once again, by Elizabeth Coldwell, and I thank her and all the other staff at NineStar Press for their good work.

And more broadly, I need to thank all those librarians, bookshop owners, and staff who have supported me in my publishing journey so far, which started out in the tough times of COVID (yee ha), with a special shout out to Andrew Sims at Gleebooks in Sydney. Without your support and enthusiasm book promotion would be impossible...and far less enjoyable.

Closer to hand I am lucky to have my own cheer squad and those who have been ready with advice, sympathy, and solutions, accompanied by a liberal dose of good humour. Mitchell Assenheim, Sam Elliott, Mary Howley, Nataša Tosic, and Trudy Whitcombe: what would I do without you?

On that note I must acknowledge all the lovely people and pets I have housesat for over the last three years who have made my impecunious, peripatetic lifestyle possible. A quiet place to create is what all writers need. Thank you in particular to Judy Betar (and Lily and Steve).

To my brother Lachlan and my mother Paula, 2023 was a challenging year for us all, but we got there in the end. Thank you both, for your love and support during this time.

And at last, Patrick, the unwritten name in every category above and more besides.

About the Author

Alicia Thompson grew up on a farm in country NSW. She has a Masters in Creative Writing from UTS and has worked as a bookkeeper, photographer, editor, adventure tour leader in the Middle East and China, spreadsheet guru, and general herder of cats. In addition to writing, she now runs a series of creative writing workshops up and down the east coast of Australia. Her published work includes numerous book reviews, travel articles, and short stories, and her debut novel *Something Else* was published in 2021 by NineStar Press. More can be found on her website www.aliciathompson.com.au and on Instagram and Facebook @aliciathompsonauthor

Website

www.aliciathompson.com.au

Instagram

www.instagram.com/aliciathompsonauthor

Facebook

www.facebook.com/aliciathompsonauthor

Other NineStar books by this author

Something Else

www.ninestarpress.com

www.facebook.com/ninestarpress

www.x.com/ninestarpress

www.instagram.com/ninestarpress

bsky.app/profile/ninestarpress.bsky.social

www.threads.net/@ninestarpress